Nerina Graye stood at the first landing of the grand staircase. Her flaming red hair and striking green eyes, her alabaster skin — now blushing with fury — had undoubtedly attracted the insolent gaze of the raven-haired stranger who stared up at her.

So this was the arrogantly handsome Sir Rupert Wroth — the most disdainful, elusive and scandalous bachelor at the court of Queen Victoria . . .

As he turned from her in a manner at once courtly and contemptuous, Nerina knew that to enslave him, to mortify such a scoundrel, would be the most difficult and important challenge of her life.

Also in Pyramid Books
by
BARBARA CARTLAND

LOVE IS
THE ENEMY

Barbara Cartland

PYRAMID BOOKS • NEW YORK

LOVE IS THE ENEMY

A PYRAMID BOOK

Pyramid edition published March 1970
    Second Printing, September 1970
    Third Printing, January 1971
    Fourth printing, June 1971
    Fifth printing, October 1972

Copyright Barbara Cartland 1952

All Rights Reserved

ISBN O-515-02824-X

Printed in the United States of America

Pyramid Books are published by Pyramid Communications, Inc.
Its trademarks, consisting of the word "Pyramid" and the
portrayal of a pyramid, are registered in the United States
Patent Office.

Pyramid Communications, Inc., 919 Third Avenue,
New York, New York 10022

1

The Queen rose and gave her hand to the Prince Consort. Sir Rupert Wroth stifled a yawn. It had been a tedious evening, as was to be expected at Buckingham Palace. He wondered how anyone could enjoy the solemnity of these long-drawn-out ceremonials, and thought that perhaps Her Majesty was the only person present who found the stiff formality entertaining.

The Queen was smiling as she began the slow, dignified promenade through the Throne-room. There was a fluster and a rustle of silk, satin, tarlatan and tulle as the ladies swept to the ground in low obeisant curtsies. There was the sparkle of Orders and Decorations as masculine heads were bowed. It would soon be over now, Sir Rupert thought, and he felt a sudden craving for a breath of fresh air after this over-heated, stifling atmosphere of starched pomposity.

But Her Majesty was not to be hurried. She stopped to speak with the Prime Minister, Lord John Russell, and now she was smiling kindly on Lord Grey, the Secretary of State for War. The Prince Consort, severe and unsmiling, made an observation to Mr. Greville which would undoubtedly be reported unflatteringly in his famous diary.

At last the Royal procession was on the move again and Sir Rupert got ready to bow, then realised somewhat to his surprise that the Queen was about to speak to him.

He looked down at her. It was extraordinary how, tiny though she was, she contrived to exude such an aura of regal dignity. It was impossible not to be in awe of her. Tonight she was smiling gaily, her eyes were bright and it was obvious that she had enjoyed the evening; but at other times that small mouth could be set in a hard line of affronted obstinacy and her eyes become steely with anger.

"It is nice to see you here, Sir Rupert," Her Majesty said in her clear, well-modulated voice, which always seemed to be a tone lower than one expected in such a diminutive person.

"I thank you, Ma'am," Sir Rupert murmured.

"But when you come again," the Queen continued, "we shall be glad to welcome at your side—a wife."

Sir Rupert had no reply ready. He was so astonished that for a moment he thought he could not have heard aright; then before he could even bow an acknowledgement of the somewhat obscure honour which was being accorded him, Her Majesty had passed on. The rippling wave of curtseying women and bowing men continued on down the room.

Sir Rupert stood very still. Indeed he felt for a moment as if his brain were paralysed, as if he could not understand or take in the full import of what had been said to him. Then as the doors were flung open by the red-liveried, gilt-laced flunkeys and the Royal procession with its attendant dignitaries and fluttering Ladies-in-Waiting disappeared from view, a murmur of voices restored his scattered senses.

The murmur grew louder and the restraint which had held the gathering silent for three hours vanished like a mist before the sun. Suddenly Sir Rupert knew that he must get away, that he must escape before those around him began to question him. It would be only a matter of seconds before someone would be bold enough to ask him what the Queen meant. Was he already betrothed? What were his matrimonial plans? Who was the fortunate lady?

They were questions he had no intention of answering, and as he turned towards the door there was an expression on his face which made those who were already approaching him shrink back abashed.

He strode quickly from the Throne-room, passing through the Green Drawing-room where refreshments were being served and down the wide crimson-carpeted stairs where the Yeomen of the Guard were on duty. Once or twice his name was called, a hand touched his arm, a friend attempted to impede his progress; yet he was blind and indifferent to everything save his own urgent desire to escape, to reach the fresh air he had craved so urgently but a short while ago and which had now become an absolute necessity.

At the door of the Palace he dismissed his carriage which was waiting for him and walked quickly past the Guard of Honour mounted in the Palace yard. Quite oblivious in his preoccupation to the big crowds waiting outside the gates he strode with long strides down the Mall.

In his Court dress, knee breeches and silk stockings, his purple-lined cloak blown back by the wind to reveal the shining decorations on his breast, he was obviously a person of distinction and as such of interest to those who had waited long hours for a glimpse of Her Majesty's guests.

But it was not his clothes which made people stare at Sir Rupert Wroth. There were one or two ribald remarks as he passed, but there were many others which were invariably complimentary softly spoken amongst the women who watched him go.

It would have been strange if they had not admired him. He was handsome enough in all conscience—tall and broad-shouldered, his clear-cut features admirably set off by his raven dark hair. There were few people who, meeting Rupert Wroth for the first time, were not impressed by his looks. But although nature might have intended him to be surpassingly and pleasingly handsome, the expression on his face was of his own making. Brooding and cynical, there was a coldness and proud disdain in his eyes which chilled the most genial gesture of friendship.

There was, too, something aggressively arrogant in the manner in which he held himself, in the way he asserted his opinion or contradicted an opponent; and there was a bitter twist to his lips which would have been more fitting in a man of middle-age than in one who had not yet reached the prime of his manhood.

And yet it was impossible to deny his attraction, and one woman in the Mall said to another with a nudge in the ribs:

"That's the sort of man I'd like to lay with, dearie, a man who is a man and looks it! Tho' something's upset his lordship for sure. There's a touch o' the Devil in his face right enough."

She was not far wrong, for as Sir Rupert walked away into the darkness he was seething with a fury beyond anything he had ever experienced. Those who had stood beside him in the Throne-room at Buckingham Palace might wonder what the Queen had meant by her remark, but he had no need to wonder. He knew; knew that Her Majesty was giving him both a warning and a command.

It had been so unexpected, something that he had not anticipated might happen in his cautious calculations; yet now that it had occurred he knew that it had been absurd to think that there would not have been those ready to spy on his private life.

There was little the Queen did not know. She had her own method of learning the most hidden secrets about people with whom she was concerned. And yet he had imagined himself too clever to be found out. Only to be publicly disillusioned. More than that, he knew that he had

7

received a direct instruction which he dare not disobey. Fool to have thought for one moment that his love affair with Clementine would pass unnoticed and not reach the ears of Court Circles!

He wondered how long the Queen had known of it— a month, two, three, or perhaps even when it started six months ago? No, not as long as that, for it was in January that Lord John Russell had spoken to him and said frankly that when Lord Palmerston resigned from the Foreign Office he would be offered the appointment.

Sir Rupert had been overwhelmed. He had planned for it, worked for it, but he had not expected the realisation of his most aspiring ambition to come so soon. His political success had already been phenomenal, there was no doubt about that. From the moment he had entered the House he had been outstanding, first as a Back Bencher and then as an Under-Secretary.

He was only twenty-seven when he had been sent on a mission to the Colonies to represent Her Majesty's Government. The Foreign Secretary had been ill and there was no one else in a ministerial capacity at that moment to take his place. Rupert Wroth had his chance of showing his capabilities, and he had not failed those who had trusted him. He had, in fact, been brilliantly successful, so successful indeed that Her Majesty had been pleased to knight him for it, and overnight he had become the most promising young man in the House of Commons.

The aptitude for diplomacy that he had shown during his mission had not been forgotten. The Prime Minister had singled him out again and again for special attention, and soon after the New Year of 1850 had been heralded with its usual train of international incidents, the threat of war and a dozen diplomatic crises, Lord John Russell had sent for Sir Rupert and told him frankly what was in his mind.

He intended, he said, to remove Lord Palmerston from the Foreign Office. The Queen, who disliked the Foreign Secretary and had repeatedly complained of his behaviour not only to Lord Palmerston himself but also to Lord John, must, the Prime Minister thought, at long last be conciliated.

"I have told Lord Palmerston so often," the Prime Minister told Sir Rupert, "that Her Majesty's uneasiness is not always groundless, but he pays no heed."

He went on to speak of the difficulties of foreign relations at such a crucial time in British history, and Sir Rupert listened attentively, forgetting for once to look aggressive. But his hopes, like the Queen's, of getting rid of Lord Palmerston were to receive a severe setback.

The Prime Minister's intention of replacing the Foreign Secretary was defeated partly by the attacks made on the foreign policy of the Government by the Opposition and also by Lord Palmerston's vindication of it in the House. It was a vindication which put him on a pedestal of popularity. Sir Rupert, listening from a back bench, knew that he would have to wait, and wait patiently—at least to all outward appearances—for office. Well aware that time was on his side, he was not unduly perturbed by this; but while he waited, he amused himself or rather, as usual, suffered a woman to amuse him.

His love affairs were already the subject of much talk and speculation, and to choose Lady Clementine Talmadge at this particular moment had been a mistake. To begin with, she was a notorious beauty and as such was very much in the public eye. Secondly, she had a reputation for being indiscreet, which was bound to bring upon her head the censure of the strait-laced and easily shocked young Queen.

Lady Clementine had spent the summer in the country, and Sir Rupert had no idea how what happened in the rural North had so speedily come to the ears of those who were in London or Windsor. He had apparently underestimated for perhaps the first time in his life both his opponents and his friends.

Striding now towards St. James's Street, he felt the first heat of his anger ebb away from him and the cool calculation of his brain taking in the situation. He was well aware that behind him those who would be leaving the Palace would be chattering about what the Queen had said.

There would be gossip of a hidden engagement, perhaps even of a secret marriage. Rumours of every fantastic sort would be rife before the morning, but only he and the Prime Minister would understand exactly what the Queen had said so clearly and unmistakably.

As plainly as if she had put it into words, Sir Rupert thought, she had told him that she would tolerate no indiscretions in his private life if he were to become Foreign Minister in place of Lord Palmerston. What was more, his present entanglement with a married woman had gone far enough. Before he came to Court again he must produce a

9

wife acceptable to Society, a bride worthy of becoming the wife of Her Majesty's Foreign Secretary.

The calm insolence of it took his breath away, and yet he could not help but admire the Queen's methods, which were invariably direct. Indeed, there was seldom any doubt left in the minds of those who listened to what Her Majesty required of them.

He had laughed often enough in the past when by sheer force of will she had discomfited those who had opposed her. And yet now, when it happened to him, he did not find it in the least humorous.

Sir Rupert stopped walking and saw where his feet had carried him. He found himself standing outside White's Club. His foot was already on the first step when a faint burst of laughter came to his ears. He had no idea at what the Members might be laughing, but it might be at himself. He pulled a watch from his pocket. It was barely ten o'clock. It was too early to go to bed and quite suddenly he decided what he must do. He must see Clementine and tell her what had occurred. It was unthinkable that she should learn of his predicament from someone else.

The Talmadges were in the country, where they had been the whole of the summer. Sir Rupert turned away impatiently from the door of the Club. He was tired of London, he would go to the country. He walked across Piccadilly and down Berkeley Square. As he went, a number of beggars and several women of easy virtue tried to attract his attention, but he neither heard nor saw them. He was making his plans with that clear, icy concentration which those who worked with him in the House of Commons knew only too well.

He was well aware that after what had occurred in the Palace this evening he must be careful. If he sought Clementine out too deliberately after what had happened, it would be playing into the hands of those who would be expecting him to do just this very thing and who would undoubtedly report it immediately to the Queen. Besides, being fastidious about such matters, Sir Rupert never, if it was possible, went to the Talmadges' house. He and Lady Clementine met secretly and disguised by incognitos which they thought were impenetrable, when they were in London or in the glades and forests surrounding Wroth, where they were quite certain no one would observe them.

But apparently they had been wrong in imagining themselves unseen, and Sir Rupert knew now as never before that they must be careful and circumspect. He would go at once to Wroth, he decided. There would be nothing wrong in that, and the fact that the Talmadges' estates matched with his could not be expected to deter him from returning to his own home.

Once there, he must contrive in some clever unobvious way to see Clementine at once. If he left tonight, he should be at Wroth before breakfast. He could then make his plans.

He entered his house in Berkeley Square, handed his cape, hat and cane to the butler, and in a calm, unhurried voice gave orders for a carriage to be prepared immediately for the journey.

"I heard at the Palace this evening," he added, "from an old friend of the family that my grandmother is far from well. I expect she has forbidden anyone to tell me of the deterioration in her health, thinking I should be busy at the House of Commons, but naturally, I shall leave for Wroth immediately."

"Very good, Sir Rupert," the butler replied. "May I venture, Sir, to express the hope that it is but a false alarm and that you will find her ladyship well?"

"I hope so indeed," Sir Rupert said, and leaving the Hall he walked into the Library.

It was an excuse, he thought, which would serve well to ward off those who enquired the following day where he had gone. He walked across the room to a table set between the windows and poured himself a drink. He felt in need of one, yet when his lips touched the wine he knew he was not thirsty. Instead, his mind was turning over and over again the thought of what lay ahead—marriage to some suitable girl. And where, he wondered, was he to find one? For his very varied experience of lovely women had not brought to his notice many marriageable *jeunes filles*.

Sir Rupert gave a sigh and put down his wineglass. Perhaps Clementine would help him to find one, unless she was foolish enough to be jealous and inclined to advise him to flout the Queen's instructions. But no, he was certain she would not be as stupid as that. She knew as well as he did what lay at stake—the post of Foreign Secretary at the age of thirty-three. To find a parallel one would have to quote Pitt who had become Chancellor of the Exchequer when he was ten years younger.

Sir Rupert took up his glass again and drank off the wine before he turned to leave the room. As he did so, his eyes caught sight of the row of invitations propped on the mantelpiece beneath the great Chippendale mirror. There were dozens of them, but one in particular, a large white card, held his attention.

"*The Earl and Countess of Cardon—At Home,*" he read, "*on July 16th, at 3 p.m. at Rowanfield Manor, Rowan.*"

Sir Rupert stared at it for some moments.

"Tomorrow at 3 p.m.," he said aloud, "and Clementine will be there."

Yes, Lady Clementine Talmadge would be there, as would most of the County, and it would be easy to meet each other quite casually and openly. Sir Rupert Wroth left the Library with the invitation card in his hand.

The drive to Rowanfield Manor was crowded with carriages of all sorts, sizes and designs, but the horses which drew them were almost uniformly finely bred. Tossing their well-combed manes and with their silver-crested harness jingling, they drew up when their turn came under the pillared portico of the mellow red-brick house where several liveried flunkeys with powdered hair were in attendance.

Nerina Graye, looking out of the mud-splashed, unpolished window of the hackney carriage which she had hired from the railway station, gave a little gasp at the sight of the other vehicles, and then shrank back into the corner of the ancient, musty-smelling cab with an expression of dismay on her face. She had forgotten that it was the day of the Garden Party; indeed why should she have remembered it as she had not intended to be there? Now she knew full well that she could not have returned to Rowanfield Manor on a more unfortunate day.

By the evening everyone would be tired and irritable. Her return, unheralded and unexpected, would be bad enough on any occasion, but today of all days it would be catastrophic! On an impulse she reached up and opened the tiny communicating window between herself and the driver.

"Cabby!" she called, "Cabby! Set me down at the back door, please."

He cupped his ear with dirty fingers swollen with arthritis.

"Th' back door, did yer say? Very good, Miss."

Nerina sat down on the seat and watched a smart dog-

12

cart with yellow and black wheels flash by them. It was driven by a young gentleman with large, well-curled side whiskers, and she recognised him for one of the most eligible bachelors in the County. Everybody would be here today, she thought miserably, and she would be the only uninvited guest and indeed the most unwelcome one.

"I could not help it, I had to come away. There was nothing else for me to do."

She said the words fiercely out loud to herself and as though the very sound of them gave her the reassurance she was needing, her chin went up a little higher and her air of dismay and dejection was replaced by a more characteristic expression of defiance. And yet her hands were cold and she knew that inside herself she was afraid.

Her aunt had been angry the last time she had returned home, but Nerina was not afraid of her Aunt Anne. It was her uncle who made her tremble. She dreaded hearing his bullying voice raised to a shout as he forced her to explain her actions! She dreaded the heckling tones he would use as he tore her explanations to ribbons, deriding her fears, and told her, as he had told her so often before, that she had got to earn her own living and the sooner she stopped being fastidious and fanciful the better.

How she loathed those scoldings, and how she shrank, although she pretended to herself she did not, from his anger, from his bullying and his jeering laughter at her efforts to preserve her chastity!

She remembered the last time when she had been forced to tell him why she had left the position of governess to the two children of a middle-aged widower. She remembered how her uncle had insisted on every detail of the amorous advances made to her by her employer, and when, shamed and humiliated by what she had to recount, she had eventually subsided into an embarrassed silence, he had laughed mockingly and told her she was making a mountain out of a mole-hill and that most of what she had resented had been nothing but the imaginings of her own love-sick mind.

This time it would be worse, much worse; and though she might resolve now to tell him as little as possible, she knew that when the moment came he would force admissions from her that she never intended to make. She knew, as she had known ever since she was a child, that he took an obscene pleasure in humiliating her. He had hated her ever since she had grown old enough to wince away from the very unpaternal kisses he had given her at bedtime. He had hated her since she had run sobbing from his Library one wet Saturday afternoon, and he had hated her, too, ever since she had grown too old for him to be able to beat her, because he had got a bestial pleasure from doing so.

Yet he was her uncle, her guardian, and her only relative. She wondered sometimes whether it was better to endure the humiliations and miseries that she encountered in the positions she had found as a governess or wiser to return home and endure others almost as bad under the roof of her uncle.

The last time she left Rowanfield Manor she had told herself that she would stay away whatever she had to suffer; yet here she was, returning in three months. It had been impossible, utterly impossible to remain in the same house as the Marquis of Droxburgh. She could see now his cruel, dissolute eyes fixed on her face, his hands reached out towards her, his tongue wetting his thin lips. He had been evil beyond anything she had imagined possible in the whole world; and she had stood it for three months, three whole months until she had known that breaking point had come and she could go on no longer.

She had not slept for weeks, she had been too frightened to do so, and all through the day when she was supposed to be teaching her charge in the schoolroom she was listening for that soft footfall outside the door. No, she could go on no longer. Flesh and blood could not stand it any more. Better to brave Uncle Herbert's anger than that, better to acknowledge herself defeated than to collapse where she was.

Another carriage passed by the window, this time an open Victoria. Nerina had a glimpse of a pretty face framed with a bonnet trimmed with roses. There was a parasol to match of flounced lace caught with rosebuds, and the girl—for she looked nothing more—was escorted by a gentleman with a curly brimmed top hat and a huge carnation buttonhole.

There was something elegant and romantic about the couple. As they flashed out of sight Nerina looked instinctively down at her own dress. It was creased and dirty from the railway train. She had been travelling since dawn and she knew that her face and her hair were smutty and that she looked generally dishevelled and untidy. She smoothed her dress impatiently and realised that there was little she could do to improve it.

14

Faded and of a shape which had been fashionable two or three years ago, it was a bright blue which Nerina had always known was unbecoming to her. But invariably she had to wear clothes which were that, because they were her cousin Elizabeth's cast-offs. Lady Elizabeth Graye was fair-haired and blue-eyed and looked her best in shades of sky-blue or blush-pink. On Elizabeth such colours were perfect, on Nerina they were disastrous.

The cousins were about the same height, but there the resemblance ended. Nerina had inherited the flaming red hair and mysterious green eyes which had made her mother an acclaimed beauty wherever she went. Indeed it was that particular combination coupled with a magnolia-white skin which had made the penniless younger brother of the Earl of Cardon run away, while he was still at Oxford, with a concert singer.

That they had been happy had abated not one iota the family's wrath and indignation; and when they were drowned while yachting off the coast of Devon eleven years later, everyone said it was exactly what they had expected to happen all along.

Nerina had been brought to Rowanfield Manor to be brought up with her cousin Elizabeth. They were the same age, and it should have been of advantage to both children to have companionship; but, as Nerina was to learn later, Lord Cardon had loathed his younger brother and was irritated almost unbearably by any remembrance of him.

Perhaps he had grudged him his happiness, perhaps it was a more obscure emotion than that, based on some twist and turn of their childhood relationship. Nerina was never to know what it was, except that as she grew older she sometimes suspected that her uncle had been repulsed by her mother and that he placated his dignity by punishing her for any humiliation he had suffered.

But whatever the reason, she only knew that from the moment she came to Rowanfield Manor she was made to feel apologetic for being alive. Everything she did was criticised, and it was almost impossible for her to do anything that was right. But as she grew to maturity she became aware that at times her uncle's interest in her was obscurely horrible. She shrank away from him, and he punished her for it swiftly and relentlessly.

She could remember all too vividly her shame at his beatings, realising subconsciously from the very first that

15

her mental humiliation was more intolerable than the physical pain she suffered.

The cab drew up at the back door. There was no one about and Nerina knew that the servants would all be busy on the lawns and in the front of the house. They were invariably short-staffed and on occasions like this Lord Cardon's meanness or penury would make him expect the work of two people from every one employed.

"If you will put my trunk in the yard," Nerina told the cabman, "I will get it taken in later."

With asthmatical wheezings and chokings and the creeking of ancient bones the cabman lifted the box from his cab on to the flagged stones of the back yard. It was not heavy, but he was an old man and he wiped the sweat from his brow when he had finished.

Impulsively Nerina added the last sixpence in her purse to the money she had ready for him in her hand. He glanced at the sum suspiciously, then seeing that she had tipped him generously, he raised a finger to his forelock.

"Thank ye, Miss, thank ye kindly."

He climbed into the box of his cab, whipped up the tired, underfed horse and turned down the drive. Nerina watched him go. She put off the moment when she must enter the house until the cab was almost out of sight; then she turned sharply and walked swiftly down the stone passage which led past the kitchen and the servants' quarters towards the green-baize door which divided it from the other part of the house.

There was no one about, but in the distance she could hear the chatter of many voices and the strains of music from a string band. It took her but a few minutes to hurry up the back stairs to the second floor and reach the big low bedroom she had shared with her cousin Elizabeth.

The room was empty, but Elizabeth's things lay scattered on the bed and over the dressing-table. The muslin gown she must have worn that morning, her stockings, frilled petticoat and hair-ribbons, a dirty handkerchief, lace mittens and a lawn chemise were all thrown down in untidy disarray, as if Elizabeth had waited until the last moment to change and her maid had had no time to tidy up before being required to help in other parts of the house.

It was unlike Elizabeth to be untidy or unpunctual, Nerina thought with a little frown, and picking up one of her ribbons from the floor, she wound it over her fingers, smoothing away its creases. As she did so she caught sight of herself in the mirror on the dressing-table and made a grimace in dismay. She had no idea she could look so dirty.

She had only been able to afford the cheapest seat in the train in an unclosed carriage. The smoke from the engine had been terrible, and the wind had blown her hair about until she looked very unlike a prim and respectable governess.

Nerina pulled her bonnet from her head. Her hair fell in heavy curls on either side of her face, framing it with a vivid fire which seemed to catch the sunlight and reflect it back again. The lashes which framed her green eyes were naturally dark and curly, but Nerina, looking at her own reflection, did not see any beauty in them or in the aristocratic perfection of her tiny, tip-tilted nose. She saw only the superficial dirt which defaced her white skin and the fear which made her lips quiver however hard she pressed them together.

"I won't be frightened, I won't," she said out loud, and suddenly her hands were clenched and she flung back her head as if she would free it from invisible shackles. "I am not afraid, I'm not. I hate men, I hate all of them! They are beasts and devils, and if I could, I would make them all suffer for what has happened to me."

She stood for a moment tense and stiff, her nails digging into the soft flesh of her palms and her eyes closed with the almost unbearable intensity of her feelings. Then she ran across the room to bury her face in the cool, clean water of the wash-hand basin.

It took her some time to wash and change, and when at length she was ready, having borrowed a clean muslin gown of her cousin's, she felt calmer and more courageous.

She decided that she would go down and brave out her arrival in front of the other guests. Perhaps if her uncle got over the first shock of seeing her while other people were there it might make it much easier for her later on when she had to give him an explanation as to why she had returned.

Slowly and purposefully Nerina walked along the passage to the Grand Staircase. Of exquisitely wrought ironwork, it had been added to the house at a later period and several rooms on all three floors had been removed to accommodate it. As she reached the first-floor landing, she

17

heard another carriage arrive at the front door and a moment later saw a man step into the Hall. She stood still for a moment, watching his arrival. He was tall and dark, and as he took his polished top hat from his raven dark hair, Nerina thought he was one of the most distinguished-looking men she had ever seen.

She watched him cross the Hall, following the footman through the Drawing-room on to the terrace where she knew her uncle and aunt would be receiving the guests. As he went, he glanced up at her as if inadvertently she had attracted his attention. For a moment she saw him full face and was surprised at his expression. It was almost as if anger smouldered behind his eyes and in the sharply etched line of his lips. There was contempt and disdain, Nerina thought, in the glance he gave her and an arrogance beyond all bearing in the way he slowly turned his head away again.

"Another bad-tempered man," Nerina thought, and knew that she hated him as she hated all others of his sex.

They were all the same, she thought, as she descended the stairs—sanctimonious hypocrites when they appeared in public amongst their own class, and all too self-revealing when it came to their relationships with other women—unprotected governesses like herself who had to earn their own living through no fault of their own.

Nerina felt a sudden desire to hurt someone as she had been hurt. She thought how she would like to wound or maim a man such as had just passed through the Hall. To know him to be in subjection to her, to know that he was mortified or abased would, she thought, be a pleasure and a satisfaction beyond any she had ever experienced. Yet even while she thought of such things she laughed at her own imagination. A man was always the master and always the conqueror. What chance had a woman against their born superiority, their natural suzerainty?

Nerina felt suddenly helpless and knew that she could not face her uncle and aunt standing on the terrace expecting to greet another County notability, their hands instinctively outstretched before they realised who she was.

Swiftly she crossed the Hall and opened the door of the Morning-room. Through the room, which was seldom used, was a conservatory with a door at the far end of it leading into the garden. No one noticed Nerina as she let herself out of the conservatory; and crossing a small part

of the flower garden, she vanished behind the rhododendron bushes which bordered the lawns.

Keeping out of sight of the crowds, Nerina made her
way by small, unfrequented grass paths behind the bushes
until she had partially encircled the garden and was facing
the house from the other side of the lawns.

The warm red brick of Rowanfield Manor which had
been built at the time of Queen Anne made a perfect
background for Lord and Lady Cardon's guests. In their
big hooped skirts the women themselves looked like in-
verted flowers as they moved gracefully amongst the
rosebeds, or stood listening to the band which, wearing
Hussar uniforms ostentatiously ornamented with gold lace,
played spirited tunes from the operas.

There was a big marquee on one side of the garden and
a croquet tournament in process on the other. Nerina
watched for a moment from the bushes, then afraid of
being seen slipped away towards a small building which lay
just ahead of her. A summer-house, it had been built by
Lord Cardon's father who had quite without justification
fancied himself as an architect. The summer-house, which
had occupied his fancy, when he was nearly eighty, was an
elaborate edifice which reminded one a little of a Japanese
pagoda with a Grecian foundation, but which had all the
damp discomfort of a religious grotto.

The mixture was not surprising for the Earl changed his
mind several times in the execution of his plans and the
local contractor and the estate carpenter had many wordy
rows as to how his lordship's wishes should best be
achieved. The resulting building, which when completed
was extremely ugly, had fortunately been mellowed by
time and a climbing honeysuckle which obscured the more
crude outlines and gave the whole edifice a somewhat tipsy
rusticity quite out of keeping with its builders' intentions.

But whatever its appearance, the summer-house had
been to Elizabeth and Nerina a source of unending joy, for
they had discovered that in lowering the roof to suit
another of the ancient Earl's requirements, a small attic
had been inadvertently contrived. This was just large
enough for the children to sit in upright, and they had
made it their secret hiding-place, having found that it was
easy to effect an entrance by a series of footholds in the
wooden panels with which the walls of the summer-house
had finally been covered.

It was here they had told each other their innermost secrets. It was here they had kept their most treasured possessions, and it was here they had feasted on food stolen from the larder or given to them by an indulgent cook. It took Nerina but a few seconds now to climb up the back of the summer-house, to open the door which gave access to the low attic, and to crawl through it, closing the door behind her.

The attic was, to her surprise, cleaner than she had expected. To its furnishings of dolls' tea-sets, tattered books and a heap of jam-jars, someone had recently added a satin-covered cushion which Nerina had never seen before. She was surprised at its appearance, but without too much speculation as to how it had come there she used it on which to sit and look out of the window.

The window had been made many years earlier when she and Elizabeth had knocked a hole in the patterned mosaic of polished wood. The honeysuckle obscured the crime and by moving some of its bugled blossom now Nerina had a panoramic view of the whole garden.

In the distance she could see her uncle and aunt standing on the terrace, a party of guests filing past them and then descending the wide grey stone steps on to the lawn. Outside the marquee Elizabeth in her new gown of frilled pink organdie was entertaining two young men. Even at this distance Nerina could see that she was nervous and her mittened hands were clasping and unclasping the handle of her sunshade.

Nerina could recognise a large number of people walking about the grounds. She could see the Lord Lieutenant of the County, pompous and loud-voiced, his face purple with the heat, his eyes searching the crowds as if he were frightened of missing someone more important than the person to whom he was speaking.

She watched the Vicar of Rowan, looking rather like a crushed black beetle as he cringed before the Bishop of the Diocese, magnificent in purple, the jewelled Cross on his fat stomach catching and reflecting the rays of the sun.

Settling herself more comfortably on the cushion and cupping her face in her hands, Nerina watched the people with enjoyment. It was nice to see and not be seen, and it was pleasant to know that it was some hours now before she need face her uncle.

It was then she became aware that two people had detached themselves from the little crowd watching the croquet tournament and were walking straight towards

20

the summer-house. She recognised the woman at once. Elizabeth had admired Lady Clementine Talmadge for years, but Nerina had always felt vaguely antagonistic to her, even though she always went out of her way to be charming to the "dear children" as she called them.

Lady Clementine was looking ravishing this afternoon in a crinoline of pale-yellow organdie over watered silk. Yellow feathers trimmed her bonnet and her shoulders were draped with a scarf of crystallised gauze.

Her dark hair framed her oval face with its long slanting eyes. There was something sensual about her which was ir- resistible, her very femininity was a challenge. Even to Nerina her beauty seemed almost deliberately provocative. It was impossible not to be aware of her small swelling breasts beneath the tight-boned bodice of her gown, and the cumbersome hoops of the crinoline succeeded on Lady Clementine in being neither modest nor a womanly protection.

There was something primitive and feline in the way she moved, in every breath she drew. She was as uncivilised be- neath the polished surface of her environment as a woman of the jungle. She was the daughter of a Duke, the respected wife of a nobleman, a person of consequence in the County, but the look she gave the man who walked beside her now was frankly and unashamedly rapacious.

Nerina, watching Lady Clementine, had not, until she intercepted that strange sidelong glance which she did not entirely understand, noticed her escort. Then as they reached the door of the summer-house she saw that it was the man who had crossed the Hall when she was about to descend the stairs—the dark man with burning hatred in his eyes, and expression of contempt and disdain.

She listened to their footsteps crossing the wooden floor beneath her, then she heard Lady Clementine say:

"But, Rupert, this is such a surprise. I had no idea that I should see you here today."

"I left London last night," Sir Rupert replied. "I had to see you immediately, something has happened."

"What is it, Rupert?" There was a note of alarm in Lady Clementine's voice. "You look strange and unlike your- self."

"There is every reason for me to look strange," Sir Rupert replied. "Clementine, I have to find myself a wife immediately."

2

Lady Clementine gave a little cry.

"Rupert! What can you mean?"

"What I say," he replied. "I have to get married and quickly."

"But why? I cannot understand! Rupert, for goodness' sake explain yourself."

"It is the Queen's command," Sir Rupert replied, and his voice was grim. "Her Majesty has obviously been informed that we have been behaving, if not improperly, at least without propriety."

"Her Majesty has been informed!" Lady Clementine repeated. "Then . . . then . . . there is only one person who can have done it—my mother-in-law. She has been spying on us. I feel certain of it. There has been something in the way she has looked at me, at the things she has said; and yet I was certain that no one suspected."

"You do not think your husband . . . ?" Sir Rupert began.

"Oh no, not Montagu! He knows nothing. Besides, he is always too drunk to notice anything even if it happened in front of his very nose. But my mother-in-law is different. She has always hated me. She swears Montagu never drank until I married him."

"And did he?" Sir Rupert enquired.

"How do I know? I wasn't there," Lady Clementine replied petulantly.

Sir Rupert laughed. It was a sound without much humour, but nevertheless it was a laugh.

"I am glad I am so amusing," Lady Clementine said in a sharp tone.

Sir Rupert laughed again.

"No, Clementine, my dear, you are not amusing," he said, "but just occasionally your very ingenuousness appeals to my sense of humour. Now, do not look cross because I am teasing you. You are far too beautiful to need any other virtues, and least of all that of being amusing."

"I wish you would not talk like that, Rupert," Lady Clementine said. "You know I do not understand in the very least what you are trying to say."

"No, I can see that," Sir Rupert said. "Let me put it

more plainly. You are a very beautiful and seductive person, Clementine."

"There, that is what I like to hear," she smiled; "but, Rupert, this command of the Queen's, what will it mean?"

"It means," he replied, "that I have got to find myself a wife and speedily. At any moment now the Prime Minister may make up his mind to ask Lord Palmerston for his resignation. There are many people who would be bitterly opposed to my taking his place, and if they had any real argument against it, I doubt if Lord John would be strong enough to support an unpopular fancy."

"Then you will have to marry," Lady Clementine said in a low voice. "I declare that I can hardly bear to think of it."

"I am not exactly enamoured of the idea myself," Sir Rupert retorted. "Besides, what do I know of these puny misses? To tell the truth, I do not number even one amongst my acquaintances."

"That I can well believe," Lady Clementine said; "and, Rupert, how you will hate holy matrimony!"

"Well, I suppose it was inevitable sooner or later," Rupert said; "but I would prefer to be older before I have to grow used to respectable domesticity."

Lady Clementine made a little sound which was neither a laugh nor a sob.

"The Queen means you to settle down. It is an appalling thought! Shall we ever be able to see each other?"

"We will contrive to do that, I promise you," Sir Rupert said rather grimly. "If you think that the whole of my life is going to be altered by a Royal command, you are much mistaken. I am not the only man who has had to provide himself with a façade of respectability. But behind it I shall be myself, to do as I wish and take my pleasures where I please."

"It is my mother-in-law who has done this," Lady Clementine said bitterly. "I could murder her, the prying old witch. I know she is great friends with at least two of Her Majesty's Women of the Bedchamber. What pleasure it must have given her to know that she was making trouble both for me and for you!"

"Does it matter?" Sir Rupert asked wearily. "The lion's share of the trouble, as you call it, appears to be mine."

"Yes indeed," Lady Clementine said sympathetically, "for you have to wed some suitable young woman. She will be *gauche*, easily shocked and a deadly bore whether she is

23

at the dining-table or in bed! Poor Rupert, how bad-tempered you will be! I declare I am almost sorry for the girl."

"Doubtless she will occupy herself at Wroth," Sir Rupert replied. "I will take her to Court for Her Majesty's approval, and then she can be packed off to the country. You must persuade Sir Montagu to reopen your London house."

"Yes indeed, I can easily do that," Lady Clementine replied, "for he much prefers to be in London where he can drink and gamble at White's. You will remember it was your idea, Rupert, that I should retire to the country so that we could see each other without there being so much gossip as there might be in London."

"An estimate which appears to have gone wrong," Sir Rupert said. "Well, we must just reverse our tactics. In the meantime . . ."

He paused.

"In the meantime?" Lady Clementine prompted, and her voice was pregnant with desire.

She looked at him out of the corners of her long slanting eyes, and her red lips were parted as she swayed a little towards him. But he was not looking at her, he was staring with unseeing eyes across the green lawns.

"You had best find me a wife," he said at length.

"Rupert, how can you ask me to do such a monstrous thing?" Lady Clementine exclaimed. "I assure you I would only have to glance at the girl you must marry to loathe her! What is more, if she loved you, as of course she would, I would want to scratch her eyes out."

"Very well then, I must choose a bride for myself," Sir Rupert said with a shrug of his broad shoulders.

"No, I cannot allow you to do that. It would make me even more jealous," Lady Clementine cried hastily. "How terrible this is! What a ghastly situation it is for you . . . and for me!" She paused suddenly then gave an exclamation. "Rupert, I have it! Look over there, the girl in the pink flounced frock with the white scarf."

"Where? What are you talking about?"

"That girl, do you see her? There, my dear, is your bride!"

"Why, and who is she?"

"Your host and hostess's daughter, Lady Elizabeth Graye," Lady Clementine said. "I have known her since she was a small child. She is pretty enough in an insipid manner and I should imagine quite docile. What else could she be with Lord Cardon as a father?"

"But . . . but . . ." Sir Rupert hesitated.

"There are no buts about it," Lady Clementine said. "The Cardons will be delighted. I know for a fact that they are extremely hard up. They even had to sell one of the farms on the Estate last year, so Lord Cardon will be looking for a wealthy son-in-law. And you are certainly that, Rupert."

"Yes, I am wealthy," Sir Rupert said. "But why do you pick on this particular girl?"

"Because, my dear, she is everything you require," Lady Clementine said. "She is stupid and placid, well-bred and of impeccable respectability. Unless I am very much mistaken, she will accept you with alacrity and make you a complacent, unsuspicious wife."

There was silence for a moment and then Sir Rupert said:

"It might be worse!"

"Much, much worse!" Lady Clementine agreed. "But as I was talking to you, I saw Elizabeth over there and realised that she is perhaps the only girl with whom I would not feel desperately and murderously jealous."

"Do you really think there would be any need for you to feel jealous of my wife, whoever she might be?" Sir Rupert asked.

"But of course," Lady Clementine answered unhesitatingly. "I shall be jealous of any other woman you must touch, any woman who bears your name. In fact, of any woman on whom your eye must rest because she is a woman! And your reputation tells me there is just cause for my jealousy."

"It is hardly fair to hold against me the things I did in the past before I met you," Sir Rupert said.

"My dear, I do not worry about your past, I assure you," Lady Clementine laughed. "It is your future which disturbs me, and with reason. Rupert, you are a very fascinating person."

"I am happy that you think so."

"Will you answer me one question, utterly truthfully?" Lady Clementine asked, and now her voice was low and unexpectedly serious.

"But of course!"

"Then tell me, Rupert, do you really love me?"

"Good gracious, what a question! Haven't we spent

much of these last months together and experienced, I believed, moments of extraordinary happiness?"

"You still have not answered my question," Lady Clementine said. "Perhaps it is unnecessary! Nevertheless I have the uneasy feeling that you do not really love me the way I love you."

"That sentence has a very familiar ring," Sir Rupert smiled.

"I am not surprised," Lady Clementine said, speaking rapidly and with the urgency of suppressed emotion. "Many women must have said the same thing to you, because, Rupert, you do not really love me or anyone else. Oh yes, I attract you, I know that. I make you feel passionate, possessive and even at times jealous; but somehow all the time we are together I know that what you feel for me is not love. I have tried to make you love me, tried so hard, Rupert, because I love you, and I mean . . . to hold you."

Her voice broke on the last words.

"Clementine, my dear, you are upsetting yourself. Besides, how can you talk such nonsense? You know I love you."

Lady Clementine drew a deep breath and moving nearer to Sir Rupert, laid her hand on his. For a moment her fingers were soft and pliable, then suddenly she dug them fiercely into his flesh.

"You are mine," she said. "I defy any woman to take you from me."

Sir Rupert raised her fingers to his lips.

"I had no idea I had engaged your feelings so successfully, Clementine. I imagined I was but another fool to lay his heart at your small but indifferent feet."

"You thought nothing of the sort," Lady Clementine replied. "I am making a scene, Rupert, and I know you dislike them, but somehow this afternoon I cannot be clever with you. For once I am telling you the truth."

"And I am replying that you are talking nonsense," Sir Rupert said, "and what is more I will prove it. Will you meet me tonight in the usual place?"

"In the arbour?" Lady Clementine asked, suddenly breathless. "Do you think we dare? Perhaps my mother-in-law spied on us there, perhaps she has employed one of the gardeners to keep watch."

"Nonsense, no one could possibly have seen us," Sir Rupert said. "Your mother-in-law's suspicions must be entirely without foundation. Say you are going to bed early and leave the house by the garden door. Wear something dark over your dress. No one will see you if you keep out of sight of the house, and I will be waiting for you as usual."

"Rupert, I want to come, you know that. It is only that I am afraid for you, for both of us. If Montagu found out, the scandal would ruin you and you know it."

"Yes, I know that," Sir Rupert replied, "but there will be no scandal. You will come?"

"Yes, I will come," Lady Clementine said hungrily. "Perhaps for the last time! If you are going to be married, I may never see you again."

"Clementine, how can you talk such rubbish? You know perfectly well that my marriage will make no difference to us. Why, you have said yourself that this girl will be a complacent, unsuspicious wife."

"Yes, I think Elizabeth will be that," Lady Clementine said. "So you intend to offer for her?"

"Of course," Sir Rupert replied. "Do not I always obey your commands?"

"As faithfully as you obey those of Her Majesty," Lady Clementine said mockingly.

"Then I will now go and have a word with my future wife," Sir Rupert said. "We have been here long enough, Clementine. Someone may have noticed our absence."

"I will go and watch the croquet; but oh, Rupert, you will come tonight?"

"Can you believe for one moment that I shall not be counting the hours?" he replied.

"I wonder if you will really do that," she said, her voice thickening. "I shall be counting them, but I often think that with you it is a very different matter."

"You under-rate your own attractions, my dear," Sir Rupert replied, "and now, as I have already said, we have been here long enough."

"Yes, of course. *Au revoir* until tonight, you wicked, fascinating, adorable lover."

He looked into her eyes and saw the flame of desire burning there unashamedly. Her face was transformed. The mask of conventional beauty vanished and in its place was a primitive yearning, an expression greedy, demanding, rapacious and almost ugly in its uncontrolled avidity.

Sir Rupert drew in his breath, and Lady Clementine knew triumphantly that she had aroused him.

"Do not keep me waiting too long tonight," he commanded, and rose to his feet.

Nerina heard them walk across the floor and down the steps on to the lawn. There, without a glance at each other, they separated, Lady Clementine moving slowly and gracefully across the grass towards the group of people still watching the croquet tournament, Sir Rupert strolling unconcernedly in the opposite direction towards the marquee.

Nerina watched them go and then, when they were out of earshot, changed her position with a violent movement as if the very roughness with which she twisted herself about in some way relieved her feelings. She was cramped, her legs had pins and needles in them, but she could hardly feel the tingling pain for she was so angry. There were two bright spots of colour burning in her cheeks, and her eyes were flashing.

Of all the disgusting, disgraceful things she had ever dreamt of this was the worst! So that was Sir Rupert Wroth, she thought! She had often heard her uncle and aunt speak of him—the rich, wealthy owner of Wroth Castle. No wonder that, when his name was mentioned, older people sometimes whispered together and shook their heads and there was a quite obvious atmosphere of disapproval to be sensed in the very way they spoke his name.

"The beast! The cad!" Nerina said out loud. "To think that he should contemplate marriage with Elizabeth, sweet, gentle Elizabeth, who, as Lady Clementine has sensed all too cleverly, would make him a complacent, unsuspicious wife. But she shan't marry him if I can help it."

Nerina felt as if the very violence of her feelings would not permit her to stay cooped up in the little attic and she crept through the hidden doorway and scrambled down to the ground.

Because she was so angry she forgot her own misdeeds, and when she came to an opening in the rhododendron bushes she walked boldly through it and hurried across the lawn in search of Elizabeth. But her cousin seemed to have disappeared, and before she had time to look around she heard a voice in which astonishment, disapproval and anger were all mingled, say:

"Nerina! What are you doing here?"

She turned round to find her aunt staring at her in startled surprise, her lorgnette raised to her eyes.

Nerina curtsied.

"I have just arrived, Aunt Anne."

"Arrived from where?" Lady Cardon asked, and then before Nerina could reply, she added: "No, there is no need to tell me. I do not know what your uncle will say to this; but until I can break the news to him, you are to go to your room at once and stay there. At once, do you understand?"

"But, Aunt Anne——" Nerina began.

"You heard me, Nerina. You are to stay in your room until I send for you. Kindly obey me."

Nerina knew when she was defeated. She curtsied and without a word walked in the direction of the house. Several of the guests whom she passed looked curiously at her as she swept by them white-faced, her chin held high. Reaching the Hall, she ran swiftly up the stairs into the sanctuary of her bedroom, slamming the door behind her.

She stood in the centre of the room quivering with rage, indignation and a sense of injustice which curiously enough for the moment seemed to invigorate rather than depress her. It was always the same, she thought. Whatever happened, she was in the wrong, even before she could speak, could even explain. She was never allowed to have a point of view, never permitted even an opinion.

"It is not fair," she said aloud, and then began to walk slowly up and down the room as if her feelings would not permit her to keep still, but must express themselves in action, any action so long as it was definite.

"It is not fair," she said again, and realised how inadequate an expression it was. Had anyone ever been fair to her? Had anything ever been fair since she had come to Rowanfield Manor?

The unwanted poor relation! The orphan who lived on charity! The one person in the house who could not call her soul her own!

She remembered her life with her father and mother. They had been miserably poor, but the tiny house in which they lived had been a place of laughter and happiness. Happiness! She had never known the meaning of the word since she came to live with her uncle and aunt. And sometimes she would fear that she might forget what it was like; forget what it had meant to live without rows, without fear and without the aching misery of knowing oneself disliked!

Never, never would she call Rowanfield Manor home. Home was a place of peace and laughter, a refuge from the outside world. Home and happiness, the two words were indivisibly linked in Nerina's miind, and yet even at home she could remember moments when there had been tears in her mother's eyes, when she had waited, tense and anxious, as the hours went by and her father had not returned at the time he was expected.

She remembered throwing her arms round her mother's neck on one such occasion and crying passionately:

"Please don't look so unhappy, Mama. I want you to be happy, I want you to laugh. It is bad and wicked of Papa to make you cry."

"I am not crying, my darling," her mother answered. "I am just worried. Your father may have had an accident, for he is late, much later than he usually is."

But Nerina was sure it was not an accident. In another hour, perhaps two, the front door would be flung open and her father would have returned. His voice would cry out her mother's name, and perhaps hers, and they would run helter-skelter into his enveloping arms. He would be warm and glowing, smelling of cigar smoke and brandy, and he would kiss them affectionately. He would ruffle Nerina's hair and ask why they were sitting round so solemn as if there were a funeral in the house.

"Mama was worried about you," Nerina would say accusingly.

"Am I late?" her father would ask innocently; then turning to his wife, he would explain. "I am sorry, darling, but I got delayed. The boys suggested a game of cards and you know how difficult it is to get away."

"I was not really worried," she would reply, and Nerina would look at her a little scornfully wondering why she did not tell him the truth.

She had learned then that men were like that, even the best of them, even the nicest of them—selfish, unthinking, inflicting pain on those who loved them. She was only seven when she decided that, although she loved her father, she loved her mother much the best. Papa was fun and exciting and there was no one like him for joking, for making the most commonplace thing an adventure, but he was not reliable. He would promise something and forget all about it. When he was playing cards, he was oblivious of everything, especially time; besides, as Nerina learned later, he could not afford to play cards. They had so very, very little money and when he lost, as he frequently did, they often went hungry and yet another of their few possessions vanished overnight.

But men were like that! Nerina was to remember that lesson when she came to Rowanfield Manor. It was hard to credit that Uncle Herbert was her father's brother. They were so unalike, and yet sometimes, when her uncle's self-ishness and unkindness were most apparent, it called to mind her mother's white face and tear-filled eyes as they waited hour after hour for a man who was playing cards.

The final incident which had orphaned Nerina had been entirely her father's fault. He had been warned that there was a storm coming on out to sea, and much more experienced men than he had advised him against taking out his yacht; but he had a bet of twenty sovereigns that he would sail along the coast for two miles, pick up a case of wine and be back in harbour before sunset.

When he told Nerina's mother of the wager he had made, she had given a little cry of horror.

"How can we afford to lose such a large amount of money?" she expostulated.

"But we aren't going to lose it; we are going to win it, and you are coming with me as my crew. You understand the boat better than anybody else. And when we win the twenty sovereigns, you shall have that gold locket we saw in the jeweller's last week."

"It is crazy!" Nerina's mother exclaimed.

"I like doing crazy things," was the reply, and Nerina felt her father's arms round her as he lifted her up to the level of his shoulders and kissed her cheek. "Good-bye, poppet, we shall be back in two hours."

He picked up his oilskin coat and ran down the garden-path. It was the last time she ever saw him or her mother alive. Even now she could not bear to think of the hours she had waited, of the procession of heavy-footed men who had come to the house long after dark and had told her what had happened.

There had been the funeral in the small unkept church-yard. She had been too numb to cry, too stunned fully to realise what had happened. Only the big, almost over-whelming figure of her uncle seemed real. She had never seen him before, but she knew he was the Earl of Cardon, whom her father had spoken of with jovial indifference and whose name had always made her mother look angry and resentful.

After the funeral her uncle had talked to her.

"Your father made a damned fool of himself," he said. "He married without the consent of his family, and he had

31

to take the consequences. If he was poor and miserable, he had nobody to blame but himself."

"We were poor," Nerina said defiantly, "but we were not miserable. We were very happy, all three of us."

"In this place!"

Lord Cardon's tone was scathing, as he looked round the tiny sitting-room of their cottage. It was the first time that Nerina had realised how shabby it was, it was the first time she had noticed the threadbare carpet, the paper peeling off the wall, the broken springs of the settee, the patched and faded coverings of the armchairs.

She had nothing to say, but she had loathed her uncle from that moment. It was as if he deliberately stripped her home naked and held it up to scorn and derision. It was, she knew later, exactly what he had wished to do. As they went back to Rowanfield together, he made her feel not only orphaned but absolutely destitute.

"Your aunt and I will give you a home," he said grandiosely, "until you are old enough to earn your own living; but you must remember that it is our charity you are living on. You must learn to be grateful. I do not care for that air in which you answer me when I speak to you. It is disrespectful. You must learn humility, my child. You must learn to be thankful for any mercies that may be accorded to you, for you are entitled to nothing."

From the very beginning he had tried to break her spirit and he had failed. Over and over again when she had defied him and was thrashed until, bruised and fainting, there was nothing she could do but apologise in the words he dictated to her, in her heart she still defied him.

Never once did she entirely capitulate, either to brute force or mental subjugation. If from sheer physical weakness she must surrender outwardly, inwardly she remained inviolable, the rebel who could still dream of revolution although she dared not express it out loud.

"It will not be like this for ever," she comforted herself, as her burning, aching body tried to find relief in her narrow bed. "One day I will get even with him, one day I will be strong enough to win."

When she was nearly eighteen her uncle had informed her that he had arranged for her to accept the post of governess to the child of an old friend of his, and she had been pleased. At last there was a chance of escape from Rowanfield Manor; and though she had been sad to leave her cousin Elizabeth, she had been thrilled and excited at the thought of being free, and of escaping from the almost active persecution by which her uncle expressed his feelings towards her now.

But her joy was quickly crushed. She had only been a week in her new position before the son of the house began to pursue her. He was an uncouth boy of twenty-two, inordinately spoilt by his mother who loved him with a possessive, jealous affection. She believed that nothing he did could possibly be wrong; and when finally she discovered him in the act of trying to kiss Nerina in the corner of the Library, she was easily convinced that it was Nerina's fault and would listen to no other explanation.

Nerina was told to pack her trunk and leave within a few hours. She had gone back to Rowanfield Manor crestfallen, but quite unprepared for the reception she received from her uncle and aunt. They too would not listen to her.

"You must have encouraged the young man," her uncle said icily, and she had known without looking at him that there was that dangerous glint in his eye. She knew then, as she had known subconsciously for a long time, that he enjoyed her sufferings, especially if they were physical ones and concerned the opposite sex. It was thus that he could be revenged upon her for the way she had fought him many years ago, for the long scars her finger-nails had left on his face, and the horror and loathing in her voice as she had cried out:

"I loathe you, you horrid, fat, ugly old man."

She had known then that he would never forgive her; and though he personally had left her alone, she knew that he was waiting for his revenge, certain that time would bring it—time and some other man not so frightened as he was of his reputation.

The next time she was employed she had returned home for the same reason, but then her persecutor had been her employer. Her uncle had cross-examined her for hours, and she had known that the inquisition gave him an obscene pleasure. But although he forced her to answer his questions, she had done so defiantly, maddening him still further. Now she knew full well what to expect this evening or tomorrow.

"What did he say to you? What did you do? When did you first notice anything in his manner? What did you feel when he touched you?"

The questions would go on and on. She knew now

33

without a doubt that her uncle had known just what he was doing when he sent her to the house of the Marquis of Droxburgh. She had listened to the servants talking, she had overheard conversations amongst the guests, and had known then that her uncle must have been well aware, as everyone else was, of the Marquis's reputation.

He was a notoriously licentious man, married to a wife who was a semi-invalid and who took no part in the household arrangements, who seldom left her own bedroom and who was to all intents and purposes as uninterested in her husband as he was in her.

Nerina had not at first guessed what awaited her. The house was lovely, a great Georgian mansion set in wide green parklands and ornamented by a chain of silver lakes. During her first week there she had believed that she would be happy. The child that she had to teach was a delicate, lonely little girl of eleven whose fragility appealed to everything that was maternal in Nerina. She had been happy planning the lessons they would do together, coaxing the child to eat and insisting that she go more often into the fresh air and sunshine. There was a peace and quietness about the place, with no one to interfere, one day succeeding another in smooth routine.

And then the Marquis came home. He brought a large party of friends with him, raffish, noisy, fashionable people who slept until luncheon and gambled the night away. The whole house appeared to Nerina to be turned upside down, the servants scurried and rushed along the corridors with hardly time to remember such trifles as the schoolroom meals, which were late, badly cooked and invariably cold.

There was the sound of music and of voices to keep both Nerina and her charge awake at night, and in the morning even the dogs seemed to creep about the house, afraid to bark lest they should waken the exhausted guests.

One afternoon, when Nerina was reading to her charge in the schoolroom, the Marquis came in. She rose politely at his entrance, curtsied, expecting him to pay little attention to her and ready after the first greeting to leave him alone with his daughter. Then as his crafty, evil eyes flickered over her and his mouth curved in a twisted, humourless smile over his darting tongue, she knew what would happen, knew it by the frightened thumping of her own heart, by the feeling of repugnance and horror which made her take a step back, made her long to run helter-skelter from the room.

That was the beginning and from that moment she had no peace. It had gone on until she could bear it no longer. The handle of her bedroom door would turn silently at night; she knew that he might be waiting for her anywhere in the darkness of a room, in the hidden curve of a staircase, in the garden or even in what she knew ought to be the sanctity of the schoolroom.

It was when the key of her bedroom door disappeared that she realised the moment had come when she could bear it no longer. For a moment she could not believe that the key had vanished. She thought it must have fallen on the floor, have been moved by some housemaid, but she had searched fruitlessly for it and had known the truth. She had been afraid as she had never been afraid before.

She spent that night locked in the child's room, sitting sleepless and alert in a chair before the dying fire, listening for a step outside, for a voice which might command her to come out. She had left before the household was awake, writing a short, incoherent note to the Marchioness and another to the child. She had made excuses—for how could she tell them the truth? There was illness at home, and she had to go at once. She regretted that she would be unable to return, and she hoped they would find someone else to take her place.

What else could she say? But it was not fair, she thought again, and caught sight of her own reflection in the mirror.

Her hair was a vivid patch of colour against the white walls of the bedroom, and somehow it seemed as if it was at the root of all her trouble. Was it her hair which caused that strange look in men's eyes as soon as they saw her, and which made them seem different as soon as she appeared? She knew the look so well, their eyes would widen as if in surprise, and then narrow as if to hide a sudden fire which gleamed red and dangerous in the secret depth of their being.

They would move towards her and almost instinctively she would move away, knowing that they longed to touch her, knowing that she had aroused their desire unwillingly, unwittingly but inevitably.

"It is unfair," she said again, and even as she said it, the door opened and she turned to find her cousin rushing towards her.

"Nerina!" Elizabeth exclaimed. "I heard Mama say you were here and I didn't believe it. I felt it couldn't be true. But I slipped away just to make sure. Oh, Nerina, I am so glad to see you."

"And I you," Nerina said, as she stepped back from her cousin's embrace. "How lovely you look! I was admiring your gown across the lawn."

"Were you down there? I didn't see you."

"I was watching you from the summer-house," Nerina said.

"From the summer-house," Elizabeth laughed. "But, Nerina, isn't that just like you to go first to our hiding-place!"

"And a good thing I did," Nerina said. "Elizabeth, I have got something to tell you."

"And I have something to tell you," Elizabeth interrupted. "Mama will be furious with me for leaving the guests, but I couldn't wait to tell you. Nerina, I am in love!"

"In love!" Nerina said sharply. "Elizabeth! . . . not with Sir Rupert Wroth?"

"Sir Rupert Wroth?" Elizabeth asked blankly. "No, of course not! Who is he? Oh, I remember; but of course it isn't him. How could you think such a thing? No, it is Adrian . . . Adrian Butler."

Nerina felt a wave of relief flood over her.

"Thank goodness! Who is he? Are you engaged?"

Elizabeth shook her head.

"No, not yet. You can imagine what Papa will say to the suggestion, for he is only a soldier. But what does it matter? I love him, and I don't care if he hasn't got a penny. I love him with all my heart and soul and . . . he loves me."

Elizabeth pulled off her bonnet as she spoke and sat down on the window-seat. Her fair curls were silhouetted against the window; and as she raised her eyes to Nerina, there was an expression of sweet seriousness on her face which made her lovelier than she had ever been in her life before. Impulsively Nerina crossed the room to kneel beside her.

"Tell me all about it, Elizabeth," she said. "I am frightened for you."

"I'm not frightened," Elizabeth said. "I love Adrian and nothing Mama or Papa can say will make me alter my mind."

"Do they know about him?" Nerina asked.

Elizabeth shook her head.

"Papa guessed that I was beginning to like him, and a fortnight ago he forbade him the house. 'Who is this young jackanapes?' he asked. 'I have never heard of him or his family. He is not to be invited here again.' Of course Mama agreed. She struck him off our visiting list but it was too late. Adrian had already told me that he loved me. We met the next afternoon in a copse at the end of the drive. He asked me to marry him and I promised him that I would."

"But, Elizabeth, your father . . . ?" Nerina cried.

"Adrian is going to see Papa at the end of this week after he has had his promotion. He will be a Captain then. Think of it, Nerina, a Captain, and he is only twenty-four. It shows how able he is. They think a lot of him in his Regiment, the Queen's Dragoon Guards, and he looks so handsome and splendid in his uniform."

"But, Elizabeth, how will you ever . . . ?" Nerina started, but was interrupted by a knock on the door.

"Come in," Elizabeth said.

The door was opened by Bessie, the maid who had waited on both the cousins since they were old enough to dispense with a nurse.

She was a middle-aged woman, short and broad in the body, who should, judging by her features, have been ugly. But there was such an expression of kindliness and good-humour on her face that anyone meeting her was instinctively attracted to her warm geniality.

She was an inveterate gossip, but she hardly ever said anything unkind or spiteful. She was the recipient of innumerable confidences, but she never revealed anything told her as a secret. Like many women who have never aroused desire, she adored romance when it happened to others, and lived vicariously through their affairs, at times half believing she herself was loved, possessed, and even deserted.

Nearer to her heart than her own family were Elizabeth and Nerina. The latter had often thought that Bessie would, if it was necessary, cut herself into small pieces or drain away her life-blood to serve them.

At the sight of Nerina now her whole face lit up.

"Miss Nerina!" she gasped in astonishment. "Well, you could knock me down with a feather, for you're the last person I expected to see here today."

"How are you, Bessie?" Nerina asked. "I have turned up again like a bad penny. Isn't that your expression?"

"Indeed it is, Miss, but I wouldn't call you a bad penny, indeed I wouldn't. Why, it was only the other day I said to Cook, 'Miss Nerina has a heart of gold' I says."

"Thank you, Bessie," Nerina answered. "It must be the only valuable thing about me."

Bessie laughed, but almost comically her laugh stopped suddenly and the expression on her face changed to one of consternation as she turned to Elizabeth.

"But I was forgetting why I came. Your ladyship is to go downstairs at once. Milady is real angry with you, I hear, for having slipped away before the guests had all gone. You are in for a row if you ask me and you had best hurry yourself."

Elizabeth got to her feet, her face rather pale.

"Is my father angry too, Bessie?"

"It was James who brought the message, and he didn't say. He only said her ladyship was asking for you and seemed to be angry because you weren't to be found. Perhaps his lordship knows nothing of it; but hurry now, for goodness' sake."

Elizabeth slipped her bonnet over her hair without looking in the glass.

"Good-bye, Nerina, I will see you later," she said. "Oh, I hope Papa isn't angry too. I have no desire to upset him just now."

She ran from the room and Bessie and Nerina looked at each other.

"Has she told you, Miss Nerina?" Bessie asked at last.

"About her young man?" Nerina enquired. "So you know, Bessie?"

"Of course I know," Bessie replied with the familiarity of a trusted and beloved servant. "Don't I wait for them every afternoon, keeping watch, as it were, in case anyone should be prying about to see what we were a-doing. It frightens me half out of my wits, I can tell you that, Miss. Every time the wind blows in the trees or a rabbit runs through the wood, I fancy it is his lordship after us."

"I can well believe that," Nerina said. "But, Bessie, what is the point? His lordship will never let them marry."

"Perhaps he will when he sees how serious they are," Bessie said confidently. "After all there's nothing against the young gentleman except that he hasn't much money.

He is of a good family, I know that for a fact. Cook's sister is in service with a cousin of his who is greatly respected in Yorkshire."

Nerina said nothing, but she was frowning. She was thinking that, as far as Lord Cardon was concerned, a family greatly respected in Yorkshire was not going to prove a formidable rival to Sir Rupert Wroth, the wealthy owner of a vast estate.

One thing she must do was to warn Elizabeth of the proposition that might be put to her. She only hoped that she would not be too late, that Lady Cardon had not called her downstairs this very moment to tell her of Sir Rupert's intentions. Then she felt that it must be impossible. Sir Rupert would not have had time to speak to Lord Cardon on such an intimate matter. Doubtless he would come over the next day, in which case there was plenty of time to warn Elizabeth and prepare her for what she must say.

"You are looking worried, Miss," Bessie said, breaking in on her thoughts. "What is perturbing you? Is it because you have had to come home again?"

"Isn't that reason enough to be worried?" Nerina asked. Bessie nodded her head.

"I guessed it would happen, Miss. I didn't want to upset you before you went; but when I heard you were going to that particular house, I cried myself to sleep night after night thinking of you."

"Bessie!" Nerina exclaimed. "You knew about it then? Why did you not warn me?"

"What could I say?" Bessie asked. "His lordship had made the arrangement. What difference would it have made had you said you didn't wish to go there?"

"That is true enough," Nerina replied. "But what do you know about Lord Droxburgh?"

"I know enough," Bessie replied, "to be certain sure that I would rather see any daughter of mine dead in her coffin than go to a house like that. We have a footman here who was in service to the Marquis both in London and in the country. The stories he told us used to make our hair stand on end. We laughed at the time and thought he was exaggerating; but when I knew you were going there, I felt as if every story he had ever told us had come alive in letters of fire. Oh, Miss Nerina, is it safe and unharmed you are?"

"Yes, safe and unharmed," Nerina said wearily.

"Thanks be to God for that," Bessie exclaimed.

39

"I don't want to think about it again," Nerina said suddenly. "But, Bessie, I hate men. They are evil, bad and cruel and wicked."

"Some are different," Bessie said quietly.

"I don't believe it," Nerina said passionately. "I hate them all, every one of them."

3

"What shall I do, Nerina?" Elizabeth asked for the thousandth time. "What shall I do?"

She knew there could be no reply to her question, and yet she repeated it again and again as if by some miracle Nerina might find an answer. All through the night they had talked together, Elizabeth at first crying bitterly, then later lying white-faced and tearless, staring into the darkness, her voice gradually dying away into silence until at last the only thing she would whisper at intermittent intervals was: "What shall I do? What shall I do?"

It did indeed seem to Nerina as if there was nothing Elizabeth could do, nothing any of them could do; and yet she refused to allow herself to accept what appeared to be inevitable. Seeing Elizabeth's distress, hearing her bitter sobs, Nerina reproached herself for not having been quick enough at least to mitigate the shock a little; but she had not had time to warn her cousin of what awaited her, and only after Elizabeth had gone downstairs and the time ticked slowly by, did she anticipate what must be happening.

Unconscious of what lay ahead, Elizabeth, fearful of her mother's anger, had sped to the Drawing-room to find Lady Cardon alone.

"Oh, here you are, Elizabeth," she said sharply. "Why did you disappear in that extraordinary ill-bred way before all our guests had departed?"

"I am indeed sorry, Mama," Elizabeth said humbly, "but I feared the tape of my petticoat had come undone and I went upstairs to set it right."

"You should be more careful," Lady Cardon said, but to Elizabeth's surprise the rebuke was made in an absent-minded tone and she realised that her mother's mind was elsewhere.

Elizabeth felt her spirits rise. She had thought as she came downstairs that she would be severely rebuked for going in search of her cousin. Gentle and sensitive, she shrank with every nerve in her body from the rows and scenes which were an all too familiar part of her home life. Her father's fits of temper terrified her, but she was almost equally distressed by her mother's anger. Lady Cardon did not rage or become physically violent as her husband did, but when anything occurred to annoy her she would scold with a nagging persistence which somehow got under the skin and which sooner or later reduced the offender to tears and a state of humiliating subservience.

She was a large woman, big-boned, who had been handsome in her youth, and it was difficult to understand how she could have given birth to anything so delicate and prettily fashioned as Elizabeth. It was indeed from her father's side of the family that Elizabeth inherited her good looks, for Lord Cardon had been an extremely handsome young man until luxurious living, too much port and an embittered disposition had taken their toll of his appearance.

One of the things which contributed more than anything else to his discontent was the fact that he had no heir. Lady Cardon had in fact presented him at varying intervals in their married life with six children, but three had died before they reached the age of seven and two at birth. It was by some miracle that Elizabeth had survived; but she was not a son, and neither her father nor her mother ever forgave her for the accident of her sex.

As Lady Cardon's small, rather protruding eyes rested on her daughter now, there was no expression of affection in them.

"Your bonnet is crooked," she said sharply after a moment. "Your brooch is undone."

"I am sorry, Mama," Elizabeth said, and with hasty trembling fingers tried to set both things right at the same moment.

Lady Cardon waited until she had finished and then she said:

"Your father wishes to see you in the Library. Go to him at once."

Elizabeth's eyes expressed her astonishment and her lips parted as if she would ask a question. But realising that it was unlikely that she would receive an adequate answer, she said nothing, but curtsied demurely and went towards the door. Lady Cardon watched her go and then without any change in her expression turned towards the window through which she could watch the servants tidying the lawns and carrying trays of dirty glasses from the marquee.

Elizabeth's fingers shook now as she turned the handle of the Library door. To her surprise, as she entered the big room almost silently, she heard the sound of voices and saw that her father was not alone. It was not to be a row,

42

then, she thought, and relief swept warmingly through her body like sunshine. It was impossible for her or Nerina ever to enter the Library without that sudden sinking of the heart, that dryness of the lips, that sudden breathlessness which comes from fear.

Only too often had they been summoned to the Library for one reason and for one reason only; and all through her life Elizabeth was to believe that hell was a big room decorated with books and furnished with leather-covered sofas and chairs.

She came into the room now so quietly that it was a moment or two before her father, standing on the hearthrug, perceived her. The expression on his face was jovial and good-humoured as he said:

"Ah, there you are, Elizabeth. Come here, my dear."

Wonderingly Elizabeth obeyed him, saw a man rise to his feet slowly from an armchair and realised that he was Sir Rupert Wroth. He had spoken to her earlier in the afternoon, claiming her acquaintance, and she had wondered for a moment who he was until someone standing by addressed him by name. It was then she recalled that she had been introduced to him two years earlier at a Hunt Ball.

It had been her first appearance in public and she was shy and frightened. No one had asked her to go down to supper and finally one of her father's cronies had taken pity on her and escorted her to the supper-room. Because he was a distinguished old gentleman, Elizabeth had found herself sitting at the most important table along with the Dowagers and dignitaries of the County.

"Do you know everyone?" her partner had enquired gruffly, and then, as she had glanced a little uncomfortably towards the man sitting on her left, he said: "You know Wroth, don't you? Rupert, this is Herbert Cardon's daughter."

Sir Rupert had been deep in conversation with a very lovely and sophisticated woman whom he had obviously escorted down to supper. At the introduction he turned his head for a moment, let his eyes flicker over Elizabeth in what seemed to her a contemptuous, disdainful manner, and then bowed so slightly that it was almost an insult rather than a courtesy.

The smile on her lips died away and she felt snubbed. Perhaps she had been absurdly sensitive, perhaps the incident had been magnified in her inexperience, but at any rate from that day she had never heard Sir Rupert's name mentioned without disliking what she remembered of him. Now, with her father's hand on her shoulder, she curtsied to him and wondered why he was smiling at her.

"Elizabeth, I have something to say to you," her father said in stentorian tones; "something which I believe will give you as much pleasure as it has given me. Sir Rupert Wroth, for whom I have a great respect and for whom I hope in the future to have a deep affection, has approached me today on a delicate and very intimate matter."

Lord Cardon cleared his throat, and as neither Sir Rupert nor Elizabeth said anything he continued:

"He has, my dear child, asked my consent to your betrothal."

For a moment Elizabeth could not understand what her father had said, the meaning did not seem to percolate into her mind. She could only stare at him, knowing that this was something of import, but finding it almost impossible to contemplate what it might be. And then, as gradually the meaning came to her poor, frightened senses, it seemed to her that her father's red face floated dizzily in front of her and Sir Rupert's dark eyes bored into hers.

"No!" she tried to say. "No! No! I can't marry you!"

But somehow the words could not force themselves between her lips. They seemed caught in her throat, and before she could say anything, before she could protest, Lord Cardon said.

"It is a surprise to you, I quite realise that, but I know that you must feel both delighted and honoured at the thought of being the wife of so eminent a politician. I have informed Sir Rupert that your mother and I are prepared to give you both our blessing and that the announcement of the betrothal shall be inserted in the *Court Circular* as soon as he wishes."

At last Elizabeth found words.

"But, Papa, I . . . can not . . ." she began, and then she felt her father's hand come down heavily on her shoulder.

"You will, of course, feel distressed at the thought of leaving your mother and me," her father said. "That is understandable, and Sir Rupert, I am sure, will make allowances for these maidenly fears and hesitations." He turned to Sir Rupert, but his hand was still hard on Elizabeth's shoulder. "You may perhaps find it convenient to call tomorrow, Wroth."

"I will ride over after luncheon," Sir Rupert said, and taking Elizabeth's trembling hand in his, he raised it to his lips. "You have made me very happy," he said and walked towards the door.

"I will see you out," Lord Cardon said. "Elizabeth, wait here until I return."

They went from the room without a backward glance and when they had gone Elizabeth stood as if turned to stone. She felt as if all her faculties were paralysed, as if it were impossible for her to move. She felt as if she were in the grip of some terrible nightmare and she could only stand there praying that she might awake and find it all a dream.

But it was no dream when her father returned. He looked at her curiously and she knew full well that he had sensed what she had tried to say, and that the way he had prevented her from speaking it had been intentional.

"You are a very fortunate girl," he said abruptly.

"Papa, I can not . . . marry him," Elizabeth stammered. "I cannot!"

"And why not?"

The question was spoken aggressively in Lord Cardon's most frightening voice, but for once Elizabeth was not cowed into silence.

"I do not love him, Papa."

"Love! What has love got to do with a good marriage?"

"I . . . I love . . . someone else," Elizabeth faltered.

"And who might that be?" her father asked, and then with his face reddening in anger and the pupils of his eyes enlarging as they did when he was most enraged, he added: "But you have no need to tell me; I can guess. It is that penniless jackanapes, that milk-faced soldier I turned out of the house last week. So you fancy yourself in love with him, do you? Well, fancy anything you like, but it is Wroth you are going to marry as soon as it can possibly be arranged."

"But . . . but, Papa . . ." Elizbaeth began.

"There are no buts about it!" Lord Cardon thundered. "Wroth is a good catch and you are damned lucky that he has offered for you. If you think I am going to let you throw yourself away on some good-for-nothing scamp without family or prospects, you are much mistaken. It is Wroth you are going to wed and if I find that young soldier lad has so much as set a foot on my land, I will thrash him within an inch of his life, and you too if you attempt to see him. Is that clear? Do you hear me?"

It would have been impossible for her not to hear him

for he was shouting at the top of his voice; and as she looked at his inflamed, crimson face, the blue veins standing out on his forehead and at the sides of his nose, Elizabeth had known that she could defy him no longer. With a piteous little cry of despair and terror she turned and ran from the room, the tears blinding her eyes so that she passed her mother in the Hall without seeing her.

Upstairs in her own bedroom Elizabeth collapsed into Nerina's arms and sobbed the story out against her cousin's shoulder.

"If only I had had time to warn you," Nerina said, "for I knew this was going to happen."

"You knew?" Elizabeth asked in astonishment, raising her tear-stained face.

"Yes," Nerina said miserably, "I was just going to tell you what I had overheard when Bessie came into the room. Elizabeth, you can't marry him. He is a brute and a beast."

"I can't marry anyone but Adrian," Elizabeth cried, "but oh, what can I do? Papa is set on it, and you know what he is."

Both girls were silent for a moment, knowing full well what Lord Cardon was like when he was determined on something; and then with an effort to control her tears Elizabeth said:

"But tell me how you know about it."

Nerina recounted what she had heard in the summerhouse. When she had finished, Elizabeth put her fingers to her eyes.

"You cannot marry him, you must not," Nerina said. "You can see now how rotten he is."

"That does not really matter," Elizabeth replied. "I don't really mind whom Sir Rupert loves or what other women he has, it is Adrian to whom I am betrothed. It is Adrian I love!"

Nerina sighed.

"What good is that if you cannot marry him?"

"But I must, I must," Elizabeth said, "even if I have to run away with him."

The cousins stared at each other as if the words quivered in the air between them and were something too fantastic to be contemplated. Then Nerina gave a laugh.

"Bravo, Elizabeth, I did not know you had it in you. Yes, of course you must run away with your Adrian!"

"And I shall be happy beyond all words, happy as I have never dreamed it possible to be."

The colour came into Elizabeth's cheeks as she spoke, and her eyes were shining; then an expression of misery crossed her face.

"But I have forgotten something, I am not of age. If Papa did not give his consent, he could even fetch me back. You remember what happened to Helen Tanner?"

Both girls were silent, remembering the elopement which had taken place the previous year when the daughter of a neighbouring squire had run away with the groom. Her father had fetched her back, the girl had been locked up in her room and brow-beaten and ill-treated until, in a moment of despair, she flung herself out of the window.

It had caused a great deal of scandal and talk, yet few people had a word of criticism for the girl's parents. They had behaved quite rightly, it was thought. The girl was better dead than contracting a *mésalliance* of such a nature.

After a moment Nerina shook herself as if trying to shake away an ever-persistent memory.

"There must be something we can do," she said after a few moments. "You must not despair."

"Perhaps Adrian will think of something," Elizabeth said trustingly, but there was little hope in her voice.

Both girls were heavy-eyed and pale when morning came, but on Nerina's advice Elizabeth decided to accept with no further protest the situation as it was.

"You will do no good by arguing with your father," Nerina said; "you will only get him into a rage and he will reduce you to tears. When Sir Rupert comes, say as little as possible."

"I can't be alone with him," Elizabeth said hastily.

"Why not?" Nerina enquired. "I should think it is unlikely that he will make love to you. We know his affections are engaged elsewhere. Just look shy and stupid, for that is all he will expect from you. What time did you arrange to meet your Adrian?"

"As soon after three o'clock as possible," Elizabeth said. "It is the time I usually go for a walk. Today I shan't have to take Bessie with me because we can go together."

"We shall have to wait until Sir Rupert has called," Nerina said practically, "but perhaps he will be early."

Her hope was justified and Sir Rupert called about half

past two. He spent a little more than ten minutes alone with Elizabeth, then rode away on a spirited black stallion which seemed to have as fiery and uncertain a temper as his own.

From behind the curtains of one of the bedroom windows Nerina watched him go. There was something in the way he handled the stallion, in the strength and breadth of his broad shoulders and in the square line of his jaw which was superbly arrogant. Watching him, so sure of himself and the complete master of his horse, Nerina prayed wordlessly in her heart that his pride and arrogance might have a fall. She knew that if Elizabeth married him she would be all Lady Clementine expected of her. She would never have a chance against a man of this sort. She could no more stand up to him or cross his wishes than she could thwart or defy her father.

It was therefore with a feeling of apprehension that twenty minutes later Nerina approached the wood where Adrian Butler would be waiting for them. Already she had pledged herself to help her cousin to marry a man she had never seen. Suppose on acquaintance she decided that he was the wrong person for Elizabeth, suppose he was another bully and a brute who would make her miserable and be unfaithful to her within a year of their marriage? What, Nerina asked herself, was she to do then? Make Elizabeth marry Sir Rupert, who despite all his vices had the virtue of being rich and important? Or allow her to marry the man of her choice, whatever he was like, knowing that by doing so she would be left with neither money nor her family's approval?

Nerina was very quiet as they neared the wood; but Elizabeth was suddenly transformed from the shrinking, miserable, white-faced girl into a radiant, glowing young woman. She pushed ahead of Nerina down the narrow mossy path beneath the beech trees into a little glade hidden in the very depth of the copse, where the sunshine percolating through the dark trees cast a pattern of gold upon a little stream. There they found Adrian Butler.

He was everything that Nerina had hoped and nothing that she had feared. Not particularly good-looking, he had nevertheless one of those charming, gentle faces which made anyone who saw him even for the first time trust him instantly. It would have been absolutely impossible to doubt either his sincerity or his honesty; and what was more, he had an easy charm of manner which bespoke his good breeding and decent upbringing as explicitly as if one had read it in the pages of *Debrett*. At the sight of him Elizabeth uttered a cry of gladness and ran to the shelter of his arms. He held her closely for a moment and it was easy to recognise the love in his eyes and the expression of tenderness on his face. Then he turned towards Nerina and reluctantly, as if she had forgotten her very existence, Elizabeth disengaged herself from Adrian's arms.

"This is my cousin, Nerina," she said. "I have told you about her, but I did not think you would meet so soon. She has returned home unexpectedly."

Nerina put her hand into Adrian Butler's warm, firm grasp.

"I am so glad you are here," he said quietly. "Both Elizabeth and I need your help."

It was as if his words recalled to Elizabeth the horror which overshadowed them.

"Adrian, my dearest, I have something to tell you," she began; but he checked the words by putting his arms round her again and saying quietly:

"And I have something to tell you, something wonderful, Elizabeth, something far better than I had dared to hope for."

"What is it?" Elizabeth asked curiously.

It was obvious that Adrian Butler was longing to share his good news, whatever it might be.

"Listen, darling," he said. "You remember I spoke to you of my cousin who lives in Yorkshire. He is the head of our family, a difficult man, I believe, but he was fond of my father. After I had met you and you had made me the happiest and luckiest man on earth, I wrote to him. I explained my position. I told him how I hesitated to approach your father because I had so little to offer save an overwhelming love and the conviction that with your help I was bound to make a success of my Army career.

"This morning I had a reply to my letter. I was half afraid to speculate even to myself on what he might do. As I have told you, he is a queer man and unaccountable in many ways. There was every likelihood that he would put my letter into the waste-paper basket and tell me to solve my own problems as best I could. Instead he has written most generously. I have the letter somewhere."

He felt in his pocket, but Elizabeth said impatiently.

"Never mind the letter, tell me what it says."

"It says," Adrian replied in a tone almost of awe, "that

he is delighted with my news. He has already made arrangements with his solicitors to send me an allowance of a thousand pounds a year. A thousand a year, Elizabeth, think of it! With my Army pay we are rich, darling, and that isn't all my news."

"What else?" Elizabeth asked.

"My Colonel sent for me last night," Adrian said, "and informed me that the Regiment was leaving for India next month."

"India!" Elizabeth exclaimed.

"No, wait," Adrian said quickly, "don't be frightened, for he went on to say that in view of the way I have conducted myself I am to be promoted immediately to the rank of a Captain. Think of it, darling, a Captain, with a thousand a year. We can be married at once. Don't you understand that Officers of the rank of Captain and over take their wives with them on foreign service? It is wonderful, my sweetest, for now I can approach your father without fear and ask permission for us to be married immediately."

"Approach my father! You think you can approach my father," Elizabeth whispered, her voice curiously dull and lifeless after Adrian's animated tones.

As she spoke she turned towards Nerina, and hiding her face in her cousin's shoulder she whispered:

"You tell him, I can't."

Adrian Butler looked from one girl to the other and slowly the excitement died from his face and a look of consternation took its place.

"What is the matter?" he asked. "Has anything happened?"

"Yes, a lot of things," Nerina answered. "I will tell you all about them, but first let us sit down, for Elizabeth is exhausted. We have been awake all night."

She looked as she spoke to where a fallen trunk of a tree afforded a comfortable seat beside the stream. Nerina led the way towards it, and when they had seated themselves Adrian, seeing that Elizabeth was in tears, drew her into the shelter of his arms and held her close.

"Listen, darling," he said in a low voice, "do not be unhappy. If something has frightened you and made you miserable, I promise I will do all in my power to set it to rights."

Elizabeth made a little convulsive sound.

"Oh, if only I could believe you," she said. "All night I

have thought to myself, 'Adrian will think of something, but what can it be?' Nerina and I are out of our minds."

"Tell me first what has occurred," Adrian said, and there was something in his strong, quiet voice which gave Nerina courage to hope for a solution even while in her heart she believed the situation was hopeless.

Quickly, in as few words as possible, she told him what had happened, and then she recounted her own part of the story, what she had heard in the summer-house.

"The man is obviously a cad," Adrian said quietly. "Whatever else happens, he shall not marry Elizabeth."

"But I shall be forced to do so," Elizabeth cried despairingly. "You know what Papa is like. I promise you I tried to defy him, but he terrorises me. When he shouts and bellows at me and his face goes crimson, I am too horror-stricken to do anything but obey. Oh, help me, Adrian, help me!"

"That is just what I am going to do," Adrian said, "and I promise you one thing, my darling, that if you marry this fellow Wroth, it will be over my dead body."

"Adrian, you are not going to fight him," Elizabeth quivered.

"No, I have thought of that," Adrian said, "but it would do no good. To begin with, he would doubtless refuse to meet me, and if I did blow a hole through him I should doubtless be arrested and spend the rest of my life in prison because he is a Minister of the Crown. It is not that I am afraid, I promise you that, it is because I am thinking of you. I shall be little use to you behind bars."

"I don't believe you are afraid of anything," Elizabeth said adoringly, "not even Papa."

"No, I am not frightened of your father," Adrian said, "and that is why I am going to give him a chance to do the right thing. I am going to see him."

"Adrian, not about us?"

"Of course," Adrian replied. "I shall tell him that I wish to marry you, inform him of my altered circumstances and say that under the circumstances I have the right to approach you."

"He will refuse you," Elizabeth said.

"Yes, indeed he will," Nerina interposed. "A thousand a year may be riches to you, but have you any idea what Sir Rupert Wroth is worth?"

"None, but I imagine he is a rich man," Adrian replied.

"You will remember that I told you Lady Clementine

said, 'the Cardons are very hard-up'. There is your answer—my uncle has need of a rich son-in-law."

But Adrian did not look dismayed.

"Then if he refuses to listen to me," he said quietly, "I must use other methods to achieve happiness for Elizabeth and myself."

"And what are those?" Nerina enquired.

"I shall have done the right thing," he replied, "in asking for Elizabeth's hand. If Lord Cardon refuses me, then I must act as I think best for both of us. Elizabeth must run away with me and we can be married before I sail for India."

"Yes, we thought of that," Nerina said. "But you forget that Elizabeth is only eighteen. If she marries before the age of twenty-one without her parents' consent, Uncle Herbert will fetch her home and the marriage can be annulled."

"It would be difficult to fetch her home from a troopship half way down the Bay of Biscay," Adrian retorted.

Elizabeth sat upright.

"You mean that Papa would not be able to catch me," she said excitedly.

"Of course he wouldn't," Adrian replied. "The whole thing is only a question of accurate timing. Once I know the date on which we sail, all the plans we make can be synchronised. I know a parson who will marry us. An uncle of mine is the Vicar of a small village church near Dover. We will call in on him on the way there, and persuade him to make us man and wife. After that I will take you aboard. If we make our plans carefully, I see no reason why we should not have a good start on your father; but just to be on the safe side, when I ask him if he will allow us to become engaged I shall not mention that my Regiment is leaving for India."

"He may find out though," Elizabeth said anxiously. "Papa has the most uncanny way of learning about things of which you would imagine he knew nothing."

"Yes, but we have got to be clever about this," Adrian said quietly. "If he refuses me—which we all seem to think likely—from that moment you must behave as if you were quite content with the situation. You must appear willing to marry Sir Rupert; you must in fact lull your father into a sense of false security."

"But, Adrian, it will be so difficult."

"Of course it will," he replied; "but you must remember

that our whole future happiness is at stake. However difficult things are, you can do them when you remember that at the end of it all we shall be together for the rest of our lives."

"I will try to do whatever you tell me," Elizabeth said humbly, "and Nerina will help me, won't you?"

"You know I will," Nerina said. "I think it is the only possible plan. Pray heaven Sir Rupert will not wish the marriage to take place before your ship sails. That is the only danger as far as I can see."

"The Colonel thought it would be about the twenty-ninth of July," Adrian said, "but I shan't know for certain for a few days."

"Then Elizabeth must say she has a passionate desire to be married in August," Nerina said.

"Oh, I only hope that I don't do anything wrong," Elizabeth murmured. "I find it so hard to lie to Papa. There is something in the way he looks at me as if he would drag my very innermost secrets from me. He seems to hypnotize me and I find myself saying things that I was quite certain I could keep from his knowledge."

"Do not worry too much," Nerina said soothingly. "Remember that if he imagines you are doing what he wants in agreeing to marry Sir Rupert, he will be extremely pleased with you. You must be prepared for one ghastly row after he has seen Mr. Butler, and after that, when he thinks he has won, everything should go smoothly."

"Of course there is always the possibility that he might prefer me as his son-in-law," Adrian said with a humourless twist of his lips.

Nerina laughed.

"I think the man himself has little to do with it," she said. "It is his bank book that counts."

"A humiliating thought," Adrian said, "but I will not say I am downcast."

He looked tenderly down at Elizabeth, whose head was resting against his shoulder. "Are you quite certain," he asked softly, "that you would not prefer to be very rich?"

Elizabeth put up her hand to touch his cheek.

"Don't you understand," she said, "that I shall be the richest and most wealthy woman in the world when I am married to you?"

He caught her fingers in his and pressed his lips to them. Nerina got to her feet.

"I am going to the edge of the wood to see that no one is
53

in sight," she said. "If you hear me call you, Elizabeth, come at once."

It was doubtful if Elizabeth heard her. She was caught into a rapturous world which included only Adrian and for the moment she had forgotten even her fears in the wonder of this new happiness.

Nerina went to the edge of the wood. There was no one in sight, only a number of pigeons and jackdaws feeding on the open field. They were as good as any sentinel and Nerina thought that, if anyone appeared even in the distance, they would rise in a warning crowd to seek the safety of the wood and the trees.

She seated herself on the stile, swinging her feet in a way which her aunt would have thought most unladylike. It was a relief to know that Adrian was a decent person who would make Elizabeth happy. Even so, Nerina wondered cynically, how long would it last? Men were all the same. When one woman tired them, they were off to seek another. Elizabeth was not clever, amusing or talented. She was just a sweet, gentle person, and having been bullied all her life, had little initiative and less courage. Would that begin to pall on a man after a time? Nerina wondered. Would he want someone more original, someone more piquant or provocative to keep him amused?

But why should a woman be nothing more or less than a plaything for a man? Was that the only existence because one was born a woman? Nerina found her thoughts turning to her own problems. Elizabeth might be settled in life, but what of herself? She was determined never to marry, no man should ever be her master.

But what alternative was there? How could she have either money, position or freedom from her uncle unless she exchanged one guardian for another and found herself a husband?

It seemed for the moment an unsolvable problem. Nerina sighed as she thought of herself going from post to post as an underpaid governess, finding perhaps the same problems in every new situation, returning to Rowanfield to be scolded and abused until perhaps as the years went by there was no longer anyone left at Rowanfield to scold her and she grew too old for the same problems to arise.

It was a gloomy thought and Nerina sighed out loud, but it turned almost immediately into a gasp of horror. Someone was coming through the wood. She could hear the sound from behind her, and by the noise of the movements she knew that it was someone riding a horse. He was moving quickly, and with a sense of dismay Nerina realised there would be hardly time for Elizabeth to reach her before the horseman, whoever he might be, appeared first. Nevertheless she called out:

"Elizabeth! Elizabeth!"

She turned round with difficulty, for the stile was high. She swung her big hooped skirt over the top bar and scrambled down inside the wood. She had only just done so when a horse appeared on the mossy path winding between the trees. It was a chestnut mare and Nerina recognised its familiar head before, with a feeling almost of suffocation, she saw whom it carried. It was her uncle! Approaching from a direction she had never suspected he might come.

4

Nerina stood paralysed with fear until her uncle came nearer; then she made an almost superhuman effort to hide her dismay at the sight of him. Moving forward, she forced a smile to her lips.

"Good afternoon, Uncle Herbert," she said.

He made no reply. His expression was ominous and his glance flickered over her as if he were looking for someone else. Still without speaking, he turned his horse down the path towards the glade where Elizabeth and Adrian Butler were locked in each other's arms. Nerina made a desperate attempt to detain him.

"Uncle Herbert, where are you going?" she cried, her voice unnaturally loud so that Elizabeth could hear and be warned.

But Lord Cardon without turning his head rode relentlessly on, and in despair Nerina followed him down the woodland path. It took them only a few seconds to reach the little clearing by the stream. Elizabeth and Adrian Butler were standing in the centre of it.

They had heard Nerina's warning call, followed almost immediately by her greeting of her uncle, and while Elizabeth in a panic had begged Adrian to hide he had stood his ground, saying he would not run away but would face her father here and now. She had little time to plead or argue with him, and there would in fact have been no time for Adrian to conceal himself, for almost before they could think Lord Cardon was upon them and Elizabeth, looking up at him astride his horse, felt as if she must faint away at the very sight of his face.

She knew the signs of his anger only too well, the ponderous knitting of his brow, which made his eyebrows meet across the top of his high nose, the narrowing of his eyes till they were merely slits of darkness; but above all, the purple flush which would rise from the base of his neck to his hair, growing alarmingly deeper and deeper until the blue veins in his forehead and nose stood out swollen and bulbous.

Lord Cardon drew his horse to a standstill. For a moment no one said anything. Elizabeth's hands fluttered like frightened birds to her breast. Adrian Butler straightened his back, but his eyes, calm and honest, met Lord Cardon's in a straightforward, unflurried manner. He looked both a man and a gentleman and Nerina hoped for one optimistic moment that his appearance might mitigate Lord Cardon's anger.

But there was no chance of appeasing his wrath, and in a voice harsh with fury he said to Elizabeth:

"So I was right in suspecting that you were deceiving me!"

It was as if the sound of his voice broke the spell which had held both Elizabeth and Adrian speechless since his appearance. Pale but dignified, Adrian stepped forward.

"You must forgive me, Sir, if we met here without your consent. I was in fact coming to call on you this very evening."

"Oh, you were, were you?" Lord Cardon said. "And for what reason?"

"This is not the place that I should have chosen to speak of such matters," Adrian Dutler replied quietly, "but since you ask me, Sir, I will answer you frankly. I wish to have your permission to marry your daughter."

Lord Cardon's face deepened in colour.

"Blast your effrontery!" he snarled. "You have the damned impertinence that I should have expected of you. Do you dare to ask for my daughter's hand in marriage when she is already affianced? She is betrothed to Sir Rupert Wroth. If she has not told you that, it merely shows that she is as ready to deceive you as she is me."

"Lady Elizabeth has informed me that Sir Rupert has offered for her," Adrian said in his quiet, even voice. "She has also told me that you, Sir, favour that gentleman's suit; but unfortunately your daughter's heart is engaged elsewhere. I am honoured, Sir, to be the recipient of her affection and I believe I can make her happy."

"Then you believe wrong," Lord Cardon shouted. "Hell and damnation, am I to sit here listening to this claptrap for some jumped-up adventurer who thinks it to his advantage to become my son-in-law? Get out of here and stay out. As for my daughter, she will marry whom I say and nobody else."

"You cannot mean that seriously, Sir," Adrian expostulated. "I am unable, it is true, to offer your daughter the worldly advantages that Sir Rupert Wroth can do, but my position is——"

"You heard what I said," Lord Cardon interrupted. "Get off my land and stay off."

He pulled at the reins of his horse as if he would leave, and impulsively Adrian Butler stepped forward and put his hand on the bridle.

"Lord Cardon," he said urgently, "you are making a very grave mistake. I beg of you in all fairness to hear me."

His action seemed to infuriate Lord Cardon beyond all bounds. With a swift movement he brought his riding whip in a smashing blow down on Adrian Butler's hand, and then as if the action shattered the last remnants of his self-control he shouted:

"Get out, I say! I'll teach you to seduce my daughter, to sneak in here and make love to her under bushes. Get out and stay out. Next time I see you I'll put a bullet through you."

Incensed now beyond all forbearance Lord Cardon brought his whip down again and again on Adrian's shoulders. The young man put up his hands to ward off the blows; but astride his horse Lord Cardon was in a position of advantage, and as the whip rained down, mercilessly cutting his cheek and hands and leaving long crimson marks on his fair skin, Adrian Butler was forced to retreat with Lord Cardon pursuing him in relentless brutality, heedless of Elizabeth's cries of horror and dismay.

"Papa . . . Papa . . . don't . . . don't . . . I beg of you," she screamed, and strove to run to Adrian's defence; but already Lord Cardon had driven him down another footpath leading from the clearing, still using his whip, still swearing at him with violent oaths which seemed to echo through the wood.

He drove the unfortunate young man before him until they reached the roadway which bounded the estate. And it was only when Adrian, blood-stained and almost unconscious, stumbled and fell over a low hedge into the ditch on the other side that Lord Cardon's whip was still. For a moment he looked down at the beaten man, whose breath was coming brokenly between his lips and whose eyes were closed in pain. Then he laughed.

"Perhaps that will teach you to leave my daughter alone," he said savagely, and turning his horse he rode swiftly back the way he had come.

Elizabeth had collapsed by the side of the stream. The tears were streaming down her white face, but her eyes were wide open and staring from the shock of what she had seen. Nerina, kneeling at her side, looked up at the sound of her uncle's approach, but Elizabeth did not turn her head.

"Get up," Lord Cardon commanded. "Get up, both of you, and go back to the house."

"Elizabeth is fainting," Nerina said, "I doubt if she can walk."

"She will walk," Lord Cardon said grimly, "or I will give her a taste of what I have given her young man." His voice rose to a shout. "Get up, blast you, and do as I say."

His violence had its effect. Almost automatically Elizabeth obeyed him although Nerina expected her to faint at any moment.

"Go on, walk ahead of me," Lord Cardon ordered, and bearing almost the full weight of her cousin Nerina started to walk back to the house.

It took nearly half an hour, and every minute of it seemed a century of misery and torture. Elizabeth dragged her feet like an old woman who had no strength left in her body. Her hands were ice cold and after a minute her teeth began to chatter. There was nothing Nerina could do but practically carry her along, encouraging her to each further effort in a low voice, hoping that her uncle could not hear what she said.

Riding behind them, driving them as a herdsman might drive his cattle to the slaughter-house, Lord Cardon said nothing until they reached the house. As a groom ran forward to take his horse, he dismounted and watched Nerina make a last desperate effort to get Elizabeth up the front steps.

She was exhausted herself for she had borne almost the whole weight of Elizabeth's body; but as a footman opened the front door he saw that something was wrong, and, hurrying forward, assisted Elizabeth into the Hall. Nerina felt that somehow she had achieved an almost superhuman task in getting Elizabeth home at all. For the moment she almost forgot the greater issues that lay ahead in the satisfaction of having achieved an immediate triumph.

She drew a deep breath of relief, and then as her uncle entered the Hall behind them her heart gave a frightened throb of terror for she saw that his anger was not in the least abated. He stood for a moment looking at Elizabeth. She was ashen-pale, swaying as she stood and kept on her feet only by Nerina's supporting arm on one side of her and the footman's on the other. Her eyes were wild and her breath came in sharp, quick pants like an animal who had been wounded. Lord Cardon looked at her for a long moment, then deliberately with his ungloved hand he slapped her hard in the face.

"Get upstairs," he said as if he were speaking to a dog. "I will deal with you later. Nerina, come into the Library."

Elizabeth did not cry out at her father's assault. Instead she crumpled up completely, and despite the arms supporting her slipped to the floor unconscious. Lord Cardon paid not the slightest attention but turned on his heel and walked towards the Library door. Nerina knew she dared not disobey him.

"Carry Lady Elizabeth upstairs to her room," she said quickly to the footman, "and call Bessie."

"Very good, Miss."

The man's expression was one of consternation. Like the rest of the household he was used to his master's tempers, but on this occasion the consequences seemed to be worse than usual. There was nothing that Nerina could do but run swiftly to the Library after her uncle. The door was open, and as she entered and closed it behind her she drew in a deep breath.

Her uncle was standing with his back to the fireplace. He watched Nerina cross the room, and she knew by the expression on his face and the breath coming quickly between his nostrils that his rage had not yet spent itself. As she looked at the crimson, dissolute face above his white cravat, seeing the purple veins swollen alarmingly on his square forehead, noting in the clear afternoon light the network of wrinkles round his eyes and the deeply etched lines running from the corners of his high nose to his tight lips, she was astonishingly no longer afraid.

It was his very ugliness which released her from her own fear. She saw him not as a monster who could terrify or subdue her by physical violence, but rather as a man who had lost not only the beauty of his youth but even the dignity of his manhood. For one moment as she advanced towards him she had a vision of what he had once been—slim and good-looking, virile and attractive to women, a man with a big position and an honoured title, a man whom any woman would have been proud to marry. But something had gone wrong, something had transformed him from a man into a beast, had made him grad-

60

ually lose all his decent qualities as he wallowed in his own egotistical sensuality.

Had it been a woman who had disappointed him? Had his marriage soured and embittered him because both happiness and an heir eluded him? It was impossible for Nerina to know the truth, and yet in that moment's vision her uncle's power over her had gone. He had always seemed to paralyse her into subservience by sheer physical supremacy. Even as she grew older she had never been quite able to escape from the feeling of being powerless in his hands and from knowing that abject, intolerable impotency from which she had suffered as a child when he had beaten her until she had been half unconscious and she had known that he enjoyed doing it.

Now it seemed to her as if he could no longer reach her. She was free of him and mentally her chains fell away from her as, with her chin held high, she faced him across the hearthrug.

"Is this your doing?" he enquired.

Nerina did not pretend to misunderstand him.

"I returned here only yesterday, as you know," she replied.

"How long has it been going on?" Lord Cardon enquired and, as Nerina hesitated, he added. "You had best tell me or I will get it out of Elizabeth quickly enough."

Nerina made up her mind to save her cousin all she could.

"I understand Elizabeth has been in love for some time."

"And she has been meeting this bounder like a servant girl, sneaking out when it is dark, behaving like a wanton with some stray ne'er-do-well who has caught her fancy."

"That is only because you forbade Mr. Butler the house, not thinking him good enough," Nerina said.

"Good enough! Of course he isn't good enough," Lord Cardon shouted. "A penniless soldier! Good God, is that the kind of son-in-law I want?"

"He is a soldier," Nerina replied, "but not penniless. He is comparatively well off, and surely it is Elizabeth's happiness that matters? She has to marry him, not you."

Lord Cardon looked at her in astonishment; then as the full import of her words percolated into his mind, he roared:

"Don't you speak to me like that, you impertinent chit, and don't you put such revolutionary ideas into Elizabeth's mind. We all know what you are like, a strumpet like your mother. Well, I won't have my daughter infected with your loose morals, do you hear me?"

Her new-found courage made Nerina say:

"Elizabeth is in love with a gentleman who is perfectly able to keep her in comfort and decency. He was waiting until he knew exactly what his prospects were before approaching you. If Elizabeth has met him in secret, there has occurred on those occasions nothing wrong, nothing which might not have taken place in Aunt Anne's drawing-room had Elizabeth been allowed to ask Mr. Butler here."

"Ask him here! Why the hell should she ask him here when I had already told her I wouldn't have him in the house? As for marrying him, the girl is an infatuated fool. Besides, she is already engaged to Wroth."

"Whom she does not love and who does not love her," Nerina said.

"What has love got to do with it?" Lord Cardon demanded. "He has offered for her, hasn't he?"

"Not because he loves her," Nerina replied, "but because the Queen has commanded him to find a wife before he next goes to Court. Apparently Her Majesty has heard of his infatuation for Lady Clementine Talmadge."

Lord Cardon stared at Nerina for a moment and then he said in a more amenable tone:

"So that's the way the wind blows! But how do you know this?"

"It happens to be the truth," Nerina parried, having no intention of telling her uncle the secret of the hiding-place over the summer-house.

"I can well believe it," Lord Cardon said. "A fellow like Wroth would not want to marry a milk-faced nincompoop like Elizabeth without a good reason for it. Well, whatever his reason, it suits me. I want him for a son-in-law and, by God, I'm going to have him."

"But, Uncle Herbert," Nerina said, "can you not understand what this will mean to Elizabeth? She will be unhappy, desperately unhappy with a man like that, a man who does not care for her in the slightest, who is making a convenience of her so as to escape from the consequences of his own indiscretions. Uncle Herbert, be kind for once and let Elizabeth marry the man she loves."

For a moment Nerina thought that her uncle might listen to her, that her plea for mercy might awaken some half-forgotten decency within himself which might respond to her appeal. Just for a second it seemed as if he hesitated and then with all his old vigour and savagery he shouted at her:

"What the devil does it matter whom she loves, she will do as she is told; and if you encourage her in defying me, it will be the worse for you, I promise you that."

His face was crimson again, and the words were spat from between his lips, with a violence which seemed to shake his whole body.

Nerina knew there was nothing more she could say or do to persuade him, and as she stood silent Lord Cardon's eyes narrowed a little.

"That's settled," he said in a somewhat different tone, "and now let us talk of you, my dear niece. Perhaps you will be good enough to inform me why you have returned here without due notice, and without, I imagine, a reference from your last employer."

As he began to speak, Nerina nerved herself as she had so often done before to withstand the fury of his onslaught, and then to her own astonishment she did not feel her heart begin to thump painfully or know that sudden nausea in her stomach which made her feel as if she would be sick from the terror which her uncle's bullying always aroused in her. Instead, she could answer him calmly.

"You know why I have returned, Uncle. I think, if you are honest, that you are surprised I have been away as long as I have."

She watched his eyes as she spoke. For an instant they flickered before hers and she knew she had struck home. It was the truth then that her uncle had known full well when he sent her to the house of the Marquis of Droxburgh what she would find there, what she would suffer. He had intended it to happen, expected it and not been displeased with the idea. It was part of his revenge, part indeed of the hatred he had always borne for her.

"What are you talking about?" he asked, and she knew that for once she had embarrassed him, pierced beneath the armour of his own self-satisfaction.

"You knew what Lord Droxburgh was like," Nerina said. "You were well aware of his reputation, and yet you were prepared to send me, unprepared and defenceless, to live under his roof. I may be an orphan, penniless and unwanted, but I am also your niece, the child of your only brother."

"The child of your mother too, the child of a play actress, of a woman who managed to ensnare a young boy even before he left Oxford," Lord Cardon sneered.

"My mother was not a play actress as you well know," Nerina retorted. "She was a concert singer and of decent breeding. She and my father fell in love with each other and they were happy together for eleven years. She gave up her career because of him. She was respectable; yes, more respectable than most of the people you acknowledge in Society, and yet because of some prudish, snobby prejudice you prefer to pillory me. Do it if you wish, continue to punish me because I was born to two people who dared to love and be happy in spite of what the world said and thought of them; but at least be honest about it, be frank and admit that you have persecuted me ever since I was a child. You want to see me disgraced, you want to see me seduced and branded as having no moral or decency, or being little better than a prostitute. That was why you sent me as governess to a child of the Marquis of Droxburgh. You knew what he was like, you knew what I might be expected to encounter in his house, yet you deliberately sent me there. Well, once again you are disappointed. I have not been seduced, I have come back to you exactly as I went; but I have learned one thing and learned it truly—that men are beasts. You are all the same, all of you. You want one thing of a woman, and one thing only."

Nerina had spoken heatedly, her eyes flashing, and there was colour in her cheeks. It seemed, too, as if her hair blazed brighter because of the anger which invaded her whole body.

Her uncle stared at her as if in stupefaction, and when she had finished speaking, the silence was broken only by the sound of her quick breathing. She thought for a moment that he would slap her in the face as he had slapped his own daughter; then strangely his anger seemed to ebb away from him. She felt his eyes flicker over her, and indeed he looked at her as if he saw her for the first time. While she waited for him to speak, conscious suddenly of the heat in her cheeks and the fact that her hands were clenched so tightly that her knuckles were white, she was aware that the atmosphere had altered. There was something new and different in her uncle's attitude, something which had never been there before; and when he spoke at last, it was in a voice which seemed to her to hold a faint, almost mocking respect rather than a bullying anger.

"So that is what you feel about men," he said slowly.

His remark seemed to call for no answer and Nerina did not reply but stood waiting for him to continue. After a moment he went on:

"So you refused Droxburgh! There aren't many women can boast at having done that."

"He is loathsome and repulsive," Nerina said.

"And you find that I am the same?" her uncle asked.

There was a queer note in his voice, almost one of appeal, but in her new-found courage she answered him truthfully.

"Yes," she said uncompromisingly.

Their eyes met and Nerina knew he was willing her gaze to fall before his. But she stared him out, conscious for the first time that in a battle of wills she was his equal if not more. For several seconds they glared at each other, and then at length in a voice low but virile with hatred her uncle said:

"You are very like your mother! Get out!"

It was only when she got outside the door that Nerina felt weak. It was as if her tension were suddenly relaxed, leaving her vulnerable and not far from tears. Then quickly, because she would escape even her own thoughts, she hurried up the stairs towards her and Elizabeth's room.

If Elizabeth had been upset the day before over Sir Rupert's proposal of marriage, it was nothing to the agony and misery she was experiencing now. Nerina held her in her arms while she cried until she could cry no more, and at length fell silent for a while from utter exhaustion. Nerina considered the situation and found it uncompromisingly dismal. It was as if Elizabeth were in a trap from which there was no chance of being released. A way had got to be found, of course, but it was not going to be easy. In fact, for the moment the difficulties seemed almost unsurmountable.

The girls had been told not to go down to dinner, and if Elizabeth had not been so desperately unhappy, Nerina might have laughed when their supper came up to them consisting only of bread and water. It was one of the old punishments they had always endured when as children they had been particularly naughty; but Nerina thought now that a diet of bread and water and being confined to their bedroom was hardly a fitting punishment for this particular crime.

But it was not a moment to indulge her sense of

humour. Elizabeth was almost delirious in her despair and Nerina had to concentrate on soothing her, finding that the only way to do so was to reassure her again and again that somehow they would be able to elude Lord Cardon and contrive that she should marry her Adrian.

A visit from Lady Cardon just before she went down to dinner did nothing to allay Elizabeth's fears. She had endured the tail end of her husband's rage and in consequence her manner towards her daughter was cold and distant. Her face bore the stiff, repressed expression which Nerina knew was an outward sign that she was suffering inwardly.

Lady Cardon's tragedy was that she loved her husband and yet had not the slightest idea of how to please him. She had been hopelessly inexperienced when she married, a girl brought up in a strict, almost puritan household, with unworldly, elderly parents who had taught her little, if anything, about the realities of life.

She was well aware that her fortune had been the main reason why Lord Cardon offered for her. It was considerable enough to attract quite a number of suitors, but until the young, handsome Earl of Cardon appeared, her father had refused them all. Sanctimonious, puritanic and in many ways a hypocrite, he was, however, honest enough to admit that Lord Cardon's reputation was not entirely one he would have chosen for his son-in-law.

"But you will reform him, my dear, you will reform him," he said to his daughter; and because she had been brought up to unquestioning obedience, she believed him.

Her tragedy had been that she had not the slightest idea from what she had to reform her husband, and in her experience she bored him to distraction even on their wedding night. On their prolonged, dismal and expensive honeymoon she was so *gauche*, so unprepossessing in her ignorance and in her home-made but serviceable trousseau that she not only bored but revolted him so much that he was unnecessarily cruel to her because of his own inner disappointment and the discovery that marriage could be so unpleasant.

Miserable and embarrassed, knowing that what she did displeased him, but not knowing why, Lady Cardon, as she stared with unseeing eyes at the beauty spots of Europe, wished she had never been born. But the Gods who torture simple people or perhaps only those who are lacking in wisdom had not finished with her yet. As a girl she had never had her feelings aroused in any way and had believed quite sincerely that affection was love and that love, as it was written about by poets, was an emotion that only happened to the unstable and the over-imaginative.

But she had fallen in love with her husband on their honeymoon with an overwhelming, passionate, possessive and jealous love which was to give her no rest and from which she was to have no respite during the whole of her married life. What was so bitter was that because of her upbringing, because of the repressions which had been hers since childhood, she was unable to express herself, unable to do more than contain that fiery emotion within her breasts and try to save herself from betraying her own weakness to the man she loved. She was ashamed of it, afraid of the desire for him which shocked her even while it made her tremble, afraid of her own thoughts, her own yearnings; and because the violence of her love seemed at times to tear her apart, she was afraid of responding to him even in their most intimate moments.

From the very beginning Lord Cardon had never understood her nor made any attempt to do so. From the very beginning she was afraid of boring him and contrived to do that very thing so completely that the gulf between them widened and widened with the years until there was never any chance of their getting to know each other or of even becoming friends and companions.

And because she loved him so desperately, because she was terrified that if once she revealed herself he would laugh and turn away from her in utter disgust, she forced herself to speak calmly and coolly at all times, made herself stiff and dignified even when she most wanted to fling herself into his arms, to pour out in a floodtide her aching, insatiable want of his body and his affection.

Then gradually this armour which she deliberately put upon herself became so much a part of her make-up that it became impossible for her to unbend or speak to anyone save in a cool, distant manner and in a voice which at times became sharp and sarcastic and as brutal in its own way as Lord Cardon's unbridled anger.

As she entered the girls' bedroom, it seemed to Nerina that Lady Cardon looked with distaste at Elizabeth's swollen eyes and trembling lips. Elizabeth sat up at the sight of her mother and instinctively, as a child that has been hurt, she held out her arms.

"Mama!" she sobbed. "Oh, Mama!"

But Lady Cardon did not draw nearer to her. She stood just inside the door, the lamplight glittering on the diamond collet she wore round her neck.

"I have talked with your father, Elizabeth," she said coldly. "He has told me how grieved he is by your outrageous behaviour. I will not speak of my own feelings; sufficient to say that I am disgusted to think that you should so far have forgotten your position in life to behave as you have. Your father has decided that as you cannot be trusted, you are not to leave the house except to walk on the lawns directly outside the Drawing-room until your marriage to Sir Rupert Wroth. Because your father has learned that Sir Rupert is anxious to marry you as soon as possible, your wedding will take place in just over three weeks from now, to be exact on the twenty-ninth of July."

Elizabeth gave a little cry of despair.

"Oh, Mama, not the twenty-ninth, not the twenty-ninth."

"The twenty-ninth," Lady Cardon repeated.

Nerina, conscious of the import of this particular date to Elizabeth, said quickly:

"But, Aunt Anne, surely people will think it very strange that Elizabeth is being married with such unseemly haste. No one, unless there is some particular reason for it, gets married three weeks after the announcement of their betrothal."

Lady Cardon looked at her, and it seemed to Nerina as if there was as much distaste in her expression as there had been when she had looked at her daughter.

"Your uncle has thought of that," she replied sharply. "He has decided that after all I have been through, after all the worry and trouble Elizabeth has given me my health has suffered. He is certain that when I see Doctor Parker, which I intend to do tomorrow, he will prescribe rest and quiet and a trip abroad as soon as it is possible for us to get away. Elizabeth's marriage will therefore be expedited so that your uncle and I can leave for a tour of the Continent."

As she finished speaking Lady Cardon opened the door.

"I hope, Elizabeth," she said, "that a night's rest will enable you to pull yourself together and that you will look your usual charming self when Sir Rupert calls tomorrow. Your father has asked me to say that otherwise he might find it necessary to call on the Colonel of Mr. Butler's Regiment. Were he to lodge a complaint of that young man's behaviour, which, of course, he is fully entitled to do, Mr. Butler would find himself cashiered and dismissed the Service. If you are as fond of this gentleman as you pretend, you would not wish that to happen."

Without waiting for an answer Lady Cardon went from the bedroom and closed the door quietly behind her. Elizabeth lay very still. Then she put her hands up to her face.

"There is no escape," she said in a low, broken voice. "Papa has thought of everything. I'm trapped, Nerina, trapped! I shall have to do what he asks."

For once Nerina had no answer. It did indeed seem that Elizabeth was right and that Lord Cardon had thought of everything.

5

It was five days before Elizabeth had any news of Adrian Butler. For five afternoons Bessie dragged Lady Cardon's asthmatic Peke for a walk along the road which bordered the wood, while Elizabeth, imprisoned in the garden, sat on the lawn in front of the house too miserable with anxiety and apprehension even to talk to Nerina.

Lord Cardon's threat to communicate with Adrian's Colonel had been extremely effective in so far as getting his own way was concerned. Elizabeth was terrified of doing anything which might hurt Adrian's chances of promotion, and with an effort of which only Nerina realised the full cost she forced herself to be pleasant to Sir Rupert when he called and to appear before her father and mother controlled and dry-eyed.

It was only when she was alone with her cousin in their bedroom that her misery need not be concealed and she could rave, at times almost crazily, against her father and his decisions. But she dare not defy Lord Cardon openly, frightened not so much for herself but for the man she loved.

If it had not been for Bessie's help and co-operation Nerina felt that Elizabeth might have had a nervous breakdown. Bessie had refused to be despondent and had been sure that once she could contact Adrian Butler he would find a solution to every problem. Elizabeth's main fear was that Adrian would think she had been overwhelmed by her father's violence, and not finding her in their usual meeting place would believe she no longer loved him.

"Now, don't you fret yourself," Bessie said comfortingly. "I'll be there to explain what's happening. Mr. Butler's a sensible gentleman and he'll know that if you can't come yourself you'll send someone you can trust. He's not to know that you are shut up here by his lordship's orders though, unless I'm very much mistaken, he'll have wits enough to guess that something of the sort will be taking place. I'll be waiting for him on the road and sure enough he'll come along sooner or later. Your ladyship can be as certain of that as that I'm standing here on my two flat feet at this very moment."

But it was five days before Bessie's confidence in Adrian Butler was justified, days in which Elizabeth grew paler and thinner and ate so little that Nerina was afraid she would waste away altogether. Every afternoon Bessie anxiously perambulated up and down the narrow dusty road, the Peke snorting and snuffing behind her, infuriated by this sudden interest in his health which took him from the comfort of the basket he loved on a walk that he heartily disliked.

"It is kind of you to take Nicky for such lovely walks," Lady Cardon said to Bessie.

"He enjoys them so much, your ladyship," Bessie said shamelessly. "It is a real pity for a beautiful dog like that to get fat for want of a bit of exercise."

Lady Cardon bent to pat her Peke. He was the one living being to which she occasionally used a term of endearment, and now as she patted him she murmured nonsensically to the wheezing animal, who turned away from her wearily, too tired to desire anything save a soft cushion. Bessie watched him with a faint smile on her lips. There was never a more unwilling messenger of love.

But when Adrian Butler finally appeared on the fifth day Bessie felt that any subterfuge and discomfort had been worth while. As he came riding down the road, Bessie could not wait until he reached her and dismounted. She rushed towards him with a cry of welcome. He looked pale and ill and his face was still scarred with the marks of Lord Cardon's whip.

"Oh, Mr. Butler, Sir, it's glad I am to see you," Bessie cried. "I've been waiting here every afternoon and praying till my jaw ached that you would come. Her ladyship is that anxious I've been thinking she would pine away altogether if she did not hear from you soon."

"I would have come before, Bessie," Adrian replied, "but I have been ill and the Doctor would not let me leave my bed however much I pleaded with him."

"We thought as how it must be something like that," Bessie said soberly, glancing at the marks on his face and the bandages on his hands.

"Tell me about her ladyship, Bessie," Adrian said quickly. "What has happened to her?"

"She is not allowed to leave the garden, Sir," Bessie answered, "and his lordship has fixed the marriage for the twenty-ninth of July."

"The twenty-ninth!" Adrian exclaimed in startled tones.

"Yes, Sir, and her ladyship is distraught about it, as you can well imagine."

"I have heard definitely that our troop-ship sails on the night of the thirtieth," Adrian said. "We have to be aboard by noon. That means that her ladyship must come away with me on the twenty-ninth."

"Yes, Sir, but how?" Bessie asked. "That is what we are all a-wondering."

"We shall have to think of something," Adrian said firmly.

" 'Tis not easy, Sir," Bessie replied. "Two days ago his lordship had a notion that her ladyship might be creeping out at night to meet you, so every evening after Lady Elizabeth and Miss Nerina have gone to bed he locks their bedroom door and it is not opened until the morning. There is no possible escape from the window, 'tis a sheer drop for two floors."

"We will think of something," Adrian repeated stubbornly. "I shall go ahead with my plans, Bessie. I shall arrange for her ladyship and me to be married on the afternoon of the twenty-ninth. That means we should leave here very early—at dawn if possible."

"His lordship keeps the key in his own room!" Bessie continued. "I'm not allowed to fetch it from him till after he has been called at half past seven."

Adrian frowned and appeared to be doing some calculations.

"If we leave immediately after that," he said, "we should reach Dover about 5 o'clock in the evening. We can go part of the way by train and the rest by carriage. We could stay the night at the local inn and go aboard first thing in the morning."

"But even when her ladyship is freed from her bedroom," Bessie went on, "it'll not be easy for her to leave the house. The servants have his lordship's most strict instructions to report to him immediately if the young ladies are seen anywhere in the grounds except on the front lawn. Oh, Sir, you'd need a flying carpet to get her away from what she calls 'this wretched prison'."

Adrian smiled and his smile seemed to light up his face and make him look little more than a boy.

"Stone walls do not a prison make . . ." he quoted, then added: "We shall have to contrive it somehow, Bessie. I will think of a plan and it may have to be a flying carpet. In the meantime will you give this to Lady Elizabeth and tell her not to despair." He drew a letter from his pocket and put it into Bessie's hands. "I hardly expected to find

72

her here this afternoon," he said, "so I was going to leave it in the hollow of the old oak tree where we have left each other notes on other occasions. If by any chance you cannot come another day, will you remember to look there?"

"Indeed I will, Sir," Bessie answered, "and oh, it grieves me to see you looking so white and ill. You must take care of yourself for her ladyship's sake."

"I am much better," Adrian replied, "and now that I know her ladyship is still thinking of me and that nothing really terrible has happened to her I shall be well in no time."

"Her ladyship asked me to give you this, Sir," Bessie said, bringing a note from the pocket of her dress. "She told me also to tell you that she would die rather than marry anyone else; and if you will not have her, her marriage bed will be a grave in the churchyard."

"She need not worry about that," Adrian replied, and his voice was suddenly strong and vigorous. "I will take her away from here even if it means killing someone to do so."

As Bessie said to Elizabeth afterwards when she repeated this remark: "It did my heart good to hear him, it did really. He looked like St. George himself ready to fight all the dragons in the world for the sake of your ladyship."

Elizabeth took Adrian's note and laid it against her cheek.

"He loves me still, Bessie," she whispered. "He loves me, that is all that matters! I was so afraid that Papa had driven him away for good."

"Such a thought never entered my head," Bessie said stoutly, though actually she had been afraid of exactly the same thing. "Why, Mr. Butler is a real gentleman. If he gives his word, he would stick to it whatever the cost to himself. But you need have no fear of his not getting his own way, m'lady. He loves you and he means to marry you, though the Devil himself should be your suitor."

"Sometimes I think he is," Elizabeth said, a little hysterically. As she spoke she turned towards Nerina who was sitting in the window, the sun making a fiery halo of her red hair. "Nerina, I am frightened of Sir Rupert. There is something about him which terrifies me! I have thought of appealing to him, of throwing myself on his mercy, of telling him that I love Adrian and begging him to break off the engagement. But though I have planned the exact words I would say, when the moment comes I cannot utter them. He paralyses my tongue. There is something inhuman about him as if he has not the feelings and emotions of an ordinary man."

"I'm not frightened of him," Nerina answered, "though I can, Elizabeth darling, understand your fears. Sir Rupert is like other men, surely enough, except that he is even more horrible than most of them. When I watch him talking to you, condescendingly pleasant, and know that before the evening is over he will be meeting Lady Clementine and making love to her, I want to strike him in the face. If only Uncle Herbert had treated him as he treated poor Adrian, I would have been glad."

Elizabeth gave a little cry and put her hands to her eyes.

"Pray do not speak of what Papa did to Adrian, I cannot bear to think of it. It haunts me always, I dream of it at night. His poor hands and face! Tell me, Bessie, are the marks still there?"

"You can hardly see them," Bessie replied, untruthfully, anxious that Elizabeth should not be upset.

Over and over again she had to repeat every word of the conversation she had had with Adrian; and when at last there was no more to tell, Elizabeth sat reading and rereading Adrian's note until Nerina was certain that she could repeat it by heart.

"Where are you going to keep it for safety?" she asked her cousin. "Uncle Herbert may easily take it into his head to have the room searched. For goodness' sake do nothing else to arouse him. If he suspects Bessie, we are finished, for without her we shall not be able to communicate with Adrian."

"I shall keep it here," Elizabeth replied with shining eyes, as she slipped the note into the bosom of her gown. "Even Papa would not dare to look for it there."

"I should not be too sure of that. He would dare anything if he felt you were disobeying him," Nerina said grimly.

"For the moment I cannot even feel frightened of Papa," Elizabeth answered. "I am so happy—unbelievably happy, Nerina, for Adrian loves me."

Nerina looked at her cousin curiously. Elizabeth's eyes were closed, her head thrown back, her hands clasped over her breasts. There was a faint smile on her lips and she looked ecstatic. Nerina wondered what it must feel like to be in love. Perhaps Adrian Butler was different from the other men she had met, and yet she knew that she was suspicious even of his quiet gentleness. However kindly and tender he might appear, he was still a man. However much he appeared to love Elizabeth now, would his love remain when she was ill or old, or when other women more attractive than she tempted him? Men were all the same, she decided. As far as she was concerned she would hate them until her dying day. Elizabeth might live in a fool's paradise for a few years, after which, when Adrian became cruel, unfaithful and perhaps bestial, she would only have her memories to look back on.

Nerina thought of Lord Droxburgh and a shudder went through her whole body. How could a woman trust any man when there were brutes like him in the world? She had known instinctively from the very first moment she had met him that he was dangerous. When he had come into the school-room, she had curtsied and stood demurely on one side, her eyes downcast which she knew befitted her position. But she had known that he was looking at her, known by the way his eyes took in every detail of her body, lingering on the curves of her small breasts, that he was thinking of one thing and one thing only.

She had not been afraid of him at that moment—that had come later—she had only known with a sense of utter dismay that this place was going to be no different from the two others she had left. And yet it was different in that it had left an ineradicable scar upon her and confirmed and strengthened her dislike of men. She had hated her uncle, loathing him for what he was and for many other things she suspected about him. She had hated the unfledged boy who had pursued her, whose mother had driven her with unjust and untrue accusations from the house, and she had despised the middle-aged widower who had pursued her persistently with a whining importunate humility.

Lord Droxburgh had been very different from all of these. The resentment and hatred which had smouldered within her towards the others flared into a vivid flame where he was concerned. There were no words in the English language strong enough to express her loathing of all he stood for. In him she recognised the very personification of lust—unbridled and uncontrolled. She knew that he desired her because she was pretty and because she attracted him, but that otherwise as a human being she had no existence whatsoever as far as he was concerned. He was selfish with an egotism which was all the more horrible because it was utterly and completely complacent.

Once and only once had she pleaded with him, striving to find some decency in a man who had grown old in the pursuit of vice.

"I am employed by your wife," she cried. "I am living here under your roof. Can you not leave me alone?"

She was breathless and agitated as she spoke, for Lord Droxburgh had cornered her in the Library where she had gone to collect some toys which the child had left behind earlier in the day. She backed away from him until she stood against one of the big bookcases, the books with their dark leather bindings making a background for her flaming hair and white face.

Her eyes were wide and dark and her red lips, despite every resolution to the contrary, quivered a little as she spoke. Lord Droxburgh watched her, a faint smile on his lips as he appraised every inch of her beauty. Her defiance appealed to him, for he loved to conquer, and the fact that he must compel a woman to his will invariably gave him exquisite pleasure.

"You are very lovely," he said, and his voice was deep with his rising passion.

"Listen to me," Nerina cried despairingly. "Do you not understand what I am saying to you? I am asking you to remember that you were at least born a gentleman. I am here in your house defenceless and without anyone to protect me. Surely you can realise that for that reason if for none other you must leave me alone?"

"You are very lovely," Lord Droxburgh repeated, and he drew nearer.

When his hands went out to touch her, Nerina screamed. But as she did so she realised how hopeless it was. The Library was far from the rest of the house. No one could hear her, and even if anyone did the servants would not interfere. Then, even as she felt Lord Droxburgh's arms go round her, saw his evil face draw nearer to hers, and felt his lips, lecherous and greedy, seeking hers, she was rescued. The door opened unexpectedly. Someone had called to see his lordship and the butler was announcing the guest's arrival.

She slipped away, but when she reached the sanctuary of her bedroom she had not cried or even trembled. She walked up and down the room, drying out in her detestation of the man who had insulted her. She had sworn then that she would be strong enough to outwit him. She would not admit herself defeated by someone whom she despised

76

so utterly. But her courage had waned. The battle had become too fierce for her and she had been forced to retreat before too strong and too powerful an enemy. She hated herself now for the weakness of her sex.

Of one thing was she resolved. She would never marry, though what would become of her she had for the moment no idea. But for Elizabeth there was no other course open and the choice was simple—marriage either with Sir Rupert Wroth or with Adrian Butler.

There was a knock on the bedroom door and Bessie went to open it.

"Madame Marcele is ready for another fitting, your ladyship," she announced.

"Another!" Elizabeth exclaimed in dismay. "I stood for three hours this morning having pins stuck into me. I am tired and I want to read Adrian's letter again."

"You had best go," Bessie said soberly. "If Madame should complain to her ladyship there will be more trouble."

Elizabeth put her hand to her forehead.

"My head aches," she said. "Oh, Bessie, it is nonsensical, fitting a lot of dresses that I have no intention of wearing. When I run away with Adrian I shall only be able to take a bundle with me, so what is the use of all those gowns?"

Nerina got to her feet.

"We are almost the same size," she said. "I will go instead of you. Madame can fit them on me. As I am never likely to have a trousseau, I may as well find out at secondhand what it feels like to be fitted for one."

Elizabeth looked up at her gratefully.

"Will you really do that for me?" she said. "I feel I cannot stand any more today, and Madame talks so much. She keeps telling me what a fine man Sir Rupert is and how lucky I am to get him."

"She's a terrible old gossip," Bessie said. "There's nothing that goes on in the County but she noses it out, going from house to house like she does. You be careful what you say to her, Miss Nerina."

"You need not be frightened," Nerina said as she went towards the door. "I shall just let her talk."

There was no difficulty in doing that, she found as Madame Marcele helped her into Elizabeth's ball gown.

"I can quite understand that her ladyship's feeling tired," Madame Marcele chattered; "but when a trousseau has to be made in such a hurry, there's nothing for it but to have

77

one fitting after another. Try as I may, Miss, one can't get a perfect fit without the help of the human body."

She tightened the waistband and stood back to admire her handiwork. She was a small withered woman, prematurely aged by years of stooping over her work, of sewing in a bad light and in airless garrets often without heat or sufficient meals. By the time she became a success and changed her name from Maggie Potts to Madame Marcele her digestion was permanently ruined and her eyesight failing. The latter was easily corrected by magnifying glasses in steel rims which cut a ridge in her nose and made the end of it permanently crimson.

The damage to her digestion, however, was irreparable and it seemed to those whose houses she visited that the only nourishment she needed was innumerable cups of strong tea, brought to her at all hours of the day, which she drank without apparently ceasing for a moment the swift movement of her fingers.

She sewed incredibly quickly, which was not surprising as Maggie Potts had started when she was little more than a baby to help her mother in the sewing of shirt buttons to cards at a penny a gross. From daylight to dusk they toiled, and as food and rent depended entirely on speed Maggie learned to be swift.

Nerina, watching her now as she knelt to tack up the hem of the gown she wore, thought she had never seen anyone wield a needle so deftly. In and out, in and out it went, and Madame Marcele slipped the pins which the tacking replaced into her mouth until her chapped lips looked like the back of a hedgehog. Once again she stood back to get the effect; her eyes, magnified through the coarse glasses, appeared enormous and in consequence her shallow face, thin and lined, seemed as withered as a mask and hardly human.

"That's all right, Miss Graye," Madame Marcele said. "I can finish that off tomorrow and her ladyship need not worry about it again. It's a lovely gown, and though I says it as shouldn't, you wouldn't find better in the whole length and breadth of Bond Street."

"Yes, it is pretty," Nerina agreed, but half heartedly, having no enthusiasm for a dress of sky-blue tulle trimmed with bunches of moss rose-buds. It was the sort of gown in which Elizabeth would look lovely and ethereal, but which on her—against her own vivid colouring—looked tawdry and garish.

78

"And now the wedding dress!" Madame Marcele said. Nerina looked surprised.

"Surely you want Lady Elizabeth for that."

"Oh, 'tis of no consequence," Madame Marcele replied. "Her ladyship has already tried it on once, and really, Miss, when it comes to measurements you're as like as two peas in a pod. Not that anyone would know you were cousins, you a red head and Lady Elizabeth yellow as a buttercup. But that's as it should be, as I was saying to her ladyship only this morning. Sir Rupert is dark and tall and she's fair and small. It's just my idea of what a couple should be."

"Dark men don't always care for fair women," Nerina replied. "What about Lady Clementine Talmadge?"

Madame Marcele gave her a sharp glance out of the corner of her eyes.

"Yes, Lady Clementine is dark," she said. "I see, Miss, as how you've been hearing things. But there, you can take it from me there's nothing in that. Her ladyship has had admirers since she was in the cradle. I was over at her place last week, making her a travelling gown, and while she was fitting we were talking of old times. I was asking after Lord Julian Shephard who was that in love with her that he wouldn't trouble to hide his feelings from anyone, whoever they might be. 'How's his lordship?' I asks. 'Lord Julian?' her ladyship enquires with a careless laugh. 'Why, I have not thought of him for ages. He may be dead for all I know.' That shows you what she's like."

"Here today and gone tomorrow!" Nerina suggested.

"But of course, Miss! And we all know what Sir Rupert is too."

"What is he?" Nerina enquired.

"I means of course as regards women," Madame Marcele explained. "It's only to be expected when he's so wealthy and so handsome. They all run after him. It makes you fair sick to hear them talking. You know, Miss, they don't mind what they say in front of me. 'It's only old Marcele,' they say, and then go on talking amongst themselves. Sometimes I think as how a man who is good-looking and attractive hasn't got a chance so far as women are concerned."

"I should think Sir Rupert is quite capable of looking after himself," Nerina said acidly.

"Yes, I admit he's a bit difficult." Madame Marcele agreed. "Not that I've ever spoken to him, but I have seen him often enough. Haughty and arrogant, as if the earth was not quite good enough for him to walk on—not that I minds a bit of pride in a man myself. And he's hard to get, that's what makes the ladies so keen on him."

"And is Lady Clementine so keen on him?" Nerina enquired.

"Now, Miss Graye, you mustn't be asking me that sort of question," Madame Marcele admonished. "It isn't fitting that a young lady like yourself should know about such things; but there, Lady Clementine always was a law unto herself. The things she's done and got away with! Well, if I told you some of them you wouldn't believe me."

"Are there a lot of people talking about Sir Rupert and Lady Clementine?"

"Oh nò," Madame Marcele replied. "They've been ever so careful. It's only that I hear about such things seeing as how my cousin's daughter is third housemaid at Wroth Castle."

"What do you think Lady Clementine will feel about Sir Rupert's marriage?" Nerina asked.

Madame Marcele gave her another of her quick, sidelong glances.

"Her ladyship doesn't concern herself with the ties her gentlemen may have," she said. "Over and over again I've heard her say, 'What's his private life to me?' I remember Lord Julian stammering something about his brother being annoyed with him—over his goings on with her ladyship, of course. And Lady Clementine gives him one of her deep looks from under her eyelashes—I was fitting her at the time and I gets a good view of it, so to speak . . . And she says, 'To hell with your carping relatives; they aren't my headache. You listen to them or me, but not both. I've no time for compromises.' Lord Julian apologised and said he'd never mention the subject again, but it shows you, doesn't it, Miss?"

"It does."

Nerina bent her head to allow Madame Marcele to slip Elizabeth's wedding gown over her shoulders. It was an exquisite dress made of flounce upon flounce of real Brussels lace, the full skirt billowing out from a tiny waist, a fichu of the same lace only partly concealing the bare shoulders of the wearer.

Nerina looked at herself in the glass and gave a little exclamation of delight.

"What a wonderful gown," she said. "You have made it beautifully."

Madame Marcele beamed her approval.

"It was a privilege to have this lace to work with," she said. "Some of it was a bit discoloured as her ladyship had kept it so long. It had been in her grandmother's trousseau, she told me, but I managed to cut out the worst of it and no one will notice where the flounces are joined."

"No, indeed," Nerina said, "it is quite lovely. Is the veil of lace, too?"

"Yes, Miss, the veil matches the dress. If you ask me, I think it's a bit heavy. It will hide her ladyship's face, but when I told her that, she didn't seem to care. Between you and I, Miss Graye, I have never known a bride take so little trouble over her appearance. I can't understand it; and believe me, Sir Rupert has never looked at a woman who was not well dressed."

"I think Lady Elizabeth is over-tired. There has been so much to arrange in such a very short space of time," Nerina said quickly.

"That is what it must be," Madame Marcele said. "Now turn a bit to the left, Miss, please. That's enough, thank you. The hem is uneven just here."

Madame Marcele's mouth was soon full of pins again, and for a moment her tongue was forced to be still least she should swallow them. Nerina regarded her own reflection in the long mirror with interest. She had never seen herself in such an expensive and exquisitely made gown before. The mellow cream of the shadowy lace was a perfect background for her skin. It made her appear both ethereal and at the same time vividly and pulsatingly beautiful. There was something ecstatic about her loveliness, and there was nothing insipid in her red hair and green eyes as there was at times in Elizabeth's pink and white cheeks and pale gold hair.

Nerina looked like a flame. It was not only her hair which seemed to light the whole room, it was something in herself, some magnetism which seemed to exude from her almost visibly.

Madame Marcele got to her feet. She spat the pins into her hands and stuck them quickly into the ancient heart-shaped velvet pin-cushion which hung from her waistband.

"There, that's finished," she said. "I shan't have to bother her ladyship with another fitting for that."

She stood back a foot or two to take in the whole picture.

"It's a lovely dress," she said, "and if you will excuse my saying so, Miss Graye, you look lovely in it yourself. It's a pity you are not to be wearing it. But there, I'll be making you a wedding gown one of these days soon."

"Never!" Nerina cried. "I shall never be married."

"That's stuff and nonsense, Miss, as well you know," Madame Marcele said. "With a face like yours you will be marrying as sure as eggs is eggs. And soon too, though I'm no fortune-teller. Why, you have only to look at yourself in the mirror to see how lovely you'd look as a bride. There's no doubt that the dress becomes you. Look at yourself now and think if you wouldn't like to be walking up the aisle to meet some handsome young man at the end of it. You may not be able to have such valuable lace, but I'll make you something pretty, I promise you that, and sew all the good wishes in the world into it."

"Thank you, Madame Marcele," Nerina said, touched by the note of sincerity in the woman's voice. And then she laughed. "But I am thanking you for nothing, for I assure you I do not intend to marry. I hate all men."

Madame Marcele looked shocked.

"There, you mustn't say such things. It sounds to me as if you have had a tiff with somebody. Ladies talk like that when they have fallen out with a gentleman. But you'll make it up again and then you'll be coming to me for a wedding dress. As I says again, you certainly look lovely in that one, it's a real pity you can't wear it."

"And marry Sir Rupert Wroth?" Nerina asked lightly. "No, thank you, Madame Marcele."

"You might go further and find worse," Madame Marcele snapped. It was obvious that Sir Rupert was rather a favourite of hers. "Men aren't born perfect, Miss, and it's no use expecting angels to be walking about in trousers."

She undid the fastening at the waist, then lifted the lace gown from off the steel-hooped petticoat.

"I do not expect angels," Nerina said when she could speak, "but surely there must be some happy medium between angels and devils?"

Madame Marcele giggled suddenly.

"You must excuse me, Miss Graye, but that's the second time I've heard Sir Rupert Wroth called a devil. I'll never forget how angry a certain lady was with him about two winters ago. I'll not mention names, for that wouldn't be right, but she was that set on Sir Rupert she could think and talk of nothing else. She used to put me through a regular cross-examination as to what I had heard of him, and what he had been doing. Of course I didn't know much, but a crumb is better than nothing when you've got a hungry heart. Then he gets tired of her. I knew that was the truth, and I knew too who his next fancy was for I was making Number Two some special dresses. They always sends for me when they wants to look special. And you wouldn't believe the amount of work that's come to me through Sir Rupert Wroth. Well, the first lady I was telling you about gradually learns that he doesn't care about her any more and she just raves about him! I've never heard anyone go on in such a way. 'He's a devil,' she screams to me, 'and one day I will kill him, you see if I don't.' It was just like a play and I was hard put to know what to say to her."

"And yet you are still prepared to say nice things about Sir Rupert," Nerina said.

She was putting on her own dress by now, tying its ribbon sash tightly round her small waist.

"And why not?" Madame Marcele enquired. "Married women as gets themselves caught up in love affairs with gentlemen like Sir Rupert know just how much it can mean and how little. They can look after themselves all right, and when things go wrong they can always fall back on their own husbands, can't they?"

Nerina did not answer. She was seeing the reasonableness of Madame Marcele's cynicism. At the same time she knew it could not be applied to Elizabeth, so gentle, so vulnerable, so easily hurt. How could Elizabeth hope to even begin to understand a man like Sir Rupert Wroth?

Nerina's lips curled a little disdainfully as she thought again of the conversation she had heard between him and Lady Clementine. If only she could have fallen in on them, have told them there and then exactly what she thought of them both. She would have enjoyed it, and for once Sir Rupert's composure might have been shattered, for once he might have been shocked out of his air of supercilious disdain.

One day, Nerina thought, Sir Rupert might get his just deserts. She wondered what he would say when he discovered that Elizabeth had run away to marry another man. It would be amusing to watch his face when he learned the news, and it would be amusing to know if for once he was humiliated.

Then as she thought of the wedding, the old familiar question began to worry her once again. How was it all to be contrived, how was Elizabeth to be spirited away without Lord Cardon's knowledge?

Even if they did manage to get Elizabeth down the drive and into a fast carriage with Adrian, Lord Cardon was bound to discover her absence within an hour or two and he would have time to catch up with the runaway couple. He would only have to find out from the Barracks where the Regiment had gone, to discover that they were due to sail from Dover, and he could be there the next day before the ship moved with the tide.

Nerina had lain awake night after night pondering over these problems, while Elizabeth slept, happy in the knowledge that Adrian loved her, confident in her belief that he would somehow arrange everything. Nerina was loathe to put too many questions to her or discuss the future too fully in case she should become too depressed to act the part which was required of her in front of Sir Rupert and her parents.

And yet the problems were there. Nerina had discussed them a thousand times with Bessie and they had come to no solution. Now as she said good-bye to Madame Marcele and prepared to leave the room, they presented themselves once more with a nagging persistence which would not be denied.

"You won't be wanting me again tonight?" Nerina enquired.

"No, Miss Graye, thank you," Madame Marcele replied. "I've got enough to keep me busy until bedtime. There's the hem of that ball gown and then I shall finish off the wedding dress completely. Her ladyship must not try it on after that, it would be bad luck and no mistake."

"Will you tell Bessie what time you want her ladyship in the morning?" Nerina said. "And if she is too tired I will come instead. She will be glad to know that I can deputise for her."

"Yes, indeed, she'll find it a real blessing," Madame Marcele replied. "There's a lot of gowns to be fitted yet. Good night, Miss, you've been a real help and don't forget how pretty you looked in that wedding dress. It will make you keen to have one of your own."

Nerina laughed.

"You're a flatterer, Madame Marcele," she said.

As she went down the passage to find Elizabeth, she felt a warm glow of satisfaction within herself. It was ridiculous, she knew, to pay much attention to what an inveterate old gossip like Madame Marcele said, and yet it was pleasant for once to be praised, to know one was pretty, to know as she looked in the glass that the words were justified.

It was not like hearing it from a man, knowing that he had some ulterior motive in praising her looks. There had been an unmistakable ring of sincerity in Madame Marcele's voice. For a moment Nerina imagined herself walking up the red-carpeted aisle, the priceless lace dress intrinsically lovely against the carved oak pews and grey stone walls of the Church. She thought of the veil covering her face, its gossamer transparency hiding a little of her shyness. Her eyes would be downcast although she would be acutely conscious of the man waiting for her at the chancel steps. She would move slowly towards him, one hand on her uncle's arm, the other holding her bouquet of flowers. Now the Priest was standing in front of her. Someone stood at her side—the unknown Bridegroom. She knew he was looking at her, and then slowly, a little daringly, she raised her eyes to his. She could see him through the folds of her veil, see the face of the man she was about to marry. . . .

The dream came to an end and Nerina found herself outside the door of her bedroom. She went in. Elizabeth was sitting where she had left her in the window seat, but the sun had long since sunk and the room was in twilight. Elizabeth was holding Adrian's letter in her hand. She looked up as Nerina came in, yet for a moment she hardly seemed to see her, for her face was alight with happiness, that bemused, rapturous inner happiness which comes to every woman when she loves for the first time.

Once again the urgent question of the future reiterated itself in Nerina's mind. How could Elizabeth marry Adrian, how could it be done? And then suddenly she knew, knew as surely as if someone had written the answer for her in letters of fire. She knew what she must do, knew, even as the solution came to her, that it was the only possible way for Elizabeth to escape—dangerous though it might be.

Galvanised into activity by the thoughts which seemed to

be burning their way through her mind, Nerina slammed the door behind her, then ran across the room to drop on her knees beside Elizabeth and put her arms protectingly round her, as if she would save her from everything, even the consequences of life itself.

"Listen, Elizabeth, listen," she said, and her voice was throbbing with excitement. "I have thought of what we can do! It has suddenly come to me! It is the only way, the only possible way. You can marry your Adrian and sail before your father finds out."

Elizabeth looked down at her dreamily, hardly aware of the stupendous decision that Nerina was making or even how vitally it concerned her future.

"It is the only way," Nerina said passionately, "the only way, Elizabeth, in which you can be safe. I must marry Sir Rupert in your place!"

6

Nerina sat on the edge of the bed listening. For a moment the house seemed very still, then in the room below she heard a housemaid scraping the ashes from the grate and in the distance the sound of curtains being pulled and the vigorous brushing of carpets.

But she was listening for another sound and the expression on her face was tense, as was every muscle in her body. So far everything had run smoothly. By this time Elizabeth would be many miles away, fleeing with Adrian towards the ship which would carry her out of reach of her parents' wrath.

But the danger was by no means past. There was still time for Lord Cardon to discover her absence and for him to prevent her sailing. He could bring her back home in disgrace, if not in time for her marriage to Sir Rupert.

Nerina looked at the clock over the mantelpiece. It was half past seven. Elizabeth had left the house at dawn and Adrian had been waiting for her at the end of the drive. To get away had required much careful thought, because Lord Cardon had persisted in locking them in their room every evening and not until he was called next morning was Bessie permitted to fetch the key from his bedside.

They had pondered for a long while how Elizabeth could be released. They had thought of forcing the lock, of trying to deceive Lord Cardon into thinking she was asleep in bed before he locked the door at night when actually she was not in the room at all, and many other ideas all of which they had discarded as being too dangerous. Nerina reiterated over and over again that if they made Lord Cardon the least bit suspicious that something was afoot, their plans were doomed to failure. Their only chance was to make everything appear quite normal so that he should be lulled into a sense of false security. Accordingly they had gone to bed in their usual fashion about ten o'clock; and when Lord Cardon had come up as was his wont half an hour later, he had opened the door, seen that both the girls were in bed and shut it decisively before turning the key in the lock.

Nerina had said nothing to him, but several times during the day she had complained to Lady Cardon of not feeling well. She had received scant sympathy; indeed her aunt had remarked tartly:

"For goodness' sake stop whining about your health, Nerina! We are all feeling tired for there has been so much to do. After Elizabeth's marriage you will be able to take things quietly until your uncle decides to find you another post, one which we hope you will not leave so precipitously as you did the last."

Sympathy or not, Nerina knew she had registered in her aunt's mind that she was not in her usual state of health. At about half past eleven that evening, when Lord Cardon was comfortably in bed, Bessie knocked on his door.

"Excuse me for disturbing your lordship," she said when he bade her enter, "but Lady Elizabeth has just rung the bell and says Miss Nerina is far from well. If your lordship will let me have the key, I will attend to her wants and bring it straight back to you."

"Damn the girl!" Lord Cardon grumbled. "Why does she want to go disturbing people at this time of night?"

"I only hope it is nothing serious, m'lord," Bessie said. "I thought to myself when I was helping the young ladies to undress that Miss Nerina looked uncommonly as if she had a temperature."

"Well, take the key," Lord Cardon commanded, who was not interested in Nerina's ailments, "but bring it back to me, mind."

"Of course, m'lord."

Bessie took the key, curtsied and hurried down the passage. Elizabeth was ready. She slipped out of the bedroom and hid in the empty schoolroom, which was on the same floor. Bessie waited a few moments and then took the key back to his lordship's room.

"I'm afraid Miss Nerina has a fever, m'lord," she said. "It would be a real shame if she has to miss the wedding tomorrow."

Lord Cardon merely grunted a reply. He had drunk his usual bottle of port after dinner and now he was feeling sleepy. He did not care what happened on the morrow provided that his daughter was married to Sir Rupert Wroth and that the very generous marriage settlement he had negotiated with the lawyers should be signed and sealed.

Bessie left Lord Cardon's room. She hurried back to Elizabeth and having locked the door of the schoolroom so that no one would disturb them, persuaded her to lie down on the sofa with a rug over her. Elizabeth did exactly as she was told. She had in the past few days shown a surprising docility about everything; in fact Nerina had been astonished at her calmness and lack of nerves. She herself in contrast was on edge the whole time, imagining every moment that their plans might be discovered or that something desperate would happen at the last minute to prevent the execution of them.

Elizabeth even slept well while Nerina lay tossing on her pillows night after night, sleepless and wide-eyed in the darkness, her brain busy with what the future held. Nerina decided finally that Elizabeth lacked imagination. She had a placid, peace-loving disposition and was designed by nature always to take the line of least resistance. Had she not happened to fall in love with Adrian, she would have married Sir Rupert Wroth at her parents' command and not questioned their right to arrange such matters or her own complacent obedience.

Elizabeth's love for Adrian was the first thing which had ever altered the even tenor of her ways. But desperate though she was, she could not change her old habit of dependence, and she was quite content, once she realised that a solution had been found for her escape, to leave every detail to Nerina and Bessie. Indeed, she hardly troubled to enquire exactly what was to be done and how they intended to do it. As long as she was assured that she would be able to reach Adrian and go away with him, nothing else mattered or concerned her in the slightest. On only one point had she been surprisingly firm, and that was that she would not leave home without her trousseau.

"But, Elizabeth," Nerina exclaimed in dismay, "how can we possibly get all those trunks and boxes out of the house."

"It must be done," Elizabeth retorted. "I cannot marry Adrian without anything to wear. Besides, what will the people on the boat think—the other officers' wives—if I arrive with only what I stand up in. They would laugh at me, Nerina. I have got to have at least some of my trousseau with me, I have really."

Nerina looked at Bessie in dismay. It was Bessie who eventually found the answer to this fresh problem. It was daring, reckless, and yet perhaps because it was both these things it succeeded.

The afternoon before the wedding Bessie informed one of the men-servants that some of her ladyship's trunks were to be sent to the station and that the luggage cart was to be brought round to the back door immediately. Bessie was an old and privileged servant and her orders were not questioned. In the meantime Bessie and Nerina had contrived to carry down from the boxroom in the attic several old trunks. They filled these with Elizabeth's trousseau, leaving her new boxes in the bedroom where Lady Cardon could see them. The old trunks were labelled and taken down the back stairs by the footman, put on the luggage cart and driven off to the station without anyone thinking it in any way extraordinary.

The new trunks were filled with old clothes and newspapers, and one which looked particularly empty even with blankets and pillows off an unused bed. Bessie waited on the road and told Adrian to pick up the luggage at the station before he came to collect Elizabeth at dawn next morning. It astonished Nerina, when there was so much at stake, that Elizabeth should mind so much about her clothes; and yet she began to realise that when a woman is in love she longs so ardently to look her best and to be admired by the man of her choice that she would risk any danger rather than that of looking unattractive.

Elizabeth had even sighed a little regretfully when she looked at her going-away gown and realised that she must at least leave that behind for Nerina. Of sapphire blue mohair trimmed with *glacé* it was an extremely elegant creation, and the bonnet, which matched, was decorated with curled ostrich plumes shading from pale pink to coral.

Nerina had insisted that Elizabeth ask the milliner to add a short veil. They were fashionable and there was no reason why she should not have one dangling gracefully from the edge of the brim. Nevertheless there had been quite an argument about it.

"You are too young!" Lady Cardon said firmly, while the milliner exclaimed that her ladyship's lovely face should not be hidden.

"I think veils are vastly becoming to married women," Elizabeth said firmly, and because Nerina had been so insistent she had continued to argue until she got her own way.

Sitting now on the edge of the bed listening for Bessie's return from Lord Cardon's room where she had gone to fetch the key as usual, Nerina looked at Elizabeth's going-away dress and her wedding gown hanging outside the wardrobe. They had not been put inside for fear of crushing them, and now in the morning light they looked almost like the ghosts of two women and for a moment Nerina fancied that they had entities of their own.

She could not believe that it would really be she who would be going up the aisle to marry Sir Rupert Wroth in Elizabeth's place. She could not believe that it would be she who would be going away with him, travelling alone with him to London where the first night of their honeymoon was to be spent.

Nerina wondered what they would say to each other during that long journey. It was not going to be an easy time, she thought, because she had already determined that she must keep up the subterfuge of being her cousin until it was quite impossible for Sir Rupert to inform Lord Cardon that he had been deceived in his bride.

At the very earliest she must not reveal the truth until they reached London. Nerina gave a deep sigh, but it was not one of depression. It was more the indrawing and the exhaling of a breath such as a boxer might when he gathered together his strength for the fight which lay ahead of him.

She heard footsteps coming down the passage and rising quickly to her feet seated herself at the dressing-table with her back to the door just in case it should be someone other than Bessie. As she did so, she saw her own reflection in the mirror and for a moment she was startled and amazed by her own appearance. She really did look like Elizabeth, with a golden wig concealing her own vivid hair, the curls, arranged in exact imitation of Elizabeth's, framing her pale cheeks.

It was really the possession of this wig which made her make the fantastic proposal that she should take Elizabeth's place. She did not know why, but as she walked from the passage into the bedroom after her fitting by Madame Marcele, she had suddenly remembered it. It had lain forgotten in one of the cupboards in the schoolroom for at least four years. She had worn it when she and Elizabeth had gone to a fancy-dress party dressed as twins. She recalled how at the time they had both thought it a ridiculous idea. They had made many other suggestions when Lady Cardon first proposed it, but as usual Lord Cardon had had the deciding vote and when they had won a prize he had taken all the credit to himself.

Lady Cardon would not have been so concerned either with the thought of a fancy-dress ball or of buying such an expensive wig if the invitation had not come from the

Duchess of Meldrum. The Duke and Duchess were seldom in residence and when they were, the whole County fell over themselves for invitations to the ducal house.

Lady Cardon was a snob like most of her friends and she was particularly anxious that Elizabeth should be friends with the Duchess's youngest daughter who was about the same age. She was, however, well aware that there were at least a dozen other mothers in the County with the same idea. The difficulty was to make Elizabeth in some way outstanding amongst the other children who would be dressed and groomed with identically the same intention.

It was the inadvertent remark of a dinner guest which put into her head the idea that Elizabeth and Nerina should go to the party as twins. He was speaking of a Grecian vase which Lord Cardon was anxious to have valued.

"You will get a good sum for it," his guest said. "It is a pity it is not a pair, for two of a kind are always far more valuable than one."

It was then the idea came to Lady Cardon, and because of what she anticipated might be achieved by the party she had sent to a famous wig-maker in London for a head of hair which was to resemble Elizabeth's exactly. There was no doubt at all, Nerina thought now, that in the wig, dressed and rearranged by Bessie's skilful fingers, anyone might mistake her for Elizabeth at a distance. That was the trouble. She had to keep all those who knew Elizabeth well at a distance, including Lord and Lady Cardon.

She heard the key turn in the lock of the door, lifted her handkerchief to her eyes, hiding her face. When she saw it was only Bessie, she turned round with a little cry of excitement.

"Was everything quite all right?" she asked.

They had arranged that Bessie should knock on the door very quietly when she came back to the house after taking Elizabeth to the drive gate, but with the door between them locked Nerina had not been able to talk to her until now.

"Everything went as smoothly as a wedding bell," Bessie said with satisfaction. "Mr. Butler was waiting and her ladyship gave a little cry and flew straight into his arms. It made the tears come to my eyes, it did, to see them both so happy. But there was no time for love-making as I told them straight enough. 'Hurry now,' I says, 'and get away from here as quick as you can. There may be someone

92

spying on us at this very instant.' Her ladyship kisses me, she jumps into the carriage, and they're away, I swear to you, Miss Nerina, I stood there watching them with the tears streaming down my face, for it was only when her ladyship turned round to wave to me that I realised I may never see her again. India is a long way from here, Miss Nerina, and you never know what those treacherous black people will be up to. But there, she'll have a husband to protect her and I suppose it is only me that is crying for a young lady whom I have loved since she was a baby."

"Poor Bessie," Nerina said, then added excitedly: "But, Bessie, it is wonderful to think that she has got away and nobody saw her go. You are quite certain none of the gardeners or game-keepers are waiting below to tell Lord Cardon that something strange has taken place?"

"I don't think anybody could see us, Miss. There's only old Mrs. Jarvis sleeping in the lodge these days since her son went to prison for poaching. She's that deaf she wouldn't hear the last trump even if they blew it right in her ear. Besides, everybody will be busy this morning getting ready for the wedding. They'll be tidying up the lawns and finding a hundred jobs to occupy their minds."

"I am sure you are right," Nerina said. "It is just that I am so afraid something may happen. If Elizabeth were brought back now I believe it would kill her."

"You're right there, Miss," Bessie agreed. "It's what I thought myself. She's been so sure that she and Mr. Adrian would be married and that she would be sailing away with him over the seas that if Lord Cardon went after her it would kill her as certain sure as if he put a bullet through her heart."

"That is what I have thought all along," Nerina said, "and that, Bessie, is exactly why I am taking her place today."

"And you'll do it cleverly enough too," Bessie smiled. "Why I promise you, Miss, you gave me a real turn when I came in just now. Just for a moment I thought it was her ladyship sitting there and my heart seemed to jump right out of my body. Then I knew it was you."

She paused for a moment and then in the soft, understanding tone which she had used when Nerina and Elizabeth were children and they had been scared of the dark or miserable after some severe punishment, she said:

"You're not frightened, are you, dearie? I have thought so often of what you have undertaken. I've said to myself,

93

'there's not a young lady in a thousand as would dare to do the things Miss Nerina has offered to do'. If you're frightened, perhaps it would be enough if you told them all the truth when you gets to the Church door."

Nerina shook her head.

"Elizabeth would not be safe even then, Bessie. His lordship would have time to get to Dover before the ship sailed. No, I have got to go through with it, and I'm not frightened . . . at least, not very."

Bessie moved forward and put out her hand to touch Nerina's shoulder. It was as if she had not words to express her feelings, and then almost sharply she said:

"But I mustn't stand here wasting my time. There's so much to be done. I'll go and get your breakfast. You had best eat a good meal or you'll be feeling faint. Be careful if anyone comes to the door. I will go and see her ladyship as soon as I get back."

Bessie bustled away while Nerina sat on at the dressing-table. For a moment Bessie's words struck a chill at the warmth of her relief in knowing that Elizabeth was safely away from the house and by the evening would be married to Adrian Butler. The first part of the programme was ended and so far all was well.

But now there was her own marriage to consider, marriage to a man with whom she had not exchanged half a dozen words since he had become engaged to her cousin. At the very thought of Sir Rupert she felt her anger rising; and her dislike and hatred of him became a physical emotion which hurt her as much as if she ached from the pain of a wound. Yes, she hated him, and her marriage to him would, she promised herself, be very different from that of Elizabeth to Adrian Butler.

As she thought of her cousin's passionate love for Adrian, Nerina's expression softened, and then with a little smile she recalled how Elizabeth had surprised her in yet another way. She had always imagined Elizabeth to be completely innocent, brought up as she had been in the sheltered, unsophisticated atmosphere of Rowanfield Manor.

There was even something very childish about Elizabeth, so much so that although Nerina and she were the same age, Nerina had always felt immeasurably older and, what was more, instinctively protective towards her cousin. Even when they were both eighteen Nerina had thought of

Elizabeth as being a mere child, someone who must be sheltered from the sharp wind of worldly things.

And then last night, as Nerina had watched her packing excitedly the little intimate possessions which she wished to carry with her on the journey into the unknown, compunction had struck her. What did Elizabeth know of life, of men, or indeed of marriage? Was it right or fair that she should go away the following day with a man who was practically a stranger, knowing nothing of what she might expect, perhaps anticipating something very different from what might be a crude, awakening reality? On an impulse Nerina sat down beside Elizabeth and took her hand in hers.

"Listen, dearest Elizabeth," she said, "there is something I must say to you before you leave here. It is difficult for me to put it into words, but somehow I must try to explain things lest you should be shocked and frightened when you discover them for yourself."

To Nerina's surprise Elizabeth had not looked at her with puzzled eyes, but had given a little laugh.

"Darling Nerina," she said, "how solemn you look! But please don't speak to me in such a manner. I have already had one little talk with Mama and I could not bear a second."

"Oh, so Aunt Anne has explained . . . er . . . marriage to you," Nerina said with a feeling of relief.

Elizabeth giggled.

"Not that one would say it was much of an explanation," she said. "She called me to her room and said in a most frightening voice: 'Elizabeth, I have something to say to you!' I thought for a moment that she had discovered everything, and then she went on. 'Tomorrow you are to be married. As you know, my dear child, marriage is a Holy Sacrament of the Church.' I was so relieved that she had not discovered about Adrian that I smiled brightly and said, 'Oh yes, Mama, I know that.' 'But that is not all,' she said in a voice of absolute gloom. Then, Nerina, she became quite extraordinary. She hummed and hawed in a way that for Mama was most strange. She did not look at me and if I didn't know Mama could never be any such thing, I would have said she was shy. She talked about one's duty towards one's husband and how one must obey him in everything he commanded, however strange and even disgusting it might seem. To tell the truth I had

95

the greatest difficulty in not laughing outright. As though anything Adrian did could be horrible or disgusting; but Mama was meandering on so, making nothing clear, in fact what she said was not even sense."

"But, Elizabeth," Nerina said in astonishment, "do you really know about such things?"

Elizabeth looked down and a little secret smile touched the corners of her lips.

"I think I do," she said, "at least enough not to be frightened at being alone with Adrian; and if there are things I don't know, then I would rather he told me about them than Mama. Poor dear. I imagine she must have been absolutely scandalised when she first married Papa."

"Elizabeth!" Nerina exclaimed, laughing at the same time, but feeling half scandalised herself that her little cousin, whom she had thought so utterly ignorant, should know so much.

There had been nothing more to say and she put her arms round Elizabeth and kissed her.

"That's my last worry disposed of," she said.

The dimples appeared in Elizabeth's cheek.

"I am not quite so stupid as to believe that babies are born under gooseberry bushes," she said, "and if you really want to know, that Meldrum girl told me a whole lot about men and babies three summers ago when she used to come over here and we played hide-and-seek in the garden."

"The Meldrum girl!" Nerina exclaimed. "And Aunt Anne thought she was always such a good influence for you."

"That is only because she was a Duke's daughter," Elizabeth said scornfully. "As a matter of fact she had an extraordinarily dirty mind. I would hate to repeat some of the things she told me."

"But why did you listen?" Nerina asked.

Elizabeth's dimple appeared again.

"I was interested," she said simply, and for once her cousin left Nerina speechless.

There was the rattle of a tray at the door and a second later Bessie entered.

"I have brought you eggs and bacon, and one of the hot rolls his lordship likes so much. You are to eat every scrap and you had best make haste about it too. I'm going along to her ladyship's room now."

Nerina looked round her, almost panic-stricken.

"Oh, Bessie, supposing she comes along here right away."

"She won't," Bessie said soothingly. "If her ladyship puts a foot out of bed before nine o'clock I'm a Dutchman. Anyway, I'll be back before she appears, so don't worry."

She went from the room and Nerina obediently began to eat the breakfast. Surprisingly she found she was hungry. The eggs were fresh and delicious, and the hot rolls, which the cook had got up at five o'clock in the morning to bake for her uncle's breakfast, were crisp and succulent. The plates were nearly empty when Bessie came back.

"Is it all right?" Nerina asked anxiously.

Bessie nodded.

"Her ladyship was only just awake. I tiptoed to the side of the bed. 'Excuse me, your ladyship, but I thought I had better tell you at once that Miss Nerina is not well. She has a temperature, your ladyship, and I don't like the look of her at all.' 'What is wrong with the tiresome child?' your aunt asked. 'Well, of course I wouldn't like to express an opinion before the Doctor sees her,' I said, 'but I have an idea, your ladyship, that it might be either measles or mumps. There's cases of both in the village, and it crossed my mind yesterday that Miss Nerina was sickening for something. She had the look.' Well, her ladyship gives a gasp of horror and sits up in bed. 'Measles or mumps, Bessie,' she cries, 'and on Lady Elizabeth's wedding day! What on earth are we to do?' 'Well, your ladyship,' I said, lowering my voice a little, 'knowing as how your ladyship and his lordship would want no fuss until after the ceremony was over, I have taken it upon myself to move Miss Nerina upstairs to the old Night Nursery. I've put her into bed there and given her a soothing syrup. It's my belief that in a few minutes she'll be fast asleep. I'll look after her, your ladyship, and she'll come to no harm. When the wedding is over, if she's no better we can send for the Doctor. We don't want to go frightening people with fear of infection.' 'No, indeed,' her ladyship says, and she lays back again on the pillows.

" 'You have done the right thing, Bessie,' she says, 'and after all it may be just a false alarm.' 'Yes, indeed, your ladyship,' I said, 'and I hopes it is, but I think it would be best if no one went near Miss Nerina save myself. I'll take her food up to her, and see that she has everything she wants. We don't want other people in the household to start spreading rumours. You know the way people go on about a bit of illness, your ladyship.' 'I leave her entirely in your hands, Bessie,' her ladyship says, and adds, 'and how is my daughter this morning?'

"At that I alters my expression to look very grave and shook my head. 'She isn't very happy, your ladyship, at the thought of going away from home,' I says. 'I'm afraid she has been crying, for her eyes are swollen; but I've made her lie down and put pads of *eau-de-Cologne* on her forehead and cool rags over her swollen eyes. She'll be all right when the time comes; but I'm hoping you and his lordship will say as little to her as possible, for she's that worried at the thought of leaving you both and I declare she will burst into another fit of crying.' 'Oh dear, how tiresome,' her ladyship says, then I comes away thinking I've given her plenty to think about."

"I had better lie down on the bed then," Nerina said hastily, finishing off her cup of coffee. "Lower the blinds, Bessie, and give me another handkerchief out of the drawer, a big one."

Nerina arranged herself on the bed. She let Bessie lay a pad of cotton wool soaked with *eau-de-Cologne* on her forehead and pads soaked in water over her eyes. This left very little of her face visible, and anyway the room was dimmed to a dusky twilight.

Nerina had slept so little during the night that now she found herself dozing a little even while her thoughts were busy with the difficulties which lay ahead.

It was nearly an hour later when she heard the door open and realised that Lady Cardon had come into the room. Hastily Nerina raised a handkerchief to her nose.

"I see you are resting, dear," Lady Cardon said. "That is very wise. Bessie will come to you when it is time to get dressed."

"Oh, Mama," Nerina said in a strangled voice.

Lady Cardon turned hastily towards the open door.

"Now you are not to upset yourself, Elizabeth," she said firmly, "try and sleep. You want to look your best today of all days."

Bessie, who had been hovering in the passage, met Lady Cardon as she came from the bedroom.

"It's terrible to see her so grief-stricken, your ladyship," she said, "not a bite of food will she eat either. I'm frightened that she'll be fainting long before she gets to the Church."

"Oh, she mustn't do that," Lady Cardon said in alarm. "His lordship would be extremely annoyed if anything occurs to upset the wedding arrangements."

"I'll do my best," Bessie said, "you know that, your ladyship, but ask his lordship not to come worrying her. I'll bring Lady Elizabeth downstairs at five minutes to twelve."

"Yes, not later," Lady Cardon said. "It will only take two or three minutes to drive to the Church, but you know how his lordship hates being kept waiting."

"Yes indeed, your ladyship," Bessie said.

Waiting in the semi-darkness until it was time to dress, Nerina felt that the hours had never gone so slowly. At any moment she expected something terrible to happen, for the door to be flung open by her uncle declaring that he knew the truth and that he had discovered the whole plot. But slowly the minutes ticked past and at last Bessie came, locking the door behind her and drawing up the blinds, saying that she must dress.

The sunlight came streaming into the room. Over Nerina's lace-trimmed petticoats Bessie lifted the wedding gown of Brussels lace. It was so lovely that for a moment Nerina forgot everything, even the fact that she should not be wearing it, as she appraised its beauty and touched it with reverent fingers. When Bessie had fastened all the dozens of tiny hooks and eyes which Madame Marcele had sewn so painstakingly down the back, she lifted the long enveloping veil and arranged it skilfully on Nerina's head under a wreath of orange blossom.

The veil was very old, an heirloom of the Cardon family, and had been handed down from generation to generation until worn by time it was no longer white, but had the soft warm shade of very old parchment. It veiled Nerina's face, giving her an elusive ethereal look, and fell at the back to the ground forming a short train.

It took Bessie some time to arrange the wreath and veil exactly as she wanted it, and when she had finished she turned Nerina round so that she could see herself in the long mirror set in the door of the wardrobe. Nerina looked at her own reflection and gave a little exclamation.

"Oh, Bessie, I look lovely. And what is more, no one for a moment would suspect that it was me, the badly dressed, poor relation who has always been shoved into the background."

"You're to take no chances, Miss," Bessie said severely. "You must keep your handkerchief to your eyes the whole time; and if you bend your head very low as well, it will be impossible for anyone to suspect it's not Lady Elizabeth herself."

"I feel so proud of myself," Nerina said, "that I would like to throw back the veil and walk up the aisle with my head held high. Oh, it is all right," she added, when she saw Bessie's look of consternation, "I am not going to take the slightest risk, you need not be frightened of that."

"You're taking quite enough without adding to them," Bessie muttered.

"That is true," Nerina said softly.

Bessie glanced at the clock.

"Seven minutes to twelve," she said. "Now sit down and hold your handkerchief in one hand and the smelling salts in the other while I ring for a footman. I'm going to send a message to his lordship that you've just fainted and that in consequence you'll be a few moments late. When you do appear, he'll be so annoyed at being kept waiting that he'll be blind and deaf to everything save his own bad temper."

Nerina laughed.

"How well you know my uncle, Bessie!"

Bessie gave the bell-pull a sharp jerk.

"My father was just the same," she said. "It doesn't matter whether they're bred in a Castle or in a cottage, men are much of a muchness wherever one finds them."

"And all of them loathsome!" Nerina added, as she raised the handkerchief to her face and waited for the footman to answer the bell.

7

Nerina lay back in the corner of the railway carriage as if she were tired and exhausted. She did not bother to hold the handkerchief to her eyes because she had done so all the afternoon and her hand felt quite weary of it. It was not very bright in the corner of the carriage and she was sure that Sir Rupert would not study her too closely.

She glanced at him out of the corner of her eye. His face was in profile to her because he was looking out of the window. His features were clear-cut and she noticed for the first time the obstinate severity of his somewhat protruding chin. It was rather exciting, she thought suddenly, to be alone with a man of whom she knew nothing save that two hours ago he had become her husband

Now that the ceremony was over and the immediate danger of discovery past, she was no longer afraid but felt almost elated that she had succeeded in what she had set out to do. It seemed in retrospect almost a miracle that no one had suspected anything and that everything had gone off exactly according to plan.

Lord Cardon had grumbled at her the whole way to the Church and had been far too incensed with the idea of being late to give her more than a perfunctory glance and to be irritated by the fact that she was apparently weeping into her handkerchief. Nerina had held a handkerchief to her eyes all the way up the aisle. She made her responses in a broken, tearful voice, and when finally they reached the Vestry and Lady Cardon stepped forward to lift her veil from her face and throw it back over the wreath of orange blossom, she sobbed out, "Mama! Mama!" in half broken tones and had apparently been shaken by a fit of weeping.

There had never been a wetter, more dismal bride, Nerina had thought to herself with a little grin of amusement as she set off down the aisle on Sir Rupert's arm to the strains of Mendelssohn's Wedding March. She could hear the murmurs of sympathy from the wedding guests and when finally she and Sir Rupert were in the carriage driving away from the Church, she knew instinctively that he was annoyed by her behaviour.

"There is no need to distress yourself, Elizabeth," he

said stiffly. "I know it is hard for you to leave your home, but I shall do my best to make you happy."

Nerina had a wild desire to laugh then, to take the handkerchief from her eyes and to answer him: "Oh, you will, will you? And what about Lady Clementine and all the other lovely ladies who will doubtless follow in her wake?" But it was too soon to say anything of the sort and she knew that she must continue to impersonate Elizabeth for at least another six or seven hours.

As had been arranged, Bessie was waiting in the Hall as they reached the Manor. Sir Rupert gave Nerina his hand to help her from the carriage and she was surprised at the warmth of his fingers. She had somehow expected any part of him to be icy cold and hard as granite. At his touch she felt for the first time that perhaps he was human. She wondered if she was treating him too badly, and then immediately the memory of his conversation with Lady Clementine in the summer-house returned and she felt that he deserved any punishment that she might inflict upon him and a great deal more.

She let him lead her up the front steps and then as she saw Bessie waiting anxiously in the hall she tottered towards her, saying in strangled tones:

"I am fainting, Bessie, I am fainting! Help me!"

She half collapsed into Bessie's arms, who, supporting her, turned to one of the footmen and said:

"James, help me carry her ladyship upstairs!"

To Nerina's surprise Sir Rupert said firmly:

"No, I will carry her ladyship."

Before she had time to realise his intentions, he had swept her high in his arms. With a little groan she hid her face against his shoulder and as he mounted the stairs she was conscious of his tremendous strength. He seemed to hold her as easily as if she had been a baby; and though he moved quickly, his breathing was just as calm and even when they reached the landing as when he had first started the climb.

"Which room?" he asked curtly of Bessie.

She led him into Lady Cardon's bedroom where Elizabeth's going-away dress was laid over an armchair, her mincing little *glacé* boots arranged beside it.

"Lay her ladyship on the bed, please, Sir," Bessie said. "She is overwrought and exhausted. It has been too much for her."

She spoke in almost a scolding tone as though she would

make Sir Rupert feel he was in the wrong. He made no reply, but laid Nerina down very gently on the bed. As she turned her face away from him, he asked:

"Shall I fetch some brandy?"

"There's some here, thank you, Sir," Bessie said. "Just leave her alone with me. She will be all right; if you would be kind enough to explain to his lordship when he arrives why her ladyship is upstairs."

"Yes, I will tell Lord Cardon," Sir Rupert replied. "You are certain there is nothing else you want?"

"Quite certain, thank you, Sir," Bessie said quickly, and followed him to the door to be quite sure he shut it behind him.

As soon as he had gone Nerina sat up in bed.

"I have done it, Bessie," she said. "I am married! Look!"

She held out her hand with the band of gold on the third finger.

"Oh, Miss Nerina, it's feared I am for you," Bessie quavered.

Nerina laughed.

"You should have seen me weeping and crying up the aisle and in the Vestry," she said. "It will do Sir Rupert's reputation no good to have people saying he has taken a reluctant bride."

She smiled again a little maliciously at the thought and then added quickly: "Pull the blinds, Bessie. It would be mad to take any risks now and Aunt Anne may be up at any moment."

"Yes, of course," Bessie replied. "What am I thinking of? It's you that has put all the sense out of me, showing me your wedding ring and talking as if what you have done this day were a trivial matter. There's a reckoning to come, Miss Nerina, and don't you forget it."

"I am ready to pay the price," Nerina replied, "so long as I can make Sir Rupert pay too. Thank goodness you are coming with me, Bessie. How soon do you think it will be before they discover there is no one in the Night Nursery?"

"I'm hoping it will be tomorrow morning," Bessie said. "I fetched some food from the kitchen after you'd gone to the Church and told Cook I was giving Miss Nerina a spoonful or two of soothing syrup. 'She'll sleep after that right enough,' I says, 'and I'm not letting anyone go barging in to wake her up. If she wants anything, she can ring for it.' I gave the housemaids my instructions and I don't think they will dare to disobey them. Anyway, they'll be celebrating the wedding tonight, so I suspect they'll not be worrying their heads about you."

"But what about Aunt Anne?" Nerina asked.

"I shall tell her ladyship the same story and advise her to be careful not to run the risk of infection. She's had neither mumps nor measles as far as I know."

"You are clever, Bessie," Nerina approved. "You seem to have thought of everything."

As she finished speaking she hastily lay down against the pillows, her handkerchief to her eyes, for she had heard a footstep outside the door.

Lady Cardon came into the room.

"What is the matter, Elizabeth?" she asked sharply. "Surely you can pull yourself together! And why are you lying here in the dark? You must come down at once to receive your guests and sit with your husband at the Wedding Breakfast."

"Oh, Mama! Mama!" Nerina wailed, her shoulders shaking as if with a tempest of tears.

"Can I speak to you outside, milady?" Bessie asked in a low voice.

Lady Cardon hesitated, then appeared to decide it was best to do as Bessie asked. She preceded her out of the room. In a few minutes Bessie came in again alone. She shut the door behind her and locked it.

"What did you say, Bessie?" Nerina asked.

"I frightened her ladyship good and proper," Bessie answered, lowering her voice. "I told her you were on the verge of collapse and that unless you were allowed to rest and take things easy you would not be in a fit state to go away on your honeymoon. Her ladyship was very upset at that, I can assure you. 'I have never known Elizabeth behave in such a ridiculous manner,' she said. 'Ah, there you are, milady,' I says, 'it's the quiet ones who feel things most deeply. It won't look well, will it, milady, if the honeymoon has to be called off. Leave things to me and I'll bring Lady Elizabeth downstairs when the carriage is round to take the bride and 'groom to the station. She's got herself that worked up that she would never be able to face the Wedding Breakfast with all those speeches. It's either that, your ladyship, or you had best send for the Doctor.' Well, that decided your aunt, Miss. She went off downstairs saying she did not know what his lordship would say about it, but it's my belief she will persuade him that leaving you here until the last moment is the best thing to do."

"Bessie, you are wonderful!" Nerina exclaimed, and lay back against the pillows in triumph, smiling at the thought of her uncle's fury and Sir Rupert's discomfiture.

Nevertheless, however brave she might pretend to be, her heart was beating apprehensively when Bessie escorted her downstairs to the Hall where Sir Rupert was waiting for her. The wedding guests had grouped themselves in the Hall and lined the front steps to the door of the carriage. There was a hush as Nerina appeared.

Slowly she came down the stairs, her head bent low as if to hide emotion, her handkerchief continually mopping her eyes. There was one dangerous moment when she had to kiss Lord and Lady Cardon good-bye, but fotunately they were so engaged in avoiding the veil, the curling ostrich feathers and the ribbons of Elizabeth's bonnet that they had no opportunity of scrutinising her face.

Amongst a roar of good wishes from the guests and a shower of rice and rose-leaves she reached the safety of the carriage. Sir Rupert jumped in beside her, the horses were whipped up and with cheers and shouts of farewell to speed them they were off.

Nerina remained for some minutes in the attitude of one who is sobbing uncontrollably, then at last she had broken the silence by saying in a faint voice:

"Would you please hand me my smelling salts?"

They were lying opposite her on the small seat where a footman had set them down with several other articles which might be required on the journey. Sir Rupert picked them up and handed them to her. As she sniffed the small cut-glass bottle, he asked courteously:

"Would you like the window a little lower?"

"Perhaps a little, thank you," Nerina replied, and when he had opened it she bent forward as if to draw in the freshness of the summer afternoon.

At length she drew back into the corner of the carriage and relaxed. They rode for about a mile in silence and then Sir Rupert turned from contemplating the view and said:

"I regret you are so distressed at leaving your home."

"It is hardly surprising," Nerina replied. "We have not known each other very long."

"No, that is true," he said in a tone of voice as if the

idea had just occurred to him. "If the haste has appeared unseemly, you must not blame me for it was necessary owing to your mother's ill-health."

"Indeed!" Nerina answered coldly. "I understood you were anxious to be married as soon as possible."

Sir Rupert was quite perceptibly startled.

"Who told you such a thing?" he asked.

Nerina hesitated.

"I . . . I cannot remember," she replied, "but I certainly had the impression that you had a good reason to speed the marriage ceremony."

She was amused to see that Sir Rupert looked slightly nonplussed, as if the conversation was unexpected and not exactly pleasant.

"Perhaps I should be honest with you," he said at length. "People gossip and you may hear further talk of this. The truth, is, my dear Elizabeth, that there is every prospect of my becoming Her Majesty's Secretary of State for Foreign Affairs on Lord Palmerston's retirement. I am extremely young to hold such a position and the Queen thinks it advisable that her Ministers, especially the younger ones, should be married men. It was of course not entirely for that reason that I proposed to you."

"No, of course not," Nerina murmured.

"As I have already told you," Sir Rupert continued, "I noticed you even when you were a child and I have heard many complimentary things about your beauty since you grew up. I should have been deaf as well as blind if I had not been aware that there was somebody exceptionally lovely living at Rowanfield Manor."

"So you fell in love with what you heard about me?" Nerina said. "How . . . precipitate!"

She noticed that Sir Rupert gave her a sharp glance, but fortunately it was impossible for him to see the expression on her face for the fine net mesh of her veil obscured her features.

"Perhaps the idea of falling in love with you was implanted in my mind by what I had heard about you," he said, for he was not a diplomat for nothing; "but it was when I came to your father's and mother's garden party a few weeks ago that I knew I wished to marry you."

"That was very kind of you," Nerina said, and though her voice was humble Sir Rupert glanced at her again in surprise.

She decided that she must be careful and not go too far. There was still time, if Sir Rupert discovered that he had been tricked, for him to turn the carriage round and drive back to Rowanfield. Lord Cardon would not be able to prevent Elizabeth from being married to Adrian, but he would, if he arrived at Dover early the following morning, be in time to prevent her from sailing to India.

'I must be careful,' Nerina thought, and folding her hands in her lap she said:

"I feel a little drowsy. Would you think it very rude of me if I slept until we reach the station?"

"No, of course not. It will be an extremely sensible thing to do," Sir Rupert said, and she heard the note of relief in his voice.

He stretched out his feet as he spoke and placed them on the seat opposite. In a few minutes' time Sir Rupert himself was asleep, while Nerina, wakeful beside him, watched his face.

It was natural for him to be sleepy, she thought. He would have drunk an enormous amount of champagne at the Wedding Breakfast. He would have eaten too much and been bored by the long stentorian speeches with which all the relations would have vied with each other in producing a welter of murky sentiment and immature wit.

'How he must have hated it!' Nerina thought with glee, and raising her veil she took a good look at him.

He looked younger when he was asleep, she thought. Younger and no longer on the defensive. When his eyes were closed, and their burning hatred and hard brilliance could not disconcert her, it was easy to notice the more gracious lines of his face. She realised that his straight nose was finely sculptured and his lips when they were not tightened in anger or resentment were full and generous.

'I wonder why he is so truculent?' Nerina asked herself, and thought suddenly that she would have plenty of time to find out.

She wondered what Elizabeth would have done in her position. She might in reality have been crying at this moment as she drove away with a man for whom, if she did not hate him, she had no liking. Nerina was certain that Elizabeth would have been both afraid and cowed. There was something about Sir Rupert which made people tremble. Nerina had noticed with amusement that even her uncle was afraid of him.

'But I am not afraid,' Nerina thought. 'I have got to keep the upper hand. Once I allow myself to be browbeaten or conquered I shall be finished.'

She pulled the veil of her bonnet over her face, and making herself comfortable in the corner of the carriage she began to plan, as she had already planned a thousand times before, what she would say to Sir Rupert when they reached London.

Their train arrived at Euston Square Terminus a few minutes after seven o'clock. A brougham was waiting outside the columned entrance and a stalwart footman in his cockaded top hat was watching for their appearance among the crowd leaving the station. As they drove away, Nerina leant forward to look out of the window, taking in the noise and bustle of London with its high houses, busy streets and innumerable noises with a joy she did not attempt to disguise.

The shops fascinated her; she stared at them with astonished eyes. There were watchmakers, haberdashers and bird-fanciers; fancy stay-makers; shawl and glove shops; jewellers, confectioners and milliners, all glittering with light yet completely eclipsed by the garish brilliance of the gaslit gin palaces. Luckily the brougham could not move quickly because of the traffic. Its progress was impeded by omnibuses filled with weary clerks, dog-carts and an occasional tandem driven by sporting swells with dashing moustaches.

The congestion was increased by rich sugar-bakers and soap-boilers in comfortable double-bodied carriages with fat horses, and hackney cabs drawn either by well-groomed animals or miserable scraggy ones with their bones rattling against broken harness. The pavements were thronged with pedestrians—yelling newspaper boys, women in voluminous crinolines, little foot pages, sailors with bronzed faces and tarry hands, their tarpaulin pancake hats stuck in defiance of all the laws of gravity on the backs of their heads; Jewish pedlars, soldiers in scarlet tunics, journeymen mechanics with their tool baskets, shopboys and flashy threadbare dandies with cheap pins in dirty cravats and long greasy hair touching their coat collars.

"The place is noisy and hot at this time of year," Sir Rupert said stiffly as Nerina leant forward to watch a crowd of children dancing gaily to a hurdy-gurdy turned by an Italian with a little withered monkey on his shoulder. "We leave for Paris the day after tomorrow. If you have never been there, it is a very elegant city and in many ways far more civilised than our own Capital."

Nerina did not answer him. She was wondering whether they would really leave for Paris the day after tomorrow or whether Sir Rupert might not bundle her back to Rowan-field Manor. She thought he would hardly dare to do such a thing, and yet there was always the possibility.

As the brougham turned into Berkeley Square Nerina had a glimpse of high plane trees moving in the evening breeze and elegant aristocratic houses surrounding a railinged garden.

"We are here at last," Sir Rupert said. "I expect the servants will be waiting to congratulate us."

He was right in his expectations. The staff at Berkeley Square were lined up in the Hall from the housekeeper in her rustling black silk apron down to the boot-boy whose cheeky, somewhat impudent grin was more reassuring to Nerina than the stiff curtsies and punctilious greetings which the others offered her. She had an almost insane desire to grin back and wink at him, but instead she shook hands solemnly and followed the housekeeper—a prim, tightlipped woman of uncertain age—upstairs.

"I expect your ladyship will want to redecorate a number of the rooms," she said as she led Nerina into a large bedroom somewhat plainly furnished. "The house has not been done up since Sir Rupert bought it eight years ago and I always think as how a lady has very different tastes to a gentleman, if you see my meaning."

"Yes, of course," Nerina said. "Has my maid arrived yet?"

"She should be here at any moment, your ladyship," the housekeeper replied; "the barouche was sent to the station to meet her and Sir Rupert's valet."

"Send her up to me the moment she comes," Nerina said.

"Yes, milady," the housekeeper said, "but if there's anything your ladyship requires in the meantime you have only to ring the bell."

"I want nothing until my maid is here."

The housekeeper curtsied and withdrew. The moment she was alone Nerina lifted her bonnet from her head and pulled off the golden wig. It was tight and the relief at being free was inexpressible. She ran her fingers through her hair and it sprang to life and began to curl around her forehead in little curls, gleaming in the light from the candles on the dressing-table.

The door opened and Bessie came in. Nerina turned with a cry of relief.

"Oh, Bessie, I am glad to see you. I was afraid you might be delayed."

"The porters were quick at getting the luggage out of the van," Bessie answered. "Has anything happened, Miss?"

"Oh, nothing," Nerina smiled reassuringly as she saw Bessie's anxious expression. "Sir Rupert slept most of the way to London and I sat thinking. But I was getting tired of this wig and it is a joy to be myself again."

"Oh, Miss Nerina, I've been worrying about you the whole way," Bessie said. "In fact I couldn't enjoy myself as I might have for all Sir Rupert's valet is a good-looking young man with plenty to say for himself. 'Something on your mind?' he asks me when we had sat silent for a while. 'You'd be surprised,' I says, and he laughs at me. But I couldn't help worrying, Miss Nerina. 'What's going to happen when we gets there?' I kept asking myself."

"You leave that to me, Bessie," Nerina said. "What time is dinner?"

"As soon as you are ready," Bessie answered.

"Then I will change at once," Nerina said, "for as it happens I am extremely hungry."

"Hungry . . . with what lies ahead of you!" Bessie exclaimed. "Are you certain Sir Rupert isn't in the least suspicious?"

"Not in the slightest," Nerina said. "Doubtless his eyes were blinded by the charms of Lady Clementine, but I don't believe he has ever really looked at Elizabeth."

"Well, her ladyship is well rid of him, if you ask me," Bessie said with a sniff.

There came a knock on the door. Bessie hurried to it and opened it a few inches.

"Wait one moment, please," she said sharply and turned back to Nerina.

"It's the luggage, Miss."

"I had forgotten that," Nerina ejaculated.

She picked up her bonnet, put it on her head and sat down at the dressing-table with her back to the door. Bessie ushered in two footmen with the trunks. They set them down and withdrew in respectful silence. When they had gone, Bessie locked the door and looked at the baggage.

"I'm blest if I can remember which has got clothes in it and which rubbish," she said.

"You put the wedding dress in the one over there," Nerina said. "I noticed it particularly because I saw that the initials were smudged."

"So they are," Bessie exclaimed. "That must have escaped his lordship's eagle eye or he would have sent it back right enough."

"It shows that when you are in too much of a hurry anyone can crook you," Nerina said, "and that also applies to Sir Rupert."

"Oh, Miss Nerina, whatever is he going to say?" Bessie exclaimed. "And what's more, I shouldn't be calling you 'Miss Nerina'. It's 'your ladyship' you are now."

"For how long, I wonder," Nerina said with a smile.

"Why, Miss, it's not a question of that," Bessie replied. "Those whom God hath joined together are married for all time. You can't be thinking of anything so wicked as divorce. Why, Parliament itself has to agree to it!"

"Yes, I know," Nerina said, "and divorce would not help Sir Rupert with his ambition of being Foreign Secretary. Just think what the Queen would say."

"I've been wondering myself what Her Majesty would say if she knew about this marriage and how Sir Rupert has been tricked into marrying the wrong young lady."

"I wonder if he would be brave enough to tell her," Nerina said. "I will wager you anything you like, Bessie, that he would rather do anything than that. It would make him look such a fool. Yes, that is one of my strongest points. It would make him look a fool."

Bessie unlocked one of the big trunks.

"What are you going to wear tonight, Miss?" she asked. "There's only your wedding dress and these old gowns of Miss Elizabeth's which she left behind. I put them in at the last moment."

"I will wear the wedding dress, of course," Nerina said. "I need to have confidence in myself and I know it suits me."

She did not speak vainly for when Bessie had finished dressing her she looked at herself in the mirror and knew that she looked lovely. If the dress had become her at the fitting before it was finished, it looked infinitely more beautiful now that her hair had been dressed by Bessie's skilful fingers. In the candlelight her shoulders gleamed

111

white as ivory against the creamy fragility of the ancient lace and her waist was small enough to be spanned by a man's two hands. Never before had Nerina been aware of her figure, but now that she saw herself for the first time in a well-fitting gown, she knew that her body with its soft curves and narrow hips was something of which she might well be proud.

She had just finished dressing when there came a knock on the door. Bessie went to open it.

"Sir Rupert's compliments," a voice said, "and he thought her ladyship might like to wear these."

Bessie came across the room carrying two jewel boxes. Nerina opened one and gave a gasp of astonishment. Lying in a bed of blue velvet was a necklace of diamonds with ear-rings and a bracelet to match. She opened the other and smaller box. It contained a ring of two huge pear-shaped diamonds surrounded by brilliants.

"Family jewels!" Nerina said.

Bessie found her voice.

"They're magnificent, Miss Nerina. Are you going to wear them?"

"Why not?" Nerina enquired. "Willy-nilly I am now one of the family. Besides, they are just the final touch that I need for my appearance."

She was right. The glittering chain round her neck and the sparkling jewels in her ears gave her a sophistication and a polish which she had lacked unadorned. When she had them all on, she stared at herself for a long moment, then impulsively she bent and kissed Bessie on the cheek.

"Now for the battle!" she whispered and swept from the room.

The housekeeper had indicated to her as they went upstairs the big Drawing-room on the first floor. The door was half open and before she entered Nerina had a glimpse of gleaming crystal chandeliers alight with tapers, elegant gilt and needlework furniture, shining mirrors and betasselled draperies of old rose velvet.

A footman flung the doors wider for her and closed them behind her. Sir Rupert was standing with his back to the door. His hands were on the mantelshelf and he was staring down at the fire. For a moment he waited and then he turned slowly with the conventional smile of greeting on his face. The smile died on his lips. For a moment he stared at Nerina and the astonishment on his face was almost ludicrous.

"Nerina Graye!" he exclaimed at length "What are you doing here?"

"What an extraordinary question to ask your wife!" Nerina replied.

She crossed the room towards him and seated herself on the sofa.

"Are you demented?" he said. "What are you doing here in this house and why are you wearing the diamonds I sent upstairs to Elizabeth?"

"You sent them to me," Nerina replied. "The message was that Sir Rupert thought her ladyship might like to wear these this evening. If you intended them for Elizabeth, they came to the wrong person."

Sir Rupert's eyebrows met across his forehead.

"I don't know what you are talking about," he said, "but I do ask for some explanation. I cannot imagine how you got here or if it was at Elizabeth's invitation, but you will oblige me by making some explanation of your presence and also by removing my family jewels which you have obviously received by mistake. They were intended for my wife."

"That is what I imagined," Nerina said, "and that is why I put them on."

Sir Rupert put his hand to his forehead and with an expression of almost unbearable irritability on his face he turned and went towards the bell-rope.

"What are you going to do?" Nerina asked.

"I am going to ask Elizabeth to come downstairs immediately," he said. "She must deal with her own relations for I assure you your behaviour is quite beyond my comprehension."

"I should not ring the bell for a moment," Nerina said quietly, and Sir Rupert stayed his hand in the very action of raising it towards the embroidered bell-pull. "Let me explain in very simple words," she went on. "Elizabeth is not in this house. She is at this moment, I confidently believe, married to a gentleman called Captain Adrian Butler. She loves him and he loves her and they will, I think, be very happy."

She had the satisfaction of seeing Sir Rupert's face grow white and stiff as if for a moment like Lot's wife he was turned into a pillar of salt. Then in a voice which seemed almost strangled in his throat he said:

"Elizabeth married! Then I . . ."

"You have married me," Nerina completed.

Sir Rupert took hold of the back of a chair.

"Do you dare to sit there and tell me this?" he said.

"Who else would you prefer to break the news?" Nerina enquired. "One of the servants?"

Sir Rupert took a step towards her.

"Have you the audacity to tell me," he thundered, "that I married you this afternoon instead of your cousin?"

"Yes indeed," Nerina replied. "I assure you that I had no wish to do so, but it was the only thing that we could do to deceive my uncle and enable Elizabeth to wed the man of her choice. We are not living in the Middle Ages, you know, and yet fathers imagine they have the power to force their daughters against their will into marriages which bring them nothing but misery and utter unhappiness."

"But your cousin agreed to marry me," Sir Rupert said.

"She did nothing of the sort," Nerina answered. "She was told she had got to marry you. It was nothing to you or to her father that she loved somebody else. You wanted her and because you were rich and powerful nothing else was considered, least of all Elizabeth's own feelings."

"But why didn't you say so? Why didn't she tell me?" Sir Rupert enquired.

"Were you really interested?" Nerina asked. "Surely marriage was a matter of convenience as far as you were concerned. All you asked for was a complacent, unsuspicious wife."

Sir Rupert started as if the words had some significance for him. But his anger would not for the moment allow him to follow another train of thought.

"But you," he said, "how can you do this? It is illegal!"

"On the contrary, I think it is entirely legal," Nerina replied. "You see, I have your wedding ring on my finger. We are in fact man and wife."

"I refuse to be made a fool of," Sir Rupert stormed. "I shall return you immediately to your uncle's home and allow him to deal with you as he thinks fit."

"I shall still be your wife in the eyes of the law and of the Church," Nerina said quietly.

"I doubt it," Sir Rupert said. "I married your cousin Elizabeth."

"You married a girl who was called Elizabeth," Nerina retorted. "As it happens, I was christened Elizabeth

114

Nerina. My mother and father always called me Elizabeth but when I went to live with my uncle and aunt at Rowanfield it was obvious that I could not be called by the same name as my cousin; and so, much against their will, they were obliged to address me by what they considered was an outlandish, fanciful name, and which, as it happens, had been my mother's."

"I don't care if the marriage is legal or illegal," Sir Rupert said. "You will go back home this very night and then we will see what your uncle has to say about it."

"And after you have taken me home," Nerina said quietly, "I presume you will come back here, visit the Palace and explain to Her Majesty exactly what has happened. Do you think that she will sanction divorce or will she consider a separation the best solution?"

Sir Rupert bit his lip.

"You appear to have a great deal to say on this matter," he said resentfully.

"What you mean is that I seem to know a lot about it. As it happens, I do. Shall I tell you why? I overheard the conversation between you and Lady Clementine Talmadge when you planned to marry my cousin Elizabeth."

"You overheard us? How?" Sir Rupert enquired.

"I see no reason to go into details," Nerina said. "Sufficient to say that I overheard your plans to find yourself a complacent wife and to continue your liaison with Lady Clementine."

"How dare you speak of such things!"

"Why?" Nerina asked. "Are you ashamed of them?"

Sir Rupert made a sound that was quite untranslatable and turned his back to stare into the fire.

"You were ready to trick Elizabeth, weren't you?" Nerina said. "This pleasant, unsuspicious girl who was to be your wife was to act as a cover for your nefarious love affairs both now and, of course, in the future. Elizabeth is a gentle, sweet person, and Lady Clementine was wise to choose her. She would have played the part well and caused you no trouble; but unfortunately she was in love with someone else. I have taken her place. I am not complacent or unsuspicious, nor do I intend to act as a dupe to suit you or your paramours."

Sir Rupert turned.

"May I ask what you do intend to do?" he enquired.

"I intend to be your wife," Nerina said. "I intend to bear your name, to spend your money and enjoy your position. I have no illusions about you, I know exactly what you are and what I must expect of you. But you will never be quite certain what you will expect from me."

"Do you imagine that I want you for my wife?" Sir Rupert enquired. "A trickster, a girl who has wormed her way by lies, subterfuge and intrigue into what must be an intolerable position as far as I am concerned!"

"And do you think that I want you for my husband?" Nerina enquired. "Let me make this very clear from the beginning. I hate you, I hate all men, I despise and detest them, and perhaps you most of all because with your great gifts, your position, wealth and political success you were prepared to destroy the happiness and trust of a young and innocent girl so long as it suited you and your evil desires for another woman. Yes, I loathe you! I am married to you, but if you ever lay so much as a finger on me I will denounce you to the Queen herself for what you are! Now we know exactly where we stand."

Nerina had risen unconsciously as she spoke, and now with the violence of her feelings her breath was coming quickly and her breasts were moving. She was forced to look up at Sir Rupert. Yet for a moment she seemed as strong and as tall as he; as they faced each other across the hearthrug, both with an expression of loathing and bitterness on their faces, their eyes darkly smouldering one at the other.

8

Sir Rupert Wroth sat at his writing-table and looked out of the window on to the garden of Berkeley quare. The sunshine made the plane trees appear as beautiful as if they were growing in the freshness of the co ntryside, and a gentle summer's breeze moved their leaves, green and golden, so that they seemed to be fanning the elegantly dressed ladies seated beneath them.

Several occupants of the Square had availed themselves of the privilege of using the enclosed garden, which was available only to those who were householders. There was the rich Miss Curzon from Number 50—a house which was considered to be haunted—whose looks and fortune had set all London speculating on whom she would marry. Dressed in a gown of sky-blue poplin she was entertaining three enraptured young noblemen, all of whom hoped to improve their impoverished estates with the help of her very considerable wealth.

Their antics were watched by Sarah, Countess of Jersey, who, nearly seventy-five and growing deaf, nevertheless managed to see a great deal more than younger people who were in possession of all their faculties. Wrapped in shawls and with the crushed and bullied companion by her side, she managed every afternoon to have a glimpse of the social world which she had ruled so long as a great beauty and one of the last patronesses of Almack's.

No one had enjoyed a fuller or more eventful life from the moment when she was married at Gretna Green, as her mother had been, until the day she inherited a fortune of £300,000 from the great Banking House of Temple Bar.

In her old age she found the younger generation dull and, as she put it, 'mealy mouthed'. She was invariably scathing about them and now as she scrutinised Miss Curzon she made remarks about her to her companion in the unmoderated tones of the deaf. As they were always uncomplimentary the companion was thrown into a flutter of embarrassment and sat with downcast eyes, flushing with mortification, a spectacle which the old lady never failed to enjoy.

There were a number of children running about with their toys and dogs while their nurses gossiped together and a straight-backed, prim-looking governess kept an eye upon them. There were flowers blooming in the flower beds, the grass was green and smooth as velvet from the careful attention it received from a number of gardeners. Indeed the Square was a little oasis of beauty and charm encircled by the busy roadway and tall grey houses.

Outside this privileged oasis and especially near the gates which led into it were the usual throng of beggars and pedlars hoping for a chance to excite the interest or the compassion of the gentry as they crossed the street from their houses to the garden or returned home after enjoying the sunshine.

But Sir Rupert, looking out through the big window hung with crimson damask, saw none of these things. He was frowning and his lips were pressed tightly together as if his thoughts were none too pleasant and his temper rising because of them. What the Marquis of Lansdowne, who had called unexpectedly, had told him a few minutes earlier was reiterating itself in his mind and should have pleased him.

"I thought you would like to know, Wroth," he said, "that two days ago Her Majesty complained to the Prime Minister that there is no question of delicacy and danger in which Lord Palmerston will not arbitrarily and without reference to his colleagues or Sovereign engage this country. The Queen, I am told, is now busy drafting a formal memorandum explaining what she expects from her Foreign Secretary."

"And what will the Prime Minister say to that?" Sir Rupert asked.

"Palmerston will go, there is not a doubt of it," Lord Lansdowne replied. "The only question is when. My advice to you, Wroth, is to do nothing but to hold yourself in readiness."

"Thank you, my lord. I shall certainly follow that advice," Sir Rupert replied.

But when the Marquis had left for his house across the Square, which was surrounded by the most beautiful garden in London, Sir Rupert continued to frown out of the window. His attention was attracted by a carriage drawing up at his own front door. It was a hackney cab, but it was open, so Sir Rupert was able to see without difficulty that it was occupied by his wife.

It took him a moment or two to recognise Nerina, however, for she looked different. Masculine-like, he did not realise that the difference was due to her clothes and

118

an alteration in the way she was doing her hair. She was indeed dressed in the very latest fashion, so up-to-date, so much the 'dernier cri' from Paris that it would have been hard for anyone to connect the elegant figure which descended from the carriage with the badly dressed, outmoded young woman whom Sir Rupert had met at Rowanfield Manor.

Nerina's dress of Chinese taffeta had been designed and fashioned by a Court dressmaker, her hat, flat and trimmed with immense ostrich plumes, was so newfangled that only a few leaders of fashion had dared as yet to appear in one. Her tiny parasol with a tasselled handle matched the bodice of her dress and was trimmed with exquisite and very expensive Viennese lace.

Nerina descended from the open carriage and as several footmen hurried forward Sir Rupert was able to see that they were required because the carriage was filled with boxes. There were boxes of every shape and size, long, short, square and round, fat and high, and they bore the names of the most expensive and exclusive Bond Street *Couturiers*. After Nerina had entered the house, the footmen went backwards and forwards for some considerable time carrying in what was obviously the spoils of a morning's shopping.

If it was possible Sir Rupert's face darkened more than ever, but he did not move from his seat at the writing-desk. He had not even turned his head to watch what was happening outside, but nothing had escaped his attention; and only when the hackney carriage had been paid and driven away, did he rise to his feet, and start pacing the floor, the time-honoured action of a man who is worried.

He could hardly believe that the predicament in which he found himself was real. He had awakened early in the morning to watch the sunlight creeping between the curtains of his bedroom and had asked himself if indeed the whole thing had not been a crazy dream. Young women did not behave in such a way, he thought. It was impossible that any man should be deceived into marrying a different girl from the one he had intended and, what was more, to find himself in the uncomfortable position of being able to do nothing whatever about it.

For what indeed could he do? Nerina's threats had not affected him half so much as his own conviction that any action he might take would make him a laughing stock. He could almost hear his enemies chuckling; even his friends

119

would be unable to hide their smiles. There were few people who do not enjoy seeing the proud laid low and the mighty fallen, and it would be hard not to laugh at a man who, having the reputation of being a Don Juan, found himself tricked by a yellow wig and some well-acted tears.

Sir Rupert had been awake for most of the night, seething with rage and indignation. He rose not only angry, but consumed with a bitter devouring fury which made him long to hurt someone, preferably the person who was troubling him the most. When he came down to breakfast, having thought out a few well-chosen remarks with which he hoped to intimidate his persecutor, he found that Nerina had already left the house.

"Her ladyship asked me to inform you, Sir, that she had gone shopping," the butler said.

He told the housekeeper afterwards in the privacy of the pantry that he had never seen anyone look less like a bridegroom or behave more disagreeably than his master. Sir Rupert was well aware that the servants were gossiping. The uncomfortable atmosphere at dinner the previous night was not likely to have passed unnoticed and the fact that the bride had gone to her bedroom and locked herself in and that Sir Rupert had slept in his own room were actions that were not likely to escape observation and comment.

But one thing Sir Rupert did not know, which might have consoled him a little, was that Nerina had adjured Bessie to say nothing as to what had happened or that she was not in fact Sir Rupert's intended bride.

"We will see how he behaves first," she said. "There will be time enough to make him feel uncomfortable and apprehensive as to what is being said once he has shown his hand. I have a feeling that it will not be in his nature to take this lying down."

"Oh, Miss Nerina," Bessie cried apprehensively. "If Sir Rupert turns nasty, whatever will you do?"

"It depends what you mean by nasty," Nerina replied. "He is not exactly going to feel friendly, that would be too much to expect. But if he is going to accept the situation as it is without too much rumpus, then I can be pleasant too."

"What about his lordship?" Bessie asked.

Nerina shrugged her shoulders.

"I am not really frightened of Uncle Herbert now," she replied. "What can he do? He will be furious, of course, mostly because he has been outwitted and out-manoeuvred.

120

He will never forgive me for that and also because he has lost a rich son-in-law. But he, too, would look extremely foolish if everyone learnt the truth."

"People are bound to talk anyway," Bessie suggested.

"Well, of course they will," Nerina said, "but supposing both Sir Rupert and Uncle Herbert brazen it out; supposing they say that they knew all along that Sir Rupert was marrying me and not Elizabeth. They can explain that there was a change of plan after the invitations had been sent out and that most of their friends had been notified. The person to whom they are speaking can always be the exception. What can outsiders do? They will be surprised and curious, but if no one appears angry or upset, what is there to say?"

"It all sounds very easy, Miss Nerina," Bessie said. "But the first person you have got to convince is Sir Rupert himself."

"Yes, I know," Nerina said, but she did not look downcast.

Instead her green eyes were twinkling and there was a smile at the corners of her mouth. For the first time in her life she was conscious of her own power. Never before had she been able to dictate to anyone, never before had she held the upper hand, never before had she known what it was to be a person of importance. Whether Sir Rupert hated her or loathed her, the fact remained that he had to reckon with her and for the moment at any rate she occupied his mind to the exclusion of all else.

She had felt her spirits rising as he sat opposite her at dinner the night before. As the butler had held back the big armchair for her at the end of the table opposite Sir Rupert, as she had faced him across the gold dishes filled with hot-house fruits and had seen the powdered footmen in their knee-breeches and gold-laced livery moving silently around the room, she had realised for the first time that she was now a woman of consequence. For better, for worse, she was Sir Rupert's wife! She was Lady Wroth, whether he detested her—as the expression on his face told her that he did—or whether on the morrow he was prepared to denounce her for the trick she had played on him. Whatever he said or did, she was still for the moment his wife, still legally joined to him by the Church and State, the symbol of it shining golden on her finger next to the heavy ring which matched the glittering diamonds round her neck.

She was offered the delicious dishes with a deference which she had never known at Rowanfield. It was thrilling to know herself exquisitely dressed and wonderously be-jewelled. As she sipped the sparkling champagne from a crystal goblet by her side, she could hardly believe that she would not hear the harsh, bullying voice of her uncle ordering her to bed.

It was freedom for the first time, a freedom she had often imagined but which she never dreamt would really become hers. It was as if a bird caught and caged suddenly found itself free to soar into the heavens and flew off, forgetful of everything and every danger save for the feel of the wind lifting its wings, the sunshine on its body. Freedom! It was an intoxication Nerina had never known before.

She seemed now to have an untrammelled radiance as she came from the street into the marble-pillared hall. The butler, taking her parasol from her, said:

"Sir Rupert is in the Library, m'lady."

Just for a moment Nerina hesitated, and then as if her courage bore her on winged feet she crossed the Hall and opened the door of the Library before an attentive footman could reach it. Sir Rupert was still pacing the carpet. He stopped at her entrance, standing still in the centre of the room, a man, it seemed to her, who was on the defensive.

She might have been a shaft of sunlight herself entering the sombre dignity of the room hung with sporting prints and paneled in oak. Her dress was the colour of very old glass. It had the same iridescent beauty and in contrast Nerina's skin was almost dazzlingly white and her eyes vividly green. She crossed the room with an air of the utmost unconcern, drawing long French suède gloves from her hands.

"I have had the most enjoyable morning," she said conversationally. "I trust that you received my message."

"I was told you had gone shopping," Sir Rupert said, his voice coming to his lips with what appeared to be a considerable effort.

"Yes, that was correct," Nerina said. "I had unfortunately nothing to wear but the gown I wore yesterday. It had been made, of course, for Elizabeth and was most unbecoming to me; otherwise my trunks contained newspapers and old blankets, hardly, you will agree, a suitable trousseau for a lady of fashion."

"So you have been buying your trousseau," Sir Rupert

said grimly, "and doubtless you expect me to pay for it."

"Indeed yes," Nerina said. "I felt sure you would be pleased to do so. I was not certain that I could obtain credit at some of the shops, but the moment I mentioned your name they allowed me to bring away anything I wanted. It appears they know you well by reputation or in some cases there has been a more personal contact. At Briggs', where I bought my sunshade, I forgot to mention that I was your wife and I found that they had obliged you with quite a considerable number of sunshades for an equal number of charming ladies. The last one, I learned, had been despatched to Lady Clementine for her to carry at Ascot. An expensive trifle with a jewelled handle set with amethysts. It must have been very pretty."

"Damn it, shops have no right to gossip in such a manner," Sir Rupert said. "I shall tell them so and close my account."

"You must not blame them too harshly," Nerina replied. "I am afraid I drew them on. I was so interested to know what your taste was like. The sunshade, for instance, that you gave to Madame Bianco when she was starring at Drury Lane was, to my mind, slightly vulgar, but I expect she was entranced by it."

"I have no desire to discuss such matters with you," Sir Rupert said stiffly.

"No?" Nerina raised her eyebrows. "What a pity! It would surely be so much better if we were frank with each other. I loathe lies and subterfuge!"

"You can hardly expect me to believe that," Sir Rupert said sarcastically.

"But why not?" Nerina enquired. "Because one has to lie or use subterfuge to gain one's ends, there is no reason to enjoy it. That is an entirely different matter. But because I am so anxious that we should be frank with each other, I think it only right to inform you that I have spent a very considerable sum of money this morning, knowing of course that you would wish me to be dressed according to my position."

"I don't care how you are dressed," Sir Rupert said angrily. "This farce has continued long enough. We have got to come to an understanding."

"That is exactly what I hoped you would say," Nerina parried, "and the sooner the better as far as I am concerned."

She looked down as she spoke, smoothed her gloves on

her lap, clasped her hands together and raised her eyes to Sir Rupert with an expression on her face of a child waiting to be praised for some outstanding achievement.

There was silence. Sir Rupert seemed to hesitate and walked across the room then back again.

"The position is intolerable," he said.

"For whom?" Nerina enquired. "Personally, I find it very pleasant. I like your house, I like being your wife."

Her bland pleasantness seemed to ignite Sir Rupert's anger.

"Damn it," he said, "you are not my wife. I did not intend to marry you, and the question with which we have got to concern ourselves is how we can unravel this cursed tangle."

"There is nothing you can do," Nerina replied. "By this time Elizabeth will be on her way to India. She at least is safe. This morning, if not before, my uncle will have discovered that I am not in the house. They will not for a moment connect my disappearance with Elizabeth's marriage. And it is very unlikely that my uncle will come posting to London to find out if we know anything of my disappearance. They will be so delighted that their daughter, as they think, is married to you that they will not want to interrupt the honeymoon, and after making all possible local enquiries they will do precisely nothing. Unless my knowledge of my uncle is very much at fault, they will carry on with their own plans to leave for the Continent tomorrow."

"Do you mean to say that they will not worry that their niece has apparently vanished overnight?"

"Oh, they will worry to a certain extent," Nerina replied, "mostly because it is so inconvenient and they will wonder what people will say. If I have got into some scrape, it might reflect on them. But if you mean will they be unhappy or anxious that something might have happened to me as a person, the answer is no. My aunt does not like me, my uncle actively dislikes me. If I had made a runaway marriage or been abducted, they would only be too delighted so long as I was not likely to turn up again and make things difficult for them."

"I cannot believe you are speaking the truth," Sir Rupert said. "After all, you are Lord Cardon's niece."

"I am the unfortunate result of his brother's marriage with what the family consider an undesirable person," Nerina said bitterly. "My mother's family had no money and she had a particularly fine voice. She used it to keep her parents from starving and to pay the Doctor's fees when her father became a helpless cripple with only a few years to live. Because she appeared on a public platform, because men and women could pay money to hear her, my uncle and aunt have always behaved as if she were no better than a common prostitute."

"But all this was hardly your fault," Sir Rupert said.

"Have you never heard that the sins of the father shall be visited upon the children?" Nerina asked with a dry smile.

"But in this case surely you are exaggerating?" Sir Rupert insisted. "Your uncle took you into his house, you were brought up with your cousin Elizabeth."

"Yes, until I was old enough to go out and earn my own living," Nerina replied. "The day of the Garden Party I returned from my third post as a child's governess. I returned to Rowanfield not because I wished to come back to the only home I had known for the last eight years, but simply because I could no longer withstand the lecherous attentions of my employer. It is not a pretty story and I will not bore you with it; sufficient to tell you that my uncle knew the sort of place to which he was sending me, knew that the gentleman who paid me would do his utmost to seduce me; and yet he sent me there, as he had previously sent me to another place of the same sort, knowingly and with intent."

"I cannot believe that," Sir Rupert said violently. "You are making out a good story for yourself. Why should I believe you?"

"It is not the slightest consequence whether you believe me or not," Nerina said. "I told you last night what I thought of you and of all the men with whom I have come in contact. You asked me a question; I have answered you truthfully. As I have already said, I dislike lies and subterfuge unless they are really necessary."

Sir Rupert bowed a little ironically.

"I apologise," he said. "I see that you do not consider my opinion is of any importance."

"No, of course not," Nerina said simply. "Yet as we are married, it is best that we should be as frank as possible with each other. I am telling you that for the moment I think it unlikely that we shall be troubled with my uncle. Later, of course, we shall have to tell him the truth."

"From the way you speak," Sir Rupert said, "I gather

you imagine that I intend to allow you to remain my wife."

"There is very little you can do about it," Nerina said. "Have you any suggestions as to how you can get rid of me?"

She was amused to see that she had silenced him. After a moment he walked towards the window to stand with his back to her.

"I refuse to go to Paris," he said at length, rather like a sulky small boy. "It would be a farce."

"I agree with you," Nerina said. "There would be little to occupy us and we should bore each other considerably. I quite understand, moreover, that you do not wish it known that you are in London. I suggest, therefore, that we stay here another day and then go to Wroth. I should like to see my future home, but let me make it clear that I have no intention of being 'packed off' there."

Sir Rupert started.

"Where were you when you overheard this unfortunate conversation of mine with Lady Clementine?" he asked.

"Does it matter?" Nerina asked.

"I suppose not," Sir Rupert muttered, "since you have heard all we said."

"It was a very revealing conversation," Nerina said. "I had not believed until that moment that men were quite so cold-blooded in their choice of a wife."

"The circumstances were unusual," Sir Rupert said. "Her Majesty had more or less commanded me not to appear at Court until I brought her a wife."

"How unfortunate that your affections were engaged elsewhere!" Nerina snapped.

"We will not talk of that, if you please," Sir Rupert said.

"Of course not, if you would rather it remained a skeleton in the cupboard," Nerina replied. "How disappointed Lady Clementine will be to see that I do not look quite so insipid as my cousin Elizabeth!"

"I have told you that we will not discuss Lady Clementine," Sir Rupert said.

"No, of course not," Nerina said pleasantly, but she wondered wickedly to herself in what words Sir Rupert would explain to his amoretta the change-over of brides.

The explanation was forced upon him sooner than either of them expected. As a lengthy luncheon drew to a close, Sir Rupert remarked that he was going to his Club.

"When will you be back?" Nerina enquired.

Sir Rupert shrugged his shoulders. Nerina looked at him speculatively.

"I expect you are trying to get away from me," she said. "But pray do not forget that we are supposed to be on our honeymoon."

"I am not likely to forget that," Sir Rupert snapped. "What do you suggest we do—hold hands in the Park?"

"I would like to go to the Opera," Nerina replied.

Sir Rupert hesitated. She saw the expression on his face and knew he was contemplating something unpleasant.

"I could call for you at your Club," she remarked.

He stared at her.

"Are you demented?" he asked. "A lady who calls at a gentleman's club would be socially damned for life."

Nerina smiled engagingly.

"I know that, and I am sure such a precipitate action will be unnecessary," she said. "In fact I think you will return here in time for dinner."

Sir Rupert muttered beneath his breath, but he knew he was defeated.

Nerina was nearly dressed that evening when Bessie, peeping from the window, told her that Sir Rupert had just returned home.

"So he is afraid of me!" she murmured to herself, and there was a smile of triumph on her lips when she swept downstairs five minutes later to wait for Sir Rupert in the Drawing-room.

Her gown was so lovely that she stood on tiptoe to peer at herself in the mirrors. A copy from Paris of one worn by the Empress Eugénie, it was of white atlas with one hundred and three tulle flounces. Under it she wore a 'Eugénie' hooped petticoat and on her hair a wreath of white roses spangled with diamond dew-drops.

Sir Rupert made no comment on her appearance, but she knew he glanced a little ironically at the wrap of white ermine trimmed with sable that she wore over her dress.

She had chosen it because it was so expensive and also because it was by far the most beautiful fur in the shop. Even though she had been intent on revenge, Nerina had been shocked at the price of this particular wrap and it had taken all her resolution to say firmly: 'I will have it' when the *vendeuse,* having extolled all its virtues with great volubility, at length lowered her voice to disclose the price.

However, Nerina forgot everything but its comfort and

the feeling it gave her of confidence as on entering Sir Rupert's box at Her Majesty's Theatre in the Haymarket she let it slip from her shoulders and knew that the diamonds round her neck were as beautiful as any of those worn by the other women present.

She was, however, quite overawed by the Opera House itself. It was more magnificent than anything she had imagined. The enormous horseshoe of the first tier boxes was crowded with all the wealth and beauty of Society. Sparkling tiaras, bare shoulders, stiff white neck-cloths, dress coats, opera cloaks, flowers, fans and long kid gloves made one realise how elegant and at the same time dramatic the English could be even when they only sought relaxation and amusement.

The Opera was Italian; but the chief stars were English, being Mr. Sim Reeves and Miss Catherine Hayes. A charming ballet was, however, led by Pocchini, who was so graceful and enchanting that Nerina wanted to join in the shouts and cheers with which the Gallery applauded her.

As the lights went up for the first interval, Nerina looked round to see that every box was filled and that practically every woman present had her head crowned with gems.

"I see that I shall have to ask you for a tiara," Nerina said to Sir Rupert with a light laugh.

As he did not answer her, she turned to look at him and saw that he was staring across the theatre. Following his gaze, her heart gave a little leap. Someone had just entered a box on the other side of the tier where three people were already sitting. It was Lady Clementine.

She was looking extremely lovely, Nerina noted. Her dress was of crimson satin cut very low in the bodice with an overskirt of gauze caught back with jewelled flowers. She wore a tiara of rubies and diamonds on her dark hair. There was a necklace of the same stones round her neck and a big bracelet of them on her wrist over her black gloves. Her gown and jewels were both beautiful, yet it was difficult to notice anything except Lady Clementine's heavy-lidded, slanted eyes and her red lips which seemed always to hold an invitation in their curves.

Nerina turned to Sir Rupert. It seemed to her that he was paler and his jaw was set square. He rose to his feet.

"Will you excuse me if I leave you for a few moments?" he asked.

Nerina hesitated.

"If you are going to see Lady Clementine," she replied after a second, "I am coming too."

He looked for a moment as if he would forbid her to do any such thing; then he said nothing, but merely opened the door of the box. They stepped outside into the red-carpeted, crystal-hung corridor.

As Nerina moved slowly through the crowds in the direction of Lady Clementine's box, Sir Rupert said suddenly:

"We will not call on Lady Clementine."

Nerina looked up at him.

"Afraid?" she asked scornfully.

She saw to her satisfaction that the shot had gone home.

"I prefer to explain to Lady Clementine what has occurred on some less public occasion," he said stiffly

Nerina laughed.

"I wonder if she is going to believe you."

"I have already told you I do not wish to discuss Lady Clementine with you," Sir Rupert retorted.

"It makes it so awkward that she keeps cropping up in our lives," Nerina said reflectively. "As she lives almost next door to Wroth, we shall doubtless see her continually. But of course I forgot, you planned for her to open her house in London so that you could meet each other while your innocent and complacent wife remained in the country."

"Be quiet, damn you!" Sir Rupert said furiously.

But Nerina only smiled as he marched her angrily back to their box.

Sir Rupert's anger seemed to continue all through the next Act, and although Nerina enjoyed the music she could not help but be conscious of it. She could feel his fury radiating from him, seeming to create an atmosphere all of its own in the small, confined space.

Quite suddenly she was sorry that he was so angry. There were things she wanted to ask him about the people present. She longed to know who everybody was, she wished to know more about the actors and actresses appearing on the stage. She was even interested in the history of the Opera House itself and she was suddenly appalled by her own ignorance of everything and everybody.

She forgot for a moment what was happening on the stage and glanced round at the boxes, at the faces of the fashionable world, paying, it seemed, in most cases little attention to the entertainment but gossiping, laughing and flirting amongst themselves.

'I am perhaps the only person here,' she thought suddenly, 'who does not know a soul in the Theatre with the exception of my husband who hates me and the woman he loves.'

She felt a surge of self pity and then severely thrust it from her. She had chosen her course, a rôle of revenge which Sir Rupert well deserved. It was ridiculous to feel weak and somehow helpless simply because Lady Clementine was opposite, watching them out of her dark, mysterious eyes.

The second interval had only just started and Sir Rupert had not even risen to his feet when the door of their box was thrown open. Nerina turned round quickly to see who it was. She had not noticed Lady Clementine leaving her box, but now she stood before them, the magnificent sweep of her crimson gown filling the doorway, her tiara glittering like a halo against the smooth darkness of her hair.

"Rupert!" she exclaimed, her hand outstretched to him. "I was so surprised to see you here. I thought you would already have left for Paris. And where is Elizabeth? Is she ill? How are you, Nerina?"

She held out her gloved hand in a perfunctory gesture, but as she did so her eye caught sight of the diamond ring on Nerina's finger and the diamonds round her neck and there was no disguising her astonishment.

"Elizabeth is, we hope, quite well," Nerina replied for Sir Rupert, "unless of course she has been sea-sick. She is on her way to India, you know."

"India!" Lady Clementine exclaimed, then added: "We must be talking at cross purposes. I am speaking of your cousin Elizabeth and of your wife, Rupert."

She favoured Sir Rupert with a provocative smile.

"But we are talking of the same person," Nerina said before Sir Rupert could reply, even if he had wished to. "You have been in London, Lady Clementine, so I am afraid you have missed all the excitement and news of the County. My cousin has married Captain Adrian Butler. Such a charming person. We all like him so much, but unfortunately his Regiment has been posted to India and they sailed yesterday."

"But . . . but I do not understand," Lady Clementine stammered. "I thought . . ." She seemed at a loss for words, then went on, ". . . that . . . that you, Rupert, were to marry Elizabeth."

"Oh no, you are quite out-of-date," Nerina said with a little laugh. "Rupert, I cannot understand why you did not let Lady Clementine know that you were marrying me."

Lady Clementine turned towards him with an expression that was half hostile and half apprehensive.

"Is this true?" she asked and her voice was low.

"Yes, it is true," Sir Rupert replied.

They were the first words he had spoken since she entered the box.

Good breeding and social education came to Lady Clementine's aid. For a second it seemed as if she would express her thoughts forcibly and without reserve, then with an effort she said in a tone that was entirely artificial:

"Then of course I must congratulate you." She turned her shoulder to Sir Rupert and addressed Nerina. "This is indeed a surprise, dear child; I was wondering whether those diamonds round your neck were real. It puzzled me for a moment as to how you could have acquired them in your very limited life—but now, of course, I understand. I hope you will both be very . . . very . . . happy."

There was no mistaking the venom in her voice as she said the last words, and turning on her heel without a single glance at Sir Rupert she swept from the box. As she left, it seemed as if he came to life from the stiffness which had held him tongue-tied and spellbound from the moment she had entered the box.

He moved forward.

"Clementine," he said. "Wait. . . ."

The door of the box slammed in his face. As he stood there, for a moment disconcerted and jerked out of his habitual aloofness, he heard Nerina laugh. It was a low, infectious laugh of genuine amusement.

9

They drove back to Berkeley Square in silence, Nerina well aware that Sir Rupert was extremely angry although he held himself in an iron control. When the carriage drew up in front of his house, he handed Nerina from it and bowing to her said in a cold voice:

"I will bid you good night."

She looked up at him. Her hair shone in the light of the gas lamp and her lips were smiling although her voice was almost as cold as his.

"I would speak with you first," she said.

"At this moment?" he enquired, his eyebrows raised a trifle. "Surely what you have to say can wait?"

"I am afraid not," Nerina replied, "but I will not keep you more than a few minutes."

He surrendered to her insistence with a bad grace, his expression frigid with suppressed fury as he followed her into the house and up the broad staircase to the Drawing-room.

The curtains were drawn, the candles lit in the chandeliers. There was a mellow beauty about the room. The furniture, pictures and crystals were the taste of a bygone age, yet it was all the lovelier because no one had troubled to bring it up-to-date, to cover the chairs with fashionable antimacassars, to clutter the hearth with beadwork stools or replace the soft romantic light of the candles with the garish brilliance of gas.

Sir Rupert closed the door behind them and standing some distance from Nerina stared at her with an obvious hostility. She did not speak for a moment, but removed her ermine and sable cape with an irritating slowness before she said:

"I am well aware that you are impatient to find Lady Clementine, and make your peace with her. But before you go, I would utter one word of warning. You were ready to marry to further your career and I should not, if I were you, destroy your chances of political advancement by telling Lady Clementine the truth about your marriage."

"If you are inferring that Lady Clementine will gossip to my disadvantage, you are much mistaken in her," Sir Rupert said with a sneer.

Nerina's green eyes were suddenly serious.

"Would you really trust Lady Clementine with anything but the vacillations of your heart?" she asked.

For a moment he met her gaze, and it was not her words which kept him silent but the frank sincerity in her eyes. Then abruptly he looked away from her and walked down the long room to one of the windows which overlooked the Square. Roughly, as if his very violence relieved his feelings, he pulled back the heavy curtains. The window was open and he stood there drawing in deep breaths of the night air. But apparently it failed to cool him for he turned suddenly and said in a voice fierce with emotion:

"This is intolerable! You twist and distort every aspect of my life. There is no reason why Lady Clementine should not know the truth."

"And when she knows it, do you imagine that she will be able to keep such an amusing, entertaining story to herself?" Nerina asked. "Even if she is exceptional enough to be able to miss the chance of being the first to relate a good story and an amusing incident, is she a saint that she can contain herself when people say in front of her that you married me because I was beautiful and witty?"

She drew a quick breath and went on before he could speak.

"For that is what I intend to be, the beautiful and witty Lady Wroth. I will not be an insipid nonentity packed off to Wroth to suit your convenience or Lady Clementine's. I will go there tomorrow—or any time you like—because I wish to inspect the house which will be mine as well as yours, but when you return to London I shall come with you. I shall take my place here among the political hostesses, but you can be certain of one thing. I am not doing this for you, but to further my own ambitions. I can destroy you easily by a few ill-considered actions, but in doing so I shall also harm my own future, my own position in Society. There is an old adage which begins: 'When thieves fall out . . .' You and I have got to sustain each other for the moment at any rate, and I would sooner trust a serpent than I would trust Lady Clementine with the story of our marriage."

As Nerina finished speaking, Sir Rupert walked down the Drawing-room towards her. When he drew near to her, he stood for a moment looking down at her small oval face, at her dark-lashed eyes raised to his, at the firm lips, at the small determined chin.

133

"I have at last realised what you are," he said at length. "You are purely and simply an adventuress, a woman out for herself without thought or feeling for anyone else."

Nerina smiled, and there was a sudden twinkle in her eyes.

"You might have called me many worse things," she said. "I am not ashamed of being an adventuress. It means to take advantage of an opportunity when it presents itself, to know what one wants from life and to be determined to get it."

"At the expense of every decency and the destruction of all self-respect," Sir Rupert said.

Nerina laughed lightly.

"It is extraordinary how very little self-respect one can have on a stipend of ten pounds a year and the knowledge that the servants despise you and your employers ignore you. I would rather be an adventuress than a governess, and I find it far easier to endure your insults than the lecherous advances of my previous employers."

"You certainly need not feel alarmed as to my feelings towards you," Sir Rupert said. "I tell you frankly that you surprise and shock me. I would not have believed it possible that any woman, let alone a girl, would behave as you have behaved in the past forty-eight hours. The woman I admire must be quiet and womanlike, gracious and tender."

"And at the same time a silly fool," Nerina added.

"On the contrary, but I would wish her to be a lady," Sir Rupert said.

Nerina acknowledged to herself that his thrust had gone home. As she faced him, her lips curved in a dry smile.

"Your choice of feminine acquaintances in the past," she said, "can hardly have possessed all the qualities you have named."

"It depends, of course, for what reason I sought their acquaintance," Sir Rupert replied. "May I say once and for all that the qualities a man seeks in a mistress are very different from those he requires in his wife."

"That was obvious in your talk with Lady Clementine," Nerina snapped.

"This sort of conversation is getting us nowhere," Sir Rupert said irritably.

"Where can it get us?" Nerina asked. "You will remember that the reason I wished to speak to you was merely to warn you against jeopardising your career."

"With you as my wife I doubt if I have one," Sir Rupert said bitterly.

"That is hardly fair," Nerina replied quietly, "unless you provoke me, I shall do nothing to do you any public harm. In private we can hate each other, we can fight and bicker and I shall show you continually, and I hope effectively, that a wife is not entirely a man's chattel, a docile creature who must shiver at his frown and tremble at a cross word. I have seen women behave like that all my life and I have realised that in loving a man they forge their own prison chains and build around themselves their own impregnable jail. I shall never be a slave to any man!"

"That is obvious," Sir Rupert said, "for when Providence fashioned you He put a flint where most women have a heart."

"What about you?" Nerina asked. "Have you ever loved anyone to the exclusion of all else? Have you ever cared enough for a woman to make sacrifices for her, to give up your egotistical desires in a sincere effort to make her happy? Have you ever honestly and truly believed that someone else was more important to you than yourself?"

Sir Rupert shrugged his shoulders.

"Is that your definition of love?" he asked mockingly.

"No," Nerina said, "not entirely, but I have yet to find a man who has the slightest conception of what love should mean. If they love anybody, it is themselves."

"Your opinion of my sex is not flattering," Sir Rupert said.

"Why should it be," Nerina asked, "when the men I have encountered have all been beasts, vile creatures to whom a woman was their natural prey? You talk about being decent and honourable, but men keep their code of decency and honesty for the times when they are within their own Clubs or associating with their own equals. I have yet to meet a man who is honourable and decent when he desires a woman, especially when she is of an inferior social standing to himself."

There was a sharpness of remembered pain in Nerina's voice and her eyes were suddenly dark with the memory of past humiliations. Watching her face, the expression on Sir Rupert's seemed suddenly softer, less aggressive. Unexpectedly he seated himself in the high-backed chair.

"You have suffered," he said quietly; "but there is no reason, because you have been hurt, to wound everyone with whom you come in contact."

135

"I wish I had power to do more than battle with my tongue," Nerina said. "Do I wound you? No, you hate me because for the moment I have prevented you from getting your own way; but because I am a woman I cannot wound you physically, I can only be a pinprick in your all-sufficient self-complacency."

She spoke with a sudden irritation, driven to it with a sense of her own impotence. Words seemed so useless, so ineffectual. They could talk and talk, but it got them nowhere. To her surprise Sir Rupert threw back his head and laughed. Nerina stared at him in astonishment, and when his merriment had ceased he said with a twist of his lips:

"I apologise for laughing, but the humorous side of all this struck me suddenly. You are such a spitfire and so very formidable for all that you are so tiny. Why, your head hardly reaches to my shoulder, yet I declare I am more frightened of you than I am of a battalion of soldiers."

Nerina eyed him warily. She was well aware that laughter was a far more dangerous weapon than hard words.

"Won't you sit down!" Sir Rupert said, seeing her hesitation. "We are, I think, behaving childishly. Let us talk things over quietly and with a reasonable amount of good-will on either side. If you agree, I will dismiss the horses. I shall not be requiring them this evening."

Nerina knew she had won the first engagement in their battle. Sir Rupert would not visit Lady Clementine this evening, and when he came to think it over fully, he would undoubtedly realise that her suggestion of keeping the circumstances of their marriage a secret was obviously sensible.

Taking her silence for consent, Sir Rupert rose to his feet and rang the bell. When a footman appeared, he gave orders that the carriage should be dismissed and commanded that a bottle of champagne be opened immediately.

They sat in silence until the butler appeared with two crystal glasses on a crested silver tray. Nerina sipped the sparkling wine, then put her glass down on a small table beside the sofa. Sir Rupert, she noticed, drank off the whole glass as if he were in need of sustenance and then refilled it from the bottle the butler had left beside him on another table.

"Now we can talk," he said, and there was something in his attitude rather than in his words which warned Nerina to be on her guard.

"You have been frank with me," he said after a moment's pause, as if he picked his words over carefully, "and I can to a certain extent understand why you embarked on this dangerous and intrepid adventure. There was your affection for your cousin Elizabeth, your fear of your uncle and hers for her father, and of course the difficulty of getting her safely out of the country without some trick or subterfuge to hide her movements. But what I cannot understand is how you can imagine that you can find any happiness for yourself in the position you have chosen as my wife. No married life can be anything but intolerable when it is based on threats, extortions and blackmail."

Nerina gave a little gasp, but did not speak. Glancing at her face Sir Rupert continued:

"The last words may seem a little strong, but you have on several occasions today and last night threatened me that if I did not agree to what you suggested you, in your turn, would do certain things which would cause me acute discomfort. That, of course, is blackmail. All this is very unpleasant and I have been wondering to myself whether you would not be wise in your own interests to take a far more decisive step. You say that you are an orphan, that your uncle and aunt have no affection for you. If therefore you were to vanish, or shall we say disappear, there would be no one to make any unpleasant enquiries as to what had happened to you."

"Do you intend to murder me?" Nerina asked.

"On the contrary! I was not suggesting that you should end your life," Sir Rupert replied, "but merely that you should live far more comfortably and a great deal more enjoyably than you have done in the past. There is only one real necessity where that is concerned and that is money—money can buy comfort, money can buy friends and even love, if one has enough of it."

"And what would you call enough?" Nerina asked.

Her voice was low and her eyes downcast. She was playing with the great diamond ring on her third finger, twirling it round, watching the diamonds catch the light and sparkle brilliantly as if within themselves they had a hidden power of their own.

"I was thinking," Sir Rupert replied in a voice slow and deliberate, "that with ten thousand pounds to her credit a
137

young woman could live in great comfort in France or Italy."

"Ten thousand pounds!" Nerina repeated.

"It is a very large sum," Sir Rupert said. "And it could be paid quarterly from one of the most reputable banks in England. There are places in Italy where one could be almost a millionairess with a fortune such as that. One could create a world of one's own where the past could be forgotten."

Nerina did not speak and after a moment, his eyes still watching her face, he said:

"What is your answer to that?"

"It is too little," Nerina said.

"Shall we say twenty thousand?" Sir Rupert said quickly. "And of course your signed undertaking as well as your word that you will never under any circumstances reveal to a living soul that by trickery and by misrepresentation you went thorugh a form of marriage with me. I should have to trust you, of course, but at the same time the money will only be paid quarterly. If you betray me, you will receive nothing."

"And how would you explain the marriage, which after all was attended by a large number of people?" Nerina asked.

"I have thought of that," Sir Rupert replied. "I shall follow your cousin Elizabeth to India. You said, I think, that the man she has married is not very rich. His Regiment will be in India for five years. I shall make it worth his while to sign on for another five years' foreign service. At the end of that time, if Lord Cardon is not dead, I shall ask them to stay away for another term. In the meantime your cousin will not communicate either with her father, her mother or any of her friends. The death of Lady Elizabeth Wroth, formerly Lady Elizabeth Cardon, will unfortunately take place on her honeymoon. She will be buried abroad and it will be found impossible to bring the body home. I shall be a widower and a free man."

"You have thought out quite a pretty plot," Nerina said. He bowed.

"I appreciate that you are an expert on such things," he said. "Do you agree then?"

Nerina looked up at him for the first time.

"Did you really think I would?" she asked. "You have called me an adventuress, you have told me that I am out entirely for my own gain. Do you really believe that you can buy me off with twenty thousand pounds?"

"Twenty-five thousand," Sir Rupert said quickly.

Nerina laughed.

"Not for a million," she said. "I was merely listening to your story to see how fantastic it could be. To begin with, it is entirely impracticable. Even if I agreed—which I have no intention of doing—to disappear into obscurity in some outlandish village in Italy, Elizabeth and Adrian would never consent to being exiled from England for ever. No, you must think of something better than that if you wish to be rid of me, for I assure you that I consider it to be worth far more than twenty-five thousand pounds to be your wife, to hold the position I intend to hold both at Wroth and at Court."

"You are intolerable," Sir Rupert said.

"You only think that because you cannot get your own way with me," Nerina replied. "I am afraid it will have to be murder. It is your only chance of being rid of me, but I should wait until you get to Wroth. You can doubtless push me off the battlements or drown me in the lake when nobody is looking."

"I promise you it will give me great pleasure to do so," Sir Rupert snapped.

"That I can well believe," Nerina retorted, "but I warn you I shall fight vigorously for life. There is one thing I would like to say to you before I retire for the night."

"What is it?" Sir Rupert asked.

"It is to say that I have never in all my life enjoyed myself so much as I have today," Nerina replied. "Good night, my lord and . . . master."

She dropped him a mocking curtsey and was gone from the room before he could open the door for her or even rise to his feet.

He sat on in the chair for a long time staring ahead of him and chewing the end of his little finger. His face bore the expression of a man who is tried beyond all bearing. It was also the face of a man who faces defeat and realises there is nothing he can do to prevent it.

The Opposition in the House of Commons would have found it hard to recognise Sir Rupert at that moment as their formidable enemy. His air of aggression and pride seemed to have left him. He sat in the chair a man not humbled but crushed, as if an unexpected and treacherous blow had laid him low and he was astonished not by the violence of it but by its treachery.

There was so much—everything he wanted and craved for—almost within his reach. He had been sure of getting it, absolutely certain within himself, and now this, this disaster of a magnitude he could not yet calculate to the full. He who had tangled and twisted other people's lives both politically and by his amorous perambulations now found his own knotted and entwined in a manner which left him little doubt that he would find it impossible to straighten it.

It had seemed so easy, so practical a step to marry a respectable young woman, to continue to enjoy his life as he had always done, and yet by one false step the whole plan had become a fiasco. Why had he been fool enough not to suspect that someone might overhear his conversation with Lady Clementine? Why had he not waited and sent her a letter asking her to meet him in their usual meeting place?

He had thought himself so clever not to put anything in writing, not to lay himself open to being spied on or watched by those who had already tittle-tattled about his behaviour to the Queen. And yet his very care had brought an avalanche down on his head. How could he have known that that damnable child with red hair was listening to his and Lady Clementine's conversation in the summer-house? How could he in his wildest imaginings have guessed that she would be crafty and clever enough to trick him into marrying her and putting him in the humiliating position of having to obey her commands because he was frightened of what she would do if he did anything else?

It was ridiculous, a situation so laughable that he knew the humorous aspect of it was the one thing he could not face should the story become public. No, he was caught; caught as neatly and as cleverly as a rabbit in a snare. He could only kick and struggle while the noose grew tighter. There was no doubt about it, struggle as he might, Nerina's suggestions as to what they should say and do were the only practical ones.

He knew in his heart it would not be safe to tell anyone the truth, least of all Lady Clementine. He was well aware there were few lengths to which she would not go if her jealousy was aroused, and he knew, too, that she was a very stupid woman. She would be furious now, abusing him with a fury that would change all too easily to an abandoned surrender of her body.

It would need only a few words from him to alter her emotions. Her eyes would still flash, her bosom heave, but for a very different reason. And yet to assuage her jealousy he would have to tell her the truth, and that was to give her a weapon which, as Nerina had seen all too clearly, would be one utterly destructive to his future career.

It was obvious what Lady Clementine believed. There was nothing else she could think but that, finding Lady Elizabeth Cardon a bore, he had transferred his attentions to her more attractive and more vivacious cousin. He had not seen Lady Clementine for three weeks, for immediately after he had become engaged to Elizabeth she had thought it prudent to leave for London. As she had pointed out, he must be circumspect, at least for the short time he was a betrothed man.

Now she would be convinced that in her absence he had found Nerina both attractive and desirable. There would be no other possible construction she could put on the change of plans. For from a worldly point of view Nerina had neither a title nor the social position of her cousin Elizabeth.

Sir Rupert bit his finger hard as he thought of the expression on Lady Clementine's face as she had left his box at the Opera House. Then with a sigh he got to his feet. There was no doubt about it, another of his love affairs had come to an abrupt end. To see Lady Clementine at this moment would be to involve himself even further into a quagmire of lies and intrigue. It was fortunate in some ways that he did not feel heartbroken, only sore and resentful that he must terminate a very pleasant acquaintance because of a red-haired chit of whose existence he had hardly been aware until yesterday evening.

Lady Clementine was an exciting, alluring and fascinating woman. He had liked making love to her because she enjoyed being possessed with the rapacious appetite of a beautiful animal. There was nothing repressive, inhibited or reserved about Clementine. And she aroused a man's virility by everything she said or did. She had the art of femininity as old as the Garden of Eden itself. There was something almost oriental in the way that she understood and practised love just as another woman might have a talent for the piano.

Yes, he would miss her, Sir Rupert decided as he crossed the Drawing-room floor, but for the moment there were other women of more importance in his life than Lady Clementine, however alluring, however desirable she might be. One was Her Majesty the Queen; the other, damn it, was his wife, Nerina!

The following morning a maid brought a note to Nerina's bedside when she was called. It was brief and had no beginning. It read:

I suggest, if you have no objection, that we leave for Wroth at mid-day. It is best to avoid both curiosity and questions by remaining in London.

Rupert Wroth.

"Tell Sir Rupert," Nerina said to the maid, "that I will be ready to leave at twelve. Pack all my clothes and send a footman immediately to Bond Street to collect the gowns which I was told would be ready this morning. Bessie will inform you of the names of the shops. The messenger must hurry, for there are quite a number of them."

"Very good, milady," the maid said and curtsied.

Nerina sat up in bed and put her arms round her knees.

'So I've won,' she thought. 'He will not visit Lady Clementine after all.'

She was elated with her victory and when Bessie came in a few minutes later she found her lying back on her pillows smiling happily at the ceiling.

"What's pleasing your ladyship?" Bessie enquired.

"Me, myself," Nerina answered. "I am the cleverest person that ever was, I am really, Bessie. I always thought I had brains, but now I am sure of it."

"Pride goes before a fall," Bessie muttered. "Is it true we are leaving for Wroth at mid-day?"

"Yes, and I am longing to see the Castle," Nerina replied. "Elizabeth did not tell me anything about it. She was so full of misery at the thought that she might have to become mistress of the place that she had no idea, when she returned, whether it was big or small, Norman or Adam."

"It is not the house that's a-worrying me," Bessie said.

"Well, what is making your face so long?" Nerina enquired affectionately.

"It's going near home again," Bessie said. "Why, we're

only fifteen miles from his lordship. What are we going to say when he comes roaring and bellowing and threatening us with all the punishments of hell because we've deceived him?"

"There is no reason for apprehension," Nerina said soothingly. "For Aunt Anne and Uncle Herbert should be on their way to Italy by now. Do you think they have dragged the lilypond to see if I have drowned myself?"

She giggled at the thought, but Bessie refused to look cheerful.

"There's trouble waiting for you, m'lady," she said grimly, "as sure as eggs is eggs."

"Well, I have endured nothing but trouble since I was a child, so I suppose I can bear a bit more. What with Sir Rupert wanting to murder me and Uncle Herbert doubtless intending to horse-whip me I wonder if I shall be alive much longer."

Bessie gave a little scream.

"Lawks, child, what terrible things you do say!"

"It is true," Nerina said, getting out of bed and standing for a moment silhouetted against the sunshine.

Her body was as firm and supple as that of a Greek Goddess. She laid her face against the window-frame and felt the sun warm on her closed eyes.

"I suppose most people want a life of peace and quiet," she said after a minute. "They want to relax in the feather-bed comfort of somebody's love and affection. It is funny, Bessie, but I am not like that. Elizabeth would be in tears if Sir Rupert had said half the things to her that he said to me last night, but I only felt like fighting him. It makes me feel excited inside. It gives me the feeling that I am fencing, a sword in my hand, and at any moment one of us may make a fatal lunge. Oh, Bessie, I am happy, happy for the first time in the whole of my life."

"Happy in fighting!" Bessie snorted in disgust. "I'd rather see you like her ladyship, bemused with love until she seemed as if she walked in a dream."

Nerina laughed suddenly.

"Goodness, Bessie, but can you see me like that? Making great sheep's eyes at Sir Rupert and saying, 'Most honoured sir, I am grieved and ashamed that I have behaved so badly. Please forgive me for marrying you. Now I will run away and drown myself so as not to inconvenience you any more.' That is what he would like me to say, but I promise you he is going to be disappointed. I am going to live and enjoy making his life a misery. Already I have got rid of Lady Clementine. He does not dare go and see her. You must admit, Bessie, that it is funny."

"Well, I'm sure I don't know," Bessie said uncertainly. "It isn't the way a young lady should behave, especially on her honeymoon. But you have always been unlike anybody else, Miss . . . m'lady, I mean . . . and I suppose those who know you will have to put up with you as you are."

"They will indeed," Nerina said, "and I will tell you one thing, Bessie. You are the only person I love in the whole world."

"Then all I can say is that it's a terrible pity," Bessie said rebukingly. "It's unnatural not to love people when you are as pretty as you are and have so many good gifts from God. You should be spreading love around you and not hatred. What you give, that is what you get back, and don't you forget it, Miss Nerina."

"You go and tell Sir Rupert that," Nerina said, "although doubtless I will tell him so myself before the day is out."

"I don't know what to say to you, I don't indeed," Bessie said as she went to the wardrobe and started to take down an armful of Nerina's dresses to be packed.

It was extraordinary how much Nerina had managed to buy in such a short space of time. Fortunately the model dresses in the shops fitted her almost to perfection. The more exclusive Court Dressmakers only made gowns to their clients' order and where she could not buy anything to wear at once she had ordered garments of every sort and description and for every possible occasion.

While they had been shopping yesterday, Bessie had exclaimed again and again at Nerina's extravagances, only to be laughed at for her pains and told that it would do Sir Rupert good to realise his responsibilities as a husband.

"He actually said, 'With all my worldly goods I thee endow'," Nerina said. "I listened for it particularly. We must find out what he is worth for I intend to spend a good part of his income on myself."

"Supposing he refuses to let you," Bessie said.

"What can he do?" Nerina asked. "He is responsible for my debts and I can always suggest that if the worst comes to the worst I can earn my own living on the stage or something equally disreputable."

Bessie looked scandalised.

"You wouldn't be threatening the poor man with such terrible things," she exclaimed.

"I shall and worse," Nerina told her. "But why worry, he will pay up."

As Bessie crossed the bedroom floor with a rainbow of taffeta, satin, brocade and tarlatan, Nerina sighed with satisfaction. No one could describe the pleasure that it gave to her to wear clothes that had been bought for her and her alone. Always she had worn Elizabeth's cast-offs or dresses of her aunt's altered and shortened by Bessie with much goodwill but little skill so that they fitted her nowhere and invariably made her appear like a child decked out in its mother's clothes.

Now to know that the exquisite creations of Bond Street's most famous designers were hers and nobody else's was an exhilaration as overwhelming as her sense of freedom and power.

There was no point in going downstairs to fight with Sir Rupert before they started for Wroth; and although Nerina was dressed quite early, she sat in her bedroom watching Bessie and the housemaids pack her trunks and exclaiming with satisfaction over further purchases—gowns, bonnets, shoes, gloves and ribbons which two footmen brought to her room about eleven o'clock.

When everything was finally packed in the trunks which had arrived at Berkeley Square filled only with rubbish, Nerina crossed to the dressing-table. Her hair had been arranged in the new style by Bessie, drawn back from her forehead and coiled low in the nape of her neck, for she had realised on reaching London that curls and ringlets were completely outmoded. The new *coiffure* made her look younger and in a way more spiritual. It gave an exquisite, almost Madonna-like serenity to the upper part of her face, but nothing could quell or subdue the brilliant sparkle of her eyes or the fascinating expressiveness of her mouth. It made her neck seem much longer, a rounded column of ivory rising from her perfectly sculptured shoulders, which were set off today by a most elegant gown of imperial green sprigged with wreaths of coloured silk.

Her flat-brimmed hat in which she intended to travel was green too, and it cast a fascinating shadow over her face, seeming at the same time to make her eyes glow more vividly. There was a travelling manteau of green velvet to cover her dress and her gloves were of soft black suède to match her tiny mincing boots.

"Everything seems to be ready now," Nerina said, as she took a last glimpse of herself in the mirror.

"Yes, everything's ready," Bessie replied, "and I'd best be going, milady. Sir Rupert's valet and I are to drive to the station with the luggage. Is there anything else you require?"

"Nothing, thank you, Bessie," Nerina replied. "I am looking forward to the journey."

She laughed as she spoke and went lightly down the stairs. She was thinking, as she went, of all the things she might say to Sir Rupert. She was ready to fence with him again, a rapier as it were already in her hand.

Just before she reached the first-floor landing she saw Sir Rupert below her entering the Drawing-room. He did not see her approaching and she wondered at his preoccupation. The expression on his face was, as usual, dark and unsmiling, but she thought, too, that he moved a little quicker than usual. She reached the landing and opened with an extravagant gesture the door of the Drawing-room which Sir Rupert had closed behind him.

She was smiling and her head was held high. Already she had thought of some provocative sentence with which to greet him, but the words died on her lips. Sir Rupert was standing in the centre of the room and beside him were her uncle and aunt—Lord and Lady Cardon!

10

For a moment there was an electrified silence. Lady Cardon spoke first:

"So this is where you are, you tiresome child, while we have been worrying ourselves as to what had happened to you. How could you be so selfish and inconsiderate?"

"It is worse than that," Lord Cardon said roughly, his voice sharp and biting as a whip. "You have obviously thrust yourself unwanted upon Sir Rupert. I cannot believe you are here at his invitation."

Nerina found her voice.

"No," she murmured. "It was not exactly at his invitation."

Her heart was beating fast after a moment of dismay and horror when it had seemed to stop beating altogether. Now quite suddenly she realised she was not so frightened as she thought she would be at seeing her uncle again. Perhaps it was her new clothes which gave her confidence, perhaps the fact that all yesterday she had felt herself free and untrammelled by the past. Whatever it was, she found she was no longer tongue-tied by that sickening sense of impotency which had assailed her in the past when faced with her uncle's anger. Slowly she crossed the room until she stood beside him, then she said quietly:

"I have something to tell you, Uncle Herbert, which I am afraid will be rather a shock."

"If you are thinking up an explanation to excuse your latest escapade, you can save your breath," Lord Cardon said sharply. "I am extremely angry with you and I shall not allow anything you may say to alter my decision to punish you as I think fit."

"I am afraid you will find it difficult to make the punishment fit the crime," Nerina replied. "You see, Elizabeth is not here. I have taken her place."

Lady Cardon gave an exclamation.

"Then she is ill!" she cried. "I was sure of it! You remember, Herbert, you said I was worrying unnecessarily; but that was why I insisted on calling here on our way across London. Elizabeth would never have behaved as she did at her wedding had she not been seriously indisposed."

"Where is my daughter?" Lord Cardon asked of Sir Rupert.

Nerina waited for Sir Rupert's answer. As she looked at him now for the first time since she entered the room, she saw by the frown on his forehead and by the very stillness of his body how much he disliked the scene into which he had unwittingly been drawn. And yet in some extraordinary way of his own he seemed to stand aloof from them all. It was characteristic of him, Nerina thought, that always, whatever happened around him, he never seemed quite a part of it but rather a lonely figure in his very contempt and disdain for the frailties of human nature.

His cold frigidity was in almost extraordinary contrast to Lord Cardon's swiftly mounting anger, which was making his face grow crimson and which, as usual, resulted in his being unable to keep still. He moved from one foot to the other, fidgeted with his fingers and was unable to control the fury of his words which seemed to burst like a tempest from between his lips. As Sir Rupert hesitated before replying, Lord Cardon repeated his question impatiently:

"Where is Elizabeth?" he demanded. "Where is she?"

"I am unable to answer that question," Sir Rupert replied at length; "your niece has more knowledge of the matter than I."

"What the devil do you mean?" Lord Cardon replied angrily. "Nerina, what nonsense is this?"

"Elizabeth is married," Nerina said quietly.

"Good God, I know that!" Lord Cardon shouted. "but where is she? Why is she not in this house?"

"Because she is with her husband, Captain Adrian Butler," Nerina replied.

Her words seemed for a moment to have a paralysing effect and for once even Lord Cardon was silenced, while the colour drained from Lady Cardon's face and she looked as if she might faint. But her habitual self-control stood her in good stead and after a few seconds' pause she said:

"It is impossible!"

The sound of her voice seemed to restore to Lord Cardon his power of speech.

"What devilish tomfoolery is this?" he bellowed. "How dare you tell me these damned lies and expect me to credit them. Wroth, why do you stand by and listen to this imbecile talking such pernicious rubbish? You should turn her out of your house. In the meantime I demand to see my daughter immediately."

"I am afraid what you have heard is the truth," Sir
148

Rupert said, and his calm, unheated tones seemed for a moment to cool the heat of Lord Cardon's anger.

"The truth," he repeated in a quieter and almost dazed manner. "But . . . how can it be the truth? Why, she married you the day before yesterday! I was there, I took her to the Church. Has everyone gone mad in this confounded place? Are you asking me to doubt the sight of my own eyes?"

"I am afraid that is exactly what I am asking you to do," Sir Rupert said.

"But then who . . . ?" Lady Cardon began, only to bite off her words and stare with dilated eyes at Nerina.

The fixity of her gaze attracted Lord Cardon's attention and he too turned to look at his niece. As neither of them spoke, Nerina felt it imperative that she should make them understand.

"I took Elizabeth's place," she said quietly.

"You!" Lord Cardon ejaculated, and then he stepped forward to seize her arm. "You little devil!" he roared. "You planned this! Elizabeth would not have had the guts to do it by herself. It is your doing, you strumpet and the daughter of one! God knows I took you into my house in sheer misguided charity. But if you think you have been clever, if you think you have succeeded in discounting me, you are mistaken. Elizabeth is not of age. She shall be brought home, beaten and kept on bread and water until she learns to behave herself. As for you, I will teach you to defy me, to disobey my commands."

He shook Nerina violently as he spoke, then raised his hand as if to strike her in the face. She did not struggle nor did she cry out. For a moment she had forgotten her new-found confidence and only remembered that she was powerless in her uncle's hands, as she had been as a child. Then suddenly she was free and astonishingly Sir Rupert was in front of her, standing between her and the fury of her uncle's anger.

"I regret, Lord Cardon," he said with great dignity, "that I cannot allow you to strike my wife."

"Your wife!"

It was Lady Cardon who voiced the words, and they sounded almost like a scream.

"What your niece has told you is the truth" Sir Rupert went on, speaking only to Lord Cardon. "She took her cousin's place and we were married as you saw for yourselves. The marriage is entirely legal, and although the circumstances in which it took place are both unfortunate and regrettable, nothing is to be gained by senseless recriminations, by violence or by any behaviour which will involve us all in unfortunate gossip or scandal. I think it would be more satisfactory if we could talk this matter over alone, my lord. If you will come with me to my study, we can leave the ladies here."

Without waiting for Lord Cardon's acceptance Sir Rupert turned on his heel and walked towards the door. It appeared that in some extraordinary manner of his own he had deflated Lord Cardon's anger and won a victory over him. Without a glance at Nerina her uncle followed Sir Rupert and she was left alone with her aunt.

As the door closed, Lady Cardon went towards the sofa and sank down on it in the manner of one whose legs would hold her no longer. She opened the reticule which she carried on her wrist, and taking out a handkerchief dabbed the corner of her lips with it before she said in a voice which Nerina knew only too well:

"You ungrateful, disgraceful girl! How could you behave in such a way?"

"If you mean why did I marry Sir Rupert," Nerina retorted "I can assure you it was the only possible manner in which I could ensure Elizabeth's escape, so that she could find happiness with the man she loves."

"Nonsense! Elizabeth hardly knew the young man," Lady Cardon said firmly. "How could she be in love with someone she hardly knew?"

"She met him every day until Lord Cardon discovered them in the wood," Nerina replied, "and love that is persecuted grows quickly."

"Your uncle will bring her back, the marriage will be declared illegal, and then we shall see what she has to say about it," Lady Cardon said almost spitefully.

"And if she has a baby, you will have made it illegitimate," Nerina said.

Lady Cardon gave a cry of horror.

"How can you speak of such things, you immodest wretch?" she exclaimed. "Hold your tongue, miss."

"You seem to forget, Aunt Anne, that I am a Miss no longer," Nerina said, "and my husband and I are at this very moment leaving for Wroth Castle."

"Your husband!" Lady Cardon exclaimed. "A pretty marriage it must be when the man has been tricked into thinking he was marrying someone else and finds himself caught by a scheming hussy, penniless and ill-bred, whom no one will keep in a respectable household."

Her aunt's words seemed to sting Nerina where her uncle's reproofs had left her unmoved.

"That is not true," she retorted. "Uncle Herbert has never sent me to a respectable household and well you know it. Deliberately, because he hated my mother, he has tried to drag me down into the gutter, to make me a creature of shame simply because he hates me."

"Your lies are so childish and ridiculous that they are not even worth answering," Lady Cardon replied. "When your uncle returns, you will learn what he intends to do with you. Until he does, you will oblige me by keeping silent for I have no desire to listen to such falsehoods."

"Very well, Aunt Anne," Nerina said, and the two women sat in silence until a few moments later when the door opened and Lord Cardon came into the room.

One glance at his crimson face and the expression in his eyes told Nerina all too clearly that he had been defeated. She felt her heart give a sudden leap for joy. Lord Cardon walked across the room to his wife.

"Come, Anne," he said. "We are leaving this house and proceeding on our journey."

Lady Cardon looked up at him in a bewildered manner.

"But, Herbert, what about Elizabeth—and Nerina?"

"I have nothing to say about either of those disreputable and reprehensible young women," Lord Cardon said grimly. "I will explain more to you when we have left. Come, the carriage is waiting."

Mechanically Lady Cardon rose to her feet. Nerina rose too, but her uncle and aunt did not so much as glance at her. They swept across the room and through the open door. Nerina watched them cross the landing and descend the stairs. Only when they had gone did she realise that her hands were trembling and that quite unexpectedly she felt suspiciously near to tears.

'It is reaction,' she told herself. 'The surprise and unexpectedness of it all has been too much for me.'

But she knew it was more than that. It was relief that Sir Rupert had taken her part and had prevented her from being manhandled. What was more, she felt certain that alone with her uncle he had put forward her own arguments for letting the whole thing remain a secret as much as possible and so preventing a scandal. There could be no other reason for the fact that her uncle had gone away, silent and deflated, abandoning her to her fate as the wife of Sir Rupert Wroth.

For a moment Nerina lifted her fingers and pressed them against her eyes. It was as if at last she really realised that the past was finished. The curtain had fallen on the First Act and it was rising for the Second. What lay ahead? What did the future hold?

In her defiance she had talked bravely to Sir Rupert. She had told him that she had planned so much, but behind her words there had been only the courage of her own imaginings. There had been no stability, no surety and indeed no confidence in the future. Always she had felt that the whole thing was a play, a fantasy as grotesque and daring as the one in which she had masqueraded as her cousin Elizabeth, but underneath it all had lain the fear and terror of what Lord Cardon would do.

He had bullied her for so long. It was his word and his alone which had ruled her life until this moment. Always he had been there, a terrible, distorted figure against whose judgment there was no appeal and from whose cruelty she had no escape. But now he was gone; he had walked out of her life across a room and disappeared round the curve of the stairs.

It was almost impossible to believe that it was true, that he had gone as casily as that, releasing her from her bondage, not by death or disaster or indeed by any form of violence, but simply at the command of another man—a man who had saved her against his own will, but who, nevertheless, was still her saviour.

She heard someone approaching and turned swiftly towards the sound of the footsteps, taking her fingers from her eyes that were suddenly alight with softness and gratitude. And then she saw it was not Sir Rupert approaching but a footman.

"The carriage is waiting, m'lady," he said.

"Thank you."

Nerina rose, glanced in the mirror over the mantelpiece and for a moment wondered if she really looked at herself. Her eyes were like stars, her mouth was warm and crimson. She went slowly down the stairs to find Sir Rupert waiting for her in the Hall. She looked up into his face as she reached his side, but he did not so much as glance at her.

"We shall miss the train if we do not hurry," he said

briefly, and she preceded him towards the waiting vehicle.

The journey to Wroth was uneventful. The train was noisy and it was impossible to talk even in the seclusion of their reserved carriage. Nerina turned over the pages of a book, but she had no idea what she read. She was indeed only conscious of the man opposite her. Sir Rupert appeared to be perusing the morning paper, but Nerina had the idea that he, too, was thinking.

She watched him. He never raised his eyes from the newspaper, and yet it seemed to her that he took a considerable time to read even one page. She had a sudden and quite absurd desire to lean forward and thank him for relieving her of her uncle and aunt; yet she knew her gratitude would mean nothing to him, for whatever he had done he had done for himself, to save his career, to protect his own ambitions.

For a moment Nerina felt a faint gleam of sympathy for him. All this must be hard to bear; and then she remembered how he and Lady Clementine had schemed against the innocent, unoffending Elizabeth and her heart was hardened again. The only hardship Sir Rupert was enduring, she told herself, was finding himself married to a difficult wife rather than a pleasant one. Otherwise his plans were not circumvented in any way; and though her uncle and aunt might decry her and seek to defame her mother's memory, from the worldly point of view Sir Rupert had married the young, innocent and well-brought-up niece of the Earl of Cardon. She would be acceptable in Court circles and that was all that Sir Rupert required of her.

It was late in the afternoon when they arrived at Pendle, a small manufacturing town which was the nearest station to Wroth. A carriage was waiting and the station-master, resplendent in gold lace and top hat, hurried forward to escort them from the platform to the station-yard. The air seemed chill and raw after the stuffiness of the carriage, and as they drove off Nerina pulled her pelisse a little more closely over her shoulders. Noticing the movement, Sir Rupert said:

"Are you cold? Would you like the carriage closed?"

Nerina shook her head.

"No indeed, I prefer it open," she replied. "I am anxious to see the countryside for I have never been in this part of the country before."

"You will find it very different from the land round Rowanfield," he replied. "There you are entirely agricultural, here there are several prosperous towns mostly engaged in weaving. You see there one of the new factories."

He pointed to a gaunt, ugly building as they passed. Its high chimneys were belching out black smoke and its windows were so small and dirty that one wondered if the light could ever percolate through them. There was something ominous and rather overpowering about the factory. For no apparent reason Nerina felt herself shudder as she passed it. All around it there were dirty, dark alleyways, squalid ancient houses most of which were so badly in need of repair that they appeared as if they might tumble down at any moment.

"Is that where the people who work in the factories live?" Nerina asked.

Sir Rupert looked in the direction in which she pointed.

"I imagine so," he replied. "Most factories in this part of the country employ children; they are cheaper."

"I read a Report the other day on the employment of children in the factories and mines," Nerina said. "It described some of their sufferings. The horrifying conditions in which they have to work, the long hours when they are flogged continually to keep them from falling asleep. Do you think that is right?"

"It is difficult to say whether such a thing is right or wrong," Sir Rupert replied. "It is necessary, if we are to keep our foreign trade, that our output in this country should be considerably greater than it is at the moment. We enter a competitive market, and as children provide us with cheap labour, then obviously to survive we must employ children."

Nerina was silent for a moment, then she said:

"You speak as if children were a race apart. Children grow up into men and women; and if they are maimed, deformed and unhealthy, then in the future Britain will become a race of unhealthy people."

"That is certainly a point of consideration in case Parliament should discuss a reform of the Employment of Children Act," Sir Rupert conceded. "Did you read that argument in the Report?"

"As a matter of fact I thought of it myself," Nerina replied. "Because one is a woman one does not read only the fashion notes in the *Ladies' Journal*."

Her voice was resentful, and unexpectedly he smiled.

"A blue-stocking as well as an adventuress," he said.

154

"Well, you are certainly unexpected both in your behaviour and in your views."

"It appears to me," Nerina said, ignoring the last remark, "that it is time women took more interest in politics. Most of them are like my aunt, who says they are beyond her. She is quite prepared to accept my uncle's views on any subject that concerns the government of the people."

"And you think differently?" Sir Rupert asked mockingly.

"I would certainly not accept any man's views as my own," Nerina said, "and from the little I know of politics and what I have heard about them it seems to me that most politicians like yourself are far too concerned with foreign affairs. You are always talking about what is happening in Turkey, Greece or Italy. How seldom you seem to be concerned with what is happening at home! A few years ago there were terrible riots. They were put down by the military. I remember my uncle's almost sadistic satisfaction that men were clubbed and shot and women were trampled to death by the horses. But riots begin because people are unhappy or are treated unjustly. There can be no justice where people are allowed to starve in a rich and prosperous land."

"I see that I am married to a reformer," Sir Rupert said. "Perhaps you would wish to reform that?"

He pointed as he spoke to where, ahead of them, the road twisted and turned to a gaunt, barren, ugly piece of country on which there were dark artificial hills created by outcast coal-dust. The very air seemed dark and dirty, and when they reached the small mining village Nerina saw that the houses were in many cases nothing but dilapidated shacks.

In the street, shuffling along in their clogs, were gaunt, ugly women wearing shawls over their heads. There were dozens of children, bare-footed and in rags, playing with garbage in the gutters or pelting each other with lumps of coal. The entrance of the mine with its big double gates was in the centre of the village. Outside it a number of men were leaning against a brick wall. They stared sullenly as the carriage went by with its well-fed horses. Several of them spat into the roadway, and Nerina thought there was a universal expression of resentfulness on their dark, dirty faces.

"What a horrible place!" she exclaimed. "Can nothing

155

be done to clean it up, to make the lives of those who live in it brighter?"

"What do you expect anyone to do?" Sir Rupert enquired. "The men get good wages if they work properly. The trouble is there are too many agitators amongst them. They make trouble, and trouble amongst workmen is never a good wage earner."

"But perhaps they feel they are unfairly treated," Nerina said.

"But they are not!"

"How do you know?"

"Because I own the mine," Sir Rupert replied.

"And the village?"

"Yes, the village, too."

Nerina was silent, and after a moment Sir Rupert said sarcastically:

"No suggestions as to how I can reform it?"

"So many that I do not know where to begin," Nerina snapped.

She was thinking of those shabbily dressed women, of the dirty, ragged children and the men with their sullen, resentful glances. Something should be done for them, but she was not certain what it should be. She suddenly felt very young and very helpless. She had always believed people in high places had great responsibilities, yet now for the moment she was beginning to be appalled at the responsibilities that might be hers. She knew in that moment that she could never submerge herself completely in a life of social ambition. She wanted to be a success in Society, she wanted to have beautiful clothes, to be courted and acclaimed a distinguished hostess, and yet she knew that ultimately these things would never satisfy her.

She wanted more, though as yet she was not certain what it was. Dimly, as if she looked at it through a fog which prevented her from seeing but the merest outline of what it enveloped, she began to think of a wider and more important ambition, began to desire something more powerful than any of the things she had imagined or dreamt of in the past. But it was impossible to put what she felt into words. It eluded her, as the memory of a dream can elude one when one first awakes while what one felt and experienced lingers in the back of the mind. She was trying so hard to formulate her own feelings to herself that she was almost startled when Sir Rupert said suddenly:

"There is Wroth!"

The flat country of the mining village had long been left behind and now they were in an undulating country of hills and dales, thick woodland and rich green pasture. As they surmounted a rise in the road and turned through two huge iron gates Nerina saw Wroth Castle for the first time.

She had expected it to be impressive, but she had not imagined it could be so beautiful. Architecturally it was a combination of building styles through the ages, and yet each succeeding generation had managed in some curious way to accord with its predecessors so that, although there was a Norman tower on one side of the Castle, the Elizabethan wing in lovely mellow red stone seemed not at variance with it.

The drive crossed a long bridge which ran over part of a chain of lakes, each with a waterful, spreading themselves like a glittering necklace in front of the house with its great grey terraces. Vast woods protected the building from the north winds and to the east and west there were formal gardens, laid out in Elizabeth's reign, containing, Nerina was to find later, some of the rarest and most exotic plants that had ever been known to blossom in Great Britain.

There was a peace and a beauty about the house which seemed a strange contrast to its owner. It was neither proud nor disdainful, and despite its grandeur it seemed almost to have a warm welcoming air about it as if, having stood for so long, it had become not only a part of the landscape but part of nature itself. Though composed of brick and stone the building gave the impression that it was impregnated with human emotion and human affections.

Nerina was suddenly aware that she had expected to hate Wroth. She had wanted to see it and yet in her heart of hearts she had thought that she would loathe it because it had always seemed to her from what she had heard of it a manifestation of power and pride.

"Why, it is lovely!"

She heard her own voice say the words involuntarily.

"Most people admire the Castle," Sir Rupert said.

"I am not surprised," Nerina replied. "You must be proud to own it. It must be wonderful to have a home which has belonged to one's ancestors and to know yourself a part of it, to feel that you really belong there."

She spoke sincerely out of her own loneliness, but to her astonishment Sir Rupert looked as if she had insulted him. There was something almost distorted in his expression as he said abruptly:

"You are quite mistaken! I was left the house and the estates, but I did not inherit."

"But your name is the same," Nerina said. "You are a Wroth of Wroth Castle."

"Some day I will satisfy your curiosity on that point," Sir Rupert said sharply, "but not now."

There was something so abrupt and rude in the way he spoke that Nerina stared at him in astonishment. What had she said to annoy him? she wondered. But as the carriage drove over the bridge and into the wide sweep of the courtyard in front of the house. Nerina forgot Sir Rupert in her wonder and amazement at what she saw around her.

The Castle was enormous, even bigger than she had imagined when she first saw it, and yet strangely enough it was not overwhelming. The Hall through which she was led on arrival was large and magnificent, but its ancient carved panelling and beautiful Persian carpets gave it almost a homely appearance.

The room in which tea had been laid for them was very much the same. Long and narrow, it had been built in the reign of Queen Anne and had windows opening out on to a rose garden. The curtains were of soft yellow brocade, the furniture-coverings of needlework, and although it was late afternoon, the room seemed full of sunshine.

Nerina drew off her gloves and laid her pelisse on a chair.

"I am longing for a cup of tea," she said. "The train always makes one's mouth so dry."

She would have liked to exclaim about the beauties of the room, but after Sir Rupert's strange behaviour about the house she was almost afraid to make any comment.

The tea-table was already laid near the fire and seeing that, as there were only two china cups and plates, no one was expected except themselves, she sat down in front of it. A moment later the butler and several footmen came in with trays laden with scones and cakes, bread-and-butter and sandwiches of every type. The silver tea-service had been fashioned in the reign of George III and the teaspoons had thin twisted handles each surmounted by an apostle.

As the servants left the room, Nerina pulled her bonnet from her head.

"I shall look untidy," she said, "and I ought to go upstairs to wash before I have a meal, but I am so thirsty that you will just have to put up with me."

"A very apt expression," Sir Rupert said.

"I gave you an opening there," Nerina said with a laugh, "I should have thought you might have been big enough not to have taken it."

The corner of his mouth twisted a little, but he did not smile.

"I, too, am waiting for a cup of tea," he said, "and then I would like to take you upstairs to meet my Grandmother."

"She is here in the house?" Nerina asked almost in consternation. "I had no idea that she still lived here."

"She is very old," Sir Rupert said, "nearly eighty, and I think you will find her an extremely interesting old lady unless, of course, you are frightened of her. But then I forgot, you are frightened of no one."

"I am not certain that you mean that as a compliment," Nerina said as she passed him a cup of tea

As he took the cup from her, their eyes met and quite suddenly he laughed.

"What are you laughing at?" Nerina enquired a little suspiciously.

"I was thinking how much had happened since I left this house two days ago," he said. "It is always difficult to laugh at one's self, but I certainly had no idea as I set out for Rowanfield Church what awaited me."

"Retribution comes to all of us in time," Nerina retorted.

"I am hoping I shall be there to see yours," Sir Rupert said. "It would, I assure you, give me great pleasure to watch you receiving your just dues."

"It is natural for you to feel vindictive," Nerina said. "I should feel the same myself. Do we tell your Grandmother the truth?"

"If we don't, she will certainly find it out," Sir Rupert said. "She is very shrewd and extremely outspoken. Now that I come to think of it, you remind me a little of her."

"I remind you of your Grandmother!" Nerina exclaimed in astonishment.

"Yes, you have the same impetuous manner of approach, the same imperious way of sweeping people aside or of forcing them to do your will. You should get on famously with each other—at least I hope so. I am sorry for anyone who makes an enemy of my Grandmother."

"You are certainly doing your best to make me apprehensive of her," Nerina said.

She took one of the succulent sandwiches from a plate of Worcester china. It was of *pâte de foie gras* and as she bit into it she had a sudden vision of the mining village. A dozen questions trembled on her tongue, but she did not speak them. There was no point in starting another controversy so soon after she had arrived. She wanted to see the house, wanted to learn so much about it and to meet Sir Rupert's grandmother. It was best not to antagonise him for the moment. Instead she smiled at him, unaware that for the first time she had deliberately set herself out to be pleasant.

When their tea was finished, Sir Rupert led the way upstairs and on reaching the first floor showed her the bedroom which was to be her own.

It was an enormous room with a huge oak four-poster bed, the ostrich feather fronds on the top of it touching the ceiling.

"What a very big room," Nerina said almost in a voice of awe.

"It is called the Bride's Bedroom," Sir Rupert said, and something in the contemptuous tone in his voice made Nerina blush despite herself.

She laid down her pelisse, hat and gloves on a chair and having taken a swift glance at herself in the mirror, said:

"Now I am ready to visit your Grandmother."

Sir Rupert led the way down a long corridor. At the end of it he turned right and Nerina realised they were in another wing of the house. Its architecture was Georgian, but the furniture and ceilings were Italian. They came to two double doors. Sir Rupert knocked on one, and a moment later Nerina found herself crossing the threshold of the most extraordinary bedroom she had ever seen. Here again was a four-poster, but a very different one from that which she was to use.

The posts were carved and ornamented with a profusion of realistically painted flowers and angels. The hangings were of white muslin tied up with blue bows. The bedspread was of white ermine over which was turned a sheet edged with wide lace and heavily embroidered with a monogram and coronet. Sitting in the centre of the bed, propped up with lace pillows, was the most fantastic old lady Nerina had ever seen.

Her face was lined and wrinkled until it looked almost like an etching rather than a human face, and yet her cheeks were rouged, her lips reddened and her eyelashes blackened. Above this she wore a wig of yellow curls so bright, so golden that it gave the impression that the whole thing must be part of a fancy dress. The old lady's hands were withered and wrinkled and blue-veined with age, but her fingers blazed with rings of every description—emeralds, diamonds, rubies and sapphires were all mingled together in a brilliant profusion, and her thin wrists were hung with bracelets, while round her neck, showing beneath a bedjacket of velvet and swansdown, were row upon row of pearls—lustrous globules so large and so numerous that they appeared almost like a shield.

For a moment Nerina was too astonished at what she saw to have any other feeling than that of confusion; then she realised that the old lady's eyes were as bright as the sapphires which glittered on her fingers. Startlingly blue, they were also shrewd and extremely observant, and she knew that they had taken in every detail of her appearance.

"How are you, Grandmother?" Sir Rupert asked, as he raised one of the old lady's hands to his lips.

"Well enough!" the old lady replied. "Is this your wife? I thought you said she had fair hair like mine?"

"I will explain about that later," Sir Rupert said hastily. "In the meantime, Grandmother, this is Nerina, my wife. Nerina, allow me to present to you my Grandmother, the Dowager Marchioness of Droxburgh."

Nerina did not stop to think, indeed she could not for the life of her check the words which came almost like an avalanche to her lips.

"But that is not her name," she heard herself cry. "It can't be!"

11

Nerina sat on the edge of the goldfish pond and dangled her fingers in the cool water. She could see the fish gleaming beneath the dark green leaves of the water-lilies whose pink-tipped blossoms opened their waxen beauty towards the sunshine. It was very quiet and peaceful and the only sounds were the songs of the birds and the splash of the water from the carved stone fountain which fed the pond.

How long she sat there she did not know for her mind was not on her surroundings. She was hardly conscious of the beauty of the gardens or the fragrance of the flowers. She was wondering, as she had wondered not once but a hundred times during the last two or three days, what was the secret that was to be revealed to her this very afternoon. She was sure it was something unpleasant. That was obvious from the very way Sir Rupert had spoken of it, from the look his Grandmother had given him and from the manner in which she had said to him in a voice deep with mystery:

"Have you told her yet?"

It would have been impossible and inhuman not to be consumed by curiosity as to what she should have been told; but Nerina had been forced to possess her soul in patience because on the very evening of her arrival the Dowager Marchioness was indisposed and the Doctor forbade her to have any visitors.

Nerina had been half afraid, when she heard this, that it had been her fault, that her behaviour had in some way agitated or perturbed the Dowager. But when she expressed these fears Sir Rupert had reassured her.

"My Grandmother thrives on excitement," he said, "and I assure you that anything unusual or extraordinary seems to give her new life and refresh rather than exhaust her. She has, however, contracted a slight chill and at her age it is always wise to take no undue risks. But I hear from her personal maid that she is very desirous to see you and as soon as the Doctor allows it she will invite you to visit her."

"I shall be glad to do so," Nerina said quietly, and indeed she was anxious to apologise for her behaviour when the shock of learning the name of Sir Rupert's

Grandmother had made her forget everything but her own astonishment and sense of dismay.

It was ridiculous, she thought now, that merely hearing the name Droxburgh should have perturbed her so much or made her lose control of herself. She imagined it must have been in reality an accumulation of things happening one after another—the anxiety over her own and Elizabeth's marriage, the shock of finding her uncle and aunt in the Drawing-room at Berkeley Square, the excitement of seeing Wroth Castle for the first time and then, on the top of it all, to hear unexpectedly the obnoxious name that she hated above all others, the name that brought back to her all too vividly the sufferings and terror she had endured under the Marquis's roof.

Even the Dowager's and Sir Rupert's surprise at her outburst had not at first brought her to her senses. She stood there in front of them, white-faced and trembling.

"It can not be true! There must be some mistake!" she whispered.

Having lost for a moment her sense of proportion and all semblance of common-sense, she felt that the fact that Sir Rupert's Grandmother bore the same name as her persecutor must in some way have delivered her into his clutches. She almost imagined that he was waiting outside the door, waiting to seize her, to prove once and for all that her efforts to escape had been foiled and that now, despite anything she could do, she was completely and absolutely in his power.

"Why do you speak like that?" the Dowager Marchioness asked at length. "I assure you that I am indeed the Dowager Marchioness of Droxburgh, for all that your husband is my grandson."

It was then that she had looked at Sir Rupert quickly with her shrewd blue eyes and lowering her voice said, nevertheless distinctly:

"Have you told her yet?"

Sir Rupert shook his head.

"No," he replied.

His Grandmother gave him a strange glance and then after a moment's hesitation as if she chose her words with care she said:

"There is, of course, plenty of time."

"Plenty!" Sir Rupert agreed frigidly.

It was this exchange of words which gave Nerina time to pull herself together. With an effort she quelled the wild beating of her heart. She forced herself to think sensibly that her fears were groundless. She was at Wroth. She was married to a strange, unaccountable man whom she heartily disliked but did not acutely loathe and did not shrink in terror with the same detestation and hatred that she had felt for the evil Marquis of Droxburgh.

He was powerless to hurt her now. He was only something slimy and terrible from which she had prudently run away. With an effort she was able to say with a tremulous smile but in a normal voice:

"Will you please forgive me for my strange behaviour? I am tired and overwrought, and although I have an explanation that I can offer, may it wait, please, until another occasion, for it is a long story and I am afraid of boring you?"

"I am seldom bored with stories as long as they are truthful," the Dowager said. "I shall look forward to hearing what you have to tell me, child, but naturally you are fatigued and want to rest after your journey. I doubt if Rupert has even suggested it to you." She looked at him and gave a little chuckling laugh. "No, of course he hasn't. All men are quite inhuman where women's feelings are concerned. Go and lie down. You and I will have a long talk on the morrow. There is much we have to say to each other."

Nerina had curtsied hastily, anxious to get from the room. She was embarrassed by what had occurred and at the same time afraid of her own feelings. She had never known herself behave in such a strange manner before. She had never lost control or cried out as she had done then without the full consent both of her brain and her will.

As she sped down the corridor towards her own bedroom, she had wondered what was the matter with herself. It was only when she was safely behind the closed door with the comforting presence of Bessie beside her that she felt she could relax. Throwing herself down on the sofa at the foot of her bed, she began to tell Bessie what had happened since she left her bedroom that morning and walked downstairs to find Lord and Lady Cardon in the Drawing-room.

She related all that had been said and done at Berkeley Square while Bessie listened goggle-eyed, punctuating the story with ejaculations of surprise, horror and excitement. But when Nerina had reached the part of her story when she and Sir Rupert had left London, the tale came to an end. Somehow not even to Bessie could Nerina explain what had happened to her just a few minutes ago when she learned the name of Sir Rupert's Grandmother. It was ridiculous, Nerina was sure of that, and yet she could not bring herself to speak of what she had felt at that strange unaccountable moment when she had heard her own voice cry out like the voice of a stranger.

All that night she lay awake wondering not only about herself but at the strangeness of the Dowager's conversation with Sir Rupert. What was it he had to tell her and why had he not done so?

She had half expected him to refer to the matter that evening. They had dined alone in great pomp and state with the butler and half a dozen footmen to wait on them. The dinner prepared by a superlative chef was in fact little less than a Royal Banquet, but as course succeeded course Nerina took only a tiny mouthful of each for appearance's sake. She wondered what Sir Rupert was thinking about as he sat at the end of the table unsmiling and with apparently as little to say as she had herself.

The Dining-room had been decorated by Robert Adam with pale-green walls enriched with Grecian plaques in the Wedgwood design; it was equipped with Chippendale furniture and mirrors and lit by huge sconces of silver each of which held a dozen glowing tapers. The room was lovely, if to the more fashionable taste somewhat severe in its design.

Nerina suddenly realised that so far she had not seen a portrait of any sort in the Castle. It struck her as surprising, for in other houses where she had lived or visited the walls had practically been covered by portraits of the owners past and present. She realised now why the walls seemed so empty both in the Dining-room and the Drawing-room, and why the panelling in the passages appeared unexpectedly severe.

She wondered what the explanation could be; and as the footmen served a dessert of peaches, luscious and velvety from the hot houses, great bunches of purple and white grapes, green figs with their crimson seeded flesh and golden nectarines which appeared to hold the warmth of the sunshine in their soft skins, she asked:

"Have you a Picture Gallery?"

Sir Rupert raised his eyebrows. "There is a Long Gallery in the east wing which has always borne that name," he replied after a moment's pause.

"Do you keep all your pictures there?" Nerina enquired.

"I have no pictures."

The reply was abrupt and uncompromising, but Nerina was too intrigued not to continue her questioning.

"No pictures?" she exclaimed. "What an extraordinary thing! I should have thought that a house like this would have been full of them."

"Then you are mistaken," Sir Rupert replied. "I have no pictures, and I think it is true to say that you will not find one in the whole of the Castle."

"But why?" Nerina asked, but something in the darkness of his expression and the frown between his eyes told her that this was forbidden ground. Hastily, because she felt uncomfortable, though it was no fault of her own, she said: "I suppose you are entitled to your own eccentricities as well as other people. I heard once of a man who burned his father's Library and refused to have a book of any sort in the house. He said they had ruined his childhood."

"Unfortunately the destruction of the books could not restore to him what he believed he had lost," Sir Rupert said.

"No, of course not," Nerina agreed.

"But there is always some satisfaction in being revengeful," Sir Rupert said sarcastically. "I am sure you have discovered that."

She felt the colour rise in her face, knowing that he was taunting her.

When dinner was finished, she rose and Sir Rupert opened the door for her to leave the room. He closed it behind her and went back to his port. She went into the Drawing-room and wondered if he would rejoin her, but although she waited for over an hour he did not come. It annoyed her that she must wait for him, and yet she could not force herself to go upstairs until she was quite certain that he did not intend to speak to her again that night.

She told herself there were many things she wished to discuss with him. Things she wanted to know which it was difficult to ask in front of the servants. It would be easier to talk, she thought, in the peace and comfort of the Drawing-room. But as the minutes ticked by and he did not come, she felt herself shiver a little and a feeling of coldness and loneliness crept over her. The Castle was so big. Was this to be her fate every evening—to sit alone by a dying fire, waiting for a man who preferred the consolation of a bottle of port to her company?

She felt a sudden sense of temerity at all she had undertaken. It was easy to be defiant, aggressive and truculent when one's enemy was present, when one could feel, as she had felt earlier that day, that she was fighting a duel; but it was difficult to feel any of these things when one was alone, when one faced not antagonism but indifference.

As the clock struck ten, Nerina gave a little exclamation of anger. He was not coming! If she waited any longer, he might learn that she still sat there and might think that she was waiting for him. She would not give him that much satisfaction. She would go up to her bedroom, go to sleep hating him as she had done so many nights previously, frightened yet fascinated by the depths of her own emotions where Sir Rupert was concerned.

In the morning she had learned of the Dowager's indisposition. In the morning, too, she had begun to realise that her fears and apprehensions of the night before were not entirely groundless. It was loneliness which sapped her strength far more effectively than any fierce, embittered exchange of words.

She had come down to breakfast only to find that Sir Rupert had already finished his and had ridden off on an inspection of the Estate. He had left word that he would not be home to luncheon as he intended to visit some of his outlying farms and would not therefore be returning until tea-time.

Nerina wandered round the gardens, then sat in the Drawing-room feeling useless and utterly unwanted. There was an efficiency in the Castle which somehow dismayed her. She had imagined that she would find a lot to do in a house that had been run by a bachelor. She had visualised making many changes, asserting herself, if only to annoy Sir Rupert, by dismissing the servants, by insisting on the things which had been left undone being undertaken immediately and on those which had been done wrong being changed, whatever the cost to tradition or lacerated feelings.

But she could find nothing that she wished to do. The gardens were wonderful. She had never dreamt that flowers could be arranged so beautifully or that so much could be contrived artificially without spoiling the natural beauties of the landscape. Inside the house everything appeared to run on greased wheels. The housekeeper was a charming, elderly woman who had been at the Castle for many years and who apparently managed to assert her authority with an unusual degree of humanity.

The housemaids were red-cheeked and smiling, the footmen in parts of the house where they could not be overheard by the gentry went about whistling. There was an atmosphere of happiness and contentment below stairs which was very recognisable, and Nerina knew at once that there would be no need for any revolutionary changes where the household were concerned.

Even to gain her own ends she would not perpetrate injustice by finding fault where there was no need for it; and when she had toured the house, she could only congratulate the housekeeper on everything she had seen and retire to the Drawing-room wishing that she too felt like whistling and not for some unaccountable reason which she could not explain even to herself perilously near to tears.

'What is the matter with me?' she asked herself. "I have got everything I wanted—a house, a position, security against poverty and having to earn my own living, yet I want more. What is it?'

She asked herself the same question now, with the coolness of the water on her fingers, the warmth of the sunshine on her bare head. Then, though she did not hear the sound of a footfall nor anything to warn her of his approach, she turned round instinctively because Sir Rupert was walking towards her across the lawn. He too was bareheaded and the snowy perfection of his frilled shirt was very white against the sapphire blue of his well-cut coat.

Nerina rose to her feet and stood waiting for him to approach her, delighted almost beyond reason that her solitude was at an end and that now there was someone to talk to, even if it was only Sir Rupert. He looked at her as he approached and she was glad that she was wearing a new gown of stiffened muslin trimmed with primrose yellow ribbons. She did not speak or welcome him, but perhaps the expression on her face was greeting enough in itself, for after standing for a moment looking down at her he said:

"Have you decided yet?"

"Decided what?" she asked in astonishment.

"Whether Wroth lives up to your expectations," he said.

"But of course! It is marvellous, you know that! How could you expect that I should think anything different?"

"I expected nothing," he said shortly, "except that if you

did not find it good enough you would order me to buy something better. Have you forgotten that a political hostess must always have a really comfortable house in which to entertain Cabinet Ministers?"

He was mocking her and yet she felt there was no real sting in his words. As she laughed, the sound, untrammelled and very young, seemed to lilt through the garden.

"Even Cabinet Ministers would find it hard to complain about Wroth," she said.

"Then it is not the place which makes them cast their invitations into the waste-paper basket," Sir Rupert said. "It might perhaps be the owner."

"You?" Nerina asked, then added: "But don't you give parties here? Political parties, I mean?"

Sir Rupert's reply was in one syllable.

"No!"

"Why not?"

She asked the question casually enough and yet she felt it was of importance. Sir Rupert hesitated, then he looked away from her to where the lakes gleamed silver in the sunshine.

"I have asked my Grandmother to explain those things to you," he said at length, his voice harsh as if it hurt him to speak.

"If there is anything to tell, I would rather you told me yourself," Nerina said quickly.

"Why?" he enquired angrily. "So that you can torture me! Oh no, you have done enough of that! There are some things on which you might go too far and regret it. I have warned you."

She stared up into his face but he did not look at her.

"You are very mysterious," she said at length.

"Am I?" He still spoke angrily. "And why not? I prefer to keep my secrets to myself, having an acute sense of self-preservation, but unfortunately a secret is not always one's own. There are invariably other people involved. But I have no intention of discussing it with you. Go to my Grandmother now, she is expecting you; and when you have heard what she has to say, you can laugh if you wish to, it is a matter of utter indifference to me."

His voice was suddenly bitter with a bitterness beyond anything she had ever heard in her life before; but before she could reply, could say anything, he had walked away down the garden, his back and the carriage of his head so uncompromising that she dared not go after him though

169

she longed to ask him for an explanation. She watched him for a long time until he was almost out of sight beyond the rose garden and where the closely cut yews formed the entrance to the maze. Then, shivering as if a sudden cold wind blew about her bare arms, she turned towards the house and found her way to the Dowager Marchioness's bedroom.

Nerina knocked and almost immediately an elderly maid came to the door and let her in. As Nerina crossed the room towards the bed, she was able to take in on this second visit a little more detail of the room which on first acquaintance had seemed to her entirely fantastic and unlike anything she had ever seen before.

Now she realised that it was not only the white muslin draperies of the bed which were so astonishing but the room itself, which was of white, gold and blue. The curtains, tasselled and draped, were of sky-blue satin, the inner curtains of frilled muslin, and a carpet of the same blue as the curtains covered the floor, while the walls were white with an intricate pattern of gold leaf both on the cornice and the dado.

The furniture was mostly gilt; the console-tables, carved bewilderingly with flowers, doves and angels, were set at intervals around the room and each held an enormous vase of blue porcelain in which were arranged hothouse flowers, every one of them white.

The elaborate and innumerable ornaments uniformly echoed the colours of blue and white. A dressing set of crystal bore a monogram and coronet of turquoise and diamonds.

As Nerina reached the great four-poster bed with its blue and white hangings and ermine cover, she saw that its occupant was also wearing blue—a sky-blue wrap of some exquisite material embroidered with silver and trimmed with white ermine and ermine tails. The old lady's hair seemed more golden than ever against the white pillows, and round it today was entwined a narrow ribbon of blue velvet.

She was covered with jewellery as she had been on Nerina's last visit. She still wore innumerable strings of pearls, and round her neck, resting on the top row, was a collet of diamonds. There were diamond and sapphire bracelets glittering on her wrists, and her fingers were almost blinding as she moved them with an exquisite little

170

gesture of welcome, a gesture which Nerina recognised as being that of a great lady receiving her guests.

It was then without being told, without any explanation being given to her, that Nerina understood. Sir Rupert's Grandmother was very old—nearly eighty, he had said—and yet her heart remained young. To herself she was still a great beauty, a famous hostess who had led Society for over half a century and who had been acclaimed by Kings and Emperors, Ambassadors and Ministers.

It is the tragedy of every woman that her face must alter quicker than her heart; but for one who had been famous for her beauty, who had known the admiration and adoration not of a few chosen friends but of all her contemporaries and indeed of a whole generation it was a tragedy almost beyond expression that age must take away everything except the memory of what one has been.

At last Nerina understood. The furnishings of the room were those suitable to a young and beautiful woman. She could almost hear people say that the room was like its owner. Blue to match her eyes, white the colour of her unblemished skin, gold to rival her golden hair. Now she understood the profusion of jewellery. It was the reward of beauty, the spoils the Marchioness had gained in the years she had reigned in the hearts of all who knew her.

It was easy to see, Nerina thought, when she looked at the Marchioness with a new insight, how beautiful she must have been. Even her wrinkled skin, discoloured now to the shade of old and yellow ivory, could not disguise the fact that once her features had been a classic in their perfection, that her eyes before they had sunk deep in her head had been large and lustrous and as blue as the sky itself.

Her grace must have been an intrinsic part of her charms. One could see it now in the way she turned her head, in the sudden movement of her neck which had once been long and white, full and rounded, in the movement of her hands, the turn of her wrists, the fluttering of her long thin fingers.

A beauty, a great beauty, to whom all the world which mattered had knelt in homage and now an old and withered woman, alone in a great four-poster bed with only her memories for company!

"Come along, child, and let me look at you," the Marchioness said, and Nerina was recalled to reality by the shrewd alertness of her voice.

She might be old, but there was little that escaped her, Nerina was certain of that. Today there was no sign of any indisposition about her, her eyes were bright, and despite the softness of the pillows behind her she held herself upright as if she scorned to accept their support.

Nerina sat down in the chair by the bedside which the maid placed for her before withdrawing and closing the door behind her. The Dowager took up a glass of champagne which stood beside her and sipped it delicately.

"That bird-witted Doctor of mine refused to allow me to see anyone these past three days," she said. "The man's an idiot and I told him so. I am too old to have what is left of my life wasted by being shut up alone with only old Maggie to talk to. I am fond of the creature, but her conversation is limited. As I have told the Doctor often enough, hell for me will be a place where I have no one to talk to. Now tell me what you have been doing."

"I have been exploring the Castle," Nerina answered, "and hoping that you would soon get well enough for me to see you. I too wanted someone to talk to."

The Dowager smiled.

"That's a nice way to talk when you are on your honeymoon. What is Rupert thinking of?" she enquired. "But there, the boy never has had much to say except when he is on his feet in the House. They tell me he can be eloquent enough there."

The Dowager set down her glass of champagne on the table beside her and then said reflectively:

"But I gather that your honeymoon is by no means a usual one. Rupert has given me a brief account of what occurred. You are a brave young woman to marry a man in such circumstances."

There was no disparagement in the Dowager's tone and Nerina smiled.

"Did Sir Rupert explain that there was no alternative?" she asked. "If I had not married him, it would have been impossible for my cousin Elizabeth to marry the man she loved."

"I was never a one to appreciate sacrificing oneself for the love of another. What do you get out of it?"

There was something in her dry shrewdness which made Nerina answer frankly:

"Security!"

"What was the alternative?" The Dowager enquired.

"A governess at a salary of ten pounds a year," Nerina said. "I have already been dismissed from three places."

The Dowager looked at her speculatively and said briefly, as she had asked the other questions:

"For what reason?" Then before Nerina could reply she added: "But you need not tell me! I know the answer. It is to be found in that red hair of yours. You are a pretty child, there is no denying that, and having married my grandson in such a cavalier fashion, what now?"

"I do not know," Nerina replied honestly. "I would like to entertain for him, I would like to be a great political hostess. It seemed easy when I thought about it, but now that I have been here and seen this house I am afraid. I doubt if I have the ability."

"A great political hostess!" the Dowager repeated, and then in quite another tone, she said: "There is something I have to tell you. Rupert should have told you himself for he had always promised me that he would tell his wife the truth lest she should learn it from some other source; but now that the moment has come he cannot bring himself to speak of it, and so I have told him that I will tell you his secret because I consider it right that you should know."

The Dowager paused and looked Nerina straight in the eye. There was something intimidating in her gaze.

"My grandson is illegitimate," she said, and her voice was harsh.

Nerina had anticipated many things but not this.

"But how?" she enquired. "Why?" Then she added impulsively: "Oh, please tell me everything!"

"That is what I intend to do," the Dowager said. "Are you shocked?"

Nerina smiled at her.

"Not in the slightest," she replied, "only very surprised. It is not in the least what I expected."

"Good gal," the Dowager approved. "I like you! I had expected someone very different when Rupert told me he was to be married to Cardon's daughter. I remember him, a tiresome conceited creature without an ounce of humour in him, and his wife a dead bore. I decided not to know them when I came to live here and I had little hope that their daughter would prove better than themselves. But that is now of no consequence. I must tell you first about Rupert and after that you shall tell me about yourself. Is that agreed?"

"Of course," Nerina replied.

173

"Very well then," the Dowager replied. "My husband was the first Marquis of Droxburgh. We had two sons, the eldest was George, the second Frederick. When my husband died, George of course inherited the title, but he chose to live here at Wroth. It was not the family seat, it had belonged to a distant cousin who borrowed a great deal of money from my father, and being unable to repay it left Wroth to me. We only came here occasionally when the boys were children, but George liked it as much as he disliked the family house in Northamptonshire.

"He was a quiet, strange boy with a love of animals which entirely surpassed his affection for human beings. He was engaged when he was quite young to the daughter of Lord Clangarron. She died from an infection of the lungs and he refused to contemplate marrying anyone else. He came up here to Wroth and spent his time laying out the gardens and grounds and keeping a menagerie of strange animals. He wandered about in old clothes and I used to hear stories of visitors mistaking him for a gamekeeper or gardener and tipping him after enquiring their way.

"I only came here once during George's lifetime because I was either in London or in Italy where I lived for some years. Then quite unexpectedly I heard that George was dead. I could not immediately get in touch with my second son, Frederick, who was in Ireland and so I myself came to Wroth to make arrangements about the funeral. I learned on my arrival that George had been killed when out riding. His horse had fallen into a quarry at the far end of the estate. The poor animal was dreadfully injured and had to be shot. George had broken his back and was already dead when they found him.

"I was shocked and distressed as you can imagine, but all the time I was being told what happened, I felt there was something else behind it, something which was being kept from me. The manner of the servants, the way they spoke, the way they could not meet my eyes made me certain that while I was being told part of the truth there was more to it than that, something was being concealed.

"I had not long to wait before I had a clue to what was being hidden. The family lawyer came to the Castle and I knew at once by his manner that something unusual was afoot. He told me that the very day of George's death he had received by hand a letter from him saying that he enclosed a new Will, that he had written it out in his own

174

hand, had it witnessed by two of the servants at the Castle, and that the Doctor would swear that he was in his right mind.

"I read the Will, which was written on a half sheet of paper, and I rang for the housekeeper. When she came, I insisted on her telling me the truth. She told me then what they had been afraid to tell me before. George, it appeared, had been living with a young woman, the daughter of a local farmer. She had come to the Castle about a year previously. She had apparently been very happy there, but she had given no orders and the servants were not required to look on her as their mistress.

"It was when they realised that she was to have a child that they wondered if anything would be changed; but everything went on in exactly the same way. She and George were overwhelmingly in love, it appeared. They were together day and night; but when he attended to affairs of the estate or received his friends, she kept to her apartments and was never seen by anyone. Finally the child was born, but although both the local doctor and the midwife were in attendance they were unable to save her life. She died, although the child was born alive.

"When George realised that she was dead, the housekeeper said, he was like a man demented. The woman he had loved so dearly was buried quietly in the private burial ground which adjoins the Castle. When that was done, George went into his Study and made out a new Will. He called the housekeeper and the butler in to witness it. He asked the Doctor over to certify that he was in his right mind; then he sent to the stables for his favourite horse. He never looked at the child, never asked to see it, and they were frightened to bring it downstairs lest the sight of it should increase his grief.

"He rode away from the front door and they never saw him alive again. It is difficult to believe it was an accident, for George knew of the existence of the quarry as everyone else on the estate did. When I had heard the housekeeper's story, I sent for the child. It was a boy, lusty and crying loudly for its foster mother who, with difficulty, had been procured from the village.

"My first impulse was, I admit, to send the child away and after making arrangements for it to be looked after to forget its very existence. Then as I looked at the baby, not meaning to give it more than a cursory glance, for I had never been very fond of children, I took it in my arms. As

I did so, the boy stopped crying and opened his eyes and in that second he reminded me clearly and unmistakably of my husband—not of my son, for as a baby I had found him almost as much a bore as when he was a grown man. No, the baby reminded me of my husband when I was first married.

"Unlike most of my contemporaries I married for love. I loved many men in my life and many men loved me, but I shall never forget the tenderness of my husband towards me on our honeymoon and the happiness I experienced during that brief golden period. I was only sixteen. Afterwards we quarrelled continually because I was headstrong and impetuous and liked all the things he most disliked. But on our honeymoon we were happy together, and somehow that small baby son of George's brought a flood of memories back to me, memories of a time when I was little more than a child myself and could suffer with all a child's intensity. Although it seemed a crazy, illogical thing to do, I made up my mind to look after George's boy myself and bring him up as if he were legally my grandson. I had made known my decision, I had made arrangements to leave the Castle when my son Frederick arrived. As George had never been married, he was, of course, the new Marquis of Droxburgh."

Nerina started.

"That is the present Marquis?" she asked.

The Dowager nodded, and then seeing the expression on Nerina's face, she asked:

"You know him?"

"My last position of governess was in his house," Nerina said.

The Dowager digested the information, then she said:

"That explains your horror when my grandson introduced us. Do not be afraid to tell me the truth as regards Frederick. I know all about him. I have heard too many stories not to know that he is a bad man. I know it and I am ashamed that any son of mine could behave in such a manner."

Nerina said nothing and after a moment the Dowager went on:

"To finish my story. Frederick arrived here and when he heard what I contemplated, he flew into a rage. There was, in fact, good reason for his temper, for George's Will had been very brief. He had written simply that he left everything he possessed to his son. Certain things were, of course, entailed to go with the title—the house in Northamptonshire, the family pictures and silver, a certain amount of money from our property in London; but the bulk of George's fortune was his own to dispose of as he wished.

"My husband had left him his wealth unconditionally, knowing that George was a sane and sensible young man who would never dissipate it away in riotous living. Frederick's anger was understandable, but knowing what his life was like even in those days I was not very sympathetic towards him. Only when he threatened to murder the child with his own hands did I tell him to behave himself.

"I shut up the Castle and took Rupert, as I had decided to call the baby, to London with me. I told the world that my nephew, who had lived for many years in China, had died and that I had adopted his son. It was a story as good as any other and after a time people forgot to question me. I went to the lawyers and I arranged legally that the baby's name should be Wroth—Rupert Wroth. By the time he was old enough to go to Eton everyone who had ever questioned the story had forgotten all about it, except one person, of course, and that was my son Frederick.

"I knew that he loathed Rupert with a deadly hatred and would do anything in his power to harm him. He watched his time, he waited until Rupert was fifteen, a charming, sensitive boy who loved me and I loved him. He meant by that time so much in my life that I had long ceased to think of him in any way save as flesh of my flesh, blood of my blood.

"I had always meant to tell Rupert the truth, but somehow the years slipped by and the opportunity did not present itself. The whole thing seemed needless and unnecessary in view of the close relationship between us and of Rupert's success wherever he went both socially and at school. He had a happy nature, was charming, good-mannered and exceedingly good-looking. What more could any boy want, what more could anyone ask for him? And then Frederick struck!

"He called at my house in London one day when I was out. Rupert was there alone. He told him most brutally and frankly and in the most horrible way who he was and where he came from. I came back to find not a broken, miserable child, but a stranger. The blow had struck at Rupert's very manhood; he was shamed, embittered and disgusted. In a few minutes Frederick had destroyed the

177

child I loved as completely as if he had murdered him, as once he had threatened to do so.

"Perhaps Rupert was unduly sensitive; perhaps, if you take away a boy's sense of security and wound his innermost decency, you destroy something that can never be replaced. Rupert and I seldom discussed the matter, but when he was much older he promised that he would tell his wife the truth before he married her. I wanted him to do this, knowing that if Frederick got the chance he would try to destroy Rupert's marriage even as he destroyed the happiness of his childhood.

"Rupert promised me he would do this, and yet I knew when he told me he was going to marry Elizabeth Cardon that there was no happiness to be destroyed in a marriage in which his heart was not involved. I talk of his heart, but I often wonder to myself if he has got one. It seems at times as if Frederick took it away from him that day in London when I came back to my house to find a sullen, resentful youth in the place of my smiling, affectionate boy.

"Perhaps I am to blame, perhaps the fault is mine; but whose ever it may be, it is now too late for Rupert to change. I believe that deep within him there is a bitter resentment against fate, against life which has given him so much with one hand and taken away his pride with the other. Since that afternoon long ago he has seemed against everything and everybody. When he smiles, his lips are twisted cynically; when he laughs, it is with a note of bitterness in it. His whole nature is warped, as if the very sun itself was less golden because of what he knows about himself."

"And yet you have done so much for him," Nerina said. "Surely he is grateful to you, surely he realises that without you things would have been much more difficult, almost impossible?"

"Yes, I think he realises that," the Dowager said reflectively, "but I can understand a little of what he feels. He is acting a part, pretending to a world which accepts him for the moment at his face value. I've often wondered—as he must—how long his political career will be allowed to continue."

"Allowed!" Nerina ejaculated.

"Yes, allowed," the Dowager repeated. "Frederick is waiting, I am sure of that, waiting for the moment when he shall strike and destroy all that Rupert has built up. And

Rupert knows it too. That is why, though he never speaks of it, I know that he does everything defiantly. It is as if he says to himself, 'one more step before I am flung down, before my pride is humbled to the dust; one step higher, and then disaster will come'. He knows it is only a question of time, you see. It is my belief that Frederick will wait until he is Foreign Secretary and then he will strike."

"But it is intolerable," Nerina cried. "How could anyone be so bestial . . . ?"

Then the words seemed to die on her lips for she knew that nothing would stop the Marquis from getting his own way. He had no decency, no code of honour. He was a man utterly without chivalry. Yes, he would strike at Sir Rupert as he had tried to strike at her. The feelings of his victims were not of the slightest consequence. There was only one thing which counted, one thing which mattered—his own desires, his own need either in lust or revenge.

Nerina put her fingers up to her eyes. She could see almost as if he stood there before her the Marquis's satisfaction if he succeeded, the way he would lick his thin dry lips, the sudden light in his dissipated eyes. She knew that Sir Rupert's political and social fall would give him as much satisfaction as if he had ravaged and despoiled a lovely woman. She felt suddenly nauseated at the very thought of it, and she looked up to see the Dowager's eyes fixed upon her, eyes which seemed to bore right into her very heart and mind.

"That is the secret I had to tell you," the Marchioness said quietly. "Perhaps, child, it will help you to understand your husband."

"My husband!" Nerina repeated almost in a whisper.

It seemed to her as if the words had never been real before.

12

Nerina dressed slowly and in silence. In fact she was so quiet that Bessie, as she moved about the bedroom, looked at her curiously as if she wondered what was amiss. Nerina was thinking deeply.

The Dowager Marchioness's story had made a deep impression on her. For the first time she was considering Sir Rupert not as a monster but as an ordinary man with ordinary human feelings. Somehow it had always been impossible to believe that he felt anything except anger. That first impression she had of him when he came to Rowanfield Manor on the day of the Garden Party had remained an unaltered portrait in her mind so that always she saw that smouldering anger on his face, the burning hatred in his eyes.

Yet now she found herself thinking of him in a very different fashion. The Dowager Marchioness's description of him when he was young had somehow a compelling and inescapable charm; and vividly, almost too vividly for her own peace of mind, Nerina could see the change which had taken place after the Marquis of Droxburgh had done his dastardly worst.

Nerina could imagine so clearly what a shock the revelation of his birth must have been to Sir Rupert. She was well aware how vulnerable, how easily hurt and how desperately sensitive one is at that age. She could recall her own agony of mind when she had first encountered brutality and hatred under her uncle's roof. She could remember her feelings when she learned that as a penniless orphan she was accorded a very different position from that she had held as the beloved only child of two adoring parents. Her own experience must in some way be comparable with what Sir Rupert had felt when his uncle told him who he was and that not even the name he bore was his own.

Nerina could visualise the darkness and the sense of isolation which must have encompassed Sir Rupert then. He would have been sleepless during the long nights; he would have been too proud to cry. He would have bitten his lips to prevent the tears flowing from his eyes. But he would have been unable to prevent the feeling of utter misery which pervaded his whole body, a feeling not only of distress but of impotency against the cruelty of fate. There had been nothing he could do but suffer; and how well Nerina knew that ghastly feeling of being helpless, of being unable to strike back at an enemy which crushed one slowly and relentlessly!

How terribly Sir Rupert must have suffered! And now for the first time Nerina could understand his air of defiance, the impression he gave of being on the defensive, ready without any excuse to be aggressive to those he encountered. It was understandable; and as Nerina thought of Lord Droxburgh waiting in the background, a dark threatening figure ready to pounce when the fancy took him, she shivered as if he menaced not only the man she had married but herself.

For a long time she sat staring unseeingly into the mirror until Bessie became half alarmed.

"You aren't feeling ill, m'lady?" she enquired, and Nerina with a start brought her thoughts back to the present.

"No, of course not, Bessie," she replied. "Do I look ill?"

"No, not ill," Bessie replied, "but strange, as if something were troubling you."

Nerina got to her feet and walked restlessly across the room.

"I am not exactly troubled, Bessie," she said. "I was just wondering if I had done the right thing in coming here."

Bessie stared at her in astonishment.

"Good gracious, m'lady, it's a bit late in the day to ask yourself that. Why, we've discussed it so often, and you were so sure, so very sure—"

"Yes, yes, I know, Bessie," Nerina said quickly. "I was just wondering, that was all."

She turned wearily and as she did so she caught sight of herself in the long gilt-framed mirror which hung between the two windows. She had been thinking of herself as she had been at Rowanfield Manor, a bullied, unwanted poor relation, and now as she saw her own reflection it took her a second to realise that she was thinking of a very different person from the self she saw reflected.

The unhappy, defiant girl whose sufferings she had been comparing with the young Sir Rupert seemed to have very little in common with the radiant figure she saw in the mirror.

Bessie had chosen the gown she was wearing tonight and Nerina, pre-occupied with her thoughts, had put it on without question; but now she saw that it was one of the loveliest gowns and much the most expensive of those she had bought in Bond Street. Of soft grey tulle, it was the colour of the morning mists over the sea. It was sprinkled with diamanté which glittered all over it like tear-drops. There were silver ribbons at the waist, and silver leaves sprinkled with diamonds made a wreath for Nerina's tiny head.

She looked as if she had stepped out of an illustration to a fairy story. She might have been an ice princess or a queen of the mists, for against the soft elusive fragility of the gown her skin was as white as alabaster and her eyes strikingly green. And yet as she looked at the loveliness of herself Nerina turned away from the mirror hastily and the expression in her eyes was one of worry.

"This . . . this dress, Bessie," she said. "If I remember rightly, it was very expensive?"

"It was indeed, m'lady," Bessie replied, but there was satisfaction in her tone. "And if you remember, there is a wrap to go with it, a pelisse of grey velvet lined with ermine."

"Yes, I remember," Nerina said in a low voice.

"Now don't you start a-worrying yourself," Bessie said sharply. "There's enough trouble in the world as it is."

There was something in her tone which made Nerina ask:

"Why do you say that, Bessie?"

Bessie sighed and looked near to tears.

"It's my soft heart, m'lady, that's what it is," she replied. "But the housekeeper's nephew has come over from Willow Hill and what he has been telling us makes me ready to cry my eyes out."

"Willow Hill!" Nerina said reflectively. "Isn't that the dreadful mining village we passed on our way here from the station?"

"That's right, m'lady, and dreadful's the right word to describe it. Sir Rupert can't know, m'lady, or he wouldn't let such things be—a decent gentleman like him."

"What is wrong?" Nerina enquired.

"Everything, m'lady; the mine's unsafe for one thing and not a penny piece is spent on it. The men takes their lives in their hands every time they goes below ground. Ten lives lost last month and twice that number injured, and not a penny of compensation. It's a real shame, m'lady, and who shall blame them for striking?"

"Are they on strike now?" Nerina asked.

"Indeed they are. A man was killed three days ago—it must have been just after we arrived—and his mate had his foot crushed to pulp. The men swear they won't go back until something is done; but, as the housekeeper's nephew says, it's hunger as defeats them."

"Hunger and bitterness," Nerina whispered. "Hunger and bitterness." She hesitated for several seconds, then she added quietly: "I'll do what I can, Bessie, but I must choose the right moment, the right approach "

She picked up a handkerchief from the dressing-table and walked towards the door. Bessie stared after her with a worried expression on her face. There was something wrong with her mistress tonight and she could not understand what it was.

Nerina went downstairs to the Drawing-room. Sir Rupert was there waiting for her. He was standing with his back to the fireplace, a glass of wine in his hand, and the moment she entered the room Nerina sensed there was something strange about him. He was scowling and as she moved gracefully down the room he did not look at her, but stared contemplatingly into his glass of wine as if he concentrated on it to the exclusion of all else.

Nerina reached his side and then, just as she would have spoken, although she had no idea what she was about to say, the butler announced that dinner was served. Sir Rupert tossed down the remainder of his glass of wine and with a gesture which was in itself somehow the action of an inner recklessness he offered Nerina his arm, still without looking at her.

It was as she took it that an explanation flashed to her mind. Quite suddenly she understood what he was feeling and she felt so relieved that she could have laughed out loud. Sir Rupert was embarrassed and apprehensive as to what might be her reaction to the story she had heard from his Grandmother. She had not expected him to care one way or another; and now that she knew that he did mind, she felt as if her entire conception of him was altered in the flash of a second.

Here was no monster, no overpoweringly arrogant man, thinking only of himself and of his own pleasures; but a man who could feel and suffer as other people felt and suffered, a man who at this moment was, although he would never confess it, shy because a young woman had learned the truth about him.

It was as if what she sensed released some hidden spring within herself and let a foundation of gaiety gush forth. As they reached the Dining-room, Nerina took her seat at the head of the table where she had sat through so many dreary meals since she had arrived at Wroth Castle; but this time she began to talk easily and amusingly as she might have conversed with Elizabeth. Always before, Nerina had found it impossible to make conversation with Sir Rupert. She had been dismally conscious that the whole thing was a farce, a piece of play-acting which they must both concede to convention because the servants were in the room. Frantically, because the silences between them had been ominous and nerve-racking, Nerina had searched her brain for one subject after another, talking unnaturally and even at times a little hysterically because the grandeur of the room and her dislike of Sir Rupert had made her feel almost light-headed.

But now she felt neither of these things. For the first time in Sir Rupert's presence she felt at ease and in some subtle way mistress of the situation. Until tonight he had been her enemy, an enemy whom she must fight every inch of the way. Yet now she knew that there was a truce between them, a truce she had declared in her heart from the moment she had left the Dowager's bedroom to walk slowly and a little dazedly to her own.

Because she now felt she was released from some spell which had bound her, she could talk without reservation. If Sir Rupert was surprised at her chatter, he at least responded to it. Nerina realised that he seldom looked directly at her, but he kept the conversation flowing and occasionally laughed at something she said. He ate very little and it struck her more than once that he was drinking a great deal. Again and again the servants filled his glass with the varied wines which were served with every course.

As they talked, Nerina had a sudden vision of herself in her sparkling dress sitting at the end of the long table in the high-backed oak chair. She thought of the many meals she had eaten in the dismal schoolrooms of other people's houses, meals brought up on a tray, usually cold and generally unappetising, meals which were prepared by a kitchen maid who thought anything was good enough for the governess. What a difference this was, the difference between misery and contentment!

When dinner was over, Nerina walked back to the Drawing-room. The fire had been lit, for it had been raining during the afternoon and it had turned chilly. Alone in the room, she sank down on the hearthrug holding out her hands to the leaping flames. The firelight glittered on the wedding ring she wore on her left hand. She was staring at it, wondering that that plain circle of gold could mean so much and yet so little, when a voice behind her said:

"Are you cold?"

She started violently. She had not heard Sir Rupert enter the room. She had not expected him to leave the Dining-room for a long time. Slowly she got to her feet. Her lips opened to make some light and trivial reply to his question, then his eyes met hers and the words died on her lips. They stared at each other, and she was conscious of some tremendous force within him, held in check and under control but only by an extreme effort of will.

The clock on the mantelpiece ticked the seconds away, and still they stared at each other; then at length in a voice harsh and raw with suffering Sir Rupert said:

"Well?"

Nerina knew it was a question. With an effort she turned her eyes away from his to stand with one hand on the mantelpiece looking down into the flames.

"I am sorry," she said in a low voice.

"For me?" Sir Rupert enquired, then added violently: "I don't want your pity."

"I am not pitying you," Nerina said quietly. "Why indeed should I do so? You have so much to be grateful for! No, I am sorry that you should have suffered at the hands of Lord Droxburgh even as I have suffered."

"You?" Sir Rupert questioned.

"Yes, I," Nerina said. "But there is no need to speak of it just now; we were talking of you."

Sir Rupert made a gesture she did not understand, then he said almost in his old aggressive tone:

"I would not have told you, had the choice been mine; but my Grandmother made me promise years ago that I would tell my wife the truth. I agreed, but I made the reservation to myself that I would tell the woman of my choice before the Ceremony and not afterwards. If she wished to leave me, she would then be free to do so."

"And yet you did not tell Elizabeth," Nerina said.

Sir Rupert hesitated.

"My conversations with your cousin were not of a very intimate nature," he said.

"And supposing, after you had married her, she had been shocked and horrified and wished to leave you?" Nerina enquired.

"In that case there would have been nothing I could have done about it," Sir Rupert said. "Are you shocked and horrified?"

"Would I have any right to be?" Nerina enquired. "Whatever horrors were revealed now, I would have no right to criticise them, no right to protest."

"You have not answered my question," Sir Rupert persisted. "Are you shocked and horrified?"

Nerina looked up at him. She was thinking of the boy who had been awake in the darkness of the night afraid to cry.

"Of course not," she said softly. "Why should it matter?"

He stared at her and she saw that his expression was one of astonishment.

"Do you mean that?" he said at length, and his voice was strangely moved.

"But of course!" Her tone was as serious as his. "We can none of us be responsible for the accident of our birth. Where you are concerned there is nothing to be ashamed of. You are your father's son. He was proud of you or he would not have left you everything he possessed."

Sir Rupert turned his head away as if he could not look into her eyes.

"Do you know what you are saying?" he questioned. "For years I have thought of this moment when my wife would have to be told, when I would be in a position to watch the expression on her face and see the contempt and disgust in her eyes. I have thought about it, dreamed about it, and now you . . you say it does not matter."

"But why should it?" Nerina asked. "You are still you! You are still Sir Rupert Wroth of Wroth Castle. You are still the man you have made yourself, a personality and a character that has been built up by all you have done and thought and been since you were a baby. Can it be of any consequence except socially and from a worldly point of view that your mother did not wear a wedding ring upon her finger? Oh, I know exactly what some people would think, I have heard women whispering in shocked tones about such things; but suppose I was suddenly told that my father and mother had never been married in the Church, would it at this moment make me any different? I should still be myself, I should still be the same person with the same feelings, the same emotions, the same desires as I had before I learned the secrets of my birth."

"That is not true!" Sir Rupert said. "You would not be the same, you would feel different! You would know yourself an outcast, you would know that if the facts were known by those who respected and honoured you, their whole attitude would be changed. Their respect would vanish and become contempt, and their affection, if they had any for you, would be altered in the passing of a second to at the best a charitable tolerance. You would find yourself an outcast whom people might pity, but whom, if they were given the choice, they would want only to ignore or forget. Do you suppose I am so stupid that I don't know that? Do you suppose I don't know that if the world learned what you have learned tonight my political career would be at an end? Socially I don't care. Knowing what I have known about myself for years, I have avoided Society as much as possible, well aware that while they fawned upon me today, tomorrow they would just as easily kick me into the gutter. It is my work that I mind, the work that I am doing for England—if that goes, all else will be lost."

"And yet you will still be yourself," Nerina said quietly. "You will still be you. Whatever happens to your position and your possessions, you are still there, the real you."

He turned then and looked at her, staring down into her small oval face, her eyes wide and serious with the effort of trying to convince him. After a moment he said:

"Are you trying to comfort me?"

"Certainly not!" Nerina's reply was almost indignant. "Why should I try to comfort you? If you need comfort, then I despise you, not for anything I have heard about you or for anything to do with your origin, but for being a weakling. Why should you need comfort? Look what you have still of your own—health, strength, good looks, wealth and great political achievements even if they must end tomorrow. Why should anyone be sorry for you, why should they want to comfort you? And besides, you have only one enemy, one person who can destroy you when it suits his evil mind; surely you can find a way to destroy him first and if not to destroy him, at least to keep him silent?"

Nerina spoke vehemently. Sir Rupert gave a little laugh.

"If I had your courage," he said, "I should doubtless conquer the whole world."

"And why not?" Nerina asked. "You have already achieved a great deal. Why not achieve much more and rid yourself of the man who hates you and who will in his own time destroy all that you value?"

"Are you suggesting that I murder my uncle?" Sir Rupert asked.

Nerina shrugged her shoulders.

"He must be silenced one way or another."

Sir Rupert smiled.

"You are a very ruthless person," he said. "If I am afraid of anyone, I think it ought to be you."

Nerina smiled back at him.

"I hoped you were already afraid of me," she said lightly. "It appears to me there are quite a large number of people in your life who are ready to blackmail you one way or another."

She moved as she spoke and the light from the candelabra glittered on her hair. It was warm by the fire and she walked across the room to a table which held a valuable collection of snuff-boxes. She picked one up, turned it over in her fingers not really intent upon it, but aware within herself of some restlessness and a need for movement. She was conscious that Sir Rupert was watching her and as she replaced the snuff-box, he said:

"Why has my uncle, the Marquis of Droxburgh, made you suffer?"

She looked up at him, and then as quickly as she had done so she looked away again.

"I have no wish to speak of it," she said. "It is over and done with, and there is no reason to recall now what happened. Sufficient to say that the Marquis of Droxburgh is loathsome, a devil in human form. I hate and despise him beyond words."

Nerina spoke vehemently, then to her astonishment Sir Rupert strode across the room to her side. Looking down at her he demanded:

"What has he done to you? Tell me!"

Nerina would have moved away from him, but she found that she was against the corner of the sofa and unable to escape. Something in Sir Rupert's peremptory tone reminded her of her uncle, and because of it she replied:

"I have told you, I do not wish to speak of Lord Droxburgh."

"I demand that you tell me the truth," Sir Rupert said.

Nerina raised her eyebrows.

"Demand!" she said. "Have you the right to demand anything of me?"

"Yes, I have," Sir Rupert retorted, and now he reached out with both his hands towards Nerina, holding her imprisoned as he said: "I command you to tell me the truth. I am your husband, I have a right to know what has occurred."

Nerina was conscious of his strength, conscious too that she was completely helpless in his hold. Then suddenly she was angry with a fierce burning anger which seemed to consume her whole body. How dare he command her! What right had he to lay a finger upon her?

"Let me go!" she cried. "How dare you try to bully me into doing what you wish? Let me go! I will tell you nothing, I promise you that."

She struggled as she spoke, trying with her hands to push him away from her and failing completely. He was stronger than she had imagined possible. He increased his hold upon her until his hands were digging deep into the soft flesh of her arms. He hurt her and yet she was too angry to realise it. His anger was as fierce as hers, his eyes were dark and smouldering with fury and when he spoke again it was through his clenched teeth.

"You shall tell me!" he said. "I know enough of the Marquis's ways with women to know that few can encounter him and remain unscathed. Has he seduced you? Answer me!"

He shook Nerina as he spoke; and as if this was the last insult to drive her to desperation, she suddenly and with an unexpected agility tore herself free of him and ran to the other side of the sofa to stand there quivering, her breasts moving tumultuously under the soft covering of grey tulle, her breath coming quickly between her parted lips, her eyes alight with anger, her hair a flaming torch of rebellion.

"How dare you question me?" she stormed. "I hate you! You are like all other men, a bully and a brute."

She turned as she finished speaking and ran from the room. The door slammed behind her and, lifting her voluminous skirts, she ran across the Hall and started up the wide staircase. She heard the Drawing-room door open, but she did not look back. She went on up the stairs, crossed the landing, and entered her own bedroom.

The fire was burning brightly but only the candles on

189

the dressing-table were lit. Much of the vast room was in darkness, a shadowy, secretive darkness which flickered and changed as the flames in the fireplace leapt or died away.

Nerina stood in the centre of the room panting. She had run quickly upstairs, but it was not only the exertion of the climb which made her breathless. Her anger still made her eyes flash and her nostrils quiver.

"How dare he bully me, how dare he?" she said aloud, then even as she said the words she saw the door open.

She watched it in fascinated horror, unable to move, unable for the moment even to collect her senses as Sir Rupert came into the bedroom and closed the door behind him.

Nerina stood very still. Slowly he advanced from the shadows into the circle of fire and candlelight. There was something menacing about him as he drew nearer. For the moment he seemed immeasurably taller and bigger, and for one split second she thought of herself as a helpless child. Then defiance flooded back into her again. Her chin went up a little higher and her fingers slowly clenched themselves as he reached her side.

"What do you want in here?" she asked.

"You!"

The monosyllable took her by surprise. For the moment she could only stare at him; stare at his dark eyes behind which she glimpsed a leaping flame; stare at the straight, almost brutal line of his lips, at the square determination of his jaw. The word he had spoken seemed to echo round the room and Nerina felt as if it repeated itself over and over again within her own body.

"What do you mean?"

Her voice was hardly above a whisper.

"What I said," he replied. "I want you. You trick me into marrying you and now you are trying to torture me. You have taunted me with the Marquis's name, but I have stood enough. You are my wife, and I demand my rights as your husband."

"Get out of here!"

Nerina's voice was low and vibrant with fury.

"How dare you come into my room and speak to me like this? Do you not understand that I hate and loathe you? I married you to save my cousin and to teach you a lesson. But if you think that because of that you are entitled to insult me, you think wrong. Leave me alone! Go back to

190

your other women, to Lady Clementine, to the other idiots who think you love them."

It was then Sir Rupert laughed, and the sound of it was more frightening to Nerina than if he had sworn at her.

"You are a little hell-cat, my dear," he said, "but you cannot frighten me away like that. You can spit and scratch all you please, but you married me and you must take the consequences. Besides, if there have been other men in your life like the Marquis, why not me?"

"If you so much as lay a finger on me, I will ruin you, I swear it," Nerina cried. "I will go to the Queen, I will expose you. I will tell her exactly who you are and what you are. I will tell her, too, about Lady Clementine and how you tried to marry a poor defenceless girl and use her as a camouflage for your illicit love affairs."

"And you can tell her also that you are my wife and that you belong to me both in name and in body," Sir Rupert replied.

As he spoke he put his arms round Nerina and drew her close to him.

"Do you really hate me as much as you hate the Marquis?" he said softly; and before she could move, his lips were on hers.

She struggled and fought, but his mouth clung to hers possessively. She felt as if his kiss sapped her very strength from her. His lips were warm, hard and brutal, and yet she could not force him away from her, could not prevent that kiss from going on, it seemed to her interminably, until she was almost fainting in his arms. When at length he released her, she could not for a moment speak, but could only look up at him gasping for breath and know in that moment a fear such as she had never known before.

It seemed to her that his face was almost unrecognisable, the face of a man possessed, a man whose passion had swept away the last control of his mind. Only one glimpse she had of him and then he was raining kisses on her face. She felt his lips on her eyes, her cheeks, her hair. Once again her mouth quivered beneath his and then she felt his kisses on her neck while his hands sought the softness of her breasts.

It was then that the weakness which had seemed to hold her utterly his prisoner for a few moments was swept away by a terror which regained for her the strength she had lost. She fought him wildly, heard her dress tear beneath his hands, and for a moment neither of them was capable of speech as they struggled one against the other, the firelight flickering on their distorted faces.

Again there was the sound of rending tulle, and then suddenly Sir Rupert swept Nerina boldly into his arms. Her breasts and shoulders were naked in the firelight as he carried her towards the great four-poster bed; and then as she struggled helplessly against him and he walked exultantly towards his goal, she reached out and caught hold of a heavy silver candlestick standing unlit on the bedside table.

Her fingers curled tightly round it, and using all her strength she brought it down violently. At the last second Sir Rupert saw the blow coming and turned his head aside so that instead of hitting him on the temple as Nerina intended the base of the candlestick caught his cheek, cutting the skin open, leaving a wide gash from which the blood instantly began to pour.

As Sir Rupert turned away from her blow, Nerina struggled from his arms. She half lay, half stood against the side of the bed, the candlestick in one hand, the other raising itself instinctively to hide her nakedness with the tattered and torn pieces of tulle which had once been the bodice of her gown.

Sir Rupert put his fingers to the gash on his cheek. As he drew them away wet with blood, he stared first at them and then at Nerina. She faced him defiantly, the candlestick half raised ready to strike again. His eyes flickered over her and seemed to take in every detail of her white face, loosened hair, and torn and dishevelled appearance; then it seemed to her that his expression became that of a devil. The blood oozing from the gash in his cheek and running down to his chin seemed to swim in a crimson flood before her eyes. She saw him take a step towards her and knew she was defeated. A darkness more terrifying than anything she had ever known encompassed her and she felt herself fall. . . .

13

Nerina opened her eyes, found she was lying on the floor, and for a moment wondered where she was and what had happened. Dizzily she sat up, staring into the darkened shadows of the room. She was alone! Beside her on the floor was a silver candlestick. For a moment she stared at it and saw again the blood dripping from Sir Rupert's cut cheek.

Unsteadily she rose to her feet, widening as she did so a jagged tear in the fullness of her skirts. Holding on to the bedpost for support, she looked down at the tattered remnants of what had once been a lovely and expensive dress. Then, as the full meaning of what had occurred swept over her in a flood-tide of terror, she ran across the room to the door. Like someone possessed she turned the key in the lock; and as she heard it click home, she gave a deep sigh of relief which seemed to come from the very depths of her being. For the moment she was safe, but for how long?

Wildly she looked around as if she would find a way of escape in the vastness of the great shadowy room; then with a sound that was suspiciously like a sob she crossed the room to the dressing-table. She stared at her face in the mirror for one second and hardly recognised herself. Her eyes were dark, her face very white, but her lips were crimson, and she knew them to be bruised and bleeding from the violence of Sir Rupert's kisses.

Feverishly with fingers that trembled Nerina undid her dress and it slid from her waist to the floor. She trampled on it as she hurried to the wardrobe and flung wide the heavy doors of carved wood. In the candlelight she could see the row of colourful gowns hanging there invitingly. At the movement of the doors the flounces, frills and ribbons fluttered a little as if they were alive. But Nerina pushed them all to one side and found what she sought.

In the far corner of the wardrobe was a gown of black crêpe. It was a dress which had originally belonged to Elizabeth when she had been in mourning for her Grandmother. It had been passed on to her cousin because Lady Cardon thought it suitable in its unpretentiousness for Nerina in her position as a governess.

Bessie had thrust it into the trunk with the other old clothes which had been packed to take the place of

Elizabeth's trousseau. It had remained there, and when Bessie unpacked at the Castle the beautiful gowns Nerina had bought in Bond Street, she had laughed when at the bottom of them all she came on the old black crêpe dress.

"You certainly won't be needing this dismal garment again, m'lady?" she smiled, and Nerina had noticed how out of place it looked against the magnificence of the panelled room with its valuable period furniture.

"Throw it away," she commanded; but as Bessie bundled the gown up roughly and threw it back into the empty trunk, Nerina changed her mind. "No, don't do that," she said. "Hang it in the wardrobe. I might need it."

"Need it, m'lady?" Bessie questioned in astonishment. "With all these lovely gowns! Why, you'll never be needing an old rag like that."

"All the same I want to keep it," Nerina answered stubbornly, and Bessie looked at her in astonishment as slowly, almost reluctantly, she took the black dress out of the trunk, put it on a hanger and hung it in the wardrobe.

Nerina could not explain even to herself why she had wished to keep the gown. Yet somehow it was a symbol of the past, something which she felt should be kept if only to remind her of what had gone, perhaps as a sheet anchor to prevent her from soaring too high or aspiring too greatly. Maybe it was that, or else it was that the black crumpled gown reminded her of what she had been herself—an unwanted orphan, a poor relation.

She knew that fine clothes, elegant dresses could not change her. She was still the same girl who had worn the faded cast-off clothing of her cousin and yet had the courage to dream dreams and to wish for a very different state of life from the one to which it had pleased God to call her.

She had kept the dress, and suddenly she knew that it was fate which had forced that very decision upon her. Now she wanted it and there was something symbolic in knowing that it was hanging there waiting.

She took it down, slipped it over her head, and buttoned it closely round her figure with hurrying, nervous fingers. Fitting snugly to her with the warm familiarity of an old friend, there was something comforting in the very ease with which she could put it on, the way she knew the position of every button, every hook and eye. Without looking in the mirror Nerina took a bonnet from the top shelf of the wardrobe and slipped it on to her head. Then she changed her shoes into black, elastic-sided boots and looked once again in the wardrobe for a manteau. There was nothing there but the elaborate, fur-trimmed velvet pelisses she had bought in Bond Street. Impatiently she turned to the drawer where Bessie had laid her shawls.

There was one of natural-coloured camel-hair which was her own having been a present to her one Christmas. She slipped it round her shoulders, taking from the same drawer her reticule. As she held it in her hand, she wondered for the first time whether she had any money. Then with an expression of relief she remembered that she was at the moment richer than she had ever been in her life before.

On the day of the wedding, just before she was starting for the Church, a footman had knocked on the door and given Bessie a letter addressed to Elizabeth. Nerina had opened it. It was, she found, from Elizabeth's godmother, an elderly lady who lived at Brighton and who was far too old to attend the wedding.

She devoted several pages of spidery writing to explaining that her health did not allow her to leave the house and she was therefore enclosing the money she would otherwise have spent on a present, suggesting that dear Elizabeth should choose herself something for her new home. The money was enclosed neatly in another envelope, and when Nerina opened this she discovered three five-pound notes.

"Heavens, a fortune!" she exclaimed to Bessie. "What shall I do with it?"

Bessie was, as usual, severely practical.

"Take it with you, Miss," she replied. "If you leave it here, his lordship will not be able to send it to her ladyship, not knowing her address, and it will be more use to you than to him."

"When Elizabeth writes to me from India, I will send it to her," Nerina replied, and Bessie had put the notes carefully away in the reticule that Nerina was to carry with her going-away outfit. Now she opened the reticule and was thankful to see that the money was there intact.

Her own purse lay inside but she found it was empty and remembered that she had given the last sixpence of her salary to the cab which had brought her back to Rowan-field. She shut the reticule and put it on her arm. Then she opened the drawer of the dressing-table and found her gloves. As she did so, the candlelight glinted on her wedding ring. She stared down at it, then violently pulled the ring from her finger and flung it down on the dressing-table.

She heard it roll amongst the brushes, handglass and ornaments, and finally clatter into silence. Then quickly, with a feverish haste, Nerina pulled open the drawers in search of a few garments which had been hers before she married. There were not many of them—several nightgowns, various articles of underwear, two or three pairs of stockings and a brush and comb.

She gathered them altogether and looked round for something to put them in. By the fireside was a bag containing her tapestry work which Bessie had brought with them from Rowanfield. Lady Cardon had been an ardent needlewoman and she had taught both Elizabeth and Nerina to work the exquisite squares of tapestry which would cover a chair or a stool.

Seeing now the plain green bag which contained her work, Nerina knew it was just what she was looking for. She tipped the unfinished piece of tapestry, the wools, needles and scissors into the armchair and in their place stuffed in the garments which she had decided to take away with her. Two nightgowns had to be left behind, but otherwise the bag accommodated everything.

Now at last she was ready. She had no idea where she was going or what she was going to do, she only knew that she must escape from this house and get away from Sir Rupert. She could not formulate her feelings, could not quell for even one moment the chaos of her thoughts. She was impelled by a force stronger than herself, stronger than common-sense or caution. She knew one thing and one thing only—that she wanted to get away, that she must escape, that she could not under any circumstances face Sir Rupert again.

This farce of a marriage was finished. It had never been real, only a pretence from the very beginning. But now her reckless action in taking Elizabeth's place had carried her too far. She could attempt no more, she could go on no longer. At the moment she could not even think of what was to happen to her. She was like an animal caught in a trap, she could only try frantically to escape with a concentration which involved the whole of her body, mind and soul.

Picking up her bag and pulling her shawl a little closer round her shoulders, Nerina went to the door. She listened for a long time before finally and with utmost caution she turned the key. When that was done, she still waited, her face tense, her whole body poised as it were on tiptoe and in dread anticipation of what she might find.

But when she opened the door there was only the quietness of a sleeping house. The candles were still lit on the stairs and in the Hall below, but the only sound was the tick of the big grandfather clock. Cautiously on tiptoe Nerina crossed the landing and looked over the banister.

There was nothing to frighten her. Quickly but silently she began to descend the staircase. As she reached the Hall she saw that the front door had been bolted and locked for the night. She was well aware that, should she attempt to undo the chains and bolts, they would make a noise and there was every chance of her being overheard. Instead she opened the door into the Library.

The room was in darkness, but by leaving the door open she was able to grope her way to the big french window. She slipped behind the curtains and it took her but a few seconds to undo the catch. Three or four marble steps led down into the herb garden on the other side of which was a small iron gate leading into the drive.

As Nerina closed the garden gate behind her, she heard the stableyard clock strike one. For a moment its booming tone frightened her; then, as it ceased, she set off quickly, walking not along the drive itself but in the shadows of the great oak trees which bordered it. She crossed the bridge which spanned the lake, knowing as she did so that she was in full sight of the house. She wanted to run and move impetuously, but she forced herself to walk at an ordinary pace, for she realised that if anyone did see her they would not be suspicious unless she behaved in a manner likely to arouse suspicion.

All the same, when she reached the other side of the bridge and could once again take to the shadow of the trees, she ran for a few minutes, and only when she was breathless and panting did she come to a standstill and lean against the trunk of a tree while she regained her breath and looked back at the Castle.

The moon was coming from the clouds which had obscured it earlier in the evening. By its light she could see the massive beauty of Wroth silhouetted against the paler sky, a star glittering precariously over one of the chimney pots. It had a grandeur that was breath-taking. At the same time even in the darkness it had a warmth and a charm which was irresistible. The moonlight on the lake turned it to molten silver, the fountains playing in the rose garden were like diamonds against the darkness of the trees.

With an effort Nerina deliberately turned away and started to walk down the drive. Her heart was still thumping against her side and she wondered if its fluttering were entirely due to the speed with which she had run. For the first time since she had started she asked herself where she was going. But her own brain would not give her an answer, while the nerves of her body cried over and over again that she must escape, she must escape.

She felt as if they excited her to a frenzy against every inclination to be calm. It was no use, she could not stay, she dared not. She must get away from Sir Rupert, whatever else lay before her.

The drive was long. As she walked steadily on, Nerina began to plan at least the first part of her journey. She would go to London. What she would do when she got there she could not think. Vaguely she imagined that she would find work. There must be a place for her in a shop or in employment of some kind which would bring her enough money to keep herself from starvation. Later perhaps her ambitions would return to her. For the moment she had only one plan, and that was to get away from Sir Rupert.

She remembered the route they had taken from the station on their arrival. Two or three miles from the Castle they had come to a cross-roads. Their carriage had pulled up to let the stage-coach pass and as Nerina watched, it began to set down its passengers outside a blacksmith's shop and to take up others. Sir Rupert had seen her interest and said,

"We are by no means isolated here. The stage-coaches from Manchester and Leeds pass three times a day—at dawn, at noon and about six o'clock at night. The coach you see is the evening mail."

"Do many people still make the journey by road?" Nerina asked.

"A large number I am told," Sir Rupert replied, "but the railways are quicker, of course, which means that in time everyone will prefer to go by rail."

Nerina remembered this conversation now. It was quicker to go by rail and therefore she must get to Pendle where she could take the train which would carry her away quicker from Sir Rupert than the stage-coach. But Pendle was another five miles further on and to get there on her feet would take too long. She would therefore pick up the stage-coach, let it carry her to Pendle and from there she would take the first train to London.

It gave her a warm glow of satisfaction to know that she had so much money in her purse. She wondered what would have happened had she been penniless, which was her usual state of finance. Yet even as the question presented itself she knew the answer. She would still have run away, still have left Wroth and the monstrous man who owned it. This was the fourth house, she thought, from which she had run away and always for the same reason. It seemed to her, as she stumbled along in the darkness, that she was fleeing not only from Sir Rupert but also from the Marquis of Droxburgh.

When she left the drive for the narrow lanes she found them rough and stony. The soles of her boots were thin and soon her feet were sore and she tried in the moonlight to pick out a smooth pathway. It seemed to her a terribly long way to the cross-roads. The bag she was carrying grew heavier and heavier; but though she longed to rest, she forced herself to go on walking, wondering more than once, as the road turned and twisted, whether she was going the right way.

At last she saw ahead of her the cross-roads and the sight of her goal spurred her lagging footsteps. She wondered what time it was and how long she had taken since leaving the Castle. As she reached the cross-roads she saw ahead of her that the blacksmith's shop was lit up from the forge within. She crossed the road and looking round the open door saw a very old man with white hair standing at the anvil, a hammer in his hand.

Nerina stepped forward into the firelight.

"Excuse me," she said, "but could you tell me what time the stage-coach will get here?"

The old man looked up in surprise at the sound of her voice, then he put down his hammer and crossed the forge towards her. When he reached her side, he gazed at her searchingly and she saw that he was very old indeed and practically blind.

"Did ye ask I something, Mistress?" he asked in a quavering voice.

"Yes," Nerina replied. "I asked you if you would be kind enough to tell me what time the stage-coach stops here."

"The stage-coach now. Weel, it depends on the time o' year and the condition o' the roads," the old man replied. "If 'tis fine weather, it should be here about half after five o' the clock; but if the roads are wet and muddy, 't will slow 'em down and they may not turn up 'til after six or nigh on seven."

"Do you know what time it is now?" Nerina enquired.

The old man looked out on the night.

"From the position o' the moon," he said, "I reckons as how it's somewhere about four in the mornin'. Ye have a long wait afore ye, Mistress. Come in and sit by the fire. 'T will keep ye warm, and that's a comfort in itself."

"It is indeed," Nerina replied. "I will be glad to wait here if I may."

"Ye're welcome, ye're welcome," the old man said, and with the skirt of the smock he wore over a pair of ancient corduroy breeches he dusted the top of a wooden stool which was standing against the wall.

Nerina sat down.

"Thank you," she said. "The coach stops at Pendle, I suppose?"

"Aye, it stops at Pendle right enough. Is it to Pendle ye're goin', Mistress?"

"No, I want to get to London, but it will be quicker to go by train than to travel all the way by coach."

"It may be slower by coach, but 'tis safer," the old man said. "I donna hold with all these new-fangled trains, belching black smoke in a man's face and smellin' as if they came from the bowels o' the earth itself. Give I the outside o' a coach on a sunny day with a nip o' frost in the air. That's the way a man should travel if he must go away from his home."

"Perhaps people only travel who have not a home to stay in," Nerina suggested.

The old man looked down at her.

"There's too many people a-journeyin' aboot the world," he said. "Home is the best place for all o' us, Mistress. Be it to your home ye are travellin' now?"

Nerina shook her head.

"I have no home."

"Then 'tis sorry I am for ye," the old man remarked. "Are ye a stranger to these parts?"

"Yes, a stranger," Nerina replied.

"Ye have been stayin' here with friends mayhap?" the old man enquired with the curiosity of a countryman who

200

wishes to know why a stranger is trespassing on what he considers his own land.

"Yes, I have been staying with friends," Nerina replied, and then for no real reason save that she liked the old man and wanted to be friendly she added, "I have come from Wroth Castle."

"Wroth Castle!" the old man repeated. " 'Tis a fine place, to be sure, though I have not seed it myself for many a long year. Did ye meet the new owner—Sir Rupert they calls him? Aye, Sir Rupert Wroth."

"Yes, I met him," Nerina said. "But why do you call him the new owner? I understand that he had been there for a long time."

"Aye, he's been there for a year or so," the old man answered with the supreme disregard of the very old for the passing of time. "But I knew his father afore him, a fine gentleman and handsome enough to attract the glances o' the women wherever he went. Many's a time I've seed him ridin' down here and all the gals o' the village peepin' at him and hopin' he'd raise his hat to em."

"Why did he come this way?" Nerina asked.

The old man gave her a sly look and chuckled to himself.

"Ah, now ye're asking I questions," he said. "There's secrets I'll be telling no one, secrets that only I knows."

"What secrets?" Nerina asked.

The old man put his finger to his mouth, glanced round the forge and sat down beside her.

"Do ye know how old I be?" he enquired.

Nerina shook her head.

"Well, I'll tell ye," he said. "I'm nigh on ninety—ninety next birthday I shall be. Aye, we're long livers in our family. Me nephie and his wife, whom I lives with here, gets cross with I. 'Ye talks too much, Uncle,' they says. 'Ye talks too much and we can't get along with our work.' Very cross they are with I at times, and so I gets up when they're asleep and I sleeps when they're awake. When I be up, I wants to talk; and when there ain't anyone there for I to talks to, then I talks to meself. So when they goes to bed I gets up and has my breakfast and I comes along here. Sometimes I talks to folks and sometimes I talks to meself. There's some as comes down here special to see I at night, some o' them be folks as don't care for the daylight and who finds night-time a better hour in which to do their work. Ye knows the type I mean, me dear."

201

The old man winked at Nerina.

Nerina laughed.

"Poachers and perhaps robbers?"

"Now that's askin' questions agin," the old man said. "There's some secrets I wouldna tell to no one. I may talk too much, but I don't tell anythin' that I oughtna. No, I keeps the secrets o' me friends to meself, I do."

"What was the secret you knew about Sir Rupert's father?" Nerina enquired.

The old man looked round the forge again as if he feared someone might be eavesdropping or that someone would admonish him for talking too much.

"Do ye really want to hear the tale?" he asked. " 'Tis a mighty strange un."

"I would love to hear it," she said.

"Weel, I'll tell ye," the old man said. " 'Tis summat I've told to no one. Nay, I've kept it to meself all these years, although sometimes I thought I would go up to the Castle and tell Sir Rupert; but there, he might not be interested and 'tis a long way for an old man to walk. Nigh on ninety I am, and God willing I'll live to see a hundred."

"I hope so," Nerina said, "but do tell me about Sir Rupert's father."

She did not know why she was interested, yet she was. It seemed so strange to come out of the darkness into the light of the forge and sit here with this friendly, white-haired old man and to hear that he knew some secret about Sir Rupert from whom she was flying in terror and hatred.

"Me nephie says I talk too much," the old man was saying, "and so I never talks to him no more. I has me other friends and they comes here to tell me their secrets, and I listens but I keeps me mouth shut about those who doesn't want I to speak o' their affairs. That's fair, Mistress. Mum's the word for the things about which I must na speak."

"Yes, one should keep silent if by speaking one would do harm," Nerina said; "but tell me about Sir Rupert's father."

"Aye, that's just what I was goin' to tell ye," the old man mumbled. "A fine upstanding man he were. A real gentleman and when he came a-ridin' past here, he always had a civil word for I and many's a guinea he has thrown this way. 'That's for you, Harry,' he would say. 'Save it against your old age.' Ah, but I wish I had followed his advice. If I had a bitta money o' me own I shouldna have to

202

live with me nephie and his wife, cross and disagreeable they are with I at times for all I am his uncle and for all I pays me way."

"And what else did Sir Rupert's father do?" Nerina asked.

"Ah, that's where the secret comes in. Courting little Nancy he were down at Weatherstone Farm. I've known little Nancy since she were born, as pretty a child as ever ye seed and growin' into a woman as pretty as her mother had been afore her were laid to rest."

"Was Nancy's father alive?" Nerina enquired.

"Nay, she lived with her old grandad, him as owned the farm. A difficult man he were, for all he was greatly respected in the neighbourhood. They say as how Nancy was never happy with him, but when I sees her she were happy enough, a smile she always had for I and a soft word. Aye, I was fond o' her. Her used to come here and watch me make the horseshoes. 'They're like gold, Harry,' she used to say when her was a little 'un, 'like gold!' I used to laugh at her and tell her that if they were I'd be that rich I wouldna have to work for me livin'."

"Were you sorry when she went away from here?" Nerina asked.

The old man shot her a strange glance.

"So ye know that her went away, do ye?" he enquired.

"I have heard people say that she went to Wroth Castle," Nerina replied.

"Aye, she did an' all. That's the truth, her went to Wroth Castle, but not afore something happened so secret that if I tell ye what it was, ye must promise to speak of it to no one."

"Oh, do tell me," Nerina said.

There was the light of mischief in the old man's eyes.

"I told ye it was old Harry who knew all the secrets about here," he said. "This secret is a very old 'un, there's none that knows it except I."

"What is it?" Nerina asked.

"I'm a-tellin' ye," the old man said, "but mind ye, I always meant to tell it only to Sir Rupert himsel'. Year after year I've looked for him to come ridin' down the road like his father, but he hasna come and as ye're interested I'll tell the secret to ye. Burnin' me lips it's been for many a long day."

"Yes, I understand that," Nerina said impatiently, "but do tell me what it is."

" 'Tis this," old Harry began. "Every 'un in this village and even Nancy's old grandad afore he died down at the Farm thought as how her went off to Wroth Castle to live with his lordship in sin. Ah, ye should hear some o' the things they said about her. 'She ain't no better than her ought to be,' they sneers; but I knows different. Old Harry knows better, he does, and I laughs to meself, laughs to think that anybody were daft enough to think such things of Nancy."

"Why, what do you mean?" Nerina said.

"I'm tellin' ye," old Harry replied. "She were wed to his lordship, she were, and who was there to witness it? Old Harry! Yes, I was there. Married they were in the little Chapel on the hill—folks call it the Shepherds' Chapel. They hold a Service in it once a year, but a right and proper little Church it is all the same. Built three hundreds o' years ago by an old woman who says our Blessed Lord were a Shepherd and why should a man who canna leave his sheep be forgotten on the Sabbath."

"They were married!" Nerina exclaimed. "Are you sure?"

"As sure as I'm a-sittin here, Mistress, for wasna I there meself? Five guineas his lordship gies me when the Service is over, five guineas! And Nancy her says to I, 'We trust ye, Harry; ye're not to tell anyone that you have been here and what ye've seen. Ye promise?' I promised and took the five guineas and thanks his lordship."

"But why did she say that?" Nerina asked.

"Aye, ye may well ask that question. It puzzled I for a time and then Nancy ups and explains. 'You see, Harry, I'm not of the same class as his lordship,' she says. 'I'm a farmer's daughter and I comes from a Farm. I'm not having all the smart people whom his lordship knows sneering and laughing at him. I love him, Harry, I love him more deeply than any woman of his own class can do, and he loves me.' I wish, Mistress, ye could have seen her face when she said that. It was as if the sunshine were bursting out of her. 'He loves me too,' she says, 'but I'll not shame him, not for anything in the world would I do that.' "

"And yet he married her?" Nerina said.

"He married her because he loved her," old Harry said. "I knows the truth of that for I seed it on their faces as they stood in the Shepherds' Chapel and made their vows afore the altar."

"But I cannot understand," Nerina exclaimed. "Why did
204

Nancy wish to keep it a secret? You would have thought she would have been proud."

"Her were proud right enough," Harry replied. "She had the love of a good man and she loved him in return, but as her said her was not a-going to shame him. She knew that the gentry wouldna accept her for one o' themselves. Why should they? She were only a farmer's girl."

"You are quite sure they were married?" Nerina insisted.

"As sure as I be that when I die I'll go to face me Maker," old Harry replied. "Haven't I seed the marriage lines with me own eyes, set in the book that lies in the Vestry of the Shepherds' Chapel? 'Tis plainly recorded there for all to see, though it doesna speak o' his lordship as being an Earl. Just write him down plain in the book by his Christian and surname as if he were nothing more than a simple man, as indeed he were in the sight of God."

"But are you sure, quite sure, that nobody except you knew of this?" Nerina asked.

"I be tellin' ye the truth, Mistress," old Harry replied. "There was only the old Parson and meself and old Tom what looked after the Chapel and kep' it clean, an' he's bin dead a time now. An' the Parson he's bin dead this thirty year. I'll wager me last penny that the secret died with him. 'Twould have died with I, but somehow when ye came along tonight I felt as ye wanted to know. I donna know why I felt that, 'tis strange now I comes to think o' it. Nigh on thirty-four years I've kept that secret to mysel', never a soul have I breathed it to, and yet ye comes along, someone I've never seed before, and I starts a-blabbing to ye. Maybe my nephie's right and I chatters too much, but I donna think so. The ways o' the Lord are queer, but ye'll find His Hand in everythin'.'"

"I still cannot quite understand it," Nerina said. "That Nancy should marry the Marquis and yet tell no one that she had done so!"

"She didn't want no one to know, I tells ye. All that mattered to Nancy was that she had made herself right with the Lord whom she worshipped. Every Sunday ever since she could toddle that girl were in our Church and many's a time I've seed her slip through the door o' a weekday. Very religious she were, as fine a lassie as you'd find anywhere. She wouldna give hersel' to a man to whom she were not married and burn in the fires o' Hell. She loved his lordship, but she made him do the right thing by

205

her afore she would surrender herself to his love. What did it matter whether anyone knew or what those chattering bodies said about her? Let 'em talk, I used to think; but if they knew our Nancy were her ladyship they'd be curtseyin' all humble like and a-beggin' her pardon. What's it matter? Nancy knew the truth and she were at peace in her own heart. That's all that matters to a decent lassie."

"At peace in her own heart," Nerina repeated softly. "Yes, I believe that is all that does matter. Other things are unimportant."

14

Owing to a series of mishaps Nerina did not arrive in London until late in the evening. The stage-coach which carried her to Pendle broke down a mile or so from the town. One of the wheels was damaged and it was several hours before a wheelwright could be found and the coach could proceed on its way. When finally Nerina did manage to catch a train, her progress was held up once more because of an accident on the line near Watford.

She had found it irksome when the stage-coach broke down, but at least she was able to walk about the road or sit comfortably on a farm gate and enjoy the sunshine and fresh air while she waited. But being shut up in a crowded third-class carriage was by no means pleasant, and by the time the line was cleared and the train at last continued its run to London Nerina felt as if she were being suffocated by the smoke and fog which prevented her even being able to see out of the tightly-closed windows.

At last, however, they drew into Euston Square Terminus and Nerina, struggling for the door with the other occupants of her carriage, thought how different her arrival today was from the last time she had disembarked at this station. Then there had been polite porters waiting to open the door of the reserved first-class carriage. There had been Bessie and Sir Rupert's valet to see to their luggage and a carriage outside the station ready to carry them to Berkeley Square. Now, jostled and pushed by the hurrying crowds, Nerina struggled to the ticket barrier, apprehensively aware that London seemed bigger, darker and more impressive than she had remembered it.

"Tickets, please," an inspector was calling, and Nerina opened her reticule to take the ticket from her purse.

She gave it to the man and passed from the platform into the big Booking Hall of the station. Here she stood for a moment staring about her, wondering which way to go. As she hesitated, she felt a sudden jerk at her arm, painful in its violence, and looking down she saw with a sense of horror that her reticule had been snatched from her arm. She caught a glimpse of a ragged youth disappearing into the crowds, her reticule being stuffed into his pocket as he disappeared. She cried out and ran after him, but her voice was drowned by the sudden shriek of an engine letting off steam and the crowds laden with luggage and children impeded her progress. In the space of a fleeting second she had lost sight of the thief.

"Help!" she cried. "Help, I have been robbed!"

One or two people passing by glanced at her curiously, but no one made any effort to speak to her or come to her assistance; and as a heavy truck piled high with luggage brought her to a standstill, she realised how hopeless it was. She could never find the boy. She had not even seen his face and the speed and agility with which he had disappeared told her all too clearly that he was an accomplished thief and not likely to be captured.

Nerina stood looking about her helplessly. Gradually, as the hurrying passengers circled around her, some of them brushing against her as if they did not even see that she was there, the desperateness of her plight was brought home to her. Weakly, with the feeling that her legs would no longer carry her, she moved to a seat placed against the wall of the Booking Hall.

She sat down, her green canvas bag on her lap, and wondered miserably what she was to do. Every penny she possessed in the world was gone and her common-sense told her it was quite useless looking for the thief or going to the Police. Besides, if she did the latter, she would have to give her name and address and account for her presence at the station.

She felt perilously near to tears. If only, she sighed, she had had the common-sense to hold her reticule tightly in her hand instead of hanging it on her arm. The thief must have watched her open her purse, seen the gleam of gold and silver as she looked for her ticket, and waited his opportunity. It would have been, Nerina thought, the sight of the gold sovereigns which had made it worth his while to snatch her reticule. She had been foolish to put temptation in his way by showing that she possessed so much money.

When she had taken her ticket at Pendle, she had cashed one of the five-pound notes which belonged to Elizabeth. The change in gold and silver had filled her purse to overflowing and there was no doubt such apparent opulence had been too much for the honesty of the boy who had snatched it from her. Unless, of course, as was far more likely, he was a habitual criminal who made a living by haunting railway stations, finding plenty of pickings amongst the flustered, frightened passengers, who were often far too harassed by their journeying to be cautious about their belongings. Whatever the reason for it, her money was gone!

Nerina put her hands up to her eyes. For a moment she could not think what to do. It was as if when walking down a road she had suddenly come to a blank wall and had no idea how to proceed. On the journey to London she had made many plans. First she would find a respectable boarding-house where she might stay the night. On the morrow she would go in search of work. She had been so sure, so confident of finding something she could do, something in which she could lose her identity and hide, for ever if need be, from Sir Rupert and the terror he inspired in her.

Now she was lost and utterly destitute. Without money she had no idea how to begin a life of independence. It was then a quiet voice beside her said:

"Can I help you?"

Startled, she took her hands from her eyes and saw that sitting beside her was a woman. Middle-aged, with a not unattractive face, she was neatly dressed in a gown of grey alpaca. She was obviously well-to-do. There was a small but well-matched string of pearls round her neck, a diamond-circled cameo brooch on her bosom. Her gloves, which matched her dress, were expensive and of the best French kid.

As Nerina, taking in those details, did not reply to the question she had been asked, the woman continued:

"I feel you must be in trouble. Have you just come off the train? Perhaps someone is meeting you?"

Nerina shook her head. Although it was not yet dusk, the lights had been lit in the Booking Hall and now as she raised her head the gaslight illuminated the red curls peeping from beneath her bonnet. She looked very young and very attractive, but there was also something wistful and pathetic about her.

"No, I am not being met," Nerina replied; and then, because she was so agitated, she added confidingly: "I am in trouble because my reticule has been stolen. A boy snatched it from my arm. It contained my purse and all my money."

The woman made an expression of sympathy.

"What a terrible thing to happen!" she exclaimed. "I am sorry for you. I came here to meet a young girl who is coming to stay with me, but I think she must have missed her train. Then I saw you sitting there. I thought for a moment you might be her; then I saw you were a stranger but obviously someone in distress."

"It is rather distressing," Nerina agreed. "I do not know quite what to do. I was going to ask a policeman if he could direct me to a respectable boarding-house, but now I have not got the money to pay for a night's lodging."

"It is the sort of thing that might happen to anyone," the stranger said comfortingly, "and of course you must let me help you. I shall be very pleased if you will stay the night in my house."

"It is very kind of you," Nerina said, "but I could not accept your hospitality because . . ."

She hesitated and was unable to end her sentence. She could see no reason why she should refuse the kindness that was being offered, yet instinctively she felt she should not make the acquaintance of an utter stranger and certainly not impose upon her in such a manner. Yet what else was there to do?

Nerina turned away from the obvious solution. She had only to go to Berkeley Square and tell the servants she had arrived in London unexpectedly. The house was empty and waiting. But it belonged to Sir Rupert and she told herself she would rather die than humiliate herself by going there.

"My carriage is outside," the strange woman was saying. "You look as if you have come a long way. You must be tired. I beg of you not to think of all the conventional excuses why you should not accept my offer of a night's rest. I am delighted to have you and there is no reason why we cannot be friends although we have met in such unusual circumstances."

"It is very kind of you," Nerina murmured almost automatically.

She did not know why, but this woman seemed to have a strange effect upon her. It was almost hypnotic. It was difficult to argue with her, so much easier to do what she wanted. Nerina supposed she must be very tired. After all, she had been awake all the night before; and though she had tried to doze in the railway carriage, it had been almost impossible owing to the noise and chatter of the other passengers.

Without further protestations she allowed herself to be led outside the station to where a closed carriage was waiting. It was not over-luxurious, but it was comfortable and with a sigh of relief Nerina leaned back against the padded cushions.

"I cannot think why you should be so good to me."

Her companion gave a little laugh.

"You must give me the credit for being a good Samaritan," she said.

Nerina smiled.

"I certainly 'fell among thieves'."

"Tell me a little about yourself," the woman suggested. "I think that, as there is no one to do it for us, we must introduce ourselves. I am Mrs. Tait—Muriel Tait is my name. And yours?"

Nerina's hesitation was almost imperceptible.

"I am Nerina . . . Butler," she said.

Adrian's name was the first which came into her mind.

"Nerina! What a pretty name!" Mrs. Tait exclaimed. "And have you many friends in London? No, that is a silly question," she answered herself. "If you had friends, you would have gone to them. I suppose your home is in the country?"

"I have no home," Nerina answered. "My father and mother are dead."

She did not know why, for in the darkness of the carriage it was impossible to see Mrs. Tait's face, but she had the impression that her answer pleased her rescuer. She decided, however, that she must have been mistaken, for in a low voice of sympathy Mrs. Tait said:

"You poor child, how terribly sad for you! And why have you come to London? You don't mind my asking you what might appear to be impertinent questions?"

"I want to find employment," Nerina answered. "Can you help me to find some? I would be more than grateful if you could."

"Of course I can help you," Mrs. Tait replied. "Don't worry your pretty head on that score. But first you must have a good night's rest. Don't trouble yourself about tomorrow. Just relax and sleep. We shall be arriving at my house in a few minutes and because you are tired I am going to take you upstairs at once and tuck you into bed. I have some nieces living with me and if you hear them laughing and talking don't let the noise perturb you. They will be full of curiosity about you, but I know you are tired and they can wait until the morning before they meet you."

"How kind you are!" Nerina said.

Her companion had spoken the truth. She was exceedingly and almost overwhelmingly weary. She wanted to sleep more than anything else in the world. She was only too glad that Mrs. Tait was wise enough to realise this. To meet a lot of strange young women tonight would have been too much of an ordeal.

The carriage drew up at a house in a quiet street which Nerina guessed was somewhere near Regent's Park. She had had a glimpse out of the windows of the carriage of trees and water. As they stepped out of the carriage she noticed that all the houses in the road were built back from the pavement and that there was a small ornamental garden in front of each one.

"I expect my nieces will be entertaining some friends," Mrs. Tait said, "so to save you from a lot of embarrassing questions we will slip in at the side door."

"Yes, I would much prefer that," Nerina replied.

She was conscious now not only of her tiredness but of her appearance. Her dress was creased and dusty from travelling and her hands and face badly in need of a wash.

Mrs. Tait led the way through a small paved garden to the side door of the house. Nerina was aware that the place was bigger than she had at first thought; then the door opened and she found herself in a dimly-lit passage, a flight of stairs in front of her. Mrs. Tait led the way. They went up two floors before she opened a baize door and they entered what Nerina guessed was the front part of the house.

Here the passage was well lit, the walls were decorated with a gay paper of lattice-work and roses and the carpet was also patterned with bunches of roses on a vivid crimson background.

"Here is your room," Mrs. Tait said, opening a door, and Nerina found herself in a bedroom which was quite unlike anything she had ever seen before.

The gas jets were lit but were heavily shaded so that the whole room was of a glowing rosy hue. The bed, which was in the Empire style, was arranged against the wall and appeared at the first glance to be more of a sofa than a bed. The curtains and hangings were of pink satin, and everywhere there were looking-glasses almost covering the walls, reflecting and re-reflecting each other and the occupants of the room until Nerina could see herself countless times in various different positions.

"I think you will find everything you want," Mrs. Tait said, indicating the brush and comb which lay ready on the dressing-table, and to Nerina's surprise there was also a nightgown and a dressing-gown laid over a chair.

As if she had asked aloud the question forming in her mind, Mrs. Tait explained:

"This room would have been used by the girl I went to meet. If she turns up later, I can find another one for her."

"It is very kind of you," Nerina said again. She felt as if there was nothing else she could say.

"And now you want something to eat," Mrs. Tait said as if everything was settled and she was impatient to get away. "Undress and get into bed and I will bring you some hot milk and a few sandwiches. You must not eat much or you will get indigestion when you are as tired as you are now. Hurry, for we can do all the talking there is to do when you are feeling fresher."

Without waiting for a reply Mrs. Tait went from the room and shut the door behind her. Nerina was too exhausted to do anything but obey. Quickly she undressed, hanging her black gown in the wardrobe and putting her shawl and bonnet on a shelf. When she had disrobed, she hesitated a moment, wondering whether to put on the nightgown that was on the chair or to unpack one of her own from her bag. Because of her fatigue she took the easier course and slipped on the nightgown which lay on the chair. As she put it over her head, she realised that it was very elaborate. It was made of the finest lawn and ornamented with row upon row of narrow lace insertion.

'Mrs. Tait much be very rich,' Nerina thought. 'Everything here seems to be done in style.'

She washed her hands and face and climbed into bed. It was soft and luxurious. She felt her tired body sink down into a mattress and pillows which seemed to be made of swansdown. She had just settled herself when the door opened and Mrs. Tait returned carrying a tray.

"Here's a chicken sandwich for you and some hot milk," she said. "Drink it up. I want you to have a really good rest tonight. You will feel much better after it in the morning."

Nerina sat up in bed and took the tray from Mrs. Tait's hands. The sandwiches were very small and she thought it was a good thing she was too tired to feel hungry. She had had nothing to eat all day and as the train had neared London she had realised that she was very hungry, but now the thought of eating was almost nauseating.

She nibbled one of the sandwiches and took up the glass of milk.

"Drink it all up," Mrs. Tait commanded.

Nerina gulped it down. It was warm and comforting, but at the same time it had a strange taste. She thought drowsily to herself that the milk in London was not very pleasant if this was a sample of it. But as Mrs. Tait was waiting, she finished the glass politely and put it back on the tray with a little murmur of thanks.

"And now you will sleep," Mrs. Tait said. "Shut your eyes and don't worry about anything until I come and see you in the morning."

Her fingers reached towards the shaded gas jets as she spoke. She turned them out. They made a series of soft pops, and then the room was in darkness.

"Good night, my dear, sleep well." Mrs. Tait said from the door, and went out, closing it behind her.

Nerina yawned and snuggled down in the pillows. Then she heard the sound of a key turning in a lock. For the moment she was startled. Several questions which had been hovering in the back of her mind ever since she had first met Mrs. Tait attempted to present themselves to her intelligence, but she knew she was too tired to question anything—even the fact that she was locked in. She was drifting away into unconsciousness and her brain could no longer withstand the overwhelming need of her tired body.

. . .

She awoke and knew even as she opened her eyes that she had slept for a long time. Her eyes felt heavy and her head rather as if it had been stuffed with cotton wool. She was very thirsty and after a moment or two she stretched and, slipping out of bed, drew back the curtains.

There was no sunshine for the day was grey and there was promise of rain in the heavy clouds. Nerina did not know why, but she felt a shiver go through her. Without more than a perfunctory glance out of the window she crossed the room to the wash-stand and poured herself out a glass of water. She drank it and immediately her mind felt clearer. Now she could look around and take stock of the room in which she stood.

To her astonishment it was by no means as attractive as it had looked the night before in the rose-shaded gaslight. There was something garish and almost dingy about it now, and Nerina saw that the pink curtains which had appeared so charming the night before were made of the cheapest sateen, and it was only their colour and their drapings which had made them appear opulent in the artificial light.

As she stood there in her white nightgown, the mirrors reflected her and she could see herself front and back and from both sides in an unending perspective almost frightening in its repetition. Hurriedly, because she felt there was something indecent in this view of herself interminably echoed and re-echoed, Nerina got back into bed. She had hardly done so when there was a knock on the door and almost simultaneously the sound of the key turning in the lock.

Nerina expected to see Mrs. Tait, but instead a maid entered. A slovenly, rather dull-witted looking girl, her greasy hair falling from under her cap and her big red hands clasping awkwardly a breakfast tray. She set it down beside Nerina, then turned without a word or even a smile of greeting.

"Thank you very much," Nerina said, but the maid did not reply and went from the room, closing and re-locking the door behind her.

The coffee and roll and butter which the tray contained were not unappetising. Nerina did not know why, but she suddenly felt apprehensive and afraid. The house was not what she expected, and yet she did not know what she had expected or indeed if she had the right to expect anything. It had been kind of Mrs. Tait to give her a bed for the night and she told herself severely that the sort of lodgings she would be able to afford on what she earned were likely to be very different indeed from this.

Yet her sense of uneasiness was not assuaged. She was pouring herself a second cup of coffee when she heard a sound outside. The key turned in the lock and the door was opened very quietly. Nerina looked up, waiting for who should come in. Then a head was thrust round the door, she saw a pair of dark eyes and heard someone say:

"She's awake, come on!"

The door opened wider and two girls entered. The one whose eyes she had seen was dark, with a pretty laughing mouth, the other was fair, with golden hair of such a strange shade of fairness that after one glance Nerina was quite certain that it was dyed. Both the girls wore wrappers of taffeta trimmed with an inordinate amount of cheap, rather showy lace. They crossed the room and standing near the bed stared down at Nerina with a curiosity which made her rather embarrassed.

215

"Who are you?" the dark girl asked.

"I am Nerina Butler," Nerina replied. "Your aunt—for I am sure you must be Mrs. Tait's nieces—was kind enough to give me a bed for the night."

Her remark, which sounded innocent enough to herself, was greeted to her astonishment with shrieks of laughter which seemed to double up her two visitors. The dark girl threw herself into an armchair, her wrapper bursting open in the front to show an elaborate lace-trimmed nightgown not unlike the one Nerina was wearing.

"Aunt!" she exclaimed. "Burst my corsets! The same old story and they all fall for it!"

The fair girl seated herself familiarly on the end of Nerina's bed.

"How old are you?" she asked.

"Eighteen, nearly nineteen," Nerina replied, trying not to show her resentment at the extraordinary behaviour of her uninvited guests.

"You look younger," the fair girl said. "I bet she thought you were, too. She likes them very young, sixteen if she can get them!"

"Yes, that's what Auntie likes," the dark-haired girl giggled, and went off into gales of laughter again. She stopped suddenly, seeing Nerina's stiff, affronted expression. "Look here, kid," she asked. "Do you know where you are?"

Nerina glanced towards the window.

"Not . . . not exactly," she replied, feeling rather stupid, "but I thought last night as we drove here that the house was somewhere near Regent's Park."

"So it is," the fair girl replied, "but that's not the point."

The dark girl got to her feet.

"Oh, stow it, Laura," she said. "What's the point of interfering? You'll have the old trout down on you like a ton of bricks if she finds out."

"I don't care," the girl who was addressed as Laura answered. "They ought to know what they're in for. I swore that after the last time when she brought that snivelling little wretch from Devonshire here I would put them wise to what was happening . . . if nothing else."

"And what difference will it make?" the dark girl enquired.

Laura shrugged her shoulders.

"None, I suppose, except that ignorance is not bliss in this game, as well you know it, Olive."

216

"Well, I imagine she's ignorant," Olive retorted, "so do your stuff, I'm not stopping you."

Nerina looked from one to the other. She could see and hear that neither of the girls was well-educated or well-bred. They both had a flashy and undeniable prettiness despite the fact that their faces were greasy and that Laura's eyelids were smeared with mascara which she had evidently forgotten to take from her eyes the night before.

Olive's hair was done up at the back in paper curlers, and the outline of her mouth was smudged with crimson lip-salve which had, however, worn away from the centre of her lips. As she looked at them Nerina felt a sudden fear within her.

"Will you please tell me what you are talking about?" she asked.

"Yes, we'll tell you," Laura said. "Tell us first how you got here."

"I . . . I arrived in London from the country late yesterday evening," Nerina replied. "On the station my reticule was stolen from my arm with every penny I had in it. I was sitting on a seat wondering what to do, for I had come to London in search of work, when your . . . when Mrs. Tait spoke to me. I told her what had happened and she invited me to stay here the night. I was very tired and she brought me in the back way. She told me that she had her nieces living with her, and that was why I referred to her as your aunt."

Olive started to giggle again, but Laura gave her a warning glance and she was silent.

"Mrs. Tait owns this house," Laura said to Nerina, "and we live here with her. There are six of us together, but we are no relation of hers; in fact some of us like you were picked up on railway stations. She makes a habit of meeting the trains. There is usually some stupid and innocent country girl arriving in London for the first time who doesn't know what to do with herself. Mrs. Tait brings her here just as she brought you."

Nerina's eyes were very wide.

"You mean . . . that this house is . . . is . . . ?"

The words seemed to be strangled in her throat.

"Exactly!" Laura said.

Nerina clasped her hands together.

"Thank you for telling me," she whispered. "I must get away at once. I never guessed, but now of course I understand how stupid I was." She looked from one girl to

217

the other, but they said nothing. "I must get away," she repeated, and got out of bed.

She walked across the room to the wardrobe, pulled open the doors and stood staring. It was empty. She turned round to find the two girls watching her. The expression on their faces was inscrutable. It seemed to Nerina they were not sympathetic, merely curious, watching her as cows in a field watch a strange one of their kind which has suddenly been put amongst them.

"My clothes have gone!" she exclaimed.

"She always takes them," Laura replied.

"But what can I do then?" Nerina asked. "How can I get away?"

"You can't," Olive ejaculated. "Now listen, kid, that's why Laura and I came to warn you. It's no use fighting. She will defeat you in the end, she always does. The girl who was in this room three weeks ago fought her. We used to hear her screaming in the morning, screaming and crying and beating her hands on the door. But 'Ma'—that's what we call Mrs. Tait—managed to break her in the end."

"How?" Nerina asked.

"Dope," Laura replied. "If you make a noise, she dopes you. I know what it is she gives you, I had some of it once. It makes you feel weak and drowsy and too lazy to make a fuss. If you have enough of it, you'll agree to anything. The world seems far away and nothing seems to matter one way or the other. Do you understand?"

"You miss it when they stop it," Olive said.

"I know you do," Laura agreed. "I used to ache for it for a bit, but it doesn't do you any good. It makes you a kind of slave to her and you feel terribly depressed when it wears off. I'm telling you this for your own good so that you won't have to have it."

"But what can I do?" Nerina asked. "I can't stay here! I won't."

Olive shrugged her shoulders.

" 'Will you walk into my parlour, said the spider to the fly,' " she quoted. "When she's got her web around you, you can't get out."

"But how is she allowed to do this?" Nerina demanded. "I thought there was a law against such things."

"Good heavens, where have you been brought up?" Olive enquired. "A law! Why, the people who come here are those who makes the laws and they wouldn't stop it if they could help it. We're very smart, in fact 'Ma' Tait's establishment is one of the best patronised in the West End. Dukes and Earls, Ambassadors and Cabinet Ministers, we entertains them all."

Nerina started. Cabinet Ministers made her think of Sir Rupert. He could rescue her, he could get her away from here. If she revealed who she was, she felt certain Mrs. Tait would send her away. Then as every nerve in her body shrank from doing such a thing, a terrible idea came to her mind. Supposing she said she was Lady Wroth, wife of Sir Rupert Wroth, and Mrs. Tait did not believe her. She knew only too well what her appearance had been like last night. Shabby and down-at-heel, there was no indication that she was likely to be the wife of a distinguished politician, in fact such a suggestion would appear not only improbable but nonsensical.

She walked across the room and sat down on the bed beside Laura.

"Can you help me?" she asked.

"To escape?" Laura enquired. "Not a hope of it! We're warning you now so that you won't make a fuss. The younger they are, as a rule the more they mind; but if Olive and I had known you were nearly nineteen we wouldn't have bothered about you. It's the young ones we're sorry for. They're little more than children if it comes to that. I was only thirteen when 'Ma' got hold of me."

"I was a year older, but I didn't mind much," Olive said. "I was a greedy little beast in those days and a square meal meant more to me than my virtue. But I've known others that feels differently."

"I for one," Nerina said violently. "What would happen if I put my head out of the window and screamed?"

"Nobody would pay any attention," Olive answered. "This room looks out on to the back anyway. The garden runs down to the Regent Canal and there's seldom anyone about. Besides, before you could scream for long, 'Ma' would give you a dose of her special medicine. You sleep like a top when you've had it."

"I suppose that's what I had last night," Nerina said, "otherwise I would have heard her come into the room and take away my clothes."

"Did she give you a glass of milk?" Laura asked.

Nerina nodded.

"You can hardly taste it in milk," Laura said. "But if you drink it straight, it's absolutely filthy."

"Oh, please help me," Nerina pleaded. "There must be some way that I can get out. Who will stop me if I go downstairs?"

"Charlie for one," Olive answered, "and besides, the doors are locked. 'Ma' sees to that before she goes to bed and Charlie takes over in the morning when she's asleep."

"How late does she sleep?" Nerina asked.

"Oh, until about one o'clock as a rule," Laura answered. "It depends on how much she's drunk the night before. If she's been very squiffy, she'll sleep until nearly opening time. That's about three o'clock, you know."

Nerina shut her eyes for a moment.

"You are quite certain?" she asked after a moment, during which it appeared as if she was trying to get her breath. "If I went downstairs and tried to get out through the front door or through the door I came in by last night, Charlie would stop me?"

"He would stop you," Olive asserted. "Besides, you can't get the doors open unless you have a key. He has one and 'Ma' has the other."

"But don't you ever go out?" Nerina enquired.

"Oh yes, when we have been here some time. We go out in twos. One of the older girls with one of the younger. We go shopping or take a walk in the park if we are not too tired from the night before. But it's only when she's quite certain she can trust you. You won't get out without her being at your heels for at least six months. She never takes any chances, she's too clever. That's why she makes such a lot of money."

"I've got to get away," Nerina cried.

She spoke desperately for she could feel the trap was closing round her.

Laura got to her feet.

"It's no use," she said. "You haven't got an earthly, so you had better make the best of a bad job."

"I'll never do that," Nerina retorted.

"Oh yes, you will," Olive replied. "We all of us get down to it sooner or later, and you won't be the exception."

She too got to her feet.

"Well, we've done the best we could for you, kid. If you take our advice, you'll avoid the dope and you'll save your breath from screaming. It's not a bad life once you're used to it; and if you're a success, well, there's always the chance that somebody will buy you out and set you up in an establishment of your own."

"Yes, indeed," Laura agreed. "Why, one of the girls from here, Rosie, got away after two months; fancy, only two months! She's got her own carriage now and sometimes she comes to see us. It's Lord Rohan as keeps her. He's old and a bit cranky, but he's ever so rich, and she has saved enough to retire if she wants to. Just think of it, only two months in this place."

"So one can be bought out," Nerina said slowly.

"If you're lucky," Olive replied, "but you don't have to count on it. Look at me, I've been here five years, and nobody has ever given me anything more expensive than a box of chocolates."

"No reason why they should," Laura said. "After all 'Ma' makes them pay through the nose."

"Yes, but what about Rosie?" Olive enquired.

"She was awfully pretty," Laura said generously, "and what's more, she was born lucky. That's better than either being good or respectable."

"Oh, come on," Olive cried. "We shall get caught if we stay here. We saw the key in the door so we thought we would come in. If 'Ma' catches us, there'll be hell to pay. Don't forget, kid, you haven't seen us, and when 'Ma' tells you what she's up to, you had best look suitably surprised."

"I won't give you away," Nerina answered, "but you are quite, quite sure you can't help me?"

"There's nothing we can do," Laura said quietly. "We've done all we can."

As if the expression on Nerina's face touched her, she put out her hand and laid it not unkindly on her shoulder.

"Cheer up," she smiled. "Perhaps you will be a success like Rosie, who knows!"

"Come on," Olive called from the door, and Laura ran across the room to join her.

The two girls let themselves out, the door closed behind them, and Nerina heard the key turn in the lock. She sat very still for a long time, then she rose to her feet and walked to the window. She could see that Olive had spoken the truth. The dingy narrow garden at the back of the house ran down to the sluggish waters of the Canal. There was nothing to be gained by screaming, in fact it was doubtful if anyone would hear.

Nerina crossed again to the bed. She sat down on it, her hands clenched together, and tried to think of some way in which she might escape. She was prepared to accept

221

Laura's and Olive's information that Charlie guarded the doors downstairs; and she shrank from the idea of being involved in a struggle with a servant, of being dragged back perhaps forcibly to her bedroom. Besides, the door of her room was now locked and the opportunity of attempting to escape even in her nightgown was now past.

She sat for a long time thinking, then gradually an idea came to her, an idea desperately dangerous but at the same time one which she felt gave her the only possible chance of escaping from the grave predicament in which she now found herself.

When Mrs. Tait entered the room an hour later, Nerina smiled at her. Mrs. Tait was not looking the quiet, respectable lady she had appeared the night before. She was wearing a dirty velvet dressing-gown which was badly in need of repair. The whole of her head was covered in curl papers and in an effort to improve her appearance she had powdered her face hastily but untidily so that patches of yellow skin showed in vivid contrast to the white powder. The lines of dissipation and debauchery were very clearly marked on her face, and Nerina looking at her now realised that she must have been crazy to have trusted such a woman the night before. But regrets and self-accusations would get her nowhere. With a great effort she made herself pleasant, telling Mrs. Tait she had slept well and enjoyed her breakfast.

Mrs. Tait seemed slightly surprised at her attitude and was even more surprised when she explained to Nerina in no uncertain terms what was expected of her and Nerina agreed without expostulation to everything she suggested.

"You are the most sensible girl I have met in a long time," Mrs. Tait said approvingly when at seven o'clock that evening she came into the bedroom to see that Nerina was dressed in the clothes which she had brought her an hour or so before.

Nerina stood in front of her wearing a frilled dress of cheap white gauze which was yet skilfully cut to make the best of her figure. There was a sash of pale-blue ribbon round her waist and Nerina realised that the whole costume was designed to make her appear as young and as unsophisticated as possible.

"You look charming," Mrs. Tait said, inspecting Nerina with a critical eye. "Loosen your hair a little. It's a little severe over the temple."

Nerina did as she was told. Mrs. Tait stood back to get

222

the effect. She herself was resplendent in a dress of crimson taffeta, ornamented with a wealth of ribbons, laces, rosebuds and cheap jewellery. She looked incredibly common and tawdry, and once again Nerina asked herself how she could have been fool enough to trust such a woman even for a moment.

"The gentleman who is coming to meet you tonight," Mrs. Tait was saying, "is a very distinguished person indeed. He is one of my best clients and I always do what I can to please him. I should not have let him see you tonight had you not convinced me how sensible and well-behaved you are. If you please him, then you will please me. There are a lot of things we might do together, my dear, a lot of things."

"Do you think I am likely to please him?" Nerina asked artlessly.

Mrs. Tait laughed unpleasantly.

"I shall be very surprised if you don't. He likes very young girls. He is always asking me to find him someone young and beautiful. It isn't always easy, but when a gentleman's purse is bottomless it isn't impossible."

"I understand," Nerina said.

Mrs. Tait stepped forward to pull out her sash.

"Now you are ready," she said. "You will meet him in the Little Salon on the first floor. You will drink together and afterwards you can, of course, bring him up here. He will doubtless tell you exactly what he wants."

"I expect he will," Nerina said.

Her tone was dry and Mrs. Tait glanced at her suspiciously, but she said nothing and led the way down the main staircase of the house to the first floor. The Little Salon was a pretentious name for a small back room. It was well furnished in an ostentatious, somewhat theatrical manner. There was a red plush sofa, an Axminster carpet and again a profusion of looking-glasses. There were bowls of artificial roses on gilt tables, and although the night was warm a fire was burning and the lights were turned very low behind shades covered with rose-pink silk.

"Sit on the sofa" Mrs. Tait commanded. "His lordship should be here soon. I will send him up as soon as he arrives. I am sure you will be sensible, my dear, for a lot depends on this."

'A lot indeed,' Nerina thought; then as the door closed behind Mrs. Tait she realised that her hands were cold and her heart beating quickly. She was more frightened than

223

she had ever been in her life before and yet she knew that only by being what Mrs. Tait called sensible could she save herself.

Mrs. Tait had let out at the last moment that it was a titled person who was expected. Nerina had prayed that he would be of great importance, for if he was, he would undoubtedly know Sir Rupert and would be compelled to take her away. There was no other course open for her, Nerina knew that, since she had decided what she must do. She had been haunted all the afternoon by the fear that the man who came might be too drunk to think coherently, but the only consolation was that both from Mrs. Tait and Laura she had learned that the establishment was a very select one. If it was true that the majority of Mrs. Tait's clients were noblemen, then Nerina knew that her plea for help would not go unanswered.

It was impossible for her to sit still, impossible for her to stay on the sofa and wait as Mrs. Tait had commanded her. She got to her feet and crossed the room. She crossed it and re-crossed it, each time more and more conscious of her rising agitation. Now her cheeks were burning and she felt as if her whole body was on fire with terror. She had a wild desire to scream for help; and even as she formulated the words she might say, she remembered that, if only Sir Rupert were here, he would rescue her effectively and without any unpleasant repercussions.

She recalled how he had protected her from her uncle and she felt again the strength of his arms as he had carried her upstairs after the wedding. If only he was with her now!

But even as she wished for him to appear, the door opened. She had her back to it and for a moment she did not turn, nerving herself to face the man who would either save or destroy her. Slowly she turned round. As she did so, her lips parted in an audible gasp of horror, for standing in the doorway, resplendent in evening clothes, a cloak lined with crimson satin hanging from his shoulders, was the Marquis of Droxburgh.

15

For a moment, as Nerina met the Marquis's dark lustful eyes, she felt the room swim around her dizzily and she knew that in another second her self-control would snap and she would run screaming from wall to wall in a vain effort to escape. Then even as her own weakness and peril flashed through her mind like a streak of lightning through a darkened sky, she knew that only by keeping her head and by an almost superhuman effort at rigid control could she save herself from the danger which threatened her.

It was perhaps the expression of astonishment on the Marquis's face which helped her more than anything else to realise that she must take the initiative. For what seemed to her a long time they stood looking at each other, and then jerkily, almost as if she were a puppet propelled by some unseen hand, Nerina ran towards him.

"Lord Droxburgh!" she exclaimed. "Thank heaven you have come! You must help me! You must save me!"

The Marquis closed the door behind him and in a voice in which surprise and satisfaction were almost equally blended he said:

"So it really is Miss Graye! For a moment I thought my eyes must be deceiving me."

"I am not surprised at your astonishment," Nerina replied. "It is, of course, a mistake that I am here, a terrible, ghastly mistake from which I know you will rescue me."

The Marquis's eyes flickered before the appeal in her eyes, raised to his with an expression of almost child-like trust. Slowly he turned away. Deliberately he took off his cloak and laid it over the back of a chair, then he put out his hand and took Nerina's. She wanted to shudder at his touch; indeed at the clasp of his long bony fingers she felt as if it were a reptile which entwined itself around her. She forced herself, however, not to shrink away but to appear to acquiesce with almost an air of willingness as the Marquis led her across the room to the red plush sofa.

They sat down, the Marquis turning sideways so as to face her, his eyes taking in every detail of her face, her figure and the all too theatrical innocence of her white dress.

"You are very lovely!" he said, and Nerina started,

remembering when she had heard him say those words before and in what circumstances.

"Let me tell you what has happened to me," she said hastily, and began her story of how she had arrived in London and how her reticule had been stolen from her at the station.

She had planned, when she was waiting for the unknown man who was to be brought to the room to make her acquaintance, that she would instantly reveal who she was and demand that he take her away. She knew now that she must change her plan. It would not impress the Marquis to learn that she was Lady Wroth. On the contrary, Nerina realised with a feeling of horror that in all probability it would make him very much less sympathetic towards her. As he disliked and despised Sir Rupert as the illegitimate son of his brother, it was not likely that he would take much account of his wife or that his desires would be set aside because of the knowledge that she was legally married to the man who he believed by his birth had defrauded him of a great fortune.

Nerina's brain was working with swiftness and clarity. She knew it was only her own wits which could save her from the terrible predicament in which she found herself and to escape she must use every faculty she possessed and strain every nerve in her body. As she spoke, telling her story clearly and with a vividness of expression which held the Marquis's attention, she was aware that he was watching her with half closed eyes and continually moistening his thin lips with the tip of his tongue.

There was no need to exaggerate or alter the tale she had to tell. She explained exactly what had happened the night before, how she had been wakened in the morning by Laura and Olive and had learned from them the sort of establishment in which she found herself and the perils which awaited her should she not acquiesce peacefully in Mrs. Tait's demands of her.

"When I knew what she would do if I resisted," Nerina said, "I decided that the only possible way of escape was to wait until I was alone with some gentleman and then to throw myself on his mercy. I was expecting, of course, a stranger, perhaps someone the worse for drink or too sunk in vice to hear my appeal. Can you imagine, my lord, what it meant to me when the door opened and you came in—you whom I already knew!"

Nerina gave a little sigh and lowered her head for a moment as if overcome with emotion. When she raised it again, it was to find the Marquis looking at her speculatively.

"So you expect me to take you away from here," he said quietly, speaking a little slower than usual as if he were thinking hard.

"But of course," Nerina answered confidently, "and when you do, you know you will earn my undying gratitude."

The Marquis did not speak for a moment. Nerina made herself put out her hands and clutch one of his convulsively.

"You will take me away, won't you?" she whispered. "Promise me you will do so. If you leave me here, I swear that I will kill myself."

She was well aware that her desperation gave him satisfaction. She could see it in the sudden glint in his eyes. Then as his fingers closed over hers he said:

"Just how grateful will you be?"

"Do I have to tell you that?" Nerina answered. "Grateful with a gratitude beyond words, grateful until the end of my life."

The Marquis smiled.

"And what will be my reward?" he questioned softly.

Nerina's eyes were wide and guileless.

"Reward?" she faltered artlessly. "But what can I give you? I have no money, nothing!"

The Marquis gave a little laugh.

"I don't want money, you stupid child, I want something far more important, something of great value which you alone can give me."

"Oh!"

Nerina's ejaculation of astonishment was a masterpiece of clever acting. She turned her head aside as if to hide her blushes and instantly the Marquis's arms went round her. With a little cry she shook herself free and sprang to her feet.

"You must not touch me here," she exclaimed. "I could not bear that anyone should even so much as hold my hand in this sordid, horrible place. The mere thought of it disgusts me. It is dirty and bestial, a house of sin!"

The Marquis looked at her flashing eyes, at the vivid beauty of her pale face framed by her glowing hair.

"You are right," he said. "The setting is not worthy of you. Nerina, my dear, you are a very beautiful creature."

"Then take me away," Nerina pleaded. "Please, please, take me away! I feel soiled and humiliated every second that I must remain here."

"And if I take you away," the Marquis said quietly, "if I place you somewhere that is worthy of your beauty and your intelligence, will you be kind to me? Will you make me a very happy man?"

"Do I have to answer that question?" Nerina parried, but her eyes were eloquent, her red lips very inviting.

The Marquis looked at her. His eyes narrowed, then he made a sound which was half a laugh and half an ejaculation of greed and excitement. Without speaking he went from the room closing the door behind him.

Nerina put her hand to her heart. The strain of the last few minutes had been almost intolerable and now she knew she was trembling. Her lips were dry and she felt it was almost impossible to draw her breath. She stood very still and then desperately, like a child who is frightened of the dark, she began to pray.

"Save me, Lord, save me!" she murmured. "I have done so many things that are wrong and bad; but if only you will save me from this, I will try to do what is right in the future. I will go back to Sir Rupert, I will humiliate myself before him, I will apologise for having tricked and deceived him. I will do anything, anything, however unpleasant; but only save me from the Marquis and from this horrible, beastly house. Please, God, save me!"

She was still praying when the door opened again. For a moment she could not raise her eyes, dare not look into the Marquis's face; when she did so, she felt her heart leap. He was in the very act of putting a gold-edged notecase away in the breast pocket of his evening coat, but it was the expression on his face more than anything else which told her what she wished to know. He held out his hand; then with a gesture which should have been dramatic but which was somehow faintly ridiculous, he threw out both his hands towards her.

"Come, my dear," he said. "You are mine!"

Nerina crossed the room to stand beside him. He looked down at her, then said:

"You have a cloak or some luggage, perhaps?"

Nerina shook her head.

"I have nothing suitable to wear," she said, "nothing that is of any consequence. Let us go . . . let us go quickly."

The Marquis slung his cloak over his shoulders and held out his arm to Nerina. She laid her fingers on it and he opened the door. Then they started to walk down the red stairway towards the hall. There was the sound of music from one of the other rooms; from the floor above there came a sudden burst of girlish laughter followed by a man's voice speaking impatiently. Nerina could not hear what was said, but somehow the sounds terrified her and instinctively she tightened her hold on the Marquis's arm.

In the hall a large and extremely ugly looking man dressed in an ornate livery was standing by the door. Nerina was in terror lest Mrs. Tait should appear; but there was no sign of her, and as if the Marquis guessed what she was thinking he said drily:

"I thought you could dispense with any fond farewells."

"Yes indeed," Nerina murmured.

The servant, whom she supposed was Charlie, handed the Marquis his hat and opened the front door. They walked down the stone pathway of the garden to the street. Nerina felt the warm night air on her bare shoulders, but the weather was sultry and there was no chance of her being chilled.

A closed brougham was waiting and Nerina saw that there were several other carriages behind it, all of luxurious appearance, the coachmen and footmen wearing the cockaded top hats of the aristocracy. The Marquis handed her into the carriage and stepped in beside her. A footman placed a warm, sable-lined rug over their knees, then the door was closed and she was alone with the man she hated most in the whole world.

She sought wildly for something to say, but before she could speak the Marquis moved a little nearer to her and she heard his voice, smooth and caressing, murmur softly:

"Now are you grateful to me?"

He would have taken her into his arms and she knew without looking at him that his lips were drawing nearer to hers. Quickly she put out both her hands to ward him off from her, to hold him away while she said wildly:

"Wait! I have something else to tell you."

"Is it more important than what I am waiting for?" the Marquis asked.

"Yes, much more important. You must listen to me," Nerina said, her voice desperate, for slowly and insidiously the Marquis was drawing her closer into his arms and all her strength could not force him to keep his distance.

229

"I have something to tell you," she repeated. "It is that I am married and my husband is someone you know, someone who is in fact your nephew."

"My nephew!"

The Marquis's hold on her slackened for a moment and she knew she had surprised him.

"Yes," Nerina said. "I am married to Sir Rupert Wroth."

"Good Lord!" There was no mistaking the astonishment in the Marquis's ejaculation. Then he added in an unpleasant tone: "So you have married the family bastard, have you? How did you contrive to do that?"

"It happened but a few days ago," Nerina replied. "I was married from my uncle's house and we came first to London on our honeymoon, then returned to Wroth."

"To Wroth?" the Marquis questioned. "But if you were at Wroth, my dear, what brought you post-haste to London and with very little money in your possession?"

Nerina had already anticipated that he might ask this question, and quickly, hoping he would believe her, she said:

"I had to come to London to see my uncle and aunt who were leaving for the Continent. It was a sudden decision and unfortunately Sir Rupert could not accompany me."

The Marquis suddenly laughed.

"Now you are lying," he said. "Do you expect me to believe that the wife of the rich and arrogant Sir Rupert Wroth would travel to London by train alone, without a companion, without a personal maid, and that, when she had her money stolen from her at the station, she was so cast down and depressed by the loss of it that she must accompany a strange woman to a house of ill-fame so that she could obtain a night's lodging?"

As he spoke, Nerina saw that her story was indeed incredible. Desperately she tried to regain the ground she had lost.

"I will be frank with you," she said. "Sir Rupert and I had quarrelled. It was only a tiff, nothing of any consequence, but because I was headstrong and foolish . . . I ran away. I thought, if I disappeared, he would be sorry for the way he had treated me. I came to London, but I meant to return to him, I meant to go back to Wroth after I had taught him a lesson."

The Marquis did not speak and after a moment she added apprehensively:

"You do believe that I am telling you the truth, that I am indeed Sir Rupert's wife?"

"Yes, I believe that," the Marquis said. "There is no reason why I should, but somehow I do believe it. But you have left him, so why bother ourselves about the fellow? He is at Wroth and we are here together, you and I."

He tightened his arms about her.

"Wait," Nerina cried. "Wait one moment! You must answer me this question."

"What is it?" the Marquis asked, and now he had forced her head back against his shoulder and he could see in the light of the street lamps the pale oval of her face looking up at him.

"Does what I have told you make no difference?" Nerina gasped. "That . . . that I am your nephew's wife?"

The Marquis laughed.

"Why should it make any difference?" he asked. "I want you, and I have indeed paid a large sum of money for you. You are mine! I have always desired you from the first moment when I saw you standing in the schoolroom, your green eyes very demure, your red hair tidy and neat. But somehow you didn't look like a governess, my dear. Shall I tell you what you looked like? You looked like a very desirable, very lovable woman, a woman who could be taught to feel passion. As for this husband of yours, he is of no consequence, especially since you have left him. Besides, if anything will add to the pleasure of taking you, it will be to know that the man who has defrauded me of many things cannot defraud me of the pleasure that you will give me."

"Do you hate him as much as that?" Nerina asked.

"Hate him!" the Marquis repeated. "What a strange question! No, I don't hate my brother's bastard. Why should I? I have him in the hollow of my hand. I am waiting, yes, waiting, so that revenge, when it comes, will be very sweet. When I strike in my own good time, I shall watch that upstart slink back to the gutter from which he has come."

There was a venom and bitterness in the Marquis's voice which was almost startling and then without any warning he pressed his lips down upon Nerina's. She felt the horror of that moment strike into her very soul. She was unable to move, unable to cry out; she only knew that his touch revolted her beyond endurance and that she must swoon

231

away through the very misery of knowing herself in his power, of feeling his mouth, bestial and obscene, striving to take possession of her.

When at last he released her, she fell back into the corner of the carriage gasping for breath, the blood drained from her face.

"Where are you taking me?" she stammered at length.

The question seemed to divert the Marquis's thoughts for a moment.

"I was about to take you to a small Hotel, but I have thought of something better," he replied. "After all, you are Lady Wroth, and you are entitled to a fitting background for what will be our night of love."

He moved forward as he spoke and pulled down the little window which communicated with the servants on the box. Through the glass Nerina could see the footman bend down attentively.

"Drive to the Ritz," the Marquis commanded and shut the window again before the man could reply.

The Marquis sat down again beside Nerina.

"We will go to the Ritz," he said. "I will explain that your maid and luggage will follow later. I will engage a suite for you and we will sup together. Over champagne and oysters you shall tell me more about your marriage to this pretentious young man who lives at Wroth Castle, and when your story is finished, I will tell you how we can both forget him and enjoy life together."

"But . . . but I do not understand," Nerina stammered. "Does it not shock you to think that I am morally . . . if not legally . . . your niece? I am married to the son of your brother. You believe that your brother, the late Marquis, was not married to the woman who became the mother of Sir Rupert; but if he had been, if in fact the marriage had been solemnised, Sir Rupert would not only be your nephew, he would also be the Marquis of Droxburgh. Would you then under those circumstances attempt to seduce his wife?"

The Marquis threw back his head and laughed.

"Shall I be frank?" he asked.

"But of course!"

"What difference do legal documents make to the fact that you are a very lovely, desirable woman and that, for the moment, we are alone together, alone in the center of London, no one knowing where we are, no one able to interrupt or part us?"

The Marquis held out his arms again.

"Come," he said. "Forget that tiresome fellow, Wroth, and remember me. Remember who I am—a man who has bought you, a man to whom you have promised to be very grateful."

Swiftly, impelled by the urgency of her fear, Nerina slipped from his arms and on to the small seat opposite. She sat there facing the Marquis and the gaslight shining through the window illuminated her hair and the white column of her throat.

"We are going to the Ritz," she said, and forced herself to speak lightly. "You must not untidy me before we arrive. They will think your story strange enough as it is, for I am sure that the wives of noblemen do not wander about London alone without luggage or a maid. If also I look dishevelled and abandoned, they will feel hesitant about giving me the suite you mentioned."

The Marquis bent forward.

"And you think my idea a good one?" he said. "You are interested in the suite and that little supper we shall enjoy together?"

"I am both hungry and thirsty," Nerina replied, and the Marquis took her hand and raised it to his lips.

"You are the most bewitching woman I have known in the whole of my life. You drive me to distraction, for I am never quite sure of you; and yet before tomorrow—I shall be sure."

Nerina's eyelashes swept against her cheeks.

"You are so impetuous," she said. "But believe me . . . I am grateful to you."

"That is all I ask," the Marquis replied.

The carriage drew up and with a sense of utter relief Nerina saw the broad circular steps of the Ritz Hotel. A gold-laced flunkey opened the door and Nerina, stepping from the carriage, preceded the Marquis up the steps and in through the high glass doors.

The Marquis followed her into the hall. A frock-coated attendant came forward bowing, his obsequious manner showing that the Marquis was well known.

"This is indeed an honour, my lord Marquis. Is there anything we can do for you?"

"Yes," the Marquis replied. "I have brought Lady Wroth here. While driving to London, her carriage unfortunately became involved in an accident. I was passing and was able by the greatest good fortune to rescue her. Unfortunately her maid and baggage had to be left behind, but I have sent my own servants to their assistance and they should arrive later in the evening. In the meantime her ladyship must be accommodated. She requires a suite, one of the best that you have."

"Certainly, my lord, we are honoured by her ladyship's request."

The receptionist turned towards the desk and spoke to the clerk in charge, who took a key from the board hanging on the wall; then he turned to Nerina.

"We have a suite on the first floor, milady," he said. "If you will be kind enough to inspect it and it meets with your approval, your baggage and maid can be sent up to you immediately on arrival."

"Thank you," Nerina said.

She followed the man up the wide, carpeted stairs; but as she went, her brain was busy seeking a way of escape. She had half formulated the idea of appealing to the management, but having seen that the Marquis was a person of importance and well known to those in attendance, she was uneasily aware that, if she did anything of the sort, she would be looked upon as demented. It was in fact problematical whether they would even listen to her.

The suite, when they reached it, consisted of an outer hall, a large sitting-room with windows overlooking the Green Park, a bedroom tastefully decorated in yellow satin, and a marble bathroom luxurious beyond anything Nerina had ever seen before. But as she appeared to have nothing to say, the Marquis appointed himself her spokesman.

"This will suit her ladyship," he said.

"It is one of the best suites in the hotel," the receptionist replied. "I feel sure her ladyship will be very comfortable here."

The Marquis glanced round the sitting-room.

"Her ladyship is a little indisposed by the accident in which she has been involved," he said. "She does not feel well enough to go down to the dining-room for supper. She will therefore sup up here. Will you send a waiter with the menu, and the wine waiter with the *Carte des Vins*?"

"Certainly, my lord, I will see it is done at once," the receptionist replied, bowing himself to the door.

Nerina watched him go and felt, as the door closed behind him, that she was a prisoner. There was nothing she could say, nothing she could do to stop herself from being left alone in this suite with the Marquis. She had escaped from one trap only to fall into another, and already she felt that rising sense of panic, that frantic desperation which seemed to numb every sense and stop even her brain from working.

As the Marquis turned towards her and she saw the expression on his face, she played for time.

"Are you quite sure we are wise to come here?" she asked. "What will they say when my luggage does not arrive and the maid about whom you have talked so glibly does not appear? Will they turn me out?"

The Marquis smiled.

"They would never dare to insult anyone whom I have introduced to the place. Besides, the maid will appear and with some luggage."

"But how?"

"I will see to it myself," the Marquis replied. "It will not unfortunately be tonight, but tomorrow morning someone will be here, I promise you that."

"But how, how can you manage it?" Nerina asked.

"These things are quite easily arranged," the Marquis said with an air of satisfaction. "What a lot you have to learn, my dear child, and how amusing it will be to teach you! Everything in this world, I promise you, is a question of money. Servants can be procured at a moment's notice if one can pay for them. Luggage is just as easy if not easier; and as for clothes, don't tell me that you are not woman enough to wish to choose your own especially when there is someone ready to pay for the expressive frills and furbelows which can make a woman look even more adorable, even more enticing."

Nerina made a little gesture with her hands.

"You make it all sound very easy," she said, "but I am doubtful."

"Then I shall have to convince you that I know best. Shall I tell you how I will do it? Come here!"

His words were a command, but Nerina made no effort to obey him. She tried to smile.

"What do you want of me?" she asked.

"I will tell you when you come to me," the Marquis replied.

Nerina shook her head.

"You frighten me," she said. "You are so used to giving orders and having people obey them. What would you do if for a change someone disobeyed you?"

"Perhaps I should punish them," the Marquis answered, "perhaps I should find another way of convincing them that I was right. You see, sooner or later I always get what I want. You ran away from me once, but now we have met again and this time you are mine."

"You sound very sure of me," Nerina said doubtfully.

The Marquis put his hands in his pockets.

"I have told you that I always get what I want. I am not an extremely lucky person. I also use my brains. There are not many men who can boast of having both luck and intelligence."

"No indeed," Nerina answered.

"And now," the Marquis continued. "Come here!"

Still Nerina hesitated, and then to her utter relief there came a knock on the door. Hastily she called out:

"Come in!"

The Marquis looked impatient, but it was two waiters who entered. One was holding a long, closely written menu in his hand, the other a gold-embossed wine list. Nerina turned towards the Marquis.

"Will you order supper?" she asked. "I would like to tidy myself. Remember I am very hungry and that you promised me champagne."

The Marquis put out his hand towards the menu.

"Let me see if there is anything fit to eat in this place," he said grandiosely to the waiter.

Nerina opened the door which led into the bedroom.

"I am hungry," she smiled, "if not a little greedy tonight."

She shut the door behind her, and a complete change came over her. The smile vanished from her lips and was replaced by an expression of tense urgency. She ran across the room on tiptoe. Very cautiously she opened the door on the other side. It led, as she had expected, into the small hall through which she and the Marquis had entered the suite. The door of the sitting-room also opened into it. The waiters had left it slightly ajar and Nerina could hear the Marquis's voice raised in interrogation. There was the respectful murmur of the men answering him. Then, so softly that she might have been a ghost flitting by, Nerina opened the outer door. A second later she was in the passage.

It was a long, straight passage running the full length of the building. She sped down it as if she moved on wings; as she reached the stairs leading down into the hall, she

236

hesitated, but only for a moment. Swiftly she ran down the broad red-carpeted stairs. She was at the bottom of the flight before the receptionist saw her. He was behind the desk, but by the time Nerina had reached the door into the street he was at her side.

"Is there anything wrong, your ladyship?" he asked. "Is there anything I can do for you?"

"Nothing, thank you," Nerina managed to say, "but his lordship would like to see you immediately. He is in the sitting-room of the suite. Will you go to him?"

"Yes, of course, your ladyship, I will go at once."

The receptionist was obviously surprised by her behaviour, but there was nothing he could do about it. As he turned away, Nerina went quickly through the door which led into the street.

The flunkey on duty came forward as if to speak to her, but she passed him by without a word. She ran down the steps and crossed Piccadilly. Fortunately there was not a great deal of traffic about at the moment, and she was not delayed for more than a second or so. Still running, she turned into Berkeley Street. Here the pavements were fairly clear save for some street hawkers and a few ladies of doubtful virtue perambulating along, their rouged cheeks and crimson mouths proclaiming their trade all too clearly.

Nerina sped past them. Fortunately the dress of white muslin was neither too full nor too cumbersome. She lifted it a little in front so as not to impede her movement; and although people stared at her in surprise, they did not attempt to stop her. She ran down Berkeley Street and into Berkeley Square.

Within four minutes of leaving the Ritz she was outside the door of Sir Rupert's house. The windows were shuttered and even the light above the door was in darkness. After she had rung the bell and thumped noisily on the knocker, a light appeared. It was only the flickering glimmer of a candle, but it gave her comfort until she heard chains and bolts being loosened and the front door was opened.

The old butler stood there, his livery coat pulled hastily round his shoulders, his eyes staring at her in surprise while the flame of the lighted candle flickered as he held it in his hand.

"M'lady!" he ejaculated. "What has happened?"

He might well ask, Nerina thought, as she pushed past him into the house and caught sight of herself in one of the great gilt mirrors which decorated the marble hall. Her hair was loosened and falling about her bare shoulders. Her breath was coming quickly and her cheeks were flushed, her eyes so large and dilated they seemed to eclipse the rest of her face completely.

"What has happened, m'lady?" the butler said again, as Nerina strove to get her breath.

Nerina tried to think of some feasible story.

"I came to London to . . . stay with friends," she said at length, "but something happened which made me decide to leave the house immediately. I have come away without my luggage and only what I stand up in. I must stay here tonight and tomorrow I shall return to Wroth."

"Sir Rupert is at Wroth, m'lady?" the butler asked.

"Yes, Sir Rupert is at Wroth," Nerina replied, "and I must join him tomorrow without fail."

The words were echoing in her brain as she went upstairs to the room she had occupied but a few days ago. The housekeeper came bustling to her, bringing a hot brick for the bed and a warm drink despite Nerina's protestations that she could eat or drink nothing. When at length in a borrowed nightgown she crept between the white sheets and was at last alone in the darkness, she turned her face into the pillow and began to cry. They were not tears of relief, they were not even tears of reaction, they were tears of sorrow.

For the first time in her life Nerina was ashamed of something she had done, was ready to accuse herself rather than anyone else for the sufferings she had experienced. She saw now how mad and crazy she had been to run away from Wroth. Somehow in the darkness of the soft bed it was difficult to recall her own indignation, horror and dislike of Sir Rupert. So much had happened since then, she had experienced so many emotions far worse, far more soul-destroying, so that now she wondered how she could have been so stupid as to relinquish the security she had found at Wroth for the horrors that had awaited her in London.

It was impossible to recapture what she had felt or the desperation which had driven her from Sir Rupert. It seemed almost fantastic that she had been conceited enough to think that she could earn her own living or that she could keep herself even for a short while on the few pounds which had been sent to Elizabeth as a wedding present.

It was neither Sir Rupert nor the Marquis who brought Nerina to her senses. It was her own honesty, her own self-examination which made her see everything in its true perspective, see how foolish she had been in everything she had done.

She wondered now how she had had the temerity to judge Sir Rupert, to set herself out to punish him with a ruthlessness which appeared now to exceed anything that he himself had contemplated. She had learnt, too, that there were far worse things in the world than making herself pleasant to the man she had tricked into marrying her.

When she thought of him, she realised that she had been not only hasty in her condemnation, but worse still, ridiculous. Gradually, as the tears abated a little, the facts of what had occurred presented themselves clearly and truthfully before her eyes, and Nerina was humbled almost to the dust.

In only one way could she make reparation—that was by saving Sir Rupert from the Marquis's long-planned and evil revenge. In that way, if in no other, she could serve him.

She remembered the prayer that she had made as she stood alone in the garish salon of Mrs. Tait's house and waited for the Marquis to return. God had indeed rescued her and now she must fulfill her part of the bargain and go back to Wroth. She would beg Sir Rupert's forgiveness and promise to do anything that he asked of her in the future.

She would go away, she thought. That was what he would want. Perhaps he would give her a little money, anyway he would see that she was not persecuted by his uncle or subjected to the licentious depravities of London that she had discovered for herself. He would be fair to her, she was sure of that, though why she should be certain of his generosity she could not tell. He would merely want to be rid of her, to find himself another wife, someone suitable to his position, someone who would behave like a lady and not like an impetuous fool rushing into trouble. She would go away.

Nerina repeated the words to herself. Suddenly with a fresh flood of tears she knew the truth. She did not want to go away from Wroth Castle; no, more than that, she did not want to leave Sir Rupert.

16

As the carriage drove over the bridge which spanned the lake, Nerina saw to her astonishment that there was a crowd of men assembled outside the front door of the Castle. It was nearly dark and some of them held flaming torches in their hands by the light of which she could see their faces, dirty, gaunt, and somehow strangely frightening.

The coachman of the hackney carriage which she had hired from Pendle was obviously as apprehensive of what he saw ahead of him as she was. He slowed the horse to a standstill. As he did so, Nerina called to him:

"Drive to the side door. You will see that the drive forks to the left a little way ahead of you."

"Very good, Ma'am."

He raised his fingers respectfully to the brim of his hat and whipping up his tired horse, drove to the west door of the Castle.

It had taken, Nerina thought, an incredible time for her to reach Wroth. She had planned to be there in the afternoon; but various things had delayed her until now the sun had set and she guessed the time to be long after eight o'clock. She had to buy a gown and bonnet before she could leave London and that had taken longer than she had intended. Being unable to go to the shops herself because she had nothing to wear but the tawdry white muslin gown in which she had been dressed by Mrs. Tait, she sent a letter of instructions to one of the shops that had attended to her previously.

A *vendeuse* had arrived at Berkeley Square an hour later with a box full of gowns for her approval and at least a dozen bonnets. In her new and sober mood Nerina picked out the most inexpensive dress and a plain straw bonnet trimmed only with ribbons. Nevertheless the purchases could not be effected very quickly and when finally she was decently clothed and ready for the journey, she found she had missed the morning train to Pendle and must wait for one which left after luncheon. Even then she would have reached the Castle sooner had she not found on arrival at Pendle that it was almost impossible to hire a carriage. The local Races were taking place that day, she was informed, and every possible vehicle in the whole town had been hired, borrowed or lent to take spectators to the race-course.

There was nothing Nerina could do but wait until the afternoon's sport was over, and she was forced to amuse herself as best she could in the dingy sitting-room of the Black Boar Hotel.

When at last a conveyance was procured for her, Nerina had sighed in relief, feeling that the last lap of her journey was nearly done. But she had reckoned without the hackney carriage. It was old and creaking and drawn by a tired, underfed horse which had already exhausted its strength in carrying a party of race-goers to and from the race-course. The miles to Wroth seemed interminable; and when eventually they turned in at the drive gates, Nerina was almost crying with exasperation and fatigue.

Yet now, as they drew up at the side door of the Castle, she felt suddenly as fresh and as full of energy as she had felt when she had woken early in the morning to find herself in Berkeley Square. Just for a moment, as consciousness returned to her and she opened her eyes, she had felt that stirring of fear which comes from uncertainty and insecurity and the poignant awareness of danger which had been hers for so long. Then with a sense of reassurance so vivid that it became inexpressible happiness she realised where she was and that she need no longer be afraid.

She had escaped from the Marquis and from Mrs. Tait! She had escaped, too, from some monster of her own imagination, some horror which had held her spellbound for far too long. She was free, free to do what she knew was the right thing and return to Wroth and to Sir Rupert.

As she stepped from the carriage she felt that the Castle welcomed her home. There was a warm glowing light in many of its windows. There was something protecting in its height and majesty. It seemed to her, too, as if the vast wings of the house spread out in a semi-circle were like arms flung wide in a spontaneous gesture of affection. The west door, which led to the stables, the Chapel and the other out-buildings, was used by members of the household as a more convenient entrance and exit to and from the house than the front door.

Nerina pulled the bell chain and at the same time turned the handle of the door. She found, as she had expected, that it was open. She walked quickly down the wide passage covered in rugs and hung with tapestry. When she was some way along it, she met a footman hurrying to answer the bell. He looked surprised at seeing her; but Nerina merely commanded him to pay her carriage, and hurried on.

She had a sudden sense of urgency, a conviction that something was very wrong, although what it was she could not imagine. Why were those men outside the front door? What did it portend? And then, even as she reached the centre of the Castle and came to the Great Hall out of which the main rooms opened, she knew the answer.

Those strange, sullen faces which she had seen by the light of the torches were familiar. She had seen men who looked like that before, and now she remembered where. They were the miners of Willow Hill, the men whom Bessie had told her about, the men who were on strike against the intolerable conditions of the mine. A fear seemed to grip Nerina by the heart, a fear quite unlike that which had possessed her for so long, a fear not for herself for once but for someone else.

Bessie had asked her help. She could hear her speaking of the miners' misery and their sense of injustice; but she had paid so little attention, thinking only of herself, of her own troubles, her own unhappiness, being not particularly concerned with the danger to others—a danger which she knew now threatened Sir Rupert.

As she crossed the Hall, the door of the Library was suddenly thrown open and Masters, the old butler, came hurrying out. He was obviously going in search of someone or something, but when he saw Nerina he stopped abruptly:

"M'lady!" he exclaimed.

"Where is Sir Rupert?" Nerina asked.

She did not wait for the man's reply. She saw the direction in which he turned his head and she moved quickly through the doorway and into the Library. There she stood very still, arrested by the scene in front of her. Sir Rupert was lying insensible on the floor. His eyes were closed and blood was pouring from his forehead. Kneeling beside him, opening a black bag, was a man whom Nerina recognised as the local Doctor who attended the Dowager Marchioness.

It seemed to her as if a long time passed before she could bring herself to speak or move. As she stood there, there was a sudden shout and a rumble of voices outside, followed by the distant crash of breaking glass.

It was then Nerina saw that on the floor beside Sir Rupert and just a little way from his head was a huge stone. It must have weighed two or three pounds. She glanced quickly from it to the great gaping hole in the glass of the window through which it had obviously been thrown. There were more yells and cat-calls outside, followed yet again by the sound of shattered glass. At last Nerina managed to speak.

"Is he hurt?" she asked, and her voice sounded strange even to herself.

The Doctor looked up. He recognised her and remarked drily:

"Oh, it is you, m'lady. Yes, Sir Rupert's hurt right enough. The piece of rock must have caught him full on the temple."

Nerina drew nearer, then suddenly she found herself on her knees beside Sir Rupert, her hand on his.

The Doctor was staunching the wound, the blood crimson against the piece of white linen he held in his hand.

"Is it serious?" Nerina asked.

"I'll not be answering that question for a moment," the Doctor replied. "You can see for yourself that it has knocked him unconscious, and I'm thinking I will have to put half a dozen stitches at least in his forehead. But he is not dead, if that is what you're worrying about."

Nerina's fingers tightened convulsively on Sir Rupert's hand, and even as she did so there came another shout from outside. Half a brick came hurtling through the window, to fall on the floor by the writing-desk. The Doctor did not turn his head, but Nerina gave a little cry.

"What is happening?" she asked.

"It is the miners," the Doctor replied. "I'll speak to them in a moment."

"They are angry," Nerina remarked.

"And not without reason!"

The Doctor's tone was grim.

"They say that the mine is unsafe!" Nerina ventured.

"And so it is!"

"What will happen if the strike continues?"

The Doctor was looking in his bag for a bandage. There was a pause before he replied:

"If Sir Rupert refuses to negotiate with them, they will have to go back. They are hungry now, and there is not a woman or a child in Willow Hill who has had a decent meal these last four days. The shops are shut and they

243

can't get credit. If they don't work, they will starve." He glanced up at the window and added: "This sort of thing will do them no good. They will merely end up in prison."

Nerina got slowly to her feet.

"You are sure that the mine is unsafe?" she asked. "I have heard people say that it is, but you know the place personally. You would know the truth."

"Yes, I know the truth," the Doctor replied. "The mine needs money spent on it. I have spoken to the Manager about it and I have spoken to Sir Rupert himself, but neither of them will pay any heed to what I say. But I have to mend the bodies that are broken when a shaft collapses, when a man is trapped for hours, perhaps days, or some poor devil loses a leg or an arm through rotten machinery."

There was silence as the Doctor finished speaking.

"You say Sir Rupert will not listen to you?" Nerina said at length.

"He won't listen to anyone," the Doctor remarked. He was binding Sir Rupert's head skilfully and with gentle fingers even while his voice was harsh. "There are people who have no loving kindness in them, no tenderness for their fellow men, and Sir Rupert is one of them."

As he spoke, Nerina saw the proud, happy schoolboy that the Marchioness had described to her so vividly; then in front of her very eyes she saw the transformation from that charming lad to a bitter resentful man—a man without kindness, a man who did not understand the meaning of the word love.

Quite suddenly it seemed to her that she understood so much. It was all clear before her as plain as if someone had written it down for her—the story of a man who had suffered and who, because of his suffering, was harsh and cruel to other people.

The door of the Library opened and the butler returned with three frightened-looking footmen.

"We will get Sir Rupert upstairs, sir," he said to the Doctor; "then I had best send a groom for the police. It's terrible the damage they're doing, sir, terrible."

The butler's voice rose in a crescendo of fear and affronted resentment. The Doctor got to his feet, picking up his black bag.

"Take him gently," he said. "Try not to move his head in any way. Get him upstairs and into bed. You may have to cut his clothes from him."

244

The footmen lifted Sir Rupert and Nerina stood watching them. As she looked at Sir Rupert's face, she remembered how young and vulnerable he had seemed when she had watched him asleep in the railway carriage after the wedding ceremony. Now his face was very pale, except for a jagged, only half-healed scar on his cheek. She flushed as she looked at it and perhaps it was the vivid crimson of the wound she had inflicted on him which in contrast made his face seem completely bloodless. He looked older and curiously spiritual.

For the first time Nerina saw that his face was extremely sensitive. When they had been fighting each other, she had been struck more than once by the strength and obstinacy of his features. Now she saw there were lines of suffering beneath his eyes. The corners of his mouth drooped a little wistfully as if in disappointment.

As the footmen carried him past her, she felt a sudden yearning within herself and knew that she wanted above all things to comfort the man she had hated, to tell him that all was well, to assure him that he no longer need be afraid of the future. And then, as the footmen carrying their burden disappeared through the Library door, Nerina knew there were other things she must do first. With an air of resolution she turned towards the Doctor.

"Will you come with me?" she said. "I am going to speak to the strikers."

The Doctor raised his eyebrows.

"And what will you be saying to them?" he enquired.

"You will hear that when I say it," Nerina replied. "I only ask that you will accompany me, and I would be grateful if you will introduce me to them for they will not know who I am."

The Doctor eyed her speculatively; then as if he were satisfied by what he saw in her face, he nodded his head and stumped across the floor.

"Come along then," he said. "You are a brave woman. I will make them listen to you."

He crossed the Hall with Nerina at his side. At the front door, which was bolted, stood one of the footmen in his livery of claret and gold. He had obviously been set there as a guard. The Doctor waved him aside and with his own hands drew back the bolts and unhooked the chains. Just as he was about to open the door, another footman came running across the Hall.

"Mr. Masters told us as how we were to keep that door shut and barred, Sir."

"It is her ladyship who gives orders here," the Doctor said gruffly, and the footman stepped back with a murmured apology.

Nerina had an idea. She turned first to one footman and then to the other.

"Each of you carry one of these silver candelabra," she said. "The Doctor and I are going out on to the steps. We want to be seen. You will hold them on either side of us."

The footmen looked dismayed, but they obeyed her. The shouts and yells from outside were rising in ferocity as if with the instinct of caged animals the men sensed that something was about to happen. The Doctor opened the door. There was a yell as they saw the light; and then as Nerina appeared with the Doctor at her side and the footmen in attendance there came a sudden silence.

Slowly the little company walked down the steps, the candlelight illuminating Nerina's face and the soft red curls peeping from beneath her bonnet.

"It's the Doctor," a man shouted, and there was a half-hearted cheer.

Nerina stopped at the bottom step. She glanced at the Doctor and he raised his voice.

"Men," he said, "I have here beside me Lady Wroth. She wishes to speak with you. I look to you to give her ladyship a fair hearing."

A little ripple went through the crowd. By the light of the torches Nerina could see the hard, suspicious expressions with which the audience regarded her. The nearest men were only a few feet away from her, the others spread out, some coming from the gardens where they had gone in search of bricks and stones to hurl at the windows. They stood now with the missiles in their hands, their coal-grimed faces sharply silhouetted against the surrounding darkness, the red handkerchiefs some of them wore around their necks showing the only glint of colour amongst their ragged dirty clothes.

"My husband, Sir Rupert Wroth, is ill," Nerina said, "otherwise he would speak to you himself."

At this there was a series of cat-calls, whistles and sounds of derision; but after a moment the noise died away and Nerina continued.

"I wish to tell you, however, on his behalf that he has considered your request regarding the mine and has decided to make immediate investigations into the safety of the seams on which you are working. New machinery and new safety devices will be ordered and used as soon as it is possible. In the meantime the Manager will be instructed that you shall work only where there is no danger and where you yourselves are convinced of safety. There will be compensation for the families of those who have been killed and badly injured and help for those who are temporarily unable to work."

There was a sudden gasp and then a great cheer arose into the night air. It was so spontaneous, so whole-hearted that Nerina felt the tears come into her eyes. The men went on cheering and cheering; and then as she raised her hand, there was a sudden silence.

"You have had a long walk to get here," she said, "and I learn from the Doctor that some of your wives and children are hungry. If you will go quietly to the kitchen door of the Castle, I will see that what food we have is distributed amongst you. There may not be enough, but at least there will be something; and when the Doctor returns tonight to the town, he will make arrangements for bread and milk to be obtained on credit until you have earned enough to pay for them."

Again the cheers went up and one old man, white-haired and with a lined and scarred face, stepped forward.

"God bless ye, m'lady," he said. "Ye'll not regret this night's work, that I promise ye."

"I am sure of that," Nerina answered; "and now will you please do as I have suggested and go to the kitchen door. The damage you have done will be forgotten; but I suggest you forget it also, for it does no good to talk of such things."

They were cheering as she walked up the steps and in through the front door. As she reached the lighted hall and the footmen closed the door behind her, she realised that she was trembling a little, not from fear but rather with relief at knowing that she had achieved what she had set out to do.

She turned to the Doctor.

"Will you see that the bread and milk are obtainable?" she asked.

"Yes, I'll see to that," he said, and then added: "But I leave the rest to you."

She knew that he was sceptical whether Sir Rupert would agree to the generous promises she had made in his

247

name, but she had no such fears. She had something to bargain with which made her supremely confident in herself. Old Harry's secret would, she was convinced, transform Sir Rupert's whole attitude.

And why not? The fear which had stalked behind him since he was a boy could be dispelled by a few words and by the possession of a piece of paper from the Vestry of the Shepherds' Chapel.

The Marquis's reign of power was finished. More than that, he was no longer the Marquis of Droxburgh. Nerina looked at the bare walls of the Great Hall. The family pictures could come back, she thought, to ornament and enrich the Castle. She longed as she had never longed for anything in the world to see Sir Rupert's expression when he learnt the truth, when she told him that he was legally his father's son and the real heir to the Marquisate. She turned quickly and eagerly towards the stairs.

Masters came forward respectfully.

"I have sent the miners to the kitchen door," Nerina told him. "They are all to be given something to take away with them. There are hams in the kitchen, cut them up. All the bread we have in the Castle is to be given away—the cooks can bake more for tomorrow. There will be milk in the dairy, have it fetched and butter too."

"Very good, m'lady."

The butler's long training prevented him from expressing in words his astonishment, but his face was eloquent with surprise. Nerina could not help smiling as she followed the Doctor upstairs.

Sir Rupert's bedroom was in semi-darkness. The only light came from the candle near his bed. His face was nearly as white as the pillow against which he lay. For a moment Nerina thought he was dead and she felt her heart give a frightened throb, a sudden horror creep over her; then as the Doctor took his pulse, she knew that he still lived.

"How long will he be unconscious?" she asked in a low voice.

The Doctor did not answer for a moment, then he laid Sir Rupert's arm gently down on the bed.

"I have no idea," he said; "and when he wakes there is the possibility that he may be delirious."

Slowly Nerina undid the ribbons of her bonnet and took it from her head.

248

"I am going to nurse him," she said quietly, "so you had best tell me exactly what I am to do."

It was two o'clock in the morning before Sir Rupert stirred. As he began to toss himself wearily from side to side, Nerina rose from the armchair near the fire where she had been resting and crossed the room to his side. She had undressed and was wearing only a peignoir of white satin trimmed with lace that she had bought in Bond Street. Her hair was unbound and her eyes were soft and heavy with sleep.

She went swiftly to Sir Rupert's side and put her cool fingers against his face. He was very hot and she knew that he had a fever. Impatiently he turned away from her hand, tossing and turning, his lips moving as if he strove to speak, but as yet he made no sound.

Nearly an hour later he began to talk out loud, at first mumbling unintelligibly and then finally crying:

"Water! Give me water!"

Nerina slipped her hand under his head and raised a glass to his lips. He took a few sips and lay back again. He had not opened his eyes and she felt that, even if he did, he would not recognise her. All at once he began to speak coherently.

"She has gone," he said. "Gone, and I have no idea where . . . I have driven her away . . . I was brutal to her . . . and she called me a devil . . . she called me a devil . . . she was right . . . she drove me mad with her red hair and those green eyes . . . Why can't I forget her? . . . she haunts me . . . she is there all the time. . . . Yes, laughing at me, mocking me, driving me mad. . . ."

He repeated the last words over and over again—"Mad! She drives me mad! Mad! Mad!"

Nerina laid her hand on his.

"You must go to sleep," she said firmly. "Do you hear me? You have been hurt, you need rest."

"I cannot rest," he replied. "I am mad . . . she drives me mad . . ."

"Forget her," Nerina said quietly. "You must sleep."

As if her command percolated into his consciousness, he was still. She felt that he obeyed her unquestionably as a child might have done. As she smoothed the sheet and made his pillows a little more comfortable, she wondered whether he was wishing for her return or whether what he had said was just a reaction from his surprise at finding that she had left the Castle.

When Nerina went back to her chair beside the fireplace, she sat looking at the flames, wondering about Sir Rupert, wondering about herself. She knew the truth now. She loved him, and she saw with a sudden clarity that the reason she had run away from him and from the Castle three days ago was not because she had been running away from the man who was legally her husband, but because she fled from love. It was love she was afraid of, love which she had known instinctively would tear her into pieces when it came to her to destroy her last feeling of independence, her last flaming rebellion against man and marriage.

When she had been a child, she had craved for love and it had been denied her. As an orphan, an unwanted poor relation who was merely an encumbrance to those who were forced to take care of her, she was starved for love. But because of some pride and an inner strength based half on reality and half on imagination she would never admit even to herself that she was hungry for affection. As she grew older, the love she had been denied began to poison her mind against all other sorts of love. She had hated her uncle and therefore she had thought that all men must be like him. She had loathed and detested the attentions paid to her by her dissolute employers and therefore she had believed that love was lust and it became as much an enemy to her as the men she despised and loathed because they desired her.

And when finally love came to her, it had come not softly and gently and tenderly, as she had imagined it would, but as a fiery cross indistinguishable from hate, twisted and tangled in her puzzled mind until she was unaware whether the emotions which consumed her were love or loathing.

Now she knew that she had begun to love Sir Rupert from that moment in Berkeley Square when he had stepped forward to protect her from her uncle. She had admired him before that under her disdain, her contempt and her desire for revenge. Yet there had been some weakness in her armour which made her long to be with him, to be happy in his presence, to feel a satisfaction even in sparring with him.

Now in retrospect she saw how much she had loved him when they had come to Wroth after their marriage. She had not understood then that the tenseness and the excitement that she felt in his presence was love and not hatred. She had not known, as she came downstairs in the morning looking for him, that it was not to tease and torture him which was important, but the mere fact of seeing him, watching his face, and knowing him near her. She had not analysed that sudden tingling within herself, that sense of exhilaration which was beyond explanation.

Now she saw it all. He had drawn and held her while she, poor fool, had all the time thought she was fighting him. He had conquered her from the very beginning while she imagined she was the triumphant conqueror. How blind she had been, how stupid! And now humbly she could cry at her very foolishness. She had wasted so much time, she had thrown away precious moments and hours which might have been golden with happiness.

Nerina hid her face in her hands. She felt herself quiver at the very intensity of her feelings. She knew at this moment that she wanted above all things to cross the room, to kneel beside Sir Rupert's bed and press her lips against his hand. It would, she knew, give her a rapture and a pleasure beyond anything she had ever known in her whole life. But she dared not do it, dared not, because she knew that, when he was himself again, she must submit herself to his will and accept from him whatever terms he dictated.

He would send her away; she would never see him again, never hear his voice or watch his face. Yet there was nothing she could do about it. Whatever it was he suggested, she knew she must agree to it, simply and solely because she loved him, because she could fight him no more. She felt the tears gather in her eyes. Softly they began to flow through her fingers. They were tears of self-pity, but she did not care. Her love was hopeless. She wished now she had never undertaken to save Elizabeth; yet even as she formulated the thought, she knew it was untrue. She would never regret what had happened because, however hard and lonely the future, she had at least known Sir Rupert—known and loved him.

With a pang of misery that was sheer physical agony she remembered how she had repulsed him when he had come to her bedroom. She wondered what would have happened if she had returned his kisses, if she had been soft and yielding in his arms instead of defiant. She felt herself tremble at the thought of his arms around her, of his mouth hard and possessive against hers; then even as she regretted that she had prevented him from taking her, that she had pitted her strength against his and won, she knew that she had been right.

It would have been a mockery of real love, a desecration of an emotion so sacred and holy that now she fell humbly on her knees before the divinity which had invaded her heart and soul. If she had allowed Sir Rupert to make her his, hungrily, lustfully, without tenderness or beauty, she knew that her love would have been desecrated. She would go away, but it would go with her, that sacrament within her heart, which was in itself the gift of God.

Her tears ceased. Still she hid her face in her hands, her head resting against the velvet black of the armchair. She did not know how long she sat there, suffering half misery, half ecstasy, conscious that her love seemed to consume her as if with a flame.

A sound from the bed startled her. She looked towards it, taking her fingers from her eyes. Sir Rupert was sitting up. He was looking around him, the white bandage showing up against the darkness at the back of the bed. Nerina got to her feet. He saw her and for a moment his eyes grew wide and dark with astonishment; then, as she advanced into the circle of light, the candle revealed the sweet curves of her figure beneath her thin peignoir, her loosened hair standing out like a halo to frame the pallor of her face and her tear-stained eyes.

"Nerina!"

Sir Rupert's voice was low and hoarse, and she saw, as he spoke, that he was no longer delirious but completely himself again.

"You have come back!" he said hoarsely.

"Yes, I have come back," Nerina said, "but you have been hurt. You must lie still."

"You have come back!" he repeated as if he did not hear the last part of her sentence. "I thought you had left me forever."

Nerina shook her head.

"No . . . I was very stupid . . . I ran away . . . then I knew that I had been foolish to do so . . . so . . . I have come back."

"To me?" Sir Rupert asked.

She did not understand what he meant and replied simply:

"Yes . . . to you! But oh, I have something to tell you, something of great importance to yourself, something I have learned which will alter the whole course of your life."

"It is of no consequence," Sir Rupert said impatiently. "There is something I must know and know at once."

"What is it?" Nerina asked wonderingly.

"Have you come back to stay?"

Nerina's eyes were puzzled, then it seemed to her as if the meaning of his question was clear, and she said:

"No, I will not stay if you wish to be rid of me. It will not be easy, I know, because legally we are married, but somehow a way can be found and now I will do what you wish. I was wrong to marry you as I did. I thought you deserved it . . . but I see that such trickery was wrong . . . and it is not for me to judge or to try to be a revenger. I am sorry for it and if I can do anything now to make things easy . . . I will do it."

"You will go away?" Sir Rupert asked.

Nerina drew a deep breath. She felt as if she passed sentence of death upon herself, but her voice was steady as she answered:

"If you want me to."

"If I want you to? Are you mad?" Sir Rupert's tone was harsh. Suddenly he reached across the bed and took Nerina's hand in his. "Don't you understand," he said, "that I am asking you to stay? On your own terms, or any terms you like, but only stay with me."

He saw Nerina's eyes widen as if she did not understand, and then her fingers clenched themselves on his.

"What are you saying?" she asked.

"I am trying to make you understand," Sir Rupert replied. "It is all very strange that you are here at this hour, dressed as you are, and I am in bed. I seem to remember a blow, to feel myself falling . . . but never mind, it does not matter what happened; this is what is of importance—that you should know how much I missed you when I found that you had gone. I could not believe it possible that you had really left me. I expected that you were tricking me, that you would come from some secret hiding-place to mock at me, driving me mad by the sight of your green eyes and red hair and the sweet disdain of your lips. I know it was crazy of me to touch you, to attempt to force myself upon you, but I could not help myself. If you knew what I had felt day after day, night after night. We had been together, sat opposite each other, talked and fenced with each other; yet all the time my heart was crying out that I wanted you—while my brain repudiated it."

As Sir Rupert spoke, he drew Nerina a little nearer to him; and now she was trembling with an ecstasy which seemed to ignite her whole body as gradually his meaning came to her. At last she found her voice.

"Do you . . . mean that . . . that . . . you . . . love me?" she whispered.

"Love you? I adore you!" Sir Rupert answered. "I have never believed it possible that I could love any woman, that I could feel like this; yet now that it has come to me I know that it is—love."

Nerina gave a little gasp and tried to free her hand from his, but he would not let it go.

"I will be gentle to you, I will be kind to you, but let me try to teach you to love me. Give me a chance to show you what I feel, to find happiness for us both."

And now he released Nerina's hands; but before she could move, his arms were round her, gently and with a tenderness she had never known and had not believed possible of him. He encircled her body. She did not resist him and her eyes were on his, searching his face as if she sought for the truth of what she had heard, hardly believing it, finding it too wonderful to credit; and then at length, as very gently he drew her down upon the bed so that she was half sitting, half lying in his arms, he looked down at her and his mouth was very near to hers.

"Will you give me a chance, my darling?" he murmured.

Still she found herself incapable of answering him. Slowly, as the sky on the horizon merges with the sea, his lips touched hers at first tentatively, then as he felt the response of her parted lips his pressure deepened.

Now at last, locked in his arms, Nerina knew the answer to all her questions. She knew, too, that the misery and loneliness which had been hers since she was a child was gone for ever. She had come home, she had found what she had sought for so long, not knowing what it was called, not even believing in its existence, but which had been waiting for her all the time.

With a little sob her arms went up around Sir Rupert's neck and she drew his head closer. She felt his heart pounding in his breast, knew that his blood had quickened and was racing wildly through his body. She felt his arms tighten round her until with the strength of them she could hardly breathe. Suddenly he released her and in a voice hoarse with emotion he said:

"Do not tempt me! I shall frighten you, and you will run away from me again!"

Nerina, looking up at him, smiled a little tumultuously for there were tears in her eyes.

"Never," she whispered. "I shall never leave you again ... for oh ... my darling ... I love you too."